Havana Nights

By

Kenneth Nowling

ISBN 979-8-89766-856-4

HAVANA NIGHTS

Written by Kenneth Nowling

Published by Nowling Manor
An imprint of Leeds Press Corp.

Contents

Acknowledgments

To my village,
This book is dedicated to you.
Thank you for trusting me with your stories.

To the countless souls who've crossed my path—each one, knowingly or not, has left an imprint on my journey. For every dreamer who dared to believe, for every teacher who inspired curiosity, and for every stranger who shared a kind word—This book is for you.

This book is dedicated to every soul whose presence, no matter how fleeting, reminded me of the boundless possibilities in life.

Chapter One

Maserati sliced through the night, its powerful engine purring like a predator in the darkness. Inside, Houston and Charlotte sat in tense silence, their faces illuminated intermittently by the passing headlights of oncoming cars. Both seemed exhausted, their expressions etched with both fatigue and apprehension.

Houston sat behind the wheel, a figure of intense focus and rugged allure. In his early 30s, he had the kind of looks that turned heads and lingered in memory. His chiseled features were defined by sharp cheekbones and a strong, angular jawline, the latter covered in a light stubble that added to his rough charm. His skin had a sun-kissed tone, suggesting time spent outdoors, engaged in activities that demanded physical exertion and skill.

His piercing blue eyes were his most striking feature. They were a shade of blue that seemed to cut through the darkness of the night, radiating an almost unsettling intensity. His gaze was unwavering, sharp, and vigilant, betraying a mind that was always calculating, always one step ahead. Beneath the surface of those eyes, there was a hint of something darker. This danger was both alluring and intimidating.

His hair, a dark brown, was cut short but stylishly tousled, giving him a perpetually windswept appearance. It framed his face perfectly, drawing attention to his features. His lips, set in a firm line, suggested a man of few words who communicated more through action and presence than through idle chatter.

Houston's physique was equally impressive. He wore a black leather jacket that hugged his broad shoulders and muscular arms, hinting at the strength beneath. The well-worn and slightly weathered jacket seemed almost like a second skin, fitting him perfectly and adding to his air of dangerous allure. Underneath, he wore a simple, fitted black t-shirt that clung to his well-defined chest and flat stomach, showcasing a body honed through years of hard living and physical discipline.

His hands, gripping the steering wheel, were large and strong, with veins visible under the skin, hands that spoke of both capability and a readiness for action. The knuckles were slightly scarred, evidence of past altercations that he had clearly come out of on top. His every movement was controlled and deliberate, exuding a sense of power and confidence.

Houston's overall demeanor was one of tense alertness. As he navigated the highway with practiced ease, his body remained taut, every muscle coiled as if ready to spring into action at a moment's notice. He exuded an aura of danger that clung to him, visible and electrifying, making it clear that he was not a man to be trifled with.

Beside him, Charlotte, known in certain circles as Brazilian Candy, was a vision of seductive beauty. In her mid-20s, she possessed a captivating allure that could command attention in any room. Her long, flowing dark hair cascaded down her back in luxurious waves, shimmering subtly even in the dim light of the car. Her striking features were a perfect blend of sharp angles and soft curves, high cheekbones, a delicate nose, and full, sensuous lips that naturally curved into a smile that could be both inviting and dangerous.

Charlotte's eyes were her most enchanting feature. Almond-shaped and framed by thick, dark lashes, they were usually alight with a playful sparkle, hinting at a mischievous spirit and an adventurous soul. But tonight, those eyes were wide and alert, darting nervously at the shadows outside the window. The usual sparkle was replaced by a steely vigilance, betraying the fear and tension that had accompanied their hasty departure.

Her attire added to her magnetism. She wore a form-fitting dress that hugged her curves, accentuating her hourglass figure with every movement. The fabric clung to her body in all the right places, enhancing her natural elegance. Despite the chaos of their escape, she managed to maintain an air of effortless grace, her posture straight, and her movements fluid. Even under stress, there was an undeniable elegance in the way she held herself, which was proof of her poise and confidence.

Charlotte's skin was flawless, with a warm, golden hue that spoke of her Brazilian heritage. It glowed faintly under the car's interior lights, adding to her bizarre charm. Her hands, delicate yet strong, rested tensely in her lap, fingers occasionally clenching in response to the adrenaline coursing through her veins.

Her presence in the car was a stark contrast to Houston's rugged, dangerous aura. Where he was all hard edges and latent power, she studied seductive elegance and controlled intensity.

Designer luggage, haphazardly stacked in the back seat, told the story of their sudden departure from where they once resided, Havana, Cuba. The city of bright lights and constant noise was now a distant memory, replaced by the oppressive silence of the open road.

Charlotte broke the silence first, her voice trembling slightly. "Houston, how much longer until we're safe?"

Houston didn't take his eyes off the road. "Couple more hours to Camagüey," he replied, his voice a deep, steady rumble. "We need to stay sharp. There's water in the back if you need it."

Candy sighed, her irritation bubbling to the surface. "Can you get it for me? I'm really struggling here."

Houston's grip on the steering wheel tightened, a flash of annoyance crossing his face. "Can't you see I'm driving? I'm just as tired as you are. Take what you need. I've got my hands full keeping us on the road."

Candy huffed but reached back, fumbling around for the water bottle. After a moment, she found it and brought it to her lips, taking a long drink. The cool water was refreshing, but it did little to ease her growing frustration.

"Hey, don't drink it all!" Houston snapped suddenly. "I need some too." He reached over and snatched the bottle from her, taking a quick swig before tossing it back into the back seat. The tension in the car was palpable, the silence thick and uncomfortable.

A few minutes later, Candy shifted in her seat, her eyes drooping. "Houston, I'm so sleepy. I need to rest, even if it's just for a little while."

Houston's jaw clenched, a mixture of concern and anger flaring in his eyes. "This is no time to fall asleep, Candy. We're not out of the woods yet."

"I just need a little sleep," Candy pleaded, her voice tinged with desperation. "Can you make the seat more comfortable for me?"

Houston let out a frustrated sigh but reached over, adjusting the seat so that it reclined slightly. "There. That's the best I can do. But you've got to stay awake. We can't afford any mistakes right now."

Candy nodded weakly, trying to keep her eyes open. "Just a little rest," she murmured, settling into the seat. "I'll be fine."

Houston glanced at her, his expression softening for a moment. "Alright, but don't fall asleep. We've got to stay sharp."

As Candy tried to get comfortable, Houston's mind raced. They were far from safety, and the road ahead was fraught with danger. He couldn't afford to let his guard down, not even for a moment.

After a while, Houston tapped Candy awake. Her eyelids fluttered open, heavy with exhaustion, and she groaned softly, turning away from him.

"Candy, wake up," Houston insisted his tone a mix of urgency and frustration.

She mumbled something incoherently, trying to burrow deeper into the seat. "I'm still so sleepy," she finally muttered, her voice thick with fatigue.

Houston glanced at the clock on the dashboard, then back at the road ahead. "We don't have time for this. You've got to stay awake."

Candy's eyes opened slightly, enough to show her lingering drowsiness. She looked at him, trying to muster the energy to comply but failing. "I can't, Houston. I need more rest."

With a resigned sigh, Houston reached into the console between them and pulled out an aluminum packet, holding it up between his fingers. "Here, hit this," he said, his voice steady and commanding.

A slow smile spread across Candy's face as she saw the packet. Her defenses lowered, and she softened, reaching over to take it from him. The sight of the familiar stimulant brought a glimmer of relief to her tired eyes.

Candy tore open the packet, her fingers trembling slightly. She glanced at Houston, exhaustion in her gaze. "Thanks," she whispered, before taking the substance close to her nose as though she wanted to inhale the contents. At that time, her eyes brightened, and she sat up straighter, the fog of sleepiness lifting from her mind.

Houston watched her, a flicker of relief crossing his face. "We've got to stay sharp, Candy. We're not out of danger yet."

She nodded, the stimulant coursing through her veins, sharpening her senses. "I'm good now," she said, her voice steadier. "Let's keep going." She wanted to stay focused in clear eye

Houston's focus returned to the road, his mind already calculating their next moves. The night stretched on, but with Candy now alert beside him.

The Maserati sped onward, its headlights cutting through the darkness, as Houston and Candy pressed forward towards Camagüey, their fate hanging in the balance.

Houston found a secluded spot off the highway and parked the Maserati, the engine ticking as it cooled. He turned to Candy, watching as she patted his hair with one hand, the half-opened aluminum packet he gave her still held carefully in the other.

"Be careful with that," he warned, his voice a low growl.

Candy nodded, a playful smile curving her lips. She sat up on her knees, leaning into the back seat to rummage through their designer luggage. Houston's eyes followed her every move, drawn to the way her perfect ass jiggled as she searched. Unable to resist, he reached out and ran his hand over her curves, then slapped her hard.

Candy arched her back, a pleased gasp escaping her lips. "Oohh, don't start it if you ain't gonna finish," she teased, glancing back at him.

Houston smirked but said nothing, his eyes dark with desire.

Candy found the bag she was looking for, a large black duffel—and unzipped it to reveal stacks of cash, millions by the looks of it. She slid out a crisp hundred-dollar bill and zipped the bag closed, settling back into her seat.

She glanced at Houston, her smile seductive. "Watch this." she purred.

Candy's fingers worked quickly and skillfully, with practiced ease, she rolled the hundred-dollar bill into a tight, makeshift straw.

She reached over and opened the glove box, placing the aluminum packet on the open door. The contents shimmered slightly in the dim light, a dangerous promise of potency within. She glanced at Houston, her eyes sparkling with a mix of mischief and anticipation. Her lips curled into a broader seductive smile as she leaned down, positioning the rolled bill at the edge of the packet.

With a quick, confident inhale, she took a long, deliberate sniff. The sound of her sharp inhalation filled the car, followed by a soft, almost imperceptible hiss as the crystals rushed through the straw.

Time seemed to slow as the glistening crystal particles raced through the narrow tube. Each tiny fragment caught the light, reflecting a dazzling array of colors. The particles moved with a mesmerizing fluidity, a sparkling river flowing toward its destination.

Candy's head snapped back as she finished the sniff, her eyes fluttering closed for a brief moment. She pulled back, the rush of the drug hitting her system with a fierce intensity. Her body reacted immediately. She rubbed her nose, trying to ease the sharp, tingling sensation that followed the initial burn. A small cough escaped her lips, and she shook her head as if to clear the fog from her mind.

Her eyes began to water, tears pooling at the corners and spilling down her cheeks. She sniffed again, a soft, involuntary sound, as the drug's effects took hold. Her pupils dilated, the once-dark orbs now wide and black, reflecting the dim light of the car's interior. Candy's breathing quickened, each inhaling shallow and rapid as her body adjusted to the sudden influx of stimulants.

She rubbed her nose again, her fingers trembling slightly. The sensation was overwhelming, both euphoria and discomfort that left her momentarily disoriented. Her senses sharpened, the world around her coming into hyper-focus. Every detail seemed more vivid, every sound more distinct.

Houston watched her closely, a mix of concern and admiration in his gaze. "Feel better?" he asked, his voice low and steady.

Candy nodded, her eyes still watering but now shining with renewed, almost manic energy. "Much better," she replied, her voice a little hoarse but filled with a new intensity.

She leaned back in her seat, her earlier exhaustion replaced with a jittery, electric alertness. The rush of the drug coursed through her veins, bringing a flush to her cheeks and a sparkle to her eyes.

Houston turned up the radio, the sudden blast of Celine Dion's "My Heart Will Go On" filling the car. The powerful ballad clashed with the tense atmosphere, creating a surreal backdrop to the unfolding drama. Candy's reaction was immediate and violent. She slammed her head back against the headrest, her entire body tightening as the music washed over her.

Her eye opened wide, the iris expanding rapidly. The drug's potency surged through her system, amplifying her physical and emotional responses to an unbearable degree.

She rubbed her nose furiously, desperate to expel the substance she had just inhaled. Her movements became frantic, and she blew out forcefully, but the stimulant had already taken hold. Her head dropped into her lap, then snapped back against the headrest with a force that sent a jolt through her body. Blood began to seep from her nose, a crimson trickle that contrasted starkly with her pale skin.

She turned towards Houston, her eyes wide and filled with a mixture of confusion and desperation. Houston glanced over, a cold smile playing on his lips. Candy let out a low moan, her head slamming against the headrest again. Her entire body convulsed violently, a final, shuddering spasm that seemed to drain life from her. Her head rolled to the side, eyes open and unseeing, as a single tear rolled down her cheek and mixed with the blood from her nose.

Houston reached down with a practiced calm, drawing out a large cigar and a lighter from the console. He lit the cigar, the end glowing bright red as he took a deep drag. The smoke curled around him, adding to the already heavy air inside the car. With a deliberate tenderness, he reached over and ran his hand over Candy's face, closing her eyes gently.

"Checkmate," he murmured, his voice low and final.

Houston then reached down and turned the volume of the radio up even higher, Celine Dion's voice soaring to a crescendo as the Maserati sped down the highway. The car's engine roared in unison with the music, a powerful, unstoppable force tearing through the night.

The haunting melody of "My Heart Will Go On" echoed through the night, a poignant counterpoint to the deadly silence that now enveloped Candy.

The Maserati raced onward, its taillights fading into the distance, leaving behind a trail of smoke and the haunting memory of what had transpired within its sleek, dark frame. The night swallowed them whole, and the road stretched endlessly ahead, promising more twists and turns for Houston as he continued his perilous journey toward Camagüey.

As the car sped away into the night, leaving the Bentley shrouded in a thick cloud of dust, Candy's almost dead sanity began to drift in her final moment. Her body lay still, but within her, thoughts raced, memories flooded back, and last-minute regrets surfaced. Each beat of her heart seemed to echo louder, amplifying the silence around her. She felt suspended in time, trapped between the past she could not change and the future she would never see.

"Damn, I never thought I'd go out this way," she mused, her thoughts clear and vivid despite the chaos of the moments prior. She remembered the first time she had seen that large sum of money.

"Well, ain't that a bitch?" Her thoughts surfaced with a bitter edge. "At least it was a Bentley. Who wants to die on vinyl?" She mussed, trying to find a sliver of humor in her grim reality. The stacks of cash had felt like the keys to a kingdom, a golden ticket to a life she had only dreamt of. Visions of a luxurious lifestyle danced before her eyes, glittering parties, designer clothes, exotic vacations, and a sense of freedom she had longed for since she was a little girl.

Candy had planned every detail meticulously. She had pictured herself lounging on white sandy beaches, the sun warming her skin as she sipped on a cocktail, the waves lapping gently at the shore. She had seen herself walking through upscale boutiques, the thrill of buying anything she desired without a second thought. She had dreamed of the independence that money would bring, the power to make her own choices, and the security to never have to rely on anyone ever again.

Her thoughts then turned to Houston, the man she had trusted implicitly. The memory of their first meeting was still fresh in her mind. He had exuded a dangerous charm, a magnetism that had drawn her in despite her better judgment. His chiseled features and piercing blue eyes had captivated her, and his promises of a shared fortune had sealed her fate.

The realization that she had been used, played like a pawn in Houston's game hit her hard. She wished she could turn back time, undo the choices that had led her to this moment. She wished she had seen through Houston's facade sooner, recognized the danger lurking behind his charming exterior.

As her mind continued to race, she thought about the last moments in the Maserati. The rush of the drug, the way her body had reacted violently, and the cruel twist of fate that had left her here, dying and alone. She remembered Houston's cold smile as he watched her, his lack of concern, his complete detachment. The man she had trusted with her life had been the one to end it, and that betrayal cut deeper than any physical pain she felt.

Her thoughts drifted back to simpler times, before the allure of fast money and dangerous men. She thought of her childhood, the innocence she had lost along the way, and the dreams she had once had. She remembered the little girl who had believed in fairy tales, who had thought that love and happiness were her destiny. That little girl seemed so far away now, buried under layers of mistakes and missteps.

Candy's mind wandered through the what-ifs and the could-have-beens. What if she had taken a different path? What if she had walked away from Houston when she had the chance? What if she had trusted her instincts instead of her greed? Each question led to more regret, more pain, as she realized that her time was running out and there was no way to change the past.

"This was not my plan… this was not my plan…" Candy's final thoughts echoed in the silence, a haunting refrain of regret and realization. She wished she could turn back time, undo the choices that had led her to this moment.

As her thoughts wandered, she could almost hear her own voice echoing in silence. "Hell, all I wanted to do was kill my husband. You shouldn't have to die snorting blood and snot for that. I mean, some husbands deserve it. Ladies, you gotta feel me here. If he deserves it, you should be able to murder your husband, right?" The irony of her situation stung. She had set out to liberate herself from one man's tyranny, only to fall victim to another's.

She thought about the people she had left behind, the friends and family who would mourn her. She wondered if they would ever understand why she had made the choices she made. She hoped they would remember her for more than just her mistakes, that they would see the girl who had tried to make something of herself, even if she had ultimately failed.

As her final moments approached, Candy felt a strange sense of peace. Her body was shutting down, but her mind was still racing. She took a deep breath, or at least she imagined she did, and tried to focus on something positive. She thought about the sunsets she had seen, the moments of joy she had experienced, and the love she had once believed in.

Candy's thoughts spiraled further into regret. She saw now how she had misread the situation, how she had been blinded by the allure of wealth and power. The realization that she had been used, played like a pawn in Houston's game, hit her hard.

As her mind continued to race, she thought about the last moments in the Bentley. The rush of the drug, the way her body had reacted violently, and the cruel twist of fate that had left her here, dying and alone. She remembered Houston's cold smile as he watched her, his lack of concern, his complete detachment. The man she had trusted with her life had been the one to end it, and that betrayal cut deeper than any physical pain she felt.

Her thoughts returned to the present, to the Bentley abandoned by the roadside, to the man who had betrayed her. She realized that while she couldn't change what had happened, she could at least find some solace in her final thoughts. She chose to remember the good times, to hold onto the hope that somewhere, somehow, she had made a difference.

Candy's last conscious thought was a simple one. She wished for peace, for herself and for those she had left behind. She hoped that her death would not be in vain, that it would serve as a lesson to others about the dangers of trusting the wrong people, of letting greed cloud one's judgment.

The world around her grew dim, and her thoughts began to fade. As she slipped away, Candy's spirit felt lighter, freed from the burdens of regret and betrayal. She was leaving behind the physical pain, the emotional turmoil, and stepping into the unknown.

In the stillness of the night, as the dust settled around the Bentley, Candy found a semblance of peace. Her journey had been fraught with danger and deception, but in her final moments, she chose to focus on the love and light she had once known. Her life might have ended tragically, but her spirit remained resilient.

The Bentley skidded to a stop behind a waiting minivan, its tires kicking up a cloud of dust and gravel. The window of the minivan rolled down, and the side mirror tilted downward as a puff of smoke wafted out, but the driver remained obscured. Houston methodically began transferring the designer luggage and the bundles of cash from the back seat of the Bentley into the rear of the van. Candy, her lifeless body still seated in the passenger seat, seemed a tragic, silent witness to his cold efficiency.

Houston raised the Bentley's top and rolled up the heavily tinted windows, sealing Candy's body inside the car. He chirped the alarm, the sound final and indifferent, then jumped into the passenger side of the minivan. The van's wheels spun, sending another plume of dirt into the air as it roared down the highway towards L.A., leaving the once beautiful Bentley covered in grime.

The Bentley remained still and quiet as the dust settled around it, alone and abandoned by the roadside. Candy found a semblance of peace in her final moments, choosing to focus on the love and light she had once known. Her life might have ended tragically, but her spirit remained resilient.

Chapter Two

(Candy's earlier life)

The nightclub was alive with energy, a pulsating heart of music and lights that seemed to draw everyone into its vibrant embrace. Among the sea of bodies, one figure stood out, commanding attention with every move. Candy, the name she had earned and worn with pride, moved with a magnetic allure that captivated everyone in her orbit. She was in her element, the center of attention, the queen of the night.

Candy's long, dark hair cascaded down her back, catching the light with each turn of her head. Her dress, a shimmering creation that hugged her curves, sparkled under the club's neon lights. She danced with abandon, her body swaying to the rhythm, her movements fluid and hypnotic. Her eyes, usually filled with a mischievous sparkle, were now focused and intense, reflecting the flashing lights around her. She was a vision of seductive beauty, every inch of her exuding confidence and allure.

The crowd around her seemed to part, making way for her as she danced, a testament to the power she held in such a space. Men and women alike watched her with a mix of admiration and desire, drawn to her like moths to a flame. Candy thrived on this attention, feeding off the energy of the crowd, her laughter mingling with the music as she twirled and swayed.

Candy had always loved the nightlife. It was her escape, her sanctuary, a place where she could forget the troubles that plagued her during the day. The flashing lights, the pounding music, the sea of bodies moving in unison, it all created a sense of euphoria that she craved. Tonight was no different, and as she danced, she let herself get lost in the rhythm, allowing the music to wash over her and cleanse her of the day's worries.

As the DJ transitioned to a new song, Candy's movements became even more intense. She was no longer just dancing, it was as though she was performing. Every step, every twist of her hips, every flick of her hair was perfectly timed to the beat. The crowd around her watched in awe, mesmerized by her energy and confidence. She was a force of nature with beauty and grace.

Eventually, the music began to slow, and Candy decided it was time for a break. She made her way through the crowd, the sea of people parting before her. She could feel their eyes on her, could hear the whispers and see the admiring glances. It gave her a sense of power, a thrill that she relished.

Candy found a plush, velvet-covered booth in the VIP section and slid into it. A server appeared almost instantly, bringing her a glass of champagne. She took a sip, savoring the bubbles as they danced on her tongue. She closed her eyes and leaned back, letting the music wash over her, the thumping bass providing a soothing backdrop to her thoughts.

It wasn't long before her moment of peace was interrupted. A man approached her booth, his presence immediately commanding her attention. He was tall and well-dressed, but there was something about him that set Candy on edge. His eyes held a predatory gleam, and his smile was more of a smirk.

"Mind if I join you?" he asked, not waiting for an answer as he slid into the booth beside her.

Candy raised an eyebrow, her expression cool and detached. "Actually, I do mind."

The man chuckled, clearly not used to being turned down. "Come on, sweetheart. Don't be like that. Let me buy you a drink."

He reached into his pocket and pulled out a wad of cash, tossing a few bills onto the table. Candy glanced at the money, then back at the man, her expression unimpressed.

"That's not enough to even fuel my ride for a single trip," she said, her voice dripping with disdain. "And it certainly won't get you a reasonable drink."

The man's smirk faltered, replaced by a look of irritation. "You think you're too good for my money?"

"I know I am," Candy replied smoothly. "Now, if you'll excuse me, I'd like to enjoy my evening in peace."

The man's face flushed with anger, but before he could respond, a bouncer appeared at the edge of the booth. "Is there a problem here?" the bouncer asked, his tone leaving no room for argument.

Candy smiled sweetly. "No problem at all. This gentleman was just leaving."

The man glared at her, but he knew better than to make a scene. He stood up and stalked away, muttering under his breath. Candy watched him go, a sense of satisfaction washing over her. She had dealt with men like him before, and she knew how to handle them.

As the night wore on, Candy continued to dance and mingle, but the encounter had left a bitter taste in her mouth. It was a reminder of the darker side of the nightlife, the predators and opportunists who lurked in the shadows. However, Candy was no damsel in distress. She was a survivor, a fighter, and she wouldn't let anyone take advantage of her.

Beneath the surface, there was restlessness, a tension that even the pulsating beats of the nightclub couldn't entirely drown out. Candy's life, as glamorous as it seemed, was far from perfect, and tonight, that reality would follow her home.

* * *

The first light of dawn was beginning to creep over the horizon as Candy slipped into her man's opulent mansion. Her movements were stealthy, almost feline, as she navigated the familiar hallways. The mansion was a sprawling estate, an architectural masterpiece that stood in stark contrast to the vibrant chaos of the nightclub she had just left behind.

Candy's boyfriend, Lorenzo, had impeccable taste, and it showed in every detail of their home. The mansion was proof of luxury and excess, filled with the finest things money could buy. Its grand facade, crafted from pale limestone, glowed softly in the early morning light, casting shadows across the wonderfully manicured grounds. Towering columns framed the entrance, each one adorned with intricate carvings that told stories of myth and legend. Above the grand doorway, an expansive balcony jutted out, its ornate wrought-iron railing curling in elegant spirals.

As Candy stepped through the massive double doors, made of rich mahogany and inlaid with gold, she was greeted by an awe-inspiring foyer. The floors were a masterpiece of Italian marble, polished to a mirror-like sheen that reflected the dazzling crystal chandelier hanging from the ceiling high above. This chandelier was a marvel in itself, a cascade of sparkling crystals that caught and refracted the light, casting tiny rainbows across the walls.

The walls of the foyer were lined with priceless artwork, each piece carefully selected to complement the overall aesthetic of the space. Rich shade depicting historical scenes hung alongside modern abstract paintings, creating a harmonious blend of the old and the new. A grand staircase dominated the room, its sweeping curve leading to the upper floors. The banister, crafted from dark, polished wood, was smooth to touch and accented with delicate gold filigree.

To the left of the foyer was the formal living room, a space designed for entertaining in grand style. The room was dominated by a massive fireplace, its mantel carved from a single piece of marble and adorned with intricate reliefs. Above it hung a portrait of Candy, her beauty immortalized in oil and canvas, her gaze alluring. Plush sofas and armchairs, upholstered in rich velvet, were arranged around the fireplace, creating intimate conversation areas. The walls were lined with bookshelves filled with rare and first-edition volumes, their leather-bound spines adding a touch of scholarly elegance to the room.

Adjacent to the living room was the dining hall, a cavernous space designed to host lavish dinner parties. A long, polished table made of dark mahogany stretched down the center of the room, capable of seating over twenty guests. The chairs, each one a work of art with intricately carved backs and cushioned seats, were arranged with military precision. Above the table, another chandelier, smaller but no less impressive than the one in the foyer. The walls were paneled in rich wood, and large windows draped in luxurious silk curtains offered a view of the expansive gardens outside.

The second floor of the mansion was equally impressive, home to the private quarters of its inhabitants. The master suite was a sanctuary of luxury, with a king-sized bed draped in the finest linens and a canopy that added a touch of old-world romance. The room was decorated in soothing tones of cream and gold, creating a serene and calming atmosphere. Large windows offered a breathtaking view of the estate, and a private balcony provided a secluded spot for quiet reflection.

The en-suite bathroom was nothing short of a spa, with a deep soaking tub positioned under a large window, allowing for relaxing baths with a view. The countertops were made of marble, and the fixtures were gold-plated, adding a touch of opulence to the space. A walk-in shower with multiple showerheads and a steam feature provided a luxurious bathing experience, while a spacious walk-in closet offered ample storage for Candy's extensive wardrobe.

The mansion also boasted a state-of-the-art security system, with discreet cameras positioned around the property and a high stone wall surrounding the estate. This was a fortress of luxury, designed to provide both comfort and security to its inhabitants.

Yet, for all its grandeur, the mansion felt like a gilded cage to Candy. The luxurious surroundings could not mask the tension and turmoil that simmered beneath the surface.

Candy moved through the mansion with the practiced ease of someone who had lived there for years. Her long, dark hair cascaded down her back, catching the soft light with each turn of her head. Her dress, a shimmering creation that hugged her curves, now felt like a costume from another life. The allure and confidence she had exuded at the nightclub seemed to fade with each step she took deeper into the mansion.

She made her way to the modern kitchen, the heart of their luxurious home. The kitchen was a chef's dream, equipped with state-of-the-art appliances and ample counter space. The countertops were made of polished granite, and the cabinets, painted a crisp white, were filled with the finest China and glassware. A large island stood in the center of the room, topped with a butcher block surface that was perfect for meal preparation. Hanging above the island was a pot rack, from which gleaming copper pots and pans were suspended.

Candy opened the SUB-ZERO refrigerator and took out a carton of orange juice. She took a long drink directly from the carton, the cold liquid a refreshing contrast to the heat of the night she had just endured. As she placed the carton back, she spotted a stalk of celery and pulled it out, gnawing absentmindedly as she moved to sit on a tall stool by the high marble counter.

Her eyes were drawn to a photo framed on the counter. It was a picture of her and Lorenzo on the last Valentine's day. They looked so happy, so in love. She stared at the image, trying to reconcile the smiling faces with the reality of their life now. The man in the photo was well-built, his dark hair neatly styled, his eyes filled with adoration. But the Lorenzo she knew now was different, his love tainted by control and anger.

Candy sighed and finished her celery, the crunching sound filling the otherwise silent kitchen. She knew she couldn't linger here forever. Gathering her resolve, she stood up and made her way to the master bedroom.

Entering the bedroom quietly, Candy began to undress. She let her clothes fall to the floor, revealing the expensive lingerie she wore underneath. She headed towards the walk-in closet, her mind focused on finding something comfortable to wear. But as she reached for the door, she was suddenly grabbed from behind.

A gasp escaped her lips as she was thrown onto the bed. She bounced and turned, her eyes widening as she saw Lorenzo standing there, shirtless and seething with anger. His muscular frame was tense, his fists clenched at his sides.

His tall frame and broad shoulders filled the doorway, casting a shadow over the room. His dark hair was neatly styled, and his tailored suit spoke of his impeccable taste. But his eyes, those piercing blue eyes that had once captivated her, now held a cold, calculating glint.

Lorenzo was a man of many contradictions. He was handsome and charismatic, with a charm that had drawn Candy to him in the first place. But he was also controlling and possessive, his temper quick to flare. Their relationship had become a series of heated arguments and bitter exchanges, each one leaving them both bruised and unsettled.

"What the hell were you doing out so late?" he demanded, his voice low and dangerous.

"Nice to see you too," Candy replied teasingly.

"Answer my question before I lose it, lady." He growled, picking up a vase from the stand nearby

Candy tried to steady her breathing, her heart racing. "I just needed some time to myself," she replied, her voice trembling slightly seeing as he was in for no joke.

Lorenzo stepped closer, his eyes blazing. "Time to yourself?

At a nightclub? Do you think I'm stupid?"

Candy pushed herself up on the bed, trying to put some distance between them. "No, Lorenzo, it's not like that. I just needed to clear my head."

"Clear your head?" Lorenzo scoffed, his anger barely contained but dropped the vase. "You've got everything here. What more do you need?"

Candy felt a surge of frustration. "I need to feel like I'm more than just your trophy. I need to feel like I have some control over my own life."

Lorenzo's expression hardened. "You're mine, Candy. Don't you forget that."

Candy's eyes filled with tears, but she refused to let them fall. "I can't live like this anymore, Lorenzo. Something has to change."

Lorenzo reached out and grabbed her arm, his grip tight. "You're not going anywhere," he said through gritted teeth.

Candy stared at him, her defiance flaring. "Watch me," she whispered, pulling her arm free.

For a moment, they stood there, locked in a silent battle of wills. Then, without another word, Candy turned and walked towards the closet. Lorenzo's eyes followed her, his expression darkening with each step she took. He watched as she reached for the closet door, his anger simmering just below the surface.

Without warning, Lorenzo stormed after her, grabbing her arm and yanking her back. His hand connected with her face in a brutal slap, the force of the blow sending her staggering. "How dare you walk away from me when I'm not done talking," he snarled, his grip tightening painfully around her wrist.

Candy's eyes flashed with both pain and fury as he shoved her back onto the bed. But this time, she was ready for him. Rising to her knees at the end of the bed, she put her arms around Lorenzo's shoulders and nuzzled his neck, trying to diffuse the situation. "Baby, you know I'm a good girl. I just wanted to have a little fun, that's all," she murmured, her voice soft and soothing.

Lorenzo's eyes narrowed, suspicion clouding his features. "Yeah… I know you alright," he said, his tone dripping with sarcasm.

Candy pressed on, her lips brushing against his skin as she spoke. "Come on, you know it's not like that. Let's not fight. Let me be good to you." She moved her lips from his neck to his chest, her hands trailing sensuously down his torso.

For a moment, Lorenzo seemed to relax, his anger dissipating under her touch. But as she continued, his expression hardened again. He snapped out of his brief reverie and shoved Candy away, slapping her once again with such force that she bounced face down on the bed, facing away from him.

Candy's head snapped up, her eyes wild with a crazed look. "Fuck you, Candy, you ain't good for anyone," Lorenzo spat, standing at the foot of the bed.

Candy looked over her shoulder, her gaze locking onto Lorenzo's. With a swift, powerful motion, she thrust her foot out, connecting with his groin. Lorenzo doubled over in pain, a guttural moan escaping his lips. Candy spun on her back and delivered a hard kick to Lorenzo's cheek, sending him crashing across the room into a large, padded chair.

In an instant, Candy sprang from the bed and stood over the groaning Lorenzo. She straddled him, pinning his hands back against the chair and kissing him hard, her lips trailing down his face to his neck. He let out another pained groan as she violently tore off his silk boxers and threw them aside.

Lorenzo's breathing grew ragged as he watched Candy, both fear and desire in his eyes. "You're fucking crazy," he muttered, his voice thick with emotion.

Candy ran her hands through her hair as she knelt in front of him, a wicked smile playing on her lips. "And you ain't interested in a good girl," she replied, digging her fingers in his back her tone low and seductive at the same time slapping her own ass.

As Candy's head disappeared from his view, Lorenzo threw his head back, a moan of pleasure replacing his earlier groans of pain. For that moment, the mansion's opulence and the night's tension melted away, leaving only the primal connection between them.

* * *

Candy entered the kitchen and poured herself a mug of coffee. Walking through the sliding door, she joined Lorenzo on the veranda. He was sitting there, eyes closed, listening to an iPod. Candy looked over the rail and then sat down. Lorenzo took out the earphones and gave her a withering look.

"Good morning, Papi," Candy said, trying to sound cheerful.

"Morning? It's fucking 3 o'clock, it's after lunch," Lorenzo retorted, his voice dripping with irritation.

"Well, it's morning to me," Candy replied, shrugging.

Lorenzo's eyes narrowed. "There's some new bitch in the living room cleaning. I guess we have a new maid. You'd think somebody would tell me what the fuck is going on around here."

"Why do you have to call her a bitch? She's not doing anything to you but cleaning up your shit. I'd think you'd be in a better mood after last night," Candy said, her tone sharp.

"After what? You whoring around all night till five in the morning or coming home and slapping my ass around? Look at my fucking face!" Lorenzo turned and showed her a nasty bruise across his jaw. Candy looked sheepish.

"That's not that bad," she muttered.

"I had to cancel an interview today because of this shit. People asking me what the hell happened, no way," Lorenzo shot back.

"It was a radio interview, you're a football player for Christ's sake," Candy countered.

"Fuck you, Candy! I got 16 games to make a mark on a shit team that ain't near making the playoffs. In a few weeks, I'm out of the fucking paper!" Lorenzo's frustration boiled over.

"I'm sorry, what do you want me to say...you started it," Candy said, showing her own not-as-bruised cheek.

"I got a meeting tonight, what the fuck am I supposed to tell those motherfuckers when they ask where I got it?" He demanded.

Candy stood up, ready to leave. "Tell them the truth...you got it getting laid."

She trailed her hand under Lorenzo's chin as she passed by. Suddenly, he grabbed her wrist, twisting her arm and pushing her face down on the table, scattering dishes and driving her cheek into a fruit bowl.

"Don't forget what you mean to me, bitch..." Lorenzo leaned down, his face near Candy's, who struggled to get free but was overpowered. "Nothing, piss me off and I got no fucking use for you."

Lorenzo released Candy, half-pushing her into a chair. As Candy looked up, eyes enraged, she saw a young woman in a maid's uniform watching from the kitchen. They locked eyes for a moment before the young woman hurried away. Lorenzo looked in the same direction but saw no one. He took out a wad of money and threw it on the table.

"I'll be leaving in the morning, be back in a couple of days. You better take the time and check that fucking attitude before I get back," Lorenzo said, walking off and leaving Candy alone on the veranda.

Candy sat in silence, the tension still crackling in the air. She could feel the sting on her wrist.

Chapter Three

Candy's eyes were transfixed on the photograph. It was a sun-drenched memory captured on glossy paper—Houston, smiling widely on a yacht, the deep blue sea behind him. As she stared, the image seemed to ripple and come alive, pulling her into the depths of her past.

Suddenly, Candy found herself back in Campeche, Mexico. The sun was beating down, the air was thick with humidity. She glanced over at a younger version of herself, sitting in the passenger seat of a dusty old car. Next to her was Houston, his eyes hidden behind aviator sunglasses, the brim of his cowboy hat casting a shadow over his face. They were driving down a bumpy dirt road, the engine rumbling beneath them.

The abandoned hangar loomed ahead, a relic from another time, rusted and weather-beaten. As they approached, Houston killed the engine and they sat in silence for a moment, the ticking of the cooling motor the only sound.

"Are you sure this is the place?" Candy asked, her voice tinged with apprehension.

Houston nodded, his gaze fixed on the hangar. "Jimmy Mack said to meet him here. He's got what we need."

Candy glanced around, the desolate landscape adding to her unease. "And you trust him?"

Houston chuckled, a low, confident sound. "As much as you can trust a hustler. But he knows his business."

They got out of the car, the gravel crunching under their boots. The hangar door was ajar, a sliver of darkness peeking through. Houston pushed it open, the metal groaning in protest. Inside, the hangar was cavernous, shadows stretching into every corner.

They stepped inside, the air cooler and musty. Candy's eyes adjusted to the dim light, and she saw stacks of crates and barrels scattered around. The place looked abandoned, but there was a sense of expectation hanging in the air.

Houston pulled out his phone, checking the time. "He should be here by now," he muttered.

Candy leaned against a crate, crossing her arms. "So, we wait."

The minutes ticked by slowly. Houston paced, his boots echoing off the concrete floor. Candy watched him, her mind racing with possibilities. What if Jimmy Mack didn't show? What if this was a setup? She pushed the thoughts away, focusing on the present.

Finally, the sound of an engine broke the silence. They both turned towards the entrance as a black SUV pulled up, its headlights cutting through the gloom. The vehicle stopped, and for a moment, there was no movement. Then, the driver's door opened, and a man stepped out.

Inside, Jimmy Mack was waiting, a smirk playing on his lips. He was a wiry figure, his clothes hanging off him like they were a size too big. He had a cigarette dangling from his lips, and his eyes darted around nervously as he approached.

"Sorry for the wait," Jimmy said, his voice a raspy whisper. "Had to make sure I wasn't followed."

Houston gave him a curt nod. "You got the goods?"

Jimmy nodded, flicking his cigarette to the ground. "Yeah, I got 'em. Follow me."

They trailed Jimmy to the back of the SUV, where he opened the rear doors. Inside were crates, similar to the ones in the hangar. Jimmy pulled one out and pried it open, revealing an assortment of weapons. Houston inspected them closely, checking for serial numbers and conditions.

"Looks good," Houston said finally. "But we need to test them."
Jimmy grinned, revealing a row of yellowed teeth. "Be my guest."

Houston selected a rifle, checking the magazine before aiming it at a distant target. He fired a few rounds, the shots echoing through the hangar. Satisfied, he nodded to Candy.

"Your turn," he said, handing her the rifle.

Candy took it, her hands were steady. She aimed and fired, hitting the target with precision. She lowered the weapon, meeting Houston's eyes with a nod.

"These will do," she said.

Jimmy looked relieved, rubbing his hands together. "Great. Now, about the payment..."

Houston pulled out a thick envelope, handing it to Jimmy. The hustler counted the bills quickly, his eyes gleaming with satisfaction.

"Pleasure doing business with you," Jimmy said, pocketing the money.

"Likewise," Houston replied. "But remember, if you double-cross us..."

Jimmy held up his hands. "No need for threats. I'm a man of my word."

With the deal done, Jimmy loaded the remaining crates into their car. Candy and Houston watched him drive away, the SUV kicking up dust as it disappeared into the distance.

"Think we can trust him?" Candy asked, breaking the silence.

Houston shrugged. "As far as we need to. We got what we came for."

They closed the hangar door behind them, the metal clanging shut. As they drove back down the dirt road, Candy glanced at

Houston, her mind still buzzing with the events of the day.

"You think this will change anything?" she asked softly.

Houston's grip tightened on the wheel. "It has to. We're in too deep to turn back now."

The sun was setting as they reached the outskirts of Campeche, the sky painted with hues of orange and pink. Candy felt a sense of foreboding, but also a strange excitement. They were playing a dangerous game, but it was one they were determined to win.

Hours later, they were parked under an overpass on the outskirts of Campeche, waiting for the buyers. The evening air was cooler, the sounds of the city muted in the distance. Candy leaned against the car, her eyes scanning the darkened landscape.

"How long do we wait?" she asked, glancing at Houston. "Not much longer," Houston replied, his eyes fixed on the road ahead. "They'll show."

As if on cue, a pair of headlights appeared in the distance, growing brighter as they approached. A black sedan pulled up beside their car, the engine idling. Two men stepped out, their movements cautious.

"Evening," one of the men called out, his voice echoing under the overpass. "You Houston?"

Houston nodded. "That's me. You got the cash?"

The man smiled, a cold, calculated expression. "Yeah, we got it. You got the merchandise?"

"Right here," Houston replied, motioning towards the trunk.

The second man stepped forward, his eyes narrowing as he inspected the crates. "Mind if we take a look?"

Houston hesitated, then nodded. "Go ahead."

Candy watched the second man closely, her instincts on high alert. Something felt off. She glanced at Houston, who was watching the first man with a steely gaze.

The second man pried open a crate, revealing the weapons inside. He picked up a rifle, inspecting it closely. Candy's heart raced as the man took longer than necessary, his eyes flicking back and forth between the weapon and the crate.

Suddenly, the first man pulled a gun from his jacket, pointing it directly at Houston. "Hands up! You're under arrest!"

Before Candy or Houston could react, the sound of sirens filled the air, and police cars swarmed the area, their lights flashing. The two men drew their weapons, revealing their badges. "Hands up!" they shouted in unison.

Candy's mind raced. This was a setup. She glanced at Houston, who was already reaching for his gun. "Run!" he shouted, firing a shot at the undercover cops.

The scene erupted into chaos. Candy ducked behind a pillar, pulling out her own weapon. She fired a few shots, trying to provide cover for Houston. The police were closing in, their shouts filling the air.

"Over here!" Houston yelled, motioning for Candy to follow him.

They sprinted towards a gap between two concrete pillars, bullets whizzing past them. Candy could hear the officers yelling, the sound of boots hitting the ground as they pursued. They reached the other side of the overpass, and Houston spotted an alleyway.

"This way!" he urged, grabbing Candy's arm.

They dashed into the alley, the narrow space providing some cover. Candy's breath came in short gasps, her adrenaline pumping. She could hear the police getting closer, their footsteps echoing off the walls.

They reached a dead end. Houston cursed under his breath, yanking a machine gun from his bag. "We have to hold them off," he said, handing Candy another weapon.

The alleyway lit up with gunfire as they unleashed a barrage of bullets, forcing the police to take cover. Candy's ears rang from the noise, but she kept firing, determined to buy them some time. The officers hesitated, pinned down by the onslaught.

"Go!" Houston shouted, reloading his weapon. "I'll cover you!"

Candy nodded, sprinting towards a fire escape ladder. She scrambled up, bullets hitting the metal steps beneath her. Houston followed, firing sporadically to keep the police at bay.

They reached the rooftop, racing across the gravel surface. Below, the police regrouped, their shouts echoing in the night. Houston led the way, leaping to the next building. Candy followed, her heart pounding.

They continued their desperate escape, jumping from rooftop to rooftop. Finally, they found a fire escape leading down to a deserted street. They slid down, landing with a thud.

"We need to split up," Houston said, his voice urgent. "We'll meet at the docks."

Candy nodded, understanding immediately. They had planned for situations like this. She turned to run in the opposite direction, but paused for a moment, meeting Houston's eyes. "Be careful," she whispered.

"You too," he replied, giving her a quick nod before disappearing down the alley.

Candy took off, her mind focused on escaping. She navigated through the maze of backstreets, her familiarity with the area guiding her steps. The sounds of pursuit gradually faded, but she didn't slow down until she was sure she had lost them.

Candy found herself in a narrow, dimly lit alley. She leaned against the wall, catching her breath. The adrenaline still pumped through her veins, making her hyper-aware of every sound around her. She heard a distant siren and knew she needed to keep moving.

She darted down another alley, her shoes slapping against the wet pavement. Her mind raced as she plotted her next move. The docks weren't too far, but getting there without being seen was the challenge. She had to stay off the main roads.

The city was a maze of backstreets and hidden passages, and Candy moved through them like a ghost. She could still hear the distant sounds of the police, but they were getting fainter. She paused at a corner, peeking around to make sure the coast was clear.

Suddenly, a police car sped past, its siren blaring. Candy pressed herself against the wall, her heart pounding. She waited until the car was out of sight before continuing. She had to get to the docks. That was their rendezvous point.

As she moved through the streets, memories of past heists and narrow escapes flooded her mind. This wasn't the first time they'd been in a tight spot, but it felt different. The stakes were higher, and the tension was palpable.

Candy finally reached the waterfront. The smell of saltwater and fish filled the air, and she could hear the gentle lapping of the waves against the docks. She stayed in the shadows, moving carefully to avoid being seen. She scanned the area, looking for any sign of Houston.

She spotted him near a row of shipping containers. He was crouched down, checking their surroundings. When he saw her, he motioned for her to join him. Candy moved quickly but quietly, her heart still racing.

"Did you lose them?" Houston asked, his voice low.

I think so," Candy replied. "But we all need to get out of here." They grabbed masks from their bags, pulling them over their faces to help them breathe underwater. Houston gave a nod, signaling for them to move. They dove into the water, the cold shock of it hitting their skin. They swam away from the shore, moving quickly and quietly. The city lights grew smaller in the distance, the vast expanse of the ocean stretching out before them.

As they swam through the water, Candy glanced at Houston, her mind racing with the events of the night. "What now?" she asked once they surfaced, bobbing in the gentle waves.

Houston's jaw tightened. "We lay low for a while. Find a place to regroup and figure out our next move."

Jimmy swam closer, his breathing heavy but controlled. "We need to find a safe spot to get out of the water. There's a cove nearby that we can use."

Candy nodded, the weight of their situation pressing down on her. But she knew they had to stay strong. They had come too far to give up now.

They swam for what felt like hours, but was probably only minutes, until they reached a secluded cove. The shoreline was hidden by rocky cliffs, and they carefully made their way onto the small, hidden beach. Houston, Jimmy, and Candy pulled off their masks, gasping for air.

"We'll hide out here for a bit," Houston said, scanning the area. "There's a resort nearby where we can blend in."

Candy climbed out of the water, her legs unsteady on the sand. She followed Houston up a narrow path, the sound of waves crashing behind them. As they approached the resort, the warm glow of lights welcomed them, a stark contrast to the chaos they had just escaped.

Houston turned to her, his expression serious. "I need you to take the money and lay low. Wire it to our contact in LA. We'll regroup there."

She hesitated, fear and uncertainty flashing in her eyes. "I don't want to be alone with the money," she said, her voice trembling. "What if I get caught?"

Before Houston could respond, the roar of engines shattered the stillness. A black SUV screeched to a halt, and armed men jumped out, guns blazing. "Go! Now!" Houston shouted, pushing her towards the resort.

Candy stumbled forward, clutching the waterproof bag. Bullets ricocheted off the rocks around them. She heard Houston and Jimmy returning to the fire, their shouts drowned out by the gunfire.

She sprinted up the path, her heart pounding. A bullet whizzed past her ear, and she ducked instinctively, diving behind a boulder. Her hands trembled as she pulled out her own weapon, firing back blindly. The resort was only a few hundred yards away, but it felt like miles.

"Candy, move!" Houston's voice cut through the chaos. She glanced back to see him and Jimmy retreating, covering her escape. She forced herself to her feet and ran, her legs burning with effort.

They reached the edge of the resort, where a tall fence blocked their path. "Over here!" Houston shouted, leading them to a gate. He kicked it open, and they slipped inside, the sounds of gunfire fading behind them.

The resort's warm glow was a stark contrast to the danger they had just escaped. They dashed through the manicured gardens, ducking behind bushes and statues. Candy's breath came in ragged gasps, her adrenaline pumping.

Houston grabbed her arm, pulling her into a shadowy alcove. "I need you to take the money and lay low. Wire it to our contact in LA. We'll regroup there."

Candy shook her head, her voice rising. "I can't do this alone, Houston. What if something goes wrong?"

"Candy, listen to me," Houston said firmly. "If we stay together, they'll catch us both. We will have a better chance if we split up. You're smart, you're careful, and you're the only one who can do this."

Tears welled up in her eyes, but she nodded slowly, understanding the gravity of the situation. Houston handed her the bag again, its weight reassuring in her hands.

"Be careful," he said, his voice softening.

"I will," she replied, stepping closer. She leaned in and kissed him, a promise and a farewell wrapped in one.

Houston and Jimmy exchanged a look, then nodded. They needed to find another way to escape, but Houston trusted her to get the money to safety.

"Stay hidden and keep your head down," Jimmy added. "We'll make it out of this."

She watched them go, her heart heavy with worry. But she knew they would find a way. They always did.

Candy made her way towards the resort, moving carefully through the shadows. She could hear distant voices and laughter, the sounds of people enjoying their evening. It was a stark contrast to the danger they were facing.

She entered the resort, blending in with the crowd. Moving through the lobby, she made her way to a quiet corner where she could gather her thoughts. She needed to stay focused. There was too much at stake.

As she navigated through the crowd, she kept her head down, blending in with the tourists and guests. The resort was lively, with people chatting, drinking, and enjoying their evening. It was hard to believe that just minutes ago, she was dodging bullets and escaping a police raid.

Candy moved quickly, slipping into the hotel's back corridors. She knew she had to avoid the main areas to stay hidden. She found a service elevator and took it to the basement, where she could find a quiet spot to plan her next move.

The basement was dimly lit and quiet, a stark contrast to the bustling resort above. Candy found an empty storage room and slipped inside, locking the door behind her. She leaned against the wall, catching her breath. The adrenaline still pumped through her veins, making her hyper-aware of every sound around her.

She knew she needed to move fast. She opened the waterproof bag and counted the money inside, her hands still trembling. She had to get to a secure location where she could wire the money safely. The docks weren't too far, but getting there without being seen was the challenge. She had to stay off the main roads and avoid any more encounters with the police or their pursuers.

Candy found a secluded spot near the pool, a quiet corner where she could gather her thoughts. She sat down and pulled out her phone, quickly typing a message to their contact in LA. She knew the transfer needed to happen fast. But didn't know how.

She checked the waterproof bag Houston had given her, ensuring everything was intact. The weight of the money felt heavy, both physically and metaphorically. Candy knew their lives depended on this.

Meanwhile, Houston and Jimmy were making their way through the dense foliage surrounding the cove. They moved quickly and quietly, aware that the police could still be searching for them.

"We need to find a place to hide until we can figure out our next move," Houston said, his voice low.

Jimmy nodded. "There's an old warehouse near the edge of town. We can lay low there for a while."

They continued on, their senses on high alert. Every rustle of leaves, every distant sound made them tense, ready for anything. The night was dark, the moon hidden behind thick clouds, making it difficult to see more than a few feet ahead.

They reached a deserted road, sticking to the shadows as they moved. The warehouse came into view, a dilapidated building that had seen better days. It was perfect for their needs: abandoned and out of sight.

Back at the resort, Candy finished her message and sent it, hoping their contact would act quickly. She tucked her phone away and tried to relax, but her mind was racing. She needed to stay calm and collected. The lobby was bustling with activity, and she knew she needed to blend in.

She approached the front desk, adopting a casual demeanor. "Excuse me," she said, smiling at the receptionist. "Could you recommend a good place to eat around here?"

The receptionist smiled back, unaware of the turmoil Candy was hiding. "Of course! We have a lovely restaurant by the beach, and there's also a great seafood place just a short walk away."

Candy thanked her and pretended to consider her options, all the while keeping an eye on the exits and entrances. She needed to stay alert even though she knew her face was not seen by the police based on the earlier encounter.

After a while, she decided to head to the beachside restaurant. It was public enough to keep her safe and give her a clear view of the surroundings.

Houston and Jimmy on the other hand slipped into the warehouse, the darkness swallowing them. It wasn't much, but it would provide some cover for the time being. The large, echoing space was filled with the remnants of forgotten goods and the musty smell of neglect. They found a corner where they could rest, keeping watch for any signs of trouble.

Houston leaned against the cold, rough wall, his mind racing as he tried to process the events of the past few days. Jimmy, younger and less experienced but equally wary, settled beside him, his eyes darting around the shadowy interior.

The silence was thick and heavy, broken only by the distant sounds of the city outside. Exhaustion began to take its toll, and despite their situation, both men drifted into a light, uneasy sleep.

It felt like only minutes had passed when Jimmy's insistent tapping pulled Houston from the edge of slumber. "Houston," Jimmy whispered urgently. "I heard something."

Instantly alert, Houston was on his feet, his senses sharpened by the adrenaline coursing through his veins. He listened intently, his eyes narrowing as he scanned the darkness. "We need to get moving," he murmured to Jimmy, his voice low and tense.

They began to gather their things, the sense of urgency growing with every passing second. Just as they were about to slip out of their hiding place, a voice echoed through the warehouse, cutting through the silence like a knife.

"It's too late! Don't move!" The voice was sharp and authoritative, coming from somewhere deep in the shadows.

Houston and Jimmy froze, their hearts pounding as they realized they were no longer alone.

Chapter Four

(Four months later)

Charlotte Glenn (Candy) stood in the bustling Mexican airport, her eyes darting around, scanning faces, searching for any signs of danger. Her past had taught her to be vigilant, the tiniest lapse in attention could mean disaster. The line moved slowly, and she shifted her weight, her nerves on edge. Each person she saw seemed like a potential threat, each moment a potential trap. Finally, she reached the counter, handed over her forged documents, and held her breath as the agent scrutinized them. After what felt like an eternity, she received her ticket to Miami. Clutching her boarding pass, she felt a mixture of relief and anxiety. The forged identity of Charlotte Glenn had held up, but she knew this was just the beginning.

As she moved through the terminal, Candy's mind wandered back to the day she decided to flee. The constant threat had become unbearable, every shadow a potential danger, every whisper a possible betrayal. She remembered the night she overheard a conversation that sealed her decision to escape, the cold and calculated words confirming her worst fears. That was the final straw. She couldn't risk another close call, another brush with disaster. The forged documents, the new identity, it was all a desperate gamble to secure her freedom and safety.

She spotted a family laughing together, a businessman engrossed in his phone, a couple arguing quietly. Each scene was a reminder of the normalcy she yearned for but couldn't afford. Candy glanced at her boarding pass again, the name Charlotte Glenn glaring back at her. It felt foreign, a mask she wore to keep her true self hidden. She thought about the risks involved in her plan. The documents had cost a fortune, but they were her ticket to freedom. She just had to make it to Miami, start over, blend in.

As she sat in the waiting area, Candy noticed a man in a dark suit standing by the gate. He seemed out of place, too attentive. Her heart raced. Was he looking for her? She forced herself to remain calm, rehearsing the details of her new identity in her mind: Charlotte Glenn, age 28, marketing consultant, no criminal record. She repeated it like a mantra, a shield against the fear threatening to overwhelm her.

To distract herself, she thought about her future. In Miami, she had a small apartment waiting, rented under her new name. It wasn't much, but it was a start. She had dreams of a quiet life, maybe even a career in marketing for real this time. But the shadow of her past loomed large, and she knew that one slip could bring everything crashing down.

The boarding announcement finally came, and Candy joined the queue. She took a deep breath, steadying herself. The next step was crucial. She handed her boarding pass to the gate agent, who scanned it without incident. As she walked down the jet bridge, she couldn't help but glance over her shoulder one last time. The man in the dark suit was gone, but her paranoia lingered.

Settling into her seat on the plane, Candy allowed herself a small sigh of relief. She was one step closer to freedom, but the journey was far from over. She gazed out the window as the plane took off, the Mexican landscape shrinking below. With each passing mile, she left behind a life of danger and deception, moving towards a future filled with uncertainty and hope.

The hum of the engines provided a strange comfort to Candy, a reminder that she was moving forward, escaping the clutches of her past. She closed her eyes, imagining a life where she could be herself again, where she didn't have to look over her shoulder constantly. It was a dream she held onto tightly, even as the reality of her situation loomed large. The weight of her past was heavy, a constant presence that threatened to pull her back. Yet, with each mile, she felt a bit lighter, a bit more hopeful.

As the plane touched down in Miami, Candy felt a mix of relief and apprehension. She collected her belongings and stepped into the warm, humid air. The city was alive with energy, a stark contrast to the small town she had fled. Here, she could disappear into the crowd, start fresh. The chaos of the airport was overwhelming, but it was a welcome distraction from her swirling thoughts.

Candy took a deep breath, the salty sea air filling her lungs. The vibrant colors of Miami's architecture, the bustling streets, and the diverse crowd were all a sensory overload, but they also represented freedom. She could blend in here, become someone new, someone without the shadows of her past haunting her every step.

Her new identity as Charlotte Glenn was more than just a name change, it was a lifeline. She had spent months planning this escape, meticulously crafting a new persona. Charlotte was confident, and assertive, everything Candy had once been but had lost in the wake of her tumultuous past. As Charlotte, she could start anew, but the fear of being discovered still lurked at the edges of her mind.

Candy hailed a cab, giving the driver the address of a modest apartment she had rented in advance. As the cab navigated through the busy streets, she watched the city pass by, a mixture of old and new, gritty and glamorous. She felt a pang of longing for the simplicity of her old life, but she quickly pushed it aside. There was no going back now.

The apartment building was unassuming, a perfect place to stay under the radar. As she climbed the stairs to her new home, her heart pounded with a mix of excitement and anxiety. The apartment was small but clean, with just enough space for her to feel comfortable. She unpacked her few belongings, arranging them methodically, creating a semblance of order in her chaotic world.

Candy sat on the edge of the bed, the reality of her situation sinking in. She was alone in a new city, with no one to rely on but herself. It was both terrifying and exhilarating. She knew she had to be careful, to avoid drawing attention to herself. Her past had taught her to be vigilant, to trust no one.

The next few days were a blur of settling in and getting to know her new surroundings. Candy, now Charlotte, explored the city, familiarizing herself with the neighborhoods, the markets, and the cafes.

She discovered local markets, where vendors sold tropical fruits and handmade crafts. She frequented small cafes, where the rich aroma of Cuban coffee mingled with the scent of fresh pastries. The diversity and vibrancy of Miami were intoxicating, a stark contrast to the monochrome palette of her past life. Candy found solace in the anonymity the city offered. Here, she was just another face in the crowd, free from the shadows that once haunted her.

It wasn't long before she discovered the vibrant nightlife that Miami had to offer. The clubs, the music, the people, it was all a whirlwind, a way to drown out the memories of her past. On weekends, she ventured into the heart of Miami's nightlife, where neon lights painted the night sky, and the thumping bass of electronic music reverberated through her chest. She danced with strangers, losing herself in the music, the motion, the moment. It was in these moments of abandon that she felt some weight lifted, if only temporarily.

One night, while exploring the nightlife, she stumbled upon a salsa club tucked away in a side street. The pulsating rhythms of the music drew her in, and she found herself captivated by the energy and passion of the dancers. She stood at the edge of the dance floor, watching couples move in perfect harmony, their bodies telling stories with each step. It reminded her of the nights she used to dance with Houston, back when life was simpler.

The club was glamorous, a place where the city's elite came to unwind. Candy blended in, letting the music and atmosphere wash over her. As she danced to the pulsating beats, Candy noticed him, Lorenzo. He was charismatic and confident, with an air of mystery that drew her in. Lorenzo was a well-known football player, and his presence commanded attention. The lights reflected off his chiseled features, creating an almost ethereal glow around him. Their eyes locked from across the dance floor, and he made his way toward her, a charming smile playing on his lips.

"Can I buy you a drink?" Lorenzo asked, his voice smooth and inviting, almost as if it were part of the music.

Candy hesitated for a moment, then nodded. "Sure, why not?" she replied, flashing him a dazzling smile, her eyes dancing with the same rhythm as the music.

As they moved to the bar, Lorenzo leaned in closer to be heard over the music. "What's your name?" he asked, his breath warm against her ear.

"Candy," she said, and then, almost as an afterthought, added, "Charlotte Glenn."

"Nice to meet you, Charlotte," he said, his eyes twinkling with intrigue. "So, what brings you to Miami?"

Candy took a sip of the drink he handed her, the cool liquid a stark contrast to the heat of the club. "A fresh start," she said with a hint of mystery. "What about you? What's a famous football player doing in a place like this?"

Lorenzo chuckled, a deep, resonant sound. "Just unwinding after a game. I love the energy of this place, don't you?"

She nodded, feeling the bass reverberate through her bones. "It's different. Vibrant. It's easy to get lost in the moment."

They spent the night talking, dancing, and laughing. Lorenzo was unlike anyone Candy had ever met. He was successful, confident, and seemed genuinely interested in her. His stories about his football career and travels were fascinating, and Candy found herself getting swept up in the excitement of it all. She learned about his rise to fame, the pressures of being in the spotlight, and the places he'd seen around the world.

"So, have you been living here for long?" Lorenzo asked as they took a break from dancing, his eyes never leaving hers.

"No," Candy said, her eyes drifting to the neon lights flickering in the distance. "I moved here recently. Needed a change of scenery."

Lorenzo looked at her thoughtfully. "Sounds like there's a story there."

Candy shrugged, smiling. "Maybe someday I'll tell you."

As the night progressed, they moved to a quieter corner of the club, where they could talk more intimately. The music was a distant thrum, allowing their conversation to flow more easily. Lorenzo's charm was undeniable, and Candy felt a connection she hadn't experienced in a long time. It was easy to forget her past when she was with him, to lose herself in the moment.

"Do you come here often?" Candy asked, swirling the remnants of her drink.

"Whenever I need a break," Lorenzo admitted. "It's a good place to let loose and be myself."

Candy raised an eyebrow. "And who is the real Lorenzo?"

He smiled, a touch of vulnerability in his eyes. "Just a guy trying to figure things out, like everyone else."

Their conversation drifted to more personal topics. Candy found herself opening up in ways she hadn't expected. She spoke of her desire to start anew, the excitement and fear that came with it. Lorenzo listened intently, his gaze unwavering, making her feel seen and heard.

As the club began to wind down, Lorenzo suggested they go somewhere quieter. They ended up at a small, secluded beach, the moonlight casting a silvery path on the waves. They walked along the shore, their footsteps the only sound in the night.

"This place is beautiful," Candy said, taking a deep breath of the salty air.

"It is," Lorenzo agreed, looking at her rather than the view. "Miami has its moments."

They sat down on the sand, the ocean stretching endlessly before them. Lorenzo turned to her, his expression serious. "You know, Charlotte, I've met a lot of people, but there's something different about you. I can't quite put my finger on it."

Candy felt a flutter in her chest. "Maybe it's because I'm not just Candy. I'm trying to be someone new, someone better."

Lorenzo reached out, brushing a strand of hair from her face. "Whatever name you go by, I like who you are right now."

"So, Candy," Lorenzo began, leaning back against the plush seat. "When you're not turning heads on the dance floor, what else do you get up to?"

Candy traced the rim of her glass, her lips curving into a playful smile. "Oh, you know, just breaking hearts at a boutique. It's nothing glamorous, but I manage."

Lorenzo's gaze was intense as he leaned in closer. "I bet you do. But I think there's more to you than meets the eye. You've got that mysterious vibe going on."

She laughed softly, feeling a blush creep up her cheeks. "Maybe I do. But what about you, Mr. Superstar? What's life like off the pitch?"

"It's a mix," Lorenzo said, his eyes sparkling. "Traveling, training, and a lot of public appearances. It can be overwhelming, but I wouldn't trade it for anything. But tonight, I think I might've found my favorite part of Miami."

Candy raised an eyebrow, her heart fluttering. "And what might that be?"

"Meeting you," he said, his voice dropping to a seductive whisper.

When the club started to wind down, Lorenzo walked Candy to a cab. "I'd love to see you again," he said, his eyes searching hers for an answer.

Candy smiled, a genuine smile that reached her eyes. "I'd like that too," she replied, feeling a flutter of hope in her chest.

As she rode back to her modest apartment, Candy replayed the evening in her mind. Meeting Lorenzo had been unexpected, but it felt like a turning point. For the first time since arriving in Miami, she felt a sense of possibility, of a future that wasn't overshadowed by her past.

The following days were filled with anticipation as she waited to hear from Lorenzo. When he finally called, inviting her to a football game, Candy felt a thrill of excitement. She knew she had to be cautious, but she couldn't deny the attraction she felt for him.

They met at the arena, and Lorenzo gave her a behind- the-scenes tour before the game. "This is where the magic happens," he said with a wink, showing her the locker room and introducing her to some of his teammates.

After the game, they went to a quiet restaurant. Lorenzo's hand brushed hers as they sat down, sending a shiver up her spine. "So, what did you think?" he asked, his voice low and intimate.

"It was amazing," Candy said, still buzzing from the excitement. "I've never been to a game like that."

Lorenzo smiled, his eyes locking onto hers. "I'm glad you enjoyed it. I wanted to share something special with you."

Several weeks later, Candy found herself in the backseat of Lorenzo's luxury car as they drove back to his house after a particularly wild party. The city lights blurred outside the window, casting a kaleidoscope of colors that danced across her vision. Candy felt a mixture of excitement and nervousness, a potent cocktail of emotions swirling inside her. The hum of the engine and the soft leather seats added to the surreal feeling of the night. Her thoughts drifted to her new life in Miami and the whirlwind of events that led her here.

As they weaved through the city's streets, Candy reflected on how drastically her life had changed. The transition from her past, where she lived in fear and uncertainty, to this glamorous existence seemed like a dream. She had adopted the name Charlotte Glenn and was determined to leave her old self, Candy, behind. Lorenzo was a part of that transformation, an escape into a world of wealth and excitement that had seemed so far out of reach.

Lorenzo parked the car in the driveway of his lavish beach- front property and turned to Candy, his eyes filled with desire. "Ready for the after-party?" he asked with a mischievous grin. Candy laughed, her earlier reservations melting away. "Always," she replied, her voice tinged with playful anticipation.

As they stepped into the grand foyer of Lorenzo's home, the sound of the waves crashing against the shore echoed in the background, providing a serene counterpoint to the wild night they had just experienced. The house was a clear reflection of Lorenzo's achievements. Marble floors, modern art on the walls, and a view of the ocean that took Candy's breath away. She marveled at the sheer opulence of her surroundings, feeling a sense of awe mixed with disbelief. How had she ended up here, in this world of luxury and privilege?

They ascended the sweeping staircase, their footsteps barely audible on the plush carpet. The house, though filled with expensive furnishings and art, had a strangely impersonal feel, as if it was more a showpiece than a home. The night wore on, and things became more intimate. The atmosphere was charged with a heady mix of passion and desire. Lorenzo's touch sent shivers down Candy's spine, and she found herself swept up in the intensity of the moment.

They started in the grand foyer, where Lorenzo pulled Candy into a deep, fervent kiss. His hands roamed over her back, sending a wave of electricity through her body. She responded eagerly, her fingers weaving through his hair as she pressed herself closer to him. The marble floor felt cool beneath her feet, a stark contrast to the heat building between them.

Lorenzo guided her into the living room, a space filled with modern art and sleek furniture. The large windows offered a stunning view of the moonlit ocean, but Candy's focus was entirely on Lorenzo. He pushed her onto the plush sofa with a firm grip, his lips never leaving hers. She could feel the intensity of his desire in every touch, every caress. The room was dimly lit, the soft glow from the recessed lights creating an intimate glow.

Their connection deepened as Lorenzo led Candy into the kitchen. The stainless-steel appliances gleamed under the soft lights, and the scent of the ocean breeze wafted through the open windows. He lifted her onto the granite countertop with a commanding force, his hands firm on her hips. Their kisses grew more urgent, more demanding. Candy's breath hitched as Lorenzo's lips trailed down her neck, sending a shiver of pleasure through her. The cool countertop against her skin heightened her senses, making every touch more vivid.

From the kitchen, they moved to the dining room. Lorenzo's hands explored every inch of Candy's body, his touch both rough and possessive. She felt a rush of emotions, desire, excitement, and a hint of vulnerability. The tablecloth rustled beneath them as Lorenzo laid her down with possessive force, his body pressing hard against hers. The sheer intensity of their connection left her breathless.

Finally, they made their way upstairs to the master bedroom. The room was a sanctuary of indulgence, with its oversized bed, silk sheets, and a panoramic view of the moonlit ocean. The air was filled with the faint scent of jasmine, adding to the room's sensual ambiance. Lorenzo pushed Candy onto the bed, his eyes locked onto hers. There was a moment of stillness, a pause where they simply gazed at each other.

Lorenzo's touch was both tender and possessive as he traced the contours of Candy's body. She closed her eyes, losing herself in the sensation. His lips followed the path of his hands, leaving a trail of fire in their wake. Candy's heart raced as Lorenzo's kisses grew more urgent, more demanding. She responded with equal fervor, her fingers digging into his shoulders as she pulled him closer.

They moved together in a rhythm that felt both new and familiar, their bodies attuned to each other's desires. The silk sheets felt cool against Candy's skin, a stark contrast to the heat building between them. She arched her back, her breath coming in short gasps as Lorenzo's touch sent waves of pleasure through her.

As the night wore on, they became lost in each other. The outside world faded away, leaving only the two of them in their private haven. Time seemed to stand still as they explored the depths of their passion, their connection growing stronger with every touch, every whisper. Candy felt a sense of completeness she had never experienced before, a feeling that transcended the physical.

In Lorenzo's arms, she found a moment of pure, unadulterated bliss. But even in the midst of their passion, a small voice in the back of her mind reminded her of the complexities of their relationship. For now, though, she pushed those thoughts aside, allowing herself to be fully present in the moment, lost in the intensity of their connection.

Candy moved in with Lorenzo shortly after. She was drawn to the luxury, the excitement, and the sense of security he provided. Her new life was filled with glamorous parties, exclusive events, and the kind of opulence she had only dreamed of. The initial thrill of her new life was intoxicating. She wore designer clothes, dined at the finest restaurants, and was a regular at high-profile social gatherings. Yet, beneath the surface of this lavish lifestyle, a sense of unease began to grow. At first, it was subtle, the way Lorenzo would control the smallest details of her life, his impatience when she didn't conform to his plans, and the possessiveness that grew more apparent with each passing day. Candy dismissed these as quirks of his personality, attributing them to his high-profile lifestyle and the pressures that came with it. She told herself that he was just protective, that his controlling nature was a sign of how much he cared about her.

But the first time he hit her, It started with an offhand comment, a casual remark about one of Lorenzo's friends that she didn't even realize was offensive until his mood shifted like a sudden storm. The room seemed to darken as Lorenzo's expression hardened, his jaw tensing with restrained fury. Before Candy could comprehend the change, his hand lashed out, striking her across the face with a force that sent her stumbling back against the wall.

"Pfft, Lorenzo, chill. What's your problem?" Candy's voice held a mix of surprise and disbelief, her hand instinctively flying to the stinging warmth spreading across her cheek. She stared at him, expecting a moment of awkward laughter to follow.

Lorenzo stood before her, his normally charming features twisted into a mask of cold indifference. His eyes, once warm and captivating, now bore into her with a chilling intensity. "You need to learn when to keep your mouth shut," he said, his voice a low growl that reverberated in the stillness of the hallway.

Candy blinked, her mind struggling to process what just happened. "You... you hit me," she murmured, her disbelief turning into a mixture of hurt and confusion.

Lorenzo's jaw clenched tighter, his fists balling at his sides. "Watch your mouth, Candy," he spat, the venom in his tone cutting through the air like a knife. "You think you can disrespect me in my own house?"

"I didn't mean to disrespect you," Candy protested, her words stumbling over the shock and pain that pulsed through her. "I didn't even realize.....,"

"Enough!" Lorenzo's voice thundered through the hallway, shaking the very walls around them. His gaze bore into her with a mixture of rage and contempt. "You're lucky I don't throw you out right now."

Candy's breath caught in her throat, the weight of his threat settling over her like a suffocating blanket. She felt a surge of anger and defiance rise within her, mingling with the hurt and confusion. "I'm not some doll you can just push around," she retorted, her voice shaking but firm.

Lorenzo's expression darkened further, his eyes narrowing dangerously. "You better watch yourself, Candy," he warned, his voice dripping with menace. "Don't test me."

With those words hanging heavy in the air, Lorenzo turned abruptly and stormed out of the mansion, leaving Candy standing in the hallway, stunned and trembling.

She didn't leave immediately. In the days that followed, Candy replayed their altercation in her mind, grappling with disbelief and confusion. When Lorenzo finally returned, it was with a flood of apologies, words drenched in remorse and promises that it would never happen again. He showered her with gifts, a diamond necklace that sparkled in the dim light of their extravagant home, and whisked her away on a surprise weekend getaway to the Bahamas. His sweet reassurances and constant declarations of love and devotion temporarily soothed her doubts.

But the cycle repeated itself. Each time, the tension grew thicker, the apologies less convincing. Candy found herself walking on eggshells, never sure when the next outburst would come.

(Kelly's Early Years)

Kelly's past was a busy one as she always assisted her frantic mother, Paloma, before she started working for Candy at her lavish home. Paloma's health had been a constant source of stress, and Kelly had grown accustomed to juggling multiple responsibilities to keep their lives afloat. The morning sun filtered through the thin curtains of their modest home, casting a gentle light on the worn furniture and faded wallpaper. It was a simple home, but it was theirs, and Kelly took pride in keeping it as welcoming as possible for her mother.

As Kelly bustled around the kitchen, she could hear Paloma's frail voice calling out, "Kelly, is there enough milk for my tea?" Kelly glanced at the nearly empty carton on the counter. "Yes, Mom, there's just enough. Don't worry about it," she replied, trying to keep her voice light. She poured the last of the milk into a small pot to warm it up.

Paloma's cough echoed down the hallway again, harsher this time. Kelly felt a pang of worry but forced a smile as she brought the tea and omelet to the small dining table. "Here you go, Mom. Made your favorite with extra cheese and veggies."

Paloma smiled weakly as she sat down, her hands trembling slightly as she picked up her fork. "Thank you, dear. You always know how to make my day a little brighter."

Kelly sat beside her, sipping her own coffee. "It's the least I can do," she said softly, watching her mother struggle with each bite. "How are you feeling today?"

Paloma sighed, setting down her fork for a moment. "A bit better than yesterday, I suppose. But this cough… it just won't go away."

"We'll get through it, Mom. One day at a time," Kelly said, squeezing her mother's hand. "I'm going to call Dr. Martinez later to see if he can adjust your medication."

Paloma nodded, her eyes filling with gratitude. "You're always so good to me, Kelly. I don't know what I'd do without you."

"You'd do just fine, Mom," Kelly said, though she wasn't sure if she believed it. "But you don't have to worry about that. I'm here, and I'll always be here."

They finished breakfast in a comfortable silence, the clinking of utensils the only sound. After breakfast, Kelly helped Paloma back to bed, adjusting the pillows and making sure her medications were within reach.

"Remember to take your medicine at noon, okay? I'll call you to remind you," Kelly said, smoothing the blanket over her mother's frail form.

"I will, sweetheart," Paloma replied, a worried look in her eyes. "But you work too hard, Kelly. You need to take care of yourself too."

Kelly forced a reassuring smile, though the lines of exhaustion around her eyes betrayed her. "I'm fine, Mom. Just a little tired. I'll be back this evening. Call me if you need anything."

Paloma grasped her hand, her grip surprisingly strong. "Promise me you'll try to rest, Kelly. You can't pour from an empty cup."

"I promise, Mom," Kelly said, though she knew it was a promise she couldn't keep. With one last look at her mother, she hurried to get ready for her job. She changed into a simple but neat outfit, grabbed her bag, and headed out the door, her heart heavy with the weight of her responsibilities.

Outside, the morning sun was already warming the air. Kelly took a deep breath, trying to shake off the worry that clung to her. She had a long day ahead, filled with work and errands, but she wouldn't let herself think about that now. She had to take it one step at a time, just like she told her mother.

As she walked to the bus stop, her phone buzzed with a text message. It was from her boss, reminding her of an early meeting. Kelly quickened her pace, her mind already racing through the day's tasks. She couldn't afford to be late.

Her first job of the day was at a local restaurant, where she worked as a cleaner. The work was hard and often thankless, but it was necessary. Kelly moved through the dining area and kitchen with practiced efficiency, scrubbing floors, wiping down tables, and making sure everything was spotless before the lunchtime rush began. The scent of cleaning products mingled with the lingering aroma of last night's dinners, creating a familiar and oddly comforting atmosphere.

As she scrubbed a particularly stubborn stain from the floor, her mind drifted back to her mother. Paloma's health had been a constant source of stress, and Kelly had grown accustomed to juggling multiple responsibilities to keep their lives afloat.

The restaurant's head chef, Carlos, walked in, his booming voice breaking Kelly's thoughts. "Morning, Kelly! How's your mom doing?"

Kelly looked up and forced a smile. "Morning, Carlos. She's hanging in there. Just trying to keep her comfortable."

Carlos nodded sympathetically. "You're doing a great job here, Kelly. I know things are tough, but if you ever need to take a day off, just let me know."

"Thanks, Carlos," Kelly said, appreciating his kindness. "But I need the hours. Every bit helps."

Carlos patted her shoulder. "I understand. Just remember to take care of yourself too."

Kelly returned to her work, the steady rhythm of cleaning provided a small measure of solace. She finished scrubbing the floors and moved on to the tables, wiping them down meticulously. Her hands moved with practiced efficiency, but her mind kept wandering back to her mother. Paloma's cough, her frail frame, the worried look in her eyes – it was all a heavy burden for Kelly to carry.

As she worked, the restaurant slowly came to life around her. The kitchen staff began arriving, chatting and laughing as they prepared for the busy day ahead. The clatter of pots and pans, the hiss of steam, and the sizzle of food hitting the grill created a lively backdrop to Kelly's solitary efforts.

Midway through cleaning the dining area, her phone buzzed in her pocket. She pulled it out and saw a message from her mother: "Don't forget your promise. Rest when you can. Love you."

Kelly's eyes filled with tears, but she quickly blinked them away. She typed a quick reply, "I will, Mom. Love you too."

She put her phone away and took a deep breath, steeling herself for the rest of the day. There was no time to dwell on her own exhaustion. She had to keep moving, keep working, for both herself and her mother.

As the morning wore on, the restaurant filled with the bustling energy of preparation. Kelly finished her cleaning tasks just as the first customers began to trickle in. She greeted them with a polite smile, her professional demeanor masking the fatigue that gnawed at her.

Once the lunch rush began, Kelly's pace quickened. She moved from table to table, clearing dishes, wiping surfaces, and ensuring that everything remained tidy. It was a constant, unrelenting cycle, but she found a strange comfort in the routine. It was predictable, unlike the uncertainty that loomed over her personal life.

By the time her shift ended, Kelly was exhausted but satisfied with her work. She said her goodbyes to the staff and stepped out into the bright afternoon sun. She had a few minutes to spare before heading to her next job, so she decided to sit on a nearby bench and rest for a moment.

Her phone buzzed again, this time with a message from Dr. Martinez: "We need to discuss your mother's treatment. Please call me when you have a moment."

Kelly sighed, knowing that conversation would be difficult. She closed her eyes for a brief moment, savoring the warmth of the sun on her face. She thought about her mother, the restaurant, and the many responsibilities that awaited her. It was a heavy load, but she was determined to carry it.

After her shift at the restaurant, Kelly caught the bus to her next job. She had recently quit working as a bartender at a nightclub. The late hours were too much to handle with Paloma's declining health, and a quarrel with a customer was the final straw. The memory of that night still stung – a heated argument over a spilled drink had escalated, leaving Kelly shaken and more determined than ever to find work that suited her situation better.

The bus ride provided a brief respite, a moment of calm between the demands of her jobs. Kelly stared out the window, her mind replaying the events of that fateful night at the nightclub. She had been exhausted, both physically and emotionally, when a customer had knocked over a drink. What should have been a minor inconvenience quickly turned into a shouting match, with the customer blaming Kelly for the spill. Despite her best efforts to defuse the situation, it had escalated, and Kelly had found herself being berated in front of a crowd. The humiliation and stress had been too much to bear.

That night, she had come home to find Paloma struggling to breathe. The sight of her mother's frail form gasping for air had been the final push Kelly needed to make a change. She couldn't afford to be exhausted and distracted, not with her mother needing her so much. She had quit the nightclub job the next day and found a more stable, albeit demanding, cleaning job at a local office building.

As the bus approached her stop, Kelly gathered her things and prepared to disembark. The office building was a short walk away, and she arrived with a few minutes to spare. The building's lobby was cool and quiet, a stark contrast to the bustling restaurant she had just left. Kelly signed in at the front desk and made her way to the janitor's closet, where she stored her cleaning supplies.

The office building was vast, with rows of cubicles and offices that needed to be cleaned meticulously. Kelly worked her way through the floors, emptying trash bins, dusting surfaces, and vacuuming carpets. The repetitive tasks allowed her mind to wander, and she found herself thinking about her mother again. Paloma's health had been steadily declining, and Kelly knew they needed to discuss the next steps with Dr. Martinez. The thought of more tests and treatments was daunting, but she couldn't ignore the reality of the situation.

By the time her shift at the office building ended, Kelly was exhausted. She said her goodbyes to the night security guard and stepped out into the evening air. The sun had already set, and the cool breeze was a welcome relief after the stuffy confines of the office. She had one more job to get to before she could finally go home and rest.

Her last job of the day was at a small, family-owned grocery store. Kelly had taken on this evening shift to make up for the hours she lost when she quit the nightclub. The work was less demanding, but it was still another few hours on her feet, stocking shelves and cleaning up before closing time.

The store's owner, Mrs. Hernandez, greeted Kelly warmly as she walked in. "Good evening, Kelly! How's your mother doing?"

Kelly smiled tiredly. "Evening, Mrs. Hernandez. She's doing okay, just trying to keep her comfortable."

Mrs. Hernandez nodded sympathetically. "You're such a good daughter, Kelly. If you ever need to take some time off, just let me know."

"Thanks, Mrs. Hernandez. I appreciate it, but I need the hours," Kelly replied, echoing the same words she had said to Carlos earlier that day.

Kelly got to work, her body protesting the continued exertion.

She stocked shelves, organized the back room, and swept the floors. The steady rhythm of work was comforting in its own way, a familiar routine that helped her push through the fatigue. She took a short break halfway through her shift, sitting in the small break room and closing her eyes for a few precious minutes of rest.

As the store's closing time approached, Kelly finished up her tasks and helped Mrs. Hernandez close up. The older woman gave her a gentle pat on the back. "Take care of yourself, Kelly. You're doing a great job."

"Thank you, Mrs. Hernandez," Kelly said, feeling a swell of gratitude for the woman's kindness.

Finally, Kelly made her way home, her steps slow and heavy. The modest house she shared with her mother came into view, and she felt a wave of relief wash over her. She unlocked the door and stepped inside, greeted by the familiar scents and sounds of home. Paloma was waiting for her in the living room, a worried look on her face.

"You're late, Kelly. Are you okay?" Paloma asked, her voice filled with concern.

Kelly managed a tired smile. "I'm fine, Mom. Just had a long day."

As she helped her mother to bed, Kelly's mind drifted back to a time when their lives had been different.

Years earlier, Kelly's life had been simpler, marked by a different kind of struggle. Before Paloma's health had deteriorated, they had lived a modest but happy life. Her father had passed away when she was young, leaving her and her mother to fend for themselves. Paloma had worked hard to provide for them, instilling in Kelly a sense of responsibility and resilience. Kelly had always been shy, more comfortable in the background than in the spotlight. She had few friends, preferring the company of books and her mother. School had been a challenge, not academically, but socially. Kelly's reserved nature made her an easy target for bullies, and she had learned to navigate the hallways with her head down, avoiding conflict. She spent her lunch breaks in the library, finding solace in the pages of novels that transported her to worlds far removed from her own.

After high school, Kelly's dreams of furthering her education had to be put on hold. Paloma's health had begun to decline, and the medical bills piled up. Kelly took on various jobs to help support her mother, each one more demanding than the last. It was during this time that she learned the true meaning of sacrifice. She watched her friends go off to college, envied their carefree lives while she juggled multiple responsibilities. It was a decision she never regretted, but it left her feeling isolated and exhausted.

One of her first jobs had been at a local diner, where she worked long hours as a waitress. The job was grueling, but the tips were decent, and she needed every penny. She would come home late at night, her feet aching and her uniform smelling grease, only to find her mother waiting up for her with a warm smile and a hot meal. Those were the moments that kept her going, the small acts of love that made the sacrifices worthwhile. As Paloma's condition worsened, Kelly found herself taking on more and more. She became adept at managing medications, scheduling doctor's appointments. The once vibrant and strong woman who had raised her was now frail and dependent, and it broke Kelly's heart to see her mother in such a state. Yet, through it all, Paloma remained strong and positive, always more concerned about Kelly's well-being than her own.

Kelly remembered the nights spent sitting by her mother's bedside, reading aloud from Paloma's favorite books. The stories were a comfort to both of them, a reminder of better times.

Even as exhaustion gnawed at her, Kelly found solace in those quiet moments of connection.

Her thoughts were interrupted by a gentle touch on her arm. Paloma looked up at her with tired eyes. "You work too hard, my dear. Promise me you'll rest."

"I promise, Mom," Kelly said, though she knew it was a promise she couldn't keep. She helped her mother settle into bed, making sure she was comfortable and had everything she needed.

As Kelly finally settled into bed herself, exhaustion overtook her. Her last thoughts before sleep claimed her were of her mother, their small home, and the unyielding responsibilities that awaited her in the morning. In the quiet darkness, Kelly allowed herself a moment of vulnerability. Tears welled up in her eyes, and she let them fall silently, the weight of her day pressing down on her. She cried for her mother, for the endless cycle of work and worry, and for the moments of peace that seemed so fleeting.

But even as the tears fell, a determination continued to form within her. Kelly knew she couldn't keep this up forever. She needed to find a more suitable job that could cover all their bills, one that wouldn't leave her drained and unable to fully care for her mother. She had to explore her options, perhaps look into furthering her education or finding work that aligned better with her skills and interests.

As the first light of dawn began to filter through the curtains, Kelly wiped her tears and took a deep breath. A new day was beginning, and she would face it with the same determination and resilience that had carried her this far. But now, she had a new resolve: to find a job that not only provided for their needs but also allowed her the time and energy to be there for her mother. She would take it one step at a time, exploring every opportunity, until she found a way to balance their lives more sustainably.

Chapter Five

Candy sat in the garage, the sharp, acrid scent of cigarette smoke swirling around her. She leaned back against the wall, exhaling a stream of smoke, and noticed Kelly passing by, her timid steps echoing in the vast space. With a mischievous glint in her eye, Candy called out, "Hey Kelly, come here for a sec."

Kelly hesitated, then approached cautiously. "Yes, Mrs.?"

Candy rolled her eyes. "It's Candy, remember? Come on, take a break. I was thinking, how about we go out for lunch today?"

Kelly looked surprised. "Lunch? With you?"

Candy laughed. "Yes, with me. Come on, it'll be fun. Besides, I need some company. And you could use a break, right?"

Kelly bit her lip, uncertainty written all over her face. "I don't know... I have a lot of work to do."

Candy waved her hand dismissively. "The work can wait. Come on, Kelly. Live a little."

After a moment's hesitation, Kelly nodded. "Alright. But I don't have anything to wear."

Candy grinned, her eyes twinkling with excitement. "Don't worry about that. I've got you covered."

They went upstairs to Candy's expansive closet, a treasure trove of designer clothes and accessories. Candy sifted through her collection, pulling out a form-fitting dress that left little to the imagination. She handed it to Kelly, who looked at it with wide eyes.

"I can't wear this," Kelly protested.

"Sure you can," Candy said, pushing the dress into her hands. "Trust me, you'll look amazing."

Candy stood by the front door, tapping her foot impatiently. "Come on already, it'll be dinner before we get there," she called out, her voice echoing through the house.

From upstairs, Kelly's voice floated down, laced with uncertainty. "I don't think this works."

"Of course it does," Candy insisted. "Come on, stop being a baby."

Candy looked up the stairs just as Kelly appeared at the top, her transformation striking. She wore a revealing mini-skirt combination, looking worlds away from the maid they knew.

"Now that's what I'm talking about. You look great," Candy said, her eyes lighting up with approval.

Kelly descended the stairs carefully, unsteady on her high heels. "I feel like a hooker. How the hell do you stay on these things?" she asked, wobbling slightly with each step.

"You get used to it," Candy replied with a shrug.

"Are you sure about this? I feel a little overdressed for lunch," Kelly said, glancing down at her outfit nervously.

"It depends where you're gonna eat," Candy responded with a mischievous smile.

They drove a sleek convertible Mercedes 600SL through the bustling streets to the Blue Door Restaurant in South Beach, a chic, upscale spot known for its vibrant atmosphere and excellent food, pulling up to a couple of waiting valets. As they walked in, Candy greeted the staff with casual familiarity. One of the waitstaff, a young woman with a knowing smile, glanced at Kelly and raised an eyebrow.

"Who's the new face?" she asked, her curiosity piqued. Candy grinned. "Hey everyone, this is Sophia," she said,

introducing Kelly with a new name. "She's joining me for lunch." Kelly, now Sophia, looked around nervously but followed Candy's lead. They were seated at a prime table by the veranda with a view, and soon they had drinks in hand. Candy raised

her glass, a sly smile on her lips.

The restaurant buzzed with life as Candy and Kelly settled into their seats. A familiar face approached their table with a broad smile.

"Miss Candy, as I live and breathe!" the waiter exclaimed. "Hi, Steven," Candy replied warmly.

Steven glanced at Kelly with a curious smile. "Who's your friend? She's cute."

"This is Sophia," Candy said, introducing Kelly. "Sophia, say hi to Steven, the only man who's never let me down."

"Oh, baby, that's so sweet," Steven cooed, clearly pleased.

A busboy appeared behind Steven, holding a tray with a single drink.

"I'm feeling… Espresso Martini," Steven announced, placing the drink in front of Candy. She took a sip and blew him a kiss. Steven turned his attention to Kelly. "You… I don't know you well enough yet… but maybe… hmm," he mused, walking away while snapping his fingers at the busboy.

Kelly watched him go, then turned to Candy with a questioning look. "Alright. Why do you keep telling people my name is

Sophia?"

"Why not? Don't you like the name?" Candy asked with a playful shrug.

"I didn't mind Kelly," Kelly replied.

Steven returned, animated and full of energy, with the busboy once again trailing behind, carrying another drink on a tray.

"I don't know, I work with minimum data. I can't be responsible for the results," Steven said, placing a drink in front of Kelly.

"Mojito," he declared.

Kelly took a tentative sip, and Steven leaned in, awaiting her reaction. She looked up and smiled brightly. "Delicious," she said.

"Ah, thank you," Steven replied, snapping his fingers again at the busboy before dashing off, clearly satisfied with his work. "To life's unpredictability," she toasted, her eyes meeting

Kelly's. "You never know what twists and turns it will take." Kelly clinked her glass against Candy's and took another sip. "So, how do you like that Mojito, huh?" Candy asked.

"It tastes like bitter lemonade," Kelly admitted, scrunching her nose slightly.

"You'll get used to it," Candy assured her with a wink.

As they proceeded to dine, Candy and Kelly's conversation flowed more freely. Candy shared stories of her wild nights and lavish lifestyle, while Kelly opened up about her dreams and the struggles she faced. They laughed, teased each other, and found a surprising connection despite their different backgrounds.

Candy's playful teasing eased Kelly's initial discomfort, and by the time they finished their meal, Kelly felt a sense of liberation she hadn't experienced in a long time. Candy's world was a stark contrast to her own, filled with risks and bold choices, but it also offered a glimpse of freedom and self-discovery.

At a corner of the table, remnants of the sumptuous meal lay scattered across the tablecloth. Candy delicately picked at a piece of dessert while Kelly, visibly tipsy, attempted to fish an olive out of her martini glass using only her tongue. She looked up to find Candy watching her with a bemused smile.

"Don't worry, I was through with that," Candy said, her eyes twinkling with amusement.

Kelly grinned, her cheeks flushed from the alcohol. "So let me get this straight...you used to be a professional cheerleader?"

Candy nodded, her expression thoughtful. "Sure was." "Wow, what's that like?" Kelly asked, her voice filled with genuine curiosity.

Candy shrugged, taking a small bite of her dessert. "Over- rated, but I did meet my boyfriend."

Kelly's eyes sparkled with a mix of envy and hope. "I could use a different life."

Candy leaned forward, her tone serious yet kind. "Be careful what you wish for, someday you just might get the chance."

With that, Candy waved to the waiter for the check. They finished their drinks and left the vibrant restaurant, stepping out into the cool night air.

Back at Candy and Lorenzo's home, the kitchen lights flickered as Candy and Kelly entered from the garage, giggling like schoolgirls. Kelly, still feeling the effects of the alcohol, stumbled toward the sink. She grabbed a glass and filled it with water, taking big, gulping sips in an attempt to sober up.

***

Houston's car rumbled along the narrow dirt road, each bumping and jolt a reminder of the rural isolation surrounding Tully's dog-breeding facility. As he approached the dimly lit entrance, the sound of barking dogs filled the night air, a noise that seemed to welcome and warn in equal measure.

Inside the barn, Tully was busy with his nightly routine. He moved with practiced efficiency, checking on the dogs one by one. Herman, his loyal guard dog, trotted at his heels, eyes bright and alert. Tully paused to give Herman an affectionate pat on the head, muttering something about "another quiet night." He didn't notice the approaching car until the headlights cut through the gloom, momentarily blinding him.

Tully straightened, his hand instinctively moving to the rifle propped against the wall. Herman growled, sensing his master's tension. As the car door creaked open, Tully tightened his grip on the rifle, ready to confront the intruder.

"Who's there?" Tully's voice was a low, threatening growl. "It's me, Tully," came the familiar voice from the shadows.

"Houston."

Tully relaxed, lowering the rifle but not entirely dropping his guard. "Damn it, Houston. You nearly got yourself shot." He chuckled, though there was an edge of genuine relief in his tone. Herman, recognizing that it was a visitor, so he wagged his tail and trotted over to greet him.

Houston stepped into the dim light spilling from the barn. "Nice to see you too, Tully," he said with a wry smile, giving Herman a pat on the head. "Didn't mean to startle you."

Tully shook his head, setting the rifle aside but keeping it within arm's reach. "You got a knack for showing up unannounced," he replied, his voice gruff but not unkind. "What brings you here in the middle of the night?"

Houston glanced around, his expression a mix of wariness and determination. "I need a place to lay low for a bit. Things in Miami are getting...complicated."

Tully raised an eyebrow, curiosity piqued. "Complicated how?" he asked, crossing his arms over his chest.

Houston sighed, running a hand through his hair. "Let's just say I made some enemies down there. Old debts and new grudges. It's safer if I stay out of sight for a while."

Tully nodded slowly, understanding the unspoken implications. "You know you're always welcome here," he said, his tone softening slightly. "But you better fill me in on the details. I don't want any surprises."

Houston leaned against the barn door, looking weary. "It's a long story, Tully. But the short version is, "I have some unfinished business with certain people, and it's time to settle it," Houston said.

Tully sighed, scratching his chin thoughtfully. "Sounds like you're diving into a real mess. But you're family, Houston. We'll figure something out."

Houston gave him a grateful look. "Thanks, Tully. I knew I could count on you."

The two men stood in silence for a moment, the weight of unspoken words hanging between them. Finally, Tully gestured towards the barn. "Come on inside. We can talk more over a drink."

Tully arched an eyebrow but didn't press further. Instead, he led Houston into the barn, where the dogs' barking had settled into a low, curious rumble. As they walked, Houston glanced around, noting the well-kept kennels and the sleek, muscular dogs within.

"Still running a tight ship, I see," Houston remarked, his voice tinged with admiration.

"Wouldn't have it any other way," Tully replied proudly. He gestured around the barn. "These dogs are my life. They deserve the best."

Houston nodded, taking in the sight of the well-cared-for animals. "You've always had a knack for this, Tully. Ever since we were kids, you were the one with the strays, the one who could calm them down with just a look."

Tully chuckled, a hint of nostalgia in his eyes. "Yeah, well, guess I found my calling early. Not everyone can say that."

They reached a large pen where a Great Dane and a Pit Bull were engaged in a careful, almost ritualistic dance. Houston watched, fascinated by the interplay between the two dogs.

"That's something you don't see every day," he commented, his eyes fixed on the animals.

Tully nodded. "Breeding season. Takes a lot of patience and a bit of luck. These two, in particular, have been tricky. But if it works out, their pups will be something special."

Houston leaned against the pen, his curiosity piqued. "How do you manage it all? The training, the breeding, keeping everything in order?"

"It's a labor of love," Tully said, a note of pride in his voice. "Early mornings, late nights. But it's worth it. Each of these dogs has a purpose, a potential that I get to help shape."

Houston glanced at Tully, a newfound respect in his eyes. "It's impressive, Tully. You've built something real here."

Tully shrugged modestly. "Just doing what I love. Speaking of which," he turned to another pen and whistled softly. A massive dog padded over, its sheer size and gentle demeanor immediately striking.

"This is Bubbles," Tully introduced, scratching the dog behind its ears. "Don't let the size fool you. She's a big softie."

Houston couldn't help but smile as Bubbles nuzzled against Tully's hand. "She's magnificent. How do you get them to be so... balanced?"

"It's all about trust," Tully explained. "You give them respect, structure, and a lot of care. They give it back tenfold."

Houston reached out cautiously, and Bubbles sniffed his hand before suddenly baring her teeth and growling. The change was instantaneous and frightening. Before Houston could react, the massive dog lunged, her jaws snapping dangerously close to his hand. He jerked back, his heart pounding in his chest.

"What the hell!" Houston exclaimed, his eyes wide with shock. "How can you name such an aggressive thing Bubbles?"

Tully was quick to intervene, stepping between them and calming Bubbles with a firm but gentle touch. "Bubbles, no! Heel!" he commanded, his voice steady and authoritative. The dog backed down, but her eyes still glinted with a hint of aggression.

"Seems like she's not too fond of strangers," Houston said, trying to mask his unease with a shaky laugh.

Tully shook his head, his expression a mix of apology and concern. "Sorry about that, Houston. She's usually gentler, but sometimes she gets a bit protective. Must be the scent of the city on you."

Houston rubbed his hand, still feeling the adrenaline rush. "Protective, huh? She almost took my hand off."

"Yeah, she's a big softie once she gets to know you," Tully said, giving Bubbles a reassuring pat. "Just needs some time to warm up, that's all."

Houston glanced at Bubbles, who was now sitting obediently by Tully's side, her eyes still watching him with a hint of suspicion. "I'll take your word for it," he muttered, still shaken.

Tully chuckled, trying to lighten the mood. "You should see her with the puppies. Gentle as a lamb. But out here, she's all business. Keeps the riff-raff away."

Houston let out a nervous laugh. "Well, she certainly made her point."

Tully's laughter echoed in the spacious barn, but it was tinged with seriousness. "Magic, hard work, same difference. You should see the rookies when they first get here. All energy and no focus. Takes time to mold that into something solid."

As they continued to walk through the barn, Tully shared more stories about the dogs, their personalities, and the various challenges he'd faced. Houston listened intently, appreciating the depth of Tully's commitment and the world he had built around these animals.

"So, what brings you back here, Houston?" Tully finally asked, his tone casual but curious. "Last I heard, you were off making a name for yourself in the big city."

Houston's expression grew seriously, a shadow crossing his features. "Business, Tully. Unfinished business. Miami has a way of pulling you back in."

Tully didn't press further, sensing the weight behind Houston's words. Instead, he clapped a hand on his friend's shoulder. "Well, whatever it is, you're always welcome here. Just don't go around stirring up too much trouble."

Houston chuckled, though it lacked genuine mirth. "Trouble has a way of finding me, Tully. But thanks. It's good to know I have a place to come back to."

They continued their tour of the barn, with Tully pointing out various dogs and explaining their roles in his breeding program. "See that one over there?" Tully said, nodding toward a sleek Doberman. "That's Duke. One of the best guard dogs I've ever trained. He's sharp as a tack and loyal to the bone."

Houston observed Duke, noting the dog's alert posture and keen eyes. "Impressive. You've really built something special here." He repeated.

Tully smiled, a clear display of pride in his expression. "It's all about finding the right balance. These dogs, they need structure and purpose. Just like us."

Houston's mind wandered as Tully spoke, the familiar surroundings and old friend's presence providing a stark contrast to the chaotic life he had left behind in Miami. "You ever think about leaving this place, doing something else?" he asked, curiosity in his voice.

Tully shook his head. "This is where I belong. Out here, with the dogs, the open space. It's a simple life, but it's mine. What about you? Ever think about settling down, finding some peace?"

Houston sighed, the weight of his past decisions heavy on his shoulders. "I've thought about it. But peace has been hard to come by. Too many loose ends, too much history."

Tully nodded, understanding without needing to press for details. "Well, just know you've got a friend here. Anytime you need to get away, this place is yours too."

"Thanks, Tully," Houston said quietly. "It means more than you know."

Tully clapped him on the back. "Anytime, Houston. Now, how about we grab those cigars and beers I promised?"

Houston grinned, the tension easing from his shoulders. "Sounds like a plan." Together, they headed toward the small office at the back of the barn

They settled into a couple of worn but comfortable chairs. Tully pulled out a couple of cigars from a wooden box, handing one to Houston. They lit up, the fragrant smoke mingling with the earthy scents of the barn. Tully cracked open a couple of beers, the hiss of the bottles opening a small but satisfying sound in the quiet evening. They sat in companionable silence for a moment, the soft sounds of the dogs and the night providing a soothing backdrop.

Tully took a sip of his beer, his eyes scanning the barn. "You know, it's not often I get visitors here, especially not ones from the old days," he said, his tone light but with an underlying curiosity.

Houston leaned back in his chair, taking a long drag from his cigar. He watched the smoke curl into the air before exhaling slowly. "Yeah, well, sometimes you just need to reconnect with what's real," he replied, his voice thoughtful.

"So, what's this business you mentioned? "Tully asked casually, though his eyes were sharp, reflecting the keen interest of someone who had seen and understood more than he let on. Houston took another sip of his beer, the cool liquid contrasting with the warm, smoky flavor of the cigar. "Got some old debts to settle in Miami. Thought I'd swing by and see an old friend first. Needed a break from the noise," he admitted, his eyes distant as if recalling the chaos he had left behind.

Tully nodded, his curiosity piqued. "Sounds like you've got a story there," he said, his tone inviting but not pressing. He knew better than to push Houston for details before he was ready.

"Maybe," Houston said with a cryptic smile, the edges of his lips curling as if he knew more than he was letting on. "But that's for another night. Tonight's about catching up, remembering the good times."

They clinked their beer bottles together, the sound ringing softly in the quiet barn. The night stretched on, filled with shared memories and quiet laughter. They talked about their childhood, the mischief they got into, and the dreams they once had. Houston shared a story about the time they tried to build a treehouse and ended up with more splinters than structure. Tully countered with a tale of their first fishing trip, where they caught more sunburn than fish.

"You ever think about those days?" Houston asked, his voice softer, almost wistful.

"All the time," Tully replied, a smile tugging at his lips. "They were simpler, in a way. But life moves on. We make do with what we have, right?"

"Yeah," Houston agreed, his gaze fixed on the horizon where the last light of the day was fading. "But sometimes it's good to remember where we came from. Keeps you grounded."

As the night grew darker, the conversation shifted to the present. Tully talked about the dogs, their breeding programs, and the challenges of maintaining the farm. Houston listened, appreciating the passion in his friend's voice.

"You've done well for yourself here, Tully," Houston said, genuine admiration in his tone. "It's not easy building something from the ground up."

Tully shrugged, though his pride was evident. "Just doing what I love. These dogs, they give me purpose. What about you, Houston? What's keeping you going?"

Houston was silent for a moment, his thoughts heavy. "It's complicated," he finally said. "But there's always something to fight for, something to protect. Even if it's just a promise you made to yourself."

Tully nodded, understanding more than he let on. "Well, whatever it is, you know you've got a place here. Anytime you need to get away, this barn, these dogs, they'll always be here for you."

Houston smiled a real, genuine smile that reached his eyes. "Thanks, Tully. That means more than you know."

They continued to talk, the hours slipping away unnoticed. The barn, filled with the gentle presence of the dogs and the comfortable silence of old friends, felt like a haven. For a brief moment, the burden of Houston's past and the uncertainty of his future seemed to lift, replaced by the simple, enduring bond of friendship.

As the night wore on, they eventually fell into a comfortable silence, the only sounds the occasional rustle of the dogs settling in for the night and the soft crackle of their cigars.

Chapter Six

Candy lay in bed, the soft glow of the moon filtering through the curtains. She had finally drifted off to sleep after a long day filled with tension and bubbles.

The house was silent, save for the gentle hum of the air conditioner.

Suddenly, a noise broke through the stillness, jolting her awake. It was faint but distinct, a soft thud coming from somewhere downstairs. Candy's eyes snapped open, her heart racing. She sat up, straining to listen, her senses on high alert.

Another thud, followed by a scraping sound, reached her ears. Her mind raced, cycling through possibilities. Lorenzo was away, and it was just her and the new maid, Kelly, in the house. Candy glanced at the clock: 12:14 AM.

She swung her legs out of bed, slipping her feet into the plush slippers waiting on the floor. Grabbing her silk robe from the chair, she wrapped it around herself, tying it securely at the waist. The cold doorknob felt like ice in her hand as she turned it, opening the door just enough to peer into the dimly lit hallway.

The house was eerily quiet. Candy tiptoed down the hall, her steps muffled by the thick carpet. Each creak of the floorboards seemed amplified in the stillness, echoing in the cavernous space. She paused at the top of the stairs, peering into the darkness below. The shadows seemed to dance and shift, playing tricks on her mind.

Candy descended the stairs cautiously, holding her breath. She reached the ground floor and moved toward the kitchen, where the sound had seemed to originate. She flicked on the light, the sudden brightness making her blink. The kitchen was pristine, nothing out of place. She let out a breath she hadn't realized she was holding, but the unease remained.

She checked the windows and doors, ensuring they were locked. Satisfied that everything was secure, she turned off the light and moved toward the living room.

The living room was bathed in shadows, the furniture hulking and unfamiliar in the dark. Candy felt a chill run down her spine as she stepped inside, her eyes scanning the room. She walked past the grand piano and the plush sofas, heading toward the glass doors that led to the veranda.

Suddenly, she heard it again, a faint whispering sound, like fabric brushing against fabric. Her breath caught in her throat as she spun around, her eyes darting to the corners of the room. Nothing. The whispering stopped as abruptly as it had started.

Candy moved to the doors, pressing her face against the glass to peer outside. The garden was still, the night air undisturbed. She unlocked the door and stepped out, the cool night breeze brushing against her skin.

Candy walked to the edge of the veranda, her eyes scanning the darkness for any sign of movement. The pool lay still, its surface reflecting the pale moonlight. She shivered, feeling exposed under the vast sky.

A rustling sound came from the bushes near the fence. Candy's heart pounded in her chest as she strained to see what had caused it. She took a tentative step forward, but a sudden gust of wind made her jump, and she realized it was just the wind stirring the leaves.

She turned to go back inside, but a feeling of being watched made her pause. She glanced over her shoulder, her eyes sweeping the garden one last time. Nothing. She shook her head, scolding herself for being so jumpy.

Back inside, Candy locked the door behind her and leaned against it, her heart still racing. She decided to check on Kelly, to make sure she was safe. She moved quietly through the house, heading toward the maid's quarters.

Candy knocked softly on Kelly's door, waiting for a response. When none came, she pushed the door open gently. The room was dark, the only light coming from the hallway. She could see Kelly's form under the covers, her breathing slow and steady. Candy felt a wave of relief wash over her. She closed the door quietly and turned to leave.

As Candy walked back to her room, she couldn't shake the feeling of unease. She paused at the foot of the stairs, glancing around one last time. The house was silent, but the feeling of being watched persisted.

She ascended the stairs quickly, her heart pounding in her ears. Once back in her bedroom, she locked the door behind her and climbed into bed. She lay there, staring at the ceiling, trying to calm her racing thoughts.

Candy closed her eyes, wanting to relax. But just as she was beginning to drift off, she heard it again—a faint, almost imperceptible sound, like a whispering voice. Her eyes snapped open, and she lay still, straining to hear.

The whispering continued, growing louder, more insistent. It seemed to be coming from inside the room. Candy's breath quickened, and she sat up, looking around wildly. The room was empty, but the whisper persisted, filling her mind with an eerie, unsettling feeling.

She threw off the covers and stood up, her heart pounding. She felt a cold sweat break on her forehead as she searched the room, trying to find the source of the noise. It was as if the very walls were whispering to her, filling her mind with a growing sense of dread.

Finally, she couldn't take it anymore. She grabbed her phone and dialed Lorenzo's number, her hands shaking. The phone rang and rang, but there was no answer. She hung up and paced the room, her mind racing.

She tried to convince herself that it was just her imagination, that the events of the night had left her jumpy and paranoid. But deep down, she knew that something was wrong, something she couldn't explain.

Candy lay back down, pulling the covers up to her chin. She closed her eyes and tried to block out the whispering, focusing on her breathing, trying to calm herself. But the feeling of unease lingered, making it impossible to find peace.

As the hours passed, the whispering gradually faded, leaving Candy in an uneasy silence. She lay awake, staring at the ceiling, her mind racing with thoughts of what could have caused the strange noises. She tried to find logical explanations, but none seemed to fit.

Just as she was beginning to calm down, a loud crash shattered the silence. It was unmistakably the sound of breaking glass coming from the kitchen. Candy's heart leaped into her throat. She bolted upright, adrenaline surging through her veins.

Without thinking, she grabbed the baseball bat she kept for protection, her hands trembling as she clutched it tightly. She hurried downstairs, her footsteps echoing in the stillness of the house. As she reached the kitchen door, she hesitated for a moment, steeling herself for whatever she might find.

Taking a deep breath, she flicked on the light and burst into the kitchen, bat raised and ready to strike.

"Kelly!" she exclaimed, her voice a mix of surprise and relief.

Kelly stood in the middle of the kitchen, shards of glass scattered around her feet. Her face was pale, and she looked just as startled as Candy.

"I'm sorry," Kelly stammered, her eyes wide with fear. "I heard a noise and came to check it out. I must have knocked over a glass."

Candy lowered the bat, her pulse still racing. She took a moment to catch her breath, the tension slowly draining from her body.

"It's okay," she said, her voice softer now. "I just... I thought someone had broken in."

Kelly nodded, her hands shaking as she began to pick up the larger pieces of glass. "I didn't mean to scare you," she said, her voice barely above a whisper.

Candy stepped forward, setting the bat down and kneeling to

help her. "No, it's not your fault. This house has been giving me the creeps all night. I heard strange noises earlier, and I guess I was just on edge."

Kelly looked even more distressed. "Maybe it was me you heard," she said, her voice trembling. "I've been trying to hide my drunk face. I felt so embarrassed, but I really needed to get some water. But I was so unsteady, I knocked the glass over."

As Kelly turned to pick up another piece of glass, Candy was about to reassure her when a hand suddenly grabbed her and spun her across the room. Her heart skipped a beat as she stumbled, and Lorenzo stepped out of the shadows, his face a mask of fury.

"What the fuck is this?" he snarled.

Candy's mind raced. "Hey baby, when did you get back? I just took Kelly out for lunch… it's, uh, her birthday. Say Happy Birthday, baby."

"Fuck that," Lorenzo spat. "You two look like a pair of hoochie fucking mamas. Who the fuck do you think you're fooling, Candy?"

Kelly, still trying to regain her composure, attempted to intervene. "Really, sir, it's not what—"

But Lorenzo's blazing eyes turned towards her. He advanced, backing Kelly up until she hit the wall. He pinned her there, his face inches from hers, radiating menace.

"Bitch, know your fucking place," he hissed. "This ain't got fuck all to do with you. You can either mind your business," Lorenzo's hands roved over Kelly's body, squeezing and groping aggressively. "Or take care of mine. Either gets you by, pick one."

Candy, horrified, moved quickly. She approached Lorenzo from behind, trying to ease his hands off Kelly. "Come on baby, you don't need to do this… it's nothing, come to me, papi."

She ran her hands over Lorenzo's chest, trailing down to his groin while kissing his neck. Lorenzo slowly released Kelly as Candy began unbuttoning his shirt.

"Come on baby…" she coaxed, her voice a mix of seduction and desperation.

She led Lorenzo out of the kitchen, casting a worried glance back at Kelly. Kelly stood there, breathing hard, her eyes wide with fear and concern. As Candy and Lorenzo disappeared down the hall, Kelly sank to the floor, her mind reeling from the night's events. She knew she had to be careful, but the dangerous undercurrent in the house was becoming increasingly hard to ignore.

Candy's mind raced as she led Lorenzo to their bedroom. She needed to calm him down and defuse the situation, but the fear gnawing at her was relentless. Once they were behind closed doors, she tried to soothe him, her touch gentleness and her words soft.

"Papi, you know I love you," she whispered, kissing his neck.

"Let's just forget about tonight and focus on us."

The bedroom was dimly lit, the soft glow of moonlight filtering through the curtains, casting delicate shadows on the walls. Lorenzo had laid sprawled on the bed, naked, his muscular form half-covered by a crumpled sheet. His eyes, dark and intense, followed Candy's every movement as she emerged from the bathroom, clad in a sheer slip that left little to the imagination.

Her gaze never left Lorenzo, their shared hunger visible in the room. With deliberate steps, she crossed to the dresser, her fingers brushing lightly over a long, silky scarf. She picked it up, wrapping it sensually around her neck as she swayed to the rhythm of the sultry music playing softly in the background.

Without breaking eye contact, Candy climbed onto the bed, her movements slow and deliberate. She straddled Lorenzo, her hips beginning a hypnotic, rhythmic motion. Lorenzo's hands roamed her body, caressing and squeezing, their touch rougher as his desire grew.

Candy's head tilted back in ecstasy, her hair cascading down her back as their actions became more frenzied. Lorenzo's grip tightened on the scarf, wrapping it around his hands, his knuckles white with the force of his passion. The scarf stretched taut between them as he pulled, Candy's breath catching in her throat.

Meanwhile, outside the bedroom door, Kelly stood silently, her heart pounding in her chest. The door was slightly ajar, allowing her a narrow view into the intimate scene unfolding within. She watched, unable to tear her eyes away, a mix of curiosity and unease swirling within her.

Through the opening, Kelly saw Candy's eyes flicker towards her. For a moment, their gazes locked, and instead of fear or embarrassment, Candy's expression seemed to intensify. She appeared to relish the presence of an observer, her movements growing more untamed, her moans louder and more desperate. Lorenzo, oblivious to their voyeur, suddenly flipped Candy over, his strong hands guiding her body as he took control. He held the scarf tightly, using it to pull her closer as he thrust into her with increasing urgency. The bed creaked under their fervent motions, the headboard tapping rhythmically against the wall.

The raw intensity of their passion was visible. The sounds of moaning and gasping filled the room, mingling with the soft strains of music, creating a symphony of lust and desire. Candy's eyes fluttered closed, her body arching in response to Lorenzo's relentless pace. Each gasp, each moan seemed to echo in the room, blending with the muffled sounds of the outside world. Her hands clutched at the sheets, her knuckles mirroring the tension of the scarf around her neck.

Lorenzo's grip on the scarf tightened further, his breathing ragged and uneven. He was lost in the moment, his entire being focused on the woman beneath him. Their bodies moved in perfect synchronization, a dance of raw, primal need.

Kelly watched, a silent witness to their passion, her own emotions, a tangled mess of fascination and apprehension. She felt like an intruder in this intimate world, yet she couldn't pull herself away. The scene before her was both mesmerizing and unsettling, a reminder of the unpredictable and often dangerous nature of human desire.

As the crescendo of their lovemaking built, the headboard shook in time with their moans. The sounds of their passion echoing in the darkness.

***

Candy closed the bathroom door behind her, feeling the cool tiles beneath her bare feet. The remnants of the night lay scattered in the bedroom, her sheer slip and the scarf, now symbols of a tangled web of emotions and desires. She turned on the harsh fluorescent light, illuminating her tired reflection in the mirror. Her eyes, still darkened with smudged makeup, stared back at her with regret.

She filled a glass with water, her hand shaking slightly. In her other hand, she held three small white pills. Candy paused, the weight of the moment pressing down on her. Taking a deep breath, she quickly swallowed the pills, washing them down with a gulp of water. The cold liquid soothed her throat but did little to calm her nerves.

Candy lingered for a moment, staring into the mirror, searching for a sense of clarity. Her reflection seemed almost foreign to her, a mask of confidence hiding the turmoil underneath. She wanted to feel in control, but the night's events had left her shaken. Her mind flashed back to the intense encounter with Lorenzo and the way Kelly had witnessed it all. The mixture of vulnerability and power she had felt still lingered, leaving her feeling unmoored.

With a resolute nod, she flushed the toilet to mask the sound and left the bathroom, stepping back into the dimly lit bedroom. The silence was heavy, and the house seemed to hold its breath.

She walked over to the window and looked out at the city lights, drawing some comfort from the distant, twinkling chaos.

The morning sun cast shadows across the veranda, highlighting the pristine luxury of their home. Lorenzo lounged in a chair, lost in the music playing through his iPod. The rhythmic beats were his sanctuary, a way to escape from the world and its complications.

Candy approached him, her face a mask of practiced calm. She stood silently for a moment, watching him, before Lorenzo finally acknowledged her presence with a terse announcement. "Team leaves today. I'll be back on Monday. Don't touch the fucking Bentley."

Candy forced a smile. "I'll miss you, Papi."

Lorenzo glanced up at her, his expression unreadable. "Yeah... right." His words were dismissive, cutting through the fragile intimacy of the moment.

Candy's heart sank a little, but she kept her composure. She watched as Lorenzo stood up, stretched, and walked away without another word, leaving her alone on the veranda. The silence that followed was oppressive, and she felt a little pang of loneliness.

Kelly wiped the counter back in the kitchen, squeezing out the sponge before placing it neatly away. She took a final look around, satisfied with her work, and began to undo her apron. Turning around, she was startled to see Candy standing there, holding a drink.

"Oh, God, you scared me," Kelly said, clutching her chest.

Candy smiled, a hint of mischief in her eyes. "Sorry about that. All done?"

"Yeah, I'll see you Monday, I guess," Kelly replied, trying to steady her nerves.

"So, what are your plans for Friday night?" Candy asked, taking a sip of her drink.

"The usual, a bath and a good book," Kelly said, her tone resigned.

Candy raised an eyebrow. "Seems like a waste. I was thinking of gliding down to the club. I would love it if you came along."

"I don't think..." Kelly started, but Candy cut her off.

"Do you realize how many times you say that? I saw you last night... Did you enjoy watching us?"

Kelly's face flushed. "Yeah... well... I, uh, I was worried, that's all."

Candy leaned in closer, her voice softening. "It's alright, I enjoyed it. Did you?"

Kelly looked down, embarrassed by Candy's directness. "No, well yes, no, I just was worried... I..."

"It's just a drink, maybe a dance. It'll do you good," Candy said, taking Kelly's hand and gently pulling her towards the door. "Besides, what's the worst that can happen?"

***

Candy's Bentley convertible that Lorenzo had asked her not to ride roared down the city streets, the bass booming from the stereo. She had later convinced Kelly to go with her to the club. She drove with a reckless abandon that made Kelly grip the seat and door tightly. As they turned a corner and entered a busy area alive with clubs and restaurants, Kelly couldn't help but ask, "Why do you do that?"

"It's fun," Candy replied with a carefree smile.

They pulled up to a red light. In the next lane, a classic Cadillac convertible with two men caught Candy's eye. The passenger leaned out, grinning. "Mm mmp, that is one fine set... of wheels. How about a ride?"

Candy exchanged a look with Kelly before turning to the man. "Excuse me," she said, her tone dripping with sarcasm. "Do you even know who you're talking to? Do you know the Goddess Night Club on Washington?"

"Uh, yeah," the passenger replied, taken aback.

"That's where I'll be. If you can get in there... I'll talk to you.

Buh-Bye," Candy said, pulling away as the light turned green.

The passenger nodded to his driver, a look of determination on his face. "See that? She wants to meet later."

The driver turned left, leaving Candy and Kelly to continue their journey.

The night was alive with energy as Candy and Kelly walked among the partiers of South Beach. Candy was vibrant, her presence commanding attention, while Kelly followed in her wake, feeling both exhilarated and out of her depth.

"Do you think those guys are gonna show up?" Kelly asked, trying to keep up.

"If they do, they'll learn a valuable lesson about applying themselves. If they don't, they'll probably tell their friends they did. Who cares?" Candy replied with a shrug.

"How do you do that?" Kelly asked, genuinely curious. "Do what?" Candy responded, stopping to face her.

"I don't know, you just seem so... alive," Kelly said, struggling to find the right words.

Candy took Kelly by the shoulders, looking her in the eyes. "Everything around you is alive. Can't you feel it? God, I love that feeling. It's the same everywhere... but always kinda different. But it's real. You can feel it. Do you feel it?"

Kelly closed her eyes, trying to tap into the energy Candy described. "There is an energy, a power in the air."

"That's it, feel that" Candy encouraged, her voice filled with passion.

Kelly opened her eyes, her expression thoughtful. "Then I think, oh, I have no idea what I'm going to do with my life and yeah, I'm broke too because I let some idiot mouth breather make me think he cared." She said all this almost in one breath.

Candy laughed softly. "Wow, you need a drink." She grabbed Kelly's hand and pulled her down the street. "Besides, what's the worst that can happen?"

The Goddess Nightclub was a pulsating haven of Latin music, spinning salsa dancers, and an animated light show. Only the beautiful and well-heeled seemed to gain entry, and Candy and Kelly were no exception. They were shown to a table overlooking the dance floor, the perfect vantage point to take in the vibrant scene.

Candy ordered drinks for them. "She'll have a Mojito, Rum and Diet Coke for me."

Kelly looked around in awe. "I love this dress. I never would have thought so, but it is kinda, I don't know... empowering?"

A slick-looking man approached their table, but Candy didn't give him a chance to speak. "Step, step, step, step," she commanded, waving him away.

The man turned to Kelly, who recoiled slightly. "Don't turn your stank eye at her, please. Get-to-stepping. Right now, come on, just... keep it moving," Candy said, her tone firm.

The man moved on, and Kelly laughed. "Of course, the power of the dress has drawbacks as well."

Candy laughed too, taking a drink as she scanned the club. Her eyes were drawn to a man standing in the shadows on the far side of the room. She tried to get a better look, but the lights kept his face hidden.

Candy's curiosity was piqued. "I'll be right back," she said, standing up.

Kelly nodded, enjoying the Latin beats. Candy navigated through the crowded club, her eyes fixed on the mysterious man. But as she pushed through a wall of people, he vanished. She looked around, shrugged, and decided to let it go for now.

The club was still alive with energy as always. Candy returned to the dance floor, pulling Kelly along and grabbing a couple of guys to dance with them. She moved with grace and confidence, her hips swaying in time with the music.

"Damn girl, put a little sway in those hips," Candy encouraged Kelly.

Kelly tried to loosen up. "I was never very good at this."

"It's not that hard, watch," Candy said, demonstrating with both guys. They moved in unison, grinding sensually. "I think I'm feeling it," Kelly said, starting to relax.

"You're not the only one," Candy replied, noticing Kelly's dance partner watching her closely.

The night continued with Candy and Kelly dancing the night away, their worries momentarily forgotten in the pulsing rhythm of the music and the vibrant atmosphere.

The Bentley pulled into the driveway and entered the garage.

Candy helped a drunken Kelly out of the car, guiding her inside. Kelly had clearly had a good time, her laughter and stumbling steps was proof of the night's adventures.

Candy took her into the maid's quarters and gently laid her on the bed, covering her with a blanket. As Candy turned to leave, Kelly bolted upright. "Yeah, I'll have a mojito," she mumbled before collapsing back onto the bed.

Candy smiled, closing the door softly behind her.

Later, Candy stood in the bathroom, wearing a silk robe and rinsing her face over the sink. She grabbed a towel and wiped her face, her senses heightened as she heard a noise from the dark bedroom. She cautiously stepped into the darkness, reaching for the light switch but unluckily the lights didn't come on.

"Shit."

Chapter Seven

The kitchen was filled with soft light of the late morning sun. The scent of freshly brewed coffee lingered in the air, mingling with the faint aroma of the cigarette. Candy was nervously puffing on. She paced back and forth, her bare feet padding softly against the cool, tiled floor. Her eyes, usually sharp and confident, now darted anxiously around the room. The smoke from her cigarette curled lazily towards the ceiling, adding to the atmosphere of tension that hung heavily in the air.

The sudden sound of the front door opening and closing made Candy startle initially. She then heard the familiar rustle of grocery bags and the soft thud of footsteps approaching. A moment later, Kelly entered the kitchen, her arms laden with bags of groceries. Her freshly styled hair framed her face, giving her a more polished look than usual.

"Where have you been?" Candy snapped, her voice tinged with impatience.

"Gee... I was having my hair done," Kelly replied, her tone light and slightly defensive. She put the grocery bags down on the counter, glancing at Candy's tense figure.

Candy stamped out her cigarette in the ashtray with a forceful twist. The acrid smell of the extinguished cigarette mixed with the lingering smoke, creating a pungent aroma. Kelly watched her, sensing that something was off.

"I had a great time last night," Kelly continued, trying to lighten the mood. "Feeling it today, though. Sorry if I got a little..."

"Sit down, I have to talk to you," Candy interrupted, her voice suddenly serious.

Kelly hesitated for a moment before pulling out a stool and sitting down. She tried to make a joke to diffuse the tension. "Okay, I guess the employer role is dominant today."

"Shut up, God damn it! This is serious!" Candy's outburst made Kelly flinch. Candy's eyes, wide and frantic, reflected the desperation of a woman on the edge.

"We need to talk. I gotta discuss something with you," Candy said, her voice trembling. She grabbed her purse from the counter and headed towards the door that led to the garage.

"Let me put the groceries away," Kelly said, standing up and reaching for the bags.

"Fuck the groceries... now!" Candy's voice was almost a shout as she stormed out the door.

Kelly, taken aback by Candy's urgency, quickly dug through the grocery bags, grabbing perishable items and throwing them into the fridge and freezer haphazardly. The rest of the groceries were left on the counter as she hurried to catch Candy.

***

The waves crashed against the rocky shore, sending up sprays of salty mist that glistened in the midday sun. The sound was both soothing and relentless, a natural rhythm that contrasted sharply with the tension between the two women. Candy and Kelly sat barefoot on the rocks, their shoes discarded nearby. Candy's eyes darted around nervously, scanning the horizon as if expecting trouble to appear at any moment.

"Well, you've got me curious, I'll say that much," Kelly said, trying to break the silence.

Candy sighed deeply, her shoulders slumping as she stared out at the ocean. "I'm fucked, Kelly. I had the whole thing worked out, and now I'm fucked."

"What do you mean?" Kelly asked, concern etched on her face.

Candy took a deep breath, the ocean breeze ruffling her hair. "You... well, you know Lorenzo isn't the easiest man to live with. I had always hoped to save enough money, get a chance, and get away. But right when I'm ready, out of nowhere, an ex appears to fuck it all up."

"An ex?" Kelly's eyebrows raised in surprise.

"Ex, ex-partner, ex-lover, expected to never see him again, ex," Candy clarified, her voice bitter.

Candy then took to narrating what happened the previous night as she stepped out of the bathroom, a towel wrapped around her body, her damp hair clinging to her neck. She reached for the light switch on the wall, but nothing happened.

"Shit," she muttered, thinking the house's electrical system was acting up again. She groped in the darkness, her fingers brushing against the cool, textured wallpaper as she made her way towards the bed.

Suddenly, a switch clicked, and a soft, yellow light from a bedside lamp flooded the room. Candy spun around, her heart pounding in her chest. Sitting casually on a chair in the corner of the room was a man she hadn't seen in years. Houston. He was holding a gun, its barrel pointed directly at her.

"Hi honey," he said, his voice smooth and menacing.

Candy's eyes widened in shock. "Houston. Oh my God," she whispered, her voice barely audible.

Houston's lips curled into a cold, humorless smile. "Nice seeing you too. You look good, nice house. Well, except for the security system. I guess you have a lot to protect, huh?"

Candy's mind raced. She had spent so many nights wondering if she would ever see him again, and now he was here, in her bedroom, with a gun. "I waited for you. I looked for you," she said, her voice trembling with a mixture of fear and disbelief.

Houston's expression darkened. "I've been looking for you too, Candy."

Candy took a hesitant step towards him, but Houston's grip on the gun tightened, and he cocked it, the click echoing ominously in the room. "Don't," he warned, his eyes narrowing.

"I... I can't believe it. Baby, I'm so glad to see you," Candy said, trying to keep her voice steady.

"Yeah, I'll bet," Houston replied, his tone dripping with sarcasm.

Candy's eyes darted to the gun in his hand. "What are you doing? Put that thing away, Houston."

"In a minute," Houston said, his voice casual. "Oh yeah, I remember now. Where's my fucking money, Candy?"

Candy's heart skipped a beat. "Houston, let me explain," she pleaded, her voice desperate.

"You always could explain things, Candy. You made the most incredible shit sound reasonable. I don't want to kill you, well... I kinda do," he said, pausing, his expression almost wistful. "It looks like you have a bank. All I want is what you took from me."

Candy's legs felt weak, and she sank down onto the edge of the bed, taking a deep breath to steady herself. "I was scared, Houston. You never called. I didn't know what to do."

"I told you what to do," Houston said, his voice cold.

"There were police, soldiers. I had a bag full of cash! Everyone I saw looked like a Fed. Houston, I waited to hear something, anything," Candy explained, her voice shaking.

"It's been a long time, Candy," Houston said, his voice low and dangerous.

Candy looked up at him, her eyes filled with a mixture of fear and regret. "I'm sorry, Houston. I didn't know what else to do."

Houston stood up slowly, the gun still pointed at her. He walked over to the window, looking out into the night. "Sorry doesn't cut it, Candy. Not after all these years."

Candy felt a tear slip down her cheek. "I didn't mean for things to turn out like this."

Houston turned back to her, his eyes cold and unyielding. "Well, they did. And now you're going to fix it."

Candy's mind raced as she tried to think of a way out of this situation. She knew Houston well enough to know that he wouldn't hesitate to pull the trigger if he didn't get what he wanted. "Houston, please. Let's just talk about this. We can figure something out."

Houston shook his head slowly. "There's nothing to talk about.

You have my money, and I want it back. All of it."

Candy swallowed hard, her mind scrambling for a solution. "Okay. I'll get you the money. Just... give me some time."

Houston's eyes narrowed. "You have two days, Candy. If I don't have my money by then, you won't like what happens next."

Candy nodded, her heart pounding in her chest. "Okay. Two days."

Houston took a step closer, his face inches from hers. "Don't make me come back here, Candy. You won't like it if I do."

Candy nodded again, tears streaming down her face. "I won't. I promise."

Houston straightened up, his expression still cold. "Good. I'll be in touch."

With that, he turned and walked out of the bedroom, leaving Candy trembling on the edge of the bed. The door closed softly behind him, and Candy let out a shaky breath, her mind reeling from the encounter. She knew she was in serious trouble, and she had no idea how she was going to get out of it. So that was the end of the flashback narration.

"So, what's the problem? Tell him to blow or introduce him to Lorenzo... that'll keep him away. What does he want, anyway?" Kelly asked, trying to find a solution.

Candy's face twisted in frustration and fear. "Five million dollars."

Kelly's eyes widened, and she let out a loud, startled exclamation. "WHAT!?"

Candy, in an attempt to divert her own growing panic, looked around at the scenery. "I love the beach," she said softly, almost to herself.

Kelly blinked, trying to process the information. "Candy, what did you say?"

"I said I love the beach. Don't you? It's so beautiful," Candy repeated, her voice distant and wistful.

Kelly shook her head, trying to focus. "About five million dollars?"

"Yeah, I kinda owe him some money," Candy admitted, her voice barely audible over the crashing waves.

"Some?" Kelly's tone was incredulous.

"Hey, some of it was supposed to be mine," Candy shot back defensively.

"Where'd you get that much money?" Kelly asked, genuinely baffled.

"It doesn't matter. If he doesn't get it, I'm dead," Candy said,

standing up abruptly. She started hopping from rock to rock, making her way down to the beach, her movements quick and almost frantic.

Kelly watched her for a moment before following, though less gracefully. "What did you do with the money?"

Not moving her gaze from the clear space. "It's a long story, girl." she replied.

"So, what are you going to do?" she called out, her voice filled with worry.

"I've been thinking about it all night. The way I figure it, I only have one choice," Candy's voice came from somewhere ahead, out of sight.

Kelly clambered down the rocks awkwardly, her eyes scanning for Candy. "What choice?" she called out, her heart pounding in her chest.

Suddenly, Candy appeared from behind a large boulder, her expression cold and matter of fact. "We're going to have to kill my husband."

Kelly froze, her eyes wide with shock. "Shit! Stop doing that!" she exclaimed, her nerves frayed by Candy's sudden appearance.

Candy stepped closer, her gaze intense. "Did you hear me? We're going to have to kill my husband."

Kelly stared at her, trying to comprehend the gravity of what Candy was saying. "Did you say 'we'?"

Candy's eyes were red rimmed from lack of sleep and stress, her hands trembling slightly as she lit another cigarette. The smoke curled upwards, creating a hazy veil between the two women. She kept mute staring into space.

Kelly's mind was racing, trying to process the bombshell Candy had just dropped on her. "Why does it have to be we? Why can't you just leave Lorenzo?"

Candy shook her head, taking a deep drag from her cigarette. "You don't understand. Lorenzo isn't just going to let me walk away. He's possessive, controlling. If I try to leave, he'll hunt me down. And now, with this ex back in the picture, it's even more complicated. If Lorenzo finds out about the money… it'll be over for me."

Kelly leaned back in her chair, her thoughts swirling. "But killing him? That's extreme, Candy. There has to be another way."

Candy's eyes filled with desperate determination. "I've thought of every other way. This is the only option. If Lorenzo is out of the picture, I can pay off the ex and finally be free."

Kelly shook her head, still unable to wrap her mind around the plan. "And you want me to help you with this? Why me?"

Candy looked at her, her expression pleading. "Because you're the only one I trust. You've seen what Lorenzo is like. You know what I'm up against. Please, Kelly, I need you."

Kelly felt a lump form in her throat. "I don't know, Candy. This is... this is a lot."

Candy reached across, grabbing Kelly's hand. Her grip was firm, almost painful. "I know it's a lot. But if you help me, we can both get out of this. We can both be free."

Kelly stared at their intertwined hands, feeling the gravity of the decision before her. She knew Candy was right about Lorenzo. He was dangerous, controlling, and wouldn't let Candy go without a fight. But was she really prepared to take such a drastic step?

Kelly's mind raced, trying to find another solution. "What if we go to the police?"

Candy laughed bitterly. "And tell them what? That my ex-criminal partner is threatening to kill me if I don't give him five million dollars that I don't have? Lorenzo has connections everywhere. The police wouldn't help us."

Kelly's head was spinning. "I don't know, Candy. This is too much. I can't... I can't be a part of this."

The silence stretched between them, heavy and oppressive. Finally, Kelly looked up, meeting Candy's gaze. "Okay," she said softly. "I'll see if I'm capable of anything."

Candy let out a breath she didn't realize she'd been holding. "Thank you, Kelly. You don't know what this means to me."

The waves continued to crash against the shore, their relentless rhythm, a stark contrast to the turmoil in Kelly's mind. She and Candy sat on the rocks, the tension between them almost palpable.

"Okay, so how do we do this?" Kelly asked, her voice barely audible over the sound of the ocean.

Candy took a deep breath, her eyes scanning the horizon as if searching for answers in the distant waves. "We need to make it look like an accident. Something that won't raise too many questions."

Kelly nodded slowly, her mind racing with possibilities. "Like what?"

Candy's gaze was intense as she turned to face Kelly. "I was thinking maybe a car accident. Lorenzo loves to drive fast. It wouldn't be hard to stage something that looks like he lost control.

Kelly's stomach churned at the thought. "A car accident? That's... that's dangerous, Candy. What if something goes wrong?"

Candy shook her head, her expression resolute. "We'll plan it carefully. Make sure everything goes off without a hitch. It's the best option."

Kelly took a deep breath, trying to steady her nerves and probably falling into the game with Candy. "Okay. But we need to be really careful. One mistake and everything could fall apart."

Candy nodded, her eyes filled with determination. "I know. We'll be careful."

Candy and Kelly discussed every detail of their plan, from the timing to the exact location where the "accident" would take place.

"We'll do it on that sharp curve near the cliffs," Candy said, pointing to a spot on the map. "It's dangerous enough that no one will question it if he goes over the edge."

Kelly nodded, her heart pounding in her chest. "And what about the car? How do you make sure it goes over?"

Candy's eyes were cold and calculating. "We'll tamper with the brakes. Make it look like they failed."

Kelly felt a shiver run down her spine. "Are you sure we can do this? And does that even sound convincing enough?"

Candy reached across the table, squeezing Kelly's hand. "We can do this. We have to. That was only a suggestion, it could be any other thing."

Kelly took a step back, shaking her head. "Candy, that's insane.

There has to be another way."

When she got no reply, she said with all strength left in her. "I'm seriously not in for this." With that, Kelly walks off to the car leaving behind her boss, her mind a whirlwind of conflicting emotions. She walked briskly towards the parking lot where Candy's convertible 600SL was parked. She needed to get away, to clear her head and think. The sound of the waves faded behind her as she approached her car, the cool metal of the door handle grounding her in reality.

As she opened the door and was about to slide into the car, she saw Candy approaching quickly. Candy's face was a mask of desperation and determination. She reached the car and leaned down, her eyes pleading so she stepped back.

"Kelly, please. Just get in the car. We need to talk about this," Candy said, her voice breaking.

Without a word, Kelly unlocked the passenger door. Candy slipped into the seat beside her, and Candy started the engine. The silence between them was thick with unspoken words and emotions. She pulled out of the parking lot, the car gliding smoothly onto the road.

The drive home was filled with a tense, oppressive silence. The wind whipped through the open roof, but it did little to dispel the heaviness that hung in the air. Both women were lost in their own thoughts, the reality of the situation sinking in.

Candy gripped the steering wheel tightly, her mind racing with possibilities and fears. She glanced over at Kelly, who stared straight ahead, her face pale and drawn. The sunlight flickered through the trees, casting fleeting shadows across Candy's face, highlighting the lines of stress and worry.

As they drove through the quiet streets, Kelly's mind kept circling back to the plan, to the sheer impossibility of what Candy was asking. The risk, the danger, the moral weight of taking a life, it was all too much to bear. Yet, she couldn't shake the image of Candy's desperate eyes, the silent plea for help.

By the time they reached Candy's house, the silence had become unbearable. For a moment, neither of them moved. They sat in the stillness, the reality of their situation pressing down on them like a physical weight.

Finally, Kelly turned to Candy, her voice barely whisper. "I need time to think, Candy. This is... this is too much. I can't just decide something like this on the spot."

Candy nodded slowly, her eyes filled with tears. "I understand, Kelly. Just... please don't take too long. We don't have much time."

Kelly nodded, her heart was heavy. She watched as Candy got out of the car and walked slowly towards the house, her shoulders slumped. Kelly sat in the car for a long moment, staring at the house, before finally getting out and following Candy inside.

The tension between them was visible as they entered the house, the weight of their conversation lingering in the air. Kelly knew that whatever happened next would change their lives forever. She just wasn't sure if she was ready to take that step.

Chapter Eight

The moon hung low in the sky, with an eerie, silvery sheen displaying over the large, fenced home by the airport. The distant roar of jet engines taking off and landing echoed through the air, a constant reminder of the proximity to the bustling airport. The house stood tall and imposing, a fortress in the night, surrounded by high walls topped with razor-sharp barbed wire glistening under the moonlight.

Houston eased his sedan to a stop behind a hulking, dark SUV parked just outside the heavy iron gate. The SUV's windows were blackened, providing no hint of what or who might be concealed within its cavernous interior, that's if there was anyone there at all. Houston's eyes flicked to the illuminated windows of the main building afar, where a dim glow seeped through the closed curtains.

Houston's heart pounded in his chest as he surveyed the area, his trained eyes scanning every corner, every shadow for any sign of movement. He knew this place well, its defenses, its routines, and its secrets. The fence, with its menacing barbed wire, was designed to keep intruders out, but Houston's concern wasn't with getting in.

He shifted the sedan into reverse, his foot gently pressing the accelerator as he backed away, the tires crunching softly on the gravel driveway. Every sound seemed amplified in the stillness of the night. Houston kept his movements slow and deliberate, ensuring he remained unnoticed.

A cool breeze whispered through the trees, rustling the leaves and sending a chill. He came to a stop a short distance away, positioning the sedan in the shadow of a large oak tree.

The night seemed to stretch on endlessly as Houston sat in the sedan, the dashboard lights casting a faint glow on his tense features.

The house remained quiet, the lights within displaying a steady glow. His muscles tensed, ready to spring into action at a moment's notice.

He glanced back at the house, trying to keep a blank mind but wasn't successful at doing that. Whatever was happening here, he needed to be ready. He reached into the glove compartment, pulling out a small, sleek handgun. He checked the magazine, ensuring it was fully loaded, and slipped it into his jacket pocket.

With one last look at the house, Houston settled back into his seat, his mind racing with possibilities. The distant hum of the airport continued to fill the air, a constant reminder of the ticking clock and the ever-present danger that surrounded him.

***

The barn, Tully's barn, stood isolated in the dead of night, its wooden frame creaking under the weight of the darkness with his main building standing far away. Moonlight filtered through the cracks in the aged wood, giving off long, ghostly shadows on the hay-strewn floor. The air was thick with the smell of damp straw, mixed with the faint, pungent scent of fear and sweat.

Inside, the atmosphere was tense. Tully was crammed inside one of the kennel cages. The metal bars pressed into his flesh, leaving marks on his skin as he tried to shift into a more comfortable position. His eyes darted nervously between the three men who surrounded him.

Two of them were muscled goons, their broad shoulders and thick arms were proof to their brute strength. They took turns poking at Tully with the ends of their batons, each jab eliciting a grunt of pain truthfully from their captive. The third man, their boss, stood slightly apart, watching with a cold, calculating gaze. He was a tall, lean figure, dressed in a sharp suit that seemed out of lace in the rustic setting. His presence exuded an air of authority and menace.

As the goons tormented Tully, the barn door creaked open, drawing their attention. Houston stepped inside, his figure silhouetted against the dim light. The sound of his boots on the wooden floor echoed through the barn, each step deliberates and measured. The goon nearest the door turned, his muscles tensing, but the boss placed a hand on his chest, signaling him to stand down.

Houston's eyes scanned the scene, taking in the sight of Tully trapped and the smirking faces of his tormentors. His expression remained impassive, but a storm brewed beneath his calm exterior. He approached the boss, who stepped forward to meet him, a smug grin playing on his lips.

For a moment, the boss's confidence wavered. He could see the fire in Houston's eyes, the promise of pain and retribution. But he quickly regained his composure, pushing Houston away with a sneer.

The goons were initially shocked as Houston stepped into the barn, his presence unexpected and imposing. Their surprise quickly turned to aggression as they began to move toward him, their intentions clear in their hostile expressions. Houston remained still, his eyes locked on the boss. He could feel the weight of the situation pressing down on him, every second ticking away like a countdown to violence. They moved closer toward him but the boss put a hand on his chest, taking a deep breath as he stepped out to meet Houston.

The air in the dimly lit room was thick with tension. "Eh, we're closed, for repair, you know," Boss said, his voice betraying a hint of nervousness.

Houston didn't respond immediately. Instead, he let his gaze linger on Tully, whose eyes pleaded silently for help. Then, slowly, he turned his attention back to the boss. His face twisted into a sneer as he stepped forward. "Shut up, dickwad." He baked at the goons and then walked towards the cage, directing the next word to its occupant. "How you doin', Tully?"

Sitting in a cage that seemed too small for his frame, Tully let out a bitter laugh. "I'm in a fucking cage. What do you think?"

Two goons, who had been standing guard, moved away from the cage and flanked their boss. Their eyes never left Houston, wary of his every move. Houston's gaze followed them before returning to the boss.

"Dickwad?" Boss repeated his attempt at indignation falling flat. "Uh, there's a debt here that needs settling... it's nothing personal, you know. To simplify, Tully here has some debts to pay"

Tully spat on the floor, his eyes burning with defiance. "Fuck you. I owe you dick."

Houston shrugged, a casual motion that contrasted sharply with the tension in the room. In a flash, he was holding two large 9mm pistols, the barrels aimed squarely at Boss and his goons. The goons, not to be outdone, drew pistols and pointed them back at Houston. But Houston ignored them, his eyes locked on Boss's. His stare was cold, hard, and unwavering.

"Now this is typical," Boss said, trying to sound amused but failing to mask his unease. "Everyone has guns. Remember when people used to settle things with their fists?"

"Tell them to drop the hardware," Houston replied, his voice calm but commanding.

Boss hesitated, his eyes darting to his men. "But... then it will be harder for them to shoot you. You drop yours."

Houston's lips curled into a smirk. "I'll make this easy for you." He stepped closer, pressing the barrel of his gun against Boss's forehead. "I only intend on shooting you. That makes them unemployed and a lot less motivated."

Boss's eyes flicked to his men, who exchanged confused glances. "You have a point. Drop him."

The goons hesitated, looking at each other for confirmation. "I said drop him!" Boss barked. Reluctantly, they let their weapons clatter to the floor and took a step back.

Boss narrowed his eyes, pushing back against the barrel of Houston's gun with his forehead. "So, what now, huh? You might want to pull that trigger, 'cause I'll remember you."

Houston's eyes didn't waver. "I'll take yours too."

The boss reached inside his jacket, drew out an impressive 357 Magnum, and dropped it on the floor with a heavy thud. Houston glanced at the weapon, a brief look of appreciation crossing his face. "Nice gun."

"Yeah," Boss said, a hint of pride in his voice. "I tell you what, I'll go get another one and be sure to show it to you. You got a name, friend?"

"Yeah, I do," Houston replied, his tone casual yet menacing. "That reminds me, before I came in, I let out a couple of Tully's more… aggressive pets. I'd try to avoid the two little nasties getting to your truck."

They all stared at each other for a few seconds, the silence thick with unspoken threats and promises of violence.

"You might not want to be the last one out the door, ya know," Houston added, his voice dripping with cold assurance.

The room held its breath as the tension hung in the air, the balance of power unmistakably shifted in Houston's favor.

As Houston moved to open the cage, the goons, including their boss, looked at each other with the same expression. Clearly frightened, the two goons who were standing guard earlier dashed for the door, a sense of self-preservation overriding any loyalty they might have had to their boss. Their boss seeing as he has been left alone and will be in more danger The sound of barking dogs grew louder as they exited, adding to the chaos.

Houston helped Tully out of the cage. Tully winced as he stretched his cramped limbs. "Hurry up, it smells like piss in here," he grumbled.

Houston couldn't help but smirk. "Well, if you'd clean this place once in a while, it wouldn't."

Tully managed a weak laugh. "Which pups did you let out? I wanna see what's left."

"I didn't let any of them out," Houston replied, picking up the boss's .357 Magnum with a gloved hand.

Tully looked confused. "Huh?"

"I just told them the dogs were out there so they'd hurry, you know, flee the scene."

Tully shook his head in disbelief. "I should have known you'd never get that close to one of my dogs."

Just as Tully turned back towards Houston, a shot rang out. Tully's leg buckled beneath him, and he crumpled to the ground, clutching his bleeding leg. "What the fuck!? Aww shit, you shot me!" he cried out in pain.

Houston walked closer, the smoking gun still in his hand. "You never told me Candy was living in Miami, Tully."

Tully tried to crawl away, using the cages for support, but the pain was too much. He slumped against a cage, his face contorted in agony. "What the fuck are you talking about?"

Houston's voice was cold, devoid of any sympathy. "You know what the fuck I'm talking about, Tully. Why the fuck didn't you tell me Candy was in Miami?"

Tully's eyes darted around, searching for an escape that didn't exist. "I don't know where the bitch is. I haven't heard from her in years."

Houston's eyes narrowed, his expression hardening into a mask of cold determination. "I can't believe you think I fell for that shit. You should have known, Tully. I settle my debts."

With those words, Houston leveled the gun and fired. The shot rang out, loud and sharp in the confined space of the barn. Tully's scream followed almost immediately, a high-pitched sound of pure agony as the bullet tore through his hand. He collapsed onto the floor, clutching his mangled hand to his chest, blood jacuzziing around him.

Houston stood over him, watching with an unfeeling gaze as Tully writhed in pain. His mind raced with memories of betrayal, of plans gone awry, and of the loved and lost. The smell of gunpowder mingled with the stench of urine and fear, creating an acrid, suffocating atmosphere.

Tully's eyes, wide and wild with pain, locked onto Houston's. "Please," he gasped, his voice barely a whisper. "Please, Hous- ton... I didn't know..."

Houston's face remained impassive. He had heard enough lies to last a lifetime. The sense of betrayal was too deep, the need for retribution too strong. "You knew," he said, his voice devoid of any sympathy. "You always knew."

Tully tried to speak, but his words were lost in another scream as Houston raised the gun once more. There was a finality in Houston's movements, a determination to end this once and for all. He aimed carefully, his finger tightening on the trigger.

For a moment, time seemed to stand still. The barn, the dogs, and the distant sounds of the night, all faded into the background. There was only Houston, Tully, and the unforgiving steel of the gun.

Houston fired one last time. The bullet hit its mark, and Tully's body jerked before falling still. Life drained from his eyes, leaving behind a vacant, glassy stare. Houston lowered the gun, the echoes of the shot still ringing in his ears.

The barn was eerily silent, save for the distant barking of dogs. Houston stood over Tully's lifeless body, feeling a strange sense of calm wash over him. He had come here seeking answers, and while he had found some, the path ahead remained shrouded in uncertainty.

With a sigh, Houston tossed the gun aside. It clattered to the floor, the sound sharp in the otherwise quiet space. He turned his attention to the machine pistols, carefully picking them up. They were heavy, their cold metal a stark contrast to the heat of the moment.

Houston glanced around the barn one last time, taking in the scene. The cages, the blood, the still form of Tully. It all seemed surreal, like a twisted tableau from a nightmare. He knew he couldn't linger. There were still many questions left unanswered, and time was not on his side.

As he exited the barn, the cool night air hit him like a refreshing wave. He took a deep breath, the fresh air cleansing his lungs of the barn's oppressive stench. The barks of the dogs grew fainter as he walked away, their sounds blending into the ambient noise of the night.

Houston climbed into his car, placing the machine pistols on the passenger seat. He took a moment to collect his thoughts, the weight of his actions settled heavily on his shoulders. The road ahead was uncertain, fraught with danger and deception. But Houston was used to that, he had always thrived in the shadows, navigating the treacherous paths that others feared to tread.

As he drove away from the barn, his mind raced with possibilities. Candy had always been a wild card, unpredictable and dangerous. But she also held the key to everything, the extremely smart one she was. Houston had already known he would find her, and he wouldn't stop until he did so the day he discovered her home and what her current lifestyle was he chose to visit her the same day.

[Flashback]

That day, the drive to Miami was long and uneventful, giving Houston plenty of time to think. Memories of his past with Candy flooded his mind, each one a reminder of the complicated relationship they had. The open road stretched out before him, a ribbon of asphalt that seemed endless, allowing his thoughts to wander freely. Each mile brought a new memory, her laugh, her smile, the way she could talk herself out of any situation. They had been partners in crime, lovers entangled in a web of deception and passion. But that was all in the past, a past he was now forced to confront.

The sun began to set as he neared the city, painting the sky in shades of orange and pink. When he finally reached Miami, the city was alive with lights and sounds. Neon signs flickered to life, illuminating the bustling streets filled with people going about their business. The contrast between Miami's vibrant nightlife and the quiet countryside he had left behind was striking. Skyscrapers towered above him, their windows reflecting the last rays of sunlight, creating a dazzling display.

Houston navigated the busy streets, his mind focused on the task at hand. He had to meet with Candy, and he had to do it quickly. The thought of seeing her again filled him with a mixture of anticipation and dread. He knew that finding her would not be easy. Candy had always been good at disappearing when she wanted to, slipping through the cracks like water through a sieve.

He had spent the last few days tracking down leads, piecing together snippets of information to find her. His search had led him to a nightclub on the outskirts of the city, a place known for its shady clientele and illicit activities. The kind of place where secrets were exchanged in dark corners, and loyalty was bought and sold like any other commodity. He parked his car a few blocks away, not wanting to draw any attention to himself.

The nightclub was a classy establishment, its exterior sleek and modern. The neon sign glowed brightly, casting a vibrant blue hue over the entrance. Houston watched from a distance, his eyes scanning the crowd for any sign of Candy. He noted everything that was going on, the people entering and leaving, the bouncers at the door, the security cameras. He needed to understand the lay of the land before making his move.

Hours passed as he kept his vigil. The night grew darker, and the club became more crowded. Finally, he saw her. Candy stepped out of a sleek black car, her bright colored dress clinging to her curves, her hair cascading down her back in soft waves. She looked just as he remembered, effortlessly beautiful and completely out of place in the gritty environment. She was also accompanied by another lady of her age, probably a friend.

Candy moved with confidence, her heels clicking on the pavement as she approached the club. Houston's heart pounded in his chest as he watched her. He took note of her interactions, the way she smiled at the bouncers, the way she seemed to know everyone. She was in her element here, and he couldn't help but feel a pang of nostalgia for the times they had spent together.

As she disappeared into the club, Houston made his move. He waited a few minutes before following her inside, blending in with the crowd. The interior of the club was dimly lit, the air thick with the smell of alcohol and cigarette smoke. Music blared from speakers, the bass thumping in his chest. He kept his distance, watching her from the shadows as she made her way to a VIP section at the back of the club.

He waited for the right moment, slipping through the crowd

and positioning himself near the VIP section. He watched as Candy excused herself from the group, heading towards the back of the club where the restrooms were located. Houston saw his opportunity and followed her, moving quickly and silently.

As the night wore on, Candy and the other lady continued to drink, their laughter growing louder and more raucous, they danced hard till they were probably tired. Houston kept his distance, sipping a drink he had no intention of finishing. His mind was focused, every detail of the club etched into his memory.

Eventually, Candy stood up once again, her movements slightly unsteady from the alcohol but not as much as the other lady. She made her way towards the restroom, and Houston saw his opportunity. He slipped into a nearby storage room, watching through a crack in the door. A few minutes later, Candy emerged, her face freshly touched up, her lipstick a bold red. She didn't notice him as she walked past, her mind elsewhere.

Houston followed her back to the VIP section, but instead of rejoining her group, the other lady came to her and they continued walking, heading towards the exit. Houston's curiosity was piqued. He followed her out of the club, staying a few steps behind to avoid detection. The other lady stumbled slightly as they walked down the street, clearly affected by the night's indulgences.

Candy reached a sleek black car parked a little way down the street and fumbled with her keys. Houston watched from the shadows, waiting until she finally managed to unlock the door and slide into the driver's seat. He waited until she pulled away from the curb, then followed at a safe distance.

The drive through the streets was uneventful, the city's nightlife slowly winding down. Candy drove in a meandering fashion, her inebriation evident in her erratic steering. Houston stayed far enough back to remain unnoticed, but close enough to keep her in sight.

Candy finally pulled into the driveway of a luxurious condo building. She parked the car haphazardly and got out, swaying slightly as she walked to the entrance. Houston parked a block away, watching as she assisted the other lady, and also fumbled with the keypad at the door before finally getting it open and disappearing inside.

He approached the building cautiously, his senses heightened. The front door had closed and locked behind Candy, but Houston was no stranger to breaking and entering. He quickly assessed the security system, noting the cameras and the keypad. It was a basic setup, nothing he couldn't handle.

Within moments, Houston had the door open and slipped inside, moving quietly through the lobby. He followed the sound of

Candy's footsteps, his own movements silent and precise.

He soon reached a designated part of the building and listened at the door before easing it open. The hallway was quiet, dimly lit by recessed lighting along the ceiling. He moved silently down the carpeted corridor, his eyes scanning for any sign of movement.

He had crept through the living room, taking in the expensive furniture and tasteful décor. It was a far cry from the gritty life they had once shared. Houston felt a pang of something – nostalgia, maybe, but quickly pushed it aside. He had a job to do.

Reaching the bedroom, Houston paused, listening. Candy was talking to herself, her voice slurred and incoherent, she had just left the kitchen where she and the other lady were discussing something he didn't know of. He could hear the sound of fabric rustling, the clink of a bottle, and the opening of another doorknob, that'd be the bathroom. Taking a deep breath, he turned the doorknob and stepped inside.

Houston slipped into Candy's room silently, the dim light from the lamp on the nightstand casting long shadows across the room. He paused, listening intently. From the bathroom, he heard the unmistakable sound of running water. She was still getting ready. He moved quickly and settled himself on the edge of the bed, his heart pounding with a mix of anticipation and anger.

As he waited, Houston took in his surroundings. The room was elegant and tastefully decorated, a stark contrast to the gritty, turbulent life they had once shared. His mind wandered briefly, recalling moments from their past, but he quickly refocused. This wasn't a social visit. This was about unfinished business.

The sound of the water stopped, and Houston knew Candy would be out any moment. He reached for the light switch on the wall and turned it off, plunging the room into near darkness. He held the portable switch tightly, ready for her reaction.

The bathroom door opened, and Candy stepped out, humming softly to herself. She paused when she noticed the room was dark. "I thought I left the light on," she muttered to herself, reaching for the switch. She flicked it, but nothing happened. Panic started to set in. "What the hell?" she whispered, her voice tinged with fear.

Houston remained silent, watching her from the shadows. He could see the confusion and fear on her face as she tried the switch again. When it still didn't work, she stepped back, her eyes scanning the dark room.

Just as she turned to head back towards the bathroom, Houston flicked the switch, and the room was bathed in light once more. Candy froze, her eyes wide with shock as they landed on him. "Houston?" she whispered, her voice trembling. "Oh my God."

He leaned back against the headboard, his expression unreadable. "Nice to see you too, Candy," he said, his voice low and steady.

[Flashback ends]

The Coconut Grove Convention Center stood majestically against the night sky, illuminated by a cascade of spotlights. The entrance was adorned with large, elegant signs that read, "WELCOME SPORTS MARKETING EXECUTIVES," announcing the night's exclusive black-tie gala. A luxurious red carpet stretched from the curb to the entrance, flanked by velvet ropes and lined with eager paparazzi, their cameras flashing incessantly as a parade of limousines arrived. Well-dressed partygoers stepped out of their vehicles, each one a picture of sophistication and glamour, adding to the spectacle of the evening.

The atmosphere buzzed with excitement and anticipation, the air filled with the murmur of conversations and the occasional shout of a photographer vying for a perfect shot. The scent of expensive perfumes and colognes mingled with the cool, salty breeze blowing in from the nearby ocean, creating an intoxicating blend that epitomized the glamour of Miami's high society.

Inside one of the sleek black limousines making its way toward the entrance, Lorenzo and Candy were the epitome of elegance and allure. Lorenzo, dressed in a tailored black tuxedo, looked every bit the powerful, charismatic mogul, while Candy, in a stunning, figure-hugging evening gown, exuded an aura of sophistication and grace. The interior of the limousine was plush and luxurious, with soft leather seats, a minibar stocked with the finest liquors, and soft ambient lighting that cast a warm glow over everything.

Lorenzo, however, seemed far from relaxed. He pressed his face against the tinted glass window, trying to get a better look at the scene outside without opening the window. His brow was furrowed with irritation, his fingers tapping restlessly on his knee.

Candy, sensing his agitation, looked at him with a mix of concern and amusement. "Papi, we'll be there in a minute," she said softly, trying to soothe him.

Lorenzo continued to glare out the window, his voice dripping with disdain. "Are you seeing this shit? It's bush league, fucking bush league. I gotta get the fuck out of this town and get to one of the coasts."

Candy sighed inwardly, taking out a compact mirror from her tiny purse to touch up her makeup. "Well, technically Miami is a coast," she remarked lightly, hoping to distract him from his foul mood.

But Lorenzo's reaction was immediate and fierce. He wheeled around, his face contorted with anger and knocked the compact out of Candy's hand. It clattered to the floor of the limo, the mirror inside shattering upon impact.

"You fucking starting shit, go ahead start shit," Lorenzo snarled, his voice low and menacing. "This ain't the fucking night, Candy. I need you to fucking be there, is that so much?"

Candy felt a surge of fear but masked it with a calm demeanor. She knew how to navigate Lorenzo's volatile temper. "Relax, ok," she said soothingly, her voice steady despite the tension.

Lorenzo's eyes softened slightly as he looked at her, a hint of vulnerability beneath the anger. "You got a pretty good life, I give you everything you fucking want. This is for us, baby. I just need you to be there for us."

He leaned in, his demeanor shifting to something almost tender as he cupped her face in his hands and peppered her with little kisses but that has never been the case it was always more of authority and power, he had over her. Candy's heart pounded with fear and not the slightest affection swirling within her. "Of course, Papi," she whispered, her voice laced with what she herself does not recognize. "Whatever you want, baby."

The limousine slowed to a stop, and the door opened, revealing the red carpet and the waiting photographers. Lorenzo stepped out first, his demeanor instantly transforming as he waved to the crowd with a practiced, confident smile. The photographers' cameras flashed, capturing his every move.

He turned and extended a hand to Candy, who took it gracefully and stepped out of the limo, her gown shimmering under the lights. She looked around, her eyes catching sight of the modestly enthusiastic crowd, and almost laughed at the absurdity of it all. But she quickly composed herself, her face lighting up with a charming smile as she linked her arm with Lorenzo's.

Together, they posed for the photographers, their smiles masking the tension that lingered just beneath the surface. Candy felt the weight of Lorenzo's grip on her arm, a silent reminder of the power he held over her. But she played her part flawlessly, the perfect picture of a devoted partner and glamorous socialite.

As they made their way inside the convention center, the noise of the crowd and the flashing cameras faded, replaced by the elegant strains of a live orchestra playing in the grand foyer. The space was adorned with crystal chandeliers and opulent floral arrangements, the very embodiment of luxury and sophistication.

Lorenzo's mood seemed to lighten as they entered, his chest puffing out slightly with pride. "Now this," he said, looking around appreciatively, "is more like it."

Candy nodded, her eyes scanning the room for familiar faces. She spotted several high-profile guests, their names and faces instantly recognizable from countless media appearances. It was a world she had grown accustomed to, a world of power, wealth, and deception.

As they mingled with the other guests, Lorenzo slipped seamlessly into his role as a charismatic businessman, shaking hands and exchanging pleasantries with ease. Candy stayed by his side, her smile never faltering, her eyes always attentive. She knew her role well—to support Lorenzo, to be his perfect companion, and to never, ever show any signs of weakness or doubt.

But beneath her composed exterior, her mind raced with thoughts of the future. She couldn't help but wonder how long she could keep up this facade, how long she could balance the demands of her relationship with Lorenzo and the secrets she kept hidden. The weight of it all pressed down on her, a constant, unyielding burden.

For now, though, she pushed those thoughts aside and focused on the present. She laughed at the right moments, made polite conversation with the other guests, and kept a watchful eye on Lorenzo. She had to appear as the perfect partner to the guests so she can be able to carry out her upcoming plan without people raising brows.

Chapter Nine

In the backyard of Candy and Lorenzo's lavish home, the sun glistened off the surface of a large jacuzzi, where Candy lay relaxing, her eyes half-closed in contentment.

The jacuzzi, nestled in a secluded corner of the sprawling backyard, was a round-shaped marvel of luxury and design. Surrounded by meticulously manicured gardens and tall privacy hedges, it offered an intimate escape from the world.

Surrounding the jacuzzi, a deck made of rich, dark teak wood added to the opulent feel. Plush, oversized towels were neatly rolled and placed in a nearby basket, alongside a small table with a chilled bottle of champagne and two fluted glasses. The entire area was covered by a retractable pergola, which could be adjusted to provide shade during the day or retracted to reveal the starry night sky.

Ambient lighting cast a warm, inviting glow, with subtle spotlights highlighting the foliage and creating a serene, almost magical atmosphere. In the evenings, the lights in the jacuzzi itself could change colors, casting a mesmerizing, shimmering effect on the water's surface. The gentle hum of the jets and the occasional splash of water added to the tranquil soundscape, making the jacuzzi a perfect retreat for relaxation and rejuvenation.

The surrounding area was thoughtfully designed for both privacy and aesthetic pleasure. Delicate, fragrant flowers bordered the space, their scents mingling with the fresh, crisp air. Comfortable lounge chairs and a small, elegant table provided additional seating and space for refreshments, making this jacuzzi not just a place for solitary relaxation, but also an ideal spot for intimate gatherings or romantic evenings under the stars.

The meticulously landscaped garden surrounding the jacuzzi was a sight of Lorenzo's wealth and their high-end lifestyle.

Kelly emerged from the house, balancing a tall glass filled with a freshly made mojito. She approached the jacuzzi with a cautious smile. "Well, I can't promise it's good, but it is a mojito," she said, holding out the drink.

Candy took the glass and sipped, savoring the strong flavor. "Hmm, strong, but I like them that way," she said, a hint of a smile playing on her lips.

Kelly sat down on a space near the jacuzzi, her mind clearly occupied. After a moment of silence, she spoke up. "I was thinking about... you know," she said hesitantly, her voice trailing off. She stood and began to pace, her agitation evident.

Candy watched her with a bemused expression. "You're pretty repressed, aren't you?" she said suddenly.

Kelly stopped in her tracks, turning to face Candy. "What?!"

"I mean, you want to live your life, but you're really afraid," Candy continued, her tone casual.

Kelly's eyes widened in disbelief. "Oh, I won't help you kill your boyfriend, and that makes me repressed?"

"Yes, it does," Candy replied coolly.

Kelly shook her head, incredulously. "I may be less adventurous than you, but that doesn't make me repressed."

Candy leaned back in the jacuzzi, her gaze piercing. "Sure it does. You watch, it's safe. You distance yourself from what you really want, and that makes you feel better about wanting the things you do. It's typical Catholic girl behavior."

"You're nuts," Kelly snapped, her frustration bubbling to the surface.

Candy remained unfazed. "Am I? What do you want, Kelly?" Kelly faltered, her bravado wavering. "What do I want? I don't know, the usual stuff."

"No, you don't," Candy said, her voice steady. "You have needs you don't want to admit. You want things you don't talk about. You watch people doing the things you want to do and stay safe in the lie that that's not who you are. You may fool yourself, but you don't fool me, Kelly."

"So I should plan a future with someone I don't love who treats me like shit just so I can have a nice house and a fancy car?" Kelly retorted, her voice rising.

"You should do what you want to do," Candy replied calmly. "Lorenzo may not be my dream guy, but he does have his advantages. I just think you want a lot more than you care to admit."

Kelly's face flushed with a mix of anger and confusion. "So what if I do? I'm not like you. I won't stop at nothing to get what I want."

Candy leaned forward, her eyes gleaming with determination. "One million dollars."

Kelly blinked, taken aback. "What?"

"One million. Help me, and you walk away with one million dollars," Candy said, her voice firm and unwavering.

Kelly stared at her, incredulous. "You're kidding, right? Was that why you were being my friend? You want me to help you kill someone?"

"I never kid about money, and the only reason you're here is because I like you," Candy said, her tone softening slightly. "It's time to take a hard look inside, Kelly. You can be whoever you want with that kind of money. Finish school, help your mom out, it's enough to last you the rest of your life."

Kelly's mind raced, the weight of Candy's words pressing down on her. "No... no... I can't, I... it's just not right."

"Life isn't right," Candy said, slowly emerging from the luxurious jacuzzi, her movements languid and graceful. The warm water cascaded off her glistening skin, creating tiny rivulets that shimmered under the soft, ambient lighting. She stepped onto the rich teak wood deck, her bare feet making soft, wet imprints.

Reaching for a plush, oversized towel nearby, she wrapped it around her shoulders, savoring the warmth and softness of the fabric against her skin. With deliberate, gentle motions, she began patting herself dry, the towel absorbing the lingering droplets of water. The air was cool against her now-drying skin, and she could feel the subtle breeze stirring the leaves and flowers around the secluded space.

Her eyes sparkled with a serene contentment, a soft smile playing at the corners of her lips. As she dried herself, she walked with relaxed confidence towards Kelly, who was sitting nearby.

Candy's hair, still damp from the jacuzzi, fell in loose, glossy waves down her back. She reached up and ran her fingers through her hair, shaking it slightly to let it fall naturally. As she approached Kelly, her smile widened, and there was a playful glint in her eyes.

Stopping just in front of Kelly, Candy leaned down slightly, bringing her face closer. Her fingers found their way into Kelly's hair, the touch tender and affectionate. She ran her hand through the silky strands, her fingers gently massaging Kelly's scalp. The sensation was both comforting and intimate, a silent gesture of connection and warmth.

"I trust you, Kelly. I need someone I trust to help me. You won't have to actually do it. I'm actually kinda looking forward to handling that myself."

Kelly's hands trembled as she ran them through her hair. "You don't know what you're asking."

Candy moved closer, her hand then moved down, the fingertips brushing against Kelly's cheek before tracing the delicate curve of her jawline. With a gentle, almost teasing motion, Candy lifted Kelly's chin, guiding her gaze upwards. Their eyes met, and for a moment, the world seemed to hold its breath. "I know exactly what I'm asking. It's time to stop making excuses and start seeing how the other half lives. Or... you can be just another member of the crew. It's your choice. Let me know by tomorrow."

Candy's fingers lingered under Kelly's chin for a moment longer before she pulled away, her gaze lingering as she straightened up. She turned and headed towards the house, leaving Kelly standing there, her words hanging in the air like a heavy fog. Just before entering, Candy paused and looked back over her shoulder. "Who knows... you might even enjoy it," she said with a knowing smile.

Kelly watched her go, her mind a series of conflicting emotions and unspoken desires. Candy's proposition lingered in her thoughts, challenging her to confront the parts of herself she had long kept hidden.

***

The night was thick with an almost tangible tension as shadows stretched across the sparsely lit streets. Moody's Pub sat at the end of the block, a neighborhood dive bar that was more a home to lowlifes and career alcoholics than a haven for the casual drinker. The weathered sign outside flickered sporadically, casting a sickly yellow glow that barely cut through the gloom. The pub itself was an old, dark building, its exterior aged by years of neglect and smoke-stained memories. Graffiti marred the brickwork, and the faint scent of stale beer and cigarette smoke lingered in the air.

Candy pushed through the heavy wooden door, her entrance drawing a few uninterested glances. She was a stark contrast to the regulars, her confident stride and striking appearance seeming almost out of place in this dingy establishment. The crowd, unimpressed, soon lost interest and turned back to their drinks, muttering amongst themselves.

Stepping inside the environment, the atmosphere didn't improve. The bar was dark and woody, a relic from another era. Dim, yellowing lights hung low over the booths and tables, casting long shadows across the room. The wooden floors creaked with every step, and the air was thick with the stench of spilled beer, sweat, and despair. Moody's was place decent folks avoided, it was a sanctuary for the broken and the damned. The patrons were a mix of hardened regulars and those just passing through, each lost in their own world of cheap liquor and shattered dreams.

The bartender, a burly man with a perpetual scowl, eyed her suspiciously as she approached the bar.

"You sure you're in the right place, lady?" he asked, his voice gruff and laden with skepticism.

Candy's eyes met his with a steely resolve. "You serve tequila?" The bartender nodded, his suspicion unwavering. "Yeah?"

"Then I'm in the right place," Candy replied. "Straight up and it better not be shit."

As she waited for her drink, Candy looked around the bar. Her gaze swept over the dark corners and the huddled figures nursing their drinks. She spotted Houston sitting alone in a corner booth, his presence both familiar and uneasy. The bartender slid a shot glass in front of her, filled with the clear liquid. Candy picked it up, her movements deliberate and smooth. She grabbed a saltshaker, dusted her hand, and licked it slowly, her eyes never leaving the bartender's face. She downed the shot with a practiced ease, savoring the burn as it went down. Picking up a wedge of lime, she sucked on it, the tartness cutting through the harshness of the tequila.

She winked at the bartender, her demeanor a mix of challenge and charm. "That'll do. Let me have the bottle."

The bartender crossed his arms, unimpressed. "Bottles cost money, sweetcheeks, and you ain't paid me for the last one yet."

Candy reached into her purse, her fingers brushing against various odds and ends before finding what she was looking for. With a slow, deliberate motion, she pulled out a crisp hundred-dollar bill, its edges sharp and unblemished, a stark contrast to the grimy, worn-down bar. She slapped it on the counter with a satisfying thwack, the sound cutting through the murmur of conversation and clinking glasses. The bartender's eyes widened slightly, a flicker of surprise crossing his otherwise impassive face. He pocketed the money quickly, a practiced move honed from years of dubious transactions. Without another word, he handed over the bottle, the amber liquid inside glinting under the dim bar lights. Candy grabbed another shot glass, its surface etched with faint scratches from countless uses, and made her way over to Houston, her movements confident and purposeful.

"What a charming place," she said, sliding into the booth opposite him. "Houston, you really know how to treat a lady. Kinda brings back old times."

Houston looked up at her, his expression unreadable. "No less than a lady like you deserves," he replied, his tone dripping with sarcasm.

Candy smirked, pouring herself a shot and one for Houston. "Still pissed, huh? I guess I can't blame you. What have you been doing all this time?"

Houston's eyes darkened. "Surviving. That was about all I could do."

Candy leaned back, her interest piqued. "But where were you?"

Houston's thought shifted abruptly to when he was no longer in the dark, smoky bar but back in the harsh reality of his past. The metallic clang of a prison cell door slamming shut echoed in his ears, a sound that still haunted him. Fast cuts and flashes of memory assaulted him as the guards was beating him, the cold concrete floor where he had lain shivering in the darkness, the suffocating smell of sweat and despair. His life had been reduced to a series of violent encounters and moments of hopelessness, each one searing into his memory like a brand.

His gaze refocused on Candy, the bitterness evident in his eyes.

"Mostly South America. Nowhere I want to visit again. When I finally made it back to the States, imagine my surprise when you were nowhere to be found."

Candy's expression softened slightly, though her eyes remained guarded. "How's Jimmy?"

Houston's jaw tightened. "As if you give a shit."

Candy sighed, her frustration evident. "Look, you have every right to be pissed, but I thought you were dead. I did the best I could. I used to think about finding you one day, I just didn't picture it like this."

"I'll bet," Houston said, his voice cold. "I've spent four years looking for you, Candy. Now I want what's mine. We had some good times, great times. That's why you're not dead right now. But fond memories can't be spent."

"So now it's all your money?" Candy asked, her tone challenging.

"Goddamn right it's my money. Four million eight hundred thousand… let's just say an even five mil. Will that be cash or check?"

Candy leaned forward, her eyes narrowing. "I need your help first."

Houston stared at her, incredulously. "You gotta be fucking kidding me. Candy, you got real balls. Why would I help you?"

"Because it's that or nothing. You wanna try me, go ahead, Houston." Candy slid closer to him, her voice dropping to a dangerous whisper. "Let me make it up to you. It's a lot better than the alternative."

Houston's eyes flashed with anger. "What's the alternative?"

Candy's expression hardened. "You never see that money. I'm at the end of my rope and really don't care anymore. You think you know me, but you have no idea what I'm capable of now."

"Fuck you," Houston spat.

"No, fuck you," Candy shot back, standing abruptly. She looked down at him, her eyes blazing. "I owe you, Houston. I'm trying to do right by you. We can help each other and both make out, or you can throw all that away because you're pissed."

Candy paused, then leaned down, inches from Houston's face. "But if you do decide to come after me, you better pack a fucking lunch."

Houston met her gaze, his eyes searching hers. He saw determination, the desperation, and something else. It was a flicker of the woman he once knew. He poured himself a shot and downed it in one go, the burn was a welcome distraction from the turmoil inside him.

"What is it you have in mind?" he asked finally, his voice rough.

Candy sat back down, pouring them both another drink. "This could take a while to explain. The first thing we'll need is a friendly environment."

Houston frowned. "A what?"

"Somewhere we won't get caught," Candy clarified, her tone serious.

"Caught doing what?" Houston's suspicion was evident.

Candy took a deep breath, her mind racing with the possibilities and dangers of what she was about to propose. She knew it was a risk, but she also knew that without Houston's help, she was as good as dead.

"Listen," Candy began, her voice steady despite the whirlwind of emotions inside her. "I've got a plan. It's risky, but it's our best shot. I need you to trust me, at least for now."

Houston's eyes narrowed, his skepticism clear. "Trust you? After everything?"

Candy nodded, her gaze unwavering. "Yes. Because this isn't just about money anymore. It's about survival. Yours and mine."

Houston leaned back, considering her words. It felt like the pub around them faded into the background as he focused on Candy. Her determination was obvious, and despite his anger, he felt a flicker of something he hadn't felt in a long time – hope.

"Alright," he said finally. "Start talking."

Candy smiled slightly, a hint of her old self shining through as she started narrating the plan in detail.

As they exited the bar after the discussion, the night air hit them with a refreshing chill, a stark contrast to the stifling atmosphere inside Moody's.

The street was quiet, the occasional distant sound of a car engine or a dog barking the only interruptions to the silence. The pavement glistened under the faint glow of the streetlights, remnants of recent rain leaving the air damp and cool. Candy walked with purpose, her heels clicking rhythmically against the wet concrete, while Houston trailed slightly behind, his eyes scanning their surroundings with practiced caution.

The neighborhood was a mix of abandoned buildings and run-down establishments, each one a testament to better days long past. Candy led Houston to a nondescript car parked a block away, its dull paint and worn tires blending perfectly into the background of urban decay. She unlocked the doors with a small remote, the car beeping softly in acknowledgment.

"I will trust you this one last time because of my money," Houston said, his voice edged with a mix of reluctance and resolve. Candy, her expression unreadable, got into her sleek, black convertible, the leather seats cool against her skin. The engine purred to life as she started it, the sound blending with the distant hum of city traffic. Houston stood there for a moment, watching her, his eyes reflecting the streetlights. He took a deep breath, the weight of his decision heavy on his shoulders, then turned and walked away, his footsteps echoing on the pavement.

Chapter Ten

Candy reclined on a plush lounge chair, basking in the intense midday sun. Her dark sunglasses shielded her eyes, and a thin layer of tanning oil glistened on her skin, enhancing the sheen of her already bronzed complexion. The backyard of her and Lorenzo's home was a private oasis, surrounded by tall hedges and tropical plants that swayed gently in the light breeze. The air was thick with humidity, creating a sauna-like atmosphere that Candy reveled in.

Kelly emerged from the house, her expression one of uncertainty as she pulled a lounge chair next to Candy's. She sat down, her movements deliberate and hesitant, the contrast between her tense demeanor and Candy's relaxed posture stark.

"It's kinda hot out here," Kelly remarked, her voice cutting through the steady hum of cicadas and distant traffic.

"It's the humidity," Candy replied without turning her head or removing her sunglasses. "I like it though…makes me feel like I'm in a sauna."

"Most people don't like that feeling," Kelly muttered, glancing around the lush backyard. The sun was relentless, beating down on them and making the air shimmer with heat.

Candy remained motionless, her face a mask of serene indifference. "Was there something you wanted?" she asked, her tone calm but with an edge that hinted at impatience.

Kelly took a deep breath, the weight of her thoughts evident in her furrowed brow. "I don't want to kill anyone."

A slight smile played on Candy's lips, hidden behind her sunglasses. "Who does?" she said softly. "Although it can be a liberating feeling."

Kelly's discomfort grew palpable. She shifted in her seat, her eyes darting towards the house as if seeking an escape. "What is it you need me to do?"

Candy finally turned her head slightly, acknowledging Kelly's presence with a faint nod. "Let's talk about it over lunch."

Kelly nodded, feeling the tension in her shoulders ease slightly, and they both stood, Candy moving with the same languid grace she always exhibited. They walked towards the house, the sun casting long shadows behind them as they left the scorching backyard.

The Blue Door Restaurant exuded an air of sophistication and exclusivity, nestled in the heart of South Beach. Dimly lit with a soft blue glow that reflected off the polished surfaces, it was the kind of place where the elite came to see and be seen. The private booth where Candy and Kelly sat was secluded, offering a perfect vantage point over the bustling restaurant while ensuring their conversation remained confidential.

Candy sipped her cocktail, a vibrant concoction that matched the lively ambiance of the restaurant. She studied Kelly over the rim of her glass, her eyes sharp and calculating. Kelly shifted uncomfortably under Candy's gaze, her own drink barely touched.

"Whens the last time you got laid?" Candy asked abruptly, her tone casual but the question jarring.

"What?!" Kelly blurted out, nearly spilling her drink.

Candy leaned in slightly, her voice lowering to a conspiratorial whisper. "Look, we're talking a million dollars here. Let's not be shy, okay? When?"

Kelly glanced around, making sure no one was within earshot. "Oh, I don't know, maybe a month or two?" she answered, her voice uncertain.

Candy's skeptical expression made it clear she wasn't buying it. "Ok, six months," Kelly admitted with a sigh, her shoulders slumping in defeat.

"Why?" Candy asked, her eyes narrowing. "Men are like cockroaches. They're everywhere whether you see them or not."

Kelly shrugged, avoiding Candy's piercing gaze. "I guess I haven't been looking."

Candy's lips curved into a sly smile. "Yet you watch others? Kinda strange, huh?"

Kelly felt a flush creep up her neck. "What does this have to do with what we're talking about?"

Candy took a slow sip of her cocktail, savoring the moment. "I need your help making Lorenzo, well, let's say distracted."

"Distracted?" Kelly echoed, her confusion growing.

Candy leaned in closer, her voice dropping to a hushed tone. "Here's the plan. We take a little vacation, somewhere tropical for Lorenzo to relax after the end of the season. You join us."

"Me? Why?" Kelly asked, her eyebrows knitting together.

"Because you're going to convince him to suggest it," Candy explained, her tone matter of fact.

Kelly's eyes widened in disbelief. "How do I do that?"

Her smile widened. "Get his libido to kick in. You just have to get him horny."

Kelly's breath caught in her throat. "And then kill him?" she whispered, her voice trembling.

Before Candy could respond, the waiter approached their table with a busboy in tow, breaking the tension. "More drinkys?" he asked, his accent thick and his demeanor professional.

"Sure, another round," Candy said smoothly, flashing a charming smile. The waiter snapped at the busboy, who hurriedly cleared their empty glasses and replaced them with fresh ones.

As the waiter and busboy moved away, Candy leaned in again, her voice barely above a whisper. "We'll have help with that. Can we just try to keep from actually mentioning that?"

Kelly swallowed hard, her mind racing. "So you want me to sleep with him?"

Candy shook her head, her expression one of mild amusement. "No, well you can if you want to. It might do you good. But all I need you to do is create the illusion, leave the rest to me."

Kelly's confusion deepened. "How do I do that?"

Candy's eyes sparkled with mischief. "It starts with a change in attitude. Lorenzo will know if you're faking it. Don't ask me how, but the guy has major slut radar. You just have to activate it."

Kelly's mouth went dry. "Ok. How do I do that?" Candy's smile turned almost predatory. "Practice."

Candy reclined back in her seat, taking a leisurely sip of her drink, her eyes never leaving Kelly's. Kelly felt a shiver run down her spine, realizing the gravity of what she was being asked to do. The plan was risky, but the promise of a million dollars hung in the air like a tantalizing prize.

As the evening wore on, Candy detailed the steps Kelly would need to take. They discussed everything from body language to conversational cues, and even down to the types of clothing that would catch Lorenzo's eye. Candy was methodical, laying out the plan with the precision of a seasoned strategist.

"You have to make him believe that you're genuinely interested," Candy said, her tone firm. "He can't suspect for a second that this is a setup."

Kelly nodded, taking mental notes, her mind a whirlwind of thoughts and emotions. She felt a mixture of fear and excitement, knowing that she was about to step into a dangerous game. But the promise of the payout kept her focused, pushing her doubts to the back of her mind.

The waiter returned with their refreshed drinks, placing them gently on the table. Kelly glanced at the glass, the contents swirling around like her chaotic thoughts. Candy raised her glass, and after a brief hesitation, Kelly followed suit, their glasses clinking softly in the dim light.

"To new beginnings," Candy said with a knowing smile.

Kelly forced a smile, her heart pounding in her chest. "To new beginnings," she echoed, the words tasting bittersweet on her tongue.

As they sipped their drinks, the conversation shifted to lighter topics, but the underlying tension remained. Kelly knew that her life was about to change in ways she couldn't fully comprehend, and the weight of her decision settled heavily on her shoulders. But for now, she allowed herself to get lost in the moment, letting Candy's confidence bolster her own resolve.

The Blue Door Restaurant buzzed with activity around them, patrons engrossed in their own conversations, oblivious to the scheme being hatched in the secluded booth. Kelly glanced around, taking in the opulent surroundings, and for a moment, she let herself believe that everything would work out as planned.

***

The night sky was a canvas of deep indigo, dotted with stars that seemed to twinkle in rhythm with the pulsing neon lights of Club Rio. The club, an upscale strip joint, radiated an air of opulence and seduction. Its façade was adorned with glowing neon signs that cast a vibrant glow, illuminating the night and beckoning patrons from all corners of the city. The parking lot was filled with sleek, expensive cars, each reflecting the bright lights in their polished surfaces.

Candy's sleek, red convertible purred as it pulled up to the entrance. The valets, sharp in their uniforms, sprang into action, scrambling to open the doors. The car, a symbol of luxury and power, mirrored the aura of its occupants.

Candy stepped out first, exuding confidence and allure. Her dress, a shimmering silver number that clung to her curves, caught the light with every move she made. She wore her hair in loose, cascading waves that framed her face, accentuating her striking features. Her makeup was impeccable, with bold red lips that hinted at danger and eyes lined with precision, making her gaze both captivating and intimidating.

Kelly followed, her movements more hesitant. She was dressed to thrill, her outfit a deep emerald green that contrasted beautifully with her auburn hair, which she had styled in soft curls for the evening. Her dress, though equally stunning, was more conservative than Candy's, hinting at her underlying nerves. She looked around, taking in the scene, her eyes wide with a mix of apprehension and excitement.

Candy shot her a sidelong glance, her lips curving into a mischievous smile. "Class is in session," she announced, her voice dripping with confidence and a hint of mischief.

Kelly swallowed hard, her nerves getting the better of her. "I don't know..." she started, her voice trailing off.

Candy, sensing her girl's hesitation, tipped the valet generously. The young man pocketed the bill with a grateful nod, but his attention was immediately drawn back to the two women as

Candy grabbed Kelly by the arm. Her grip was firm but not

unkind, and with a gentle tug, she pulled Kelly out of the car and towards the club's entrance.

"Alright, now let's just cut the whole repressed thing, alright?" Candy said, her tone a mix of encouragement and impatience. "It's time to party!"

The doors of Club Rio swung open, releasing a wave of music and energy into the night. The bass thumped rhythmically, reverberating through the ground and up into their bodies. Candy led the way with a confident stride, her heels clicking against the pavement with each step. Kelly followed, her steps more tentative, her mind racing with thoughts of what the night might hold.

As they approached the entrance, the doorman, a hulking figure dressed in a sharp suit, gave them a once-over. His stern expression softened into a smirk as he recognized Candy. "Evening, ladies," he greeted, stepping aside to let them pass.

Candy winked at him, her smile dazzling. "Evening, Sam," she replied smoothly. Kelly managed to make a nervous smile, her heart pounding in her chest.

Inside, the club was a sensory overload. The interior was bathed in dim, seductive lighting, with neon accents casting vibrant hues across the room. The air was thick with the scent of expensive perfume and the faint hint of cigar smoke. The music, a blend of sultry rhythms and pulsing beats, created an atmosphere that was both electrifying and intoxicating.

The main floor was dominated by a large stage, where dancers moved with grace and sensuality, their bodies shimmering under the stage lights. Around the stage, patrons lounged in plush seating, their eyes glued to the performances. Waitresses in skimpy outfits weaved through the crowd, balancing trays of drinks with practiced ease.

Candy navigated the room with the confidence of someone who belonged, her eyes scanning the crowd for familiar faces. Kelly stayed close, her initial nervousness slowly giving way to a sense of curiosity and excitement. She could feel the eyes of the patrons on them, sensing the energy they brought into the room.

Candy led them to a table near the stage, where the music was loudest and the atmosphere most charged. She slid into a seat with the grace of a practiced performer, motioning for Kelly to do the same. A waitress appeared almost instantly, a bright smile plastered on her face.

"Two tequila shots, top shelf," Candy ordered without missing a beat.

The waitress nodded and disappeared into the crowd. Kelly looked at Candy, her eyes wide with a mix of admiration and anxiety. "Are you sure about this?" she asked, her voice barely audible over the music.

Candy leaned in, her expression serious for the first time that night. "Kelly, you need to relax. Trust me, tonight is about letting go and having fun. Just follow my lead, and you'll be fine."

She nodded, taking a deep breath to steady herself. The waitress returned with their drinks, setting the shots down with a flourish. Candy picked up her glass, raising it in a toast. "To new experiences," she said, her eyes locking onto Kelly's.

Kelly picked up her glass, the cool weight of the glass grounding her. "To new experiences," she echoed, clinking her glass against Candy's.

They downed their shots in unison, the burn of the tequila spreading warmth through their bodies. Candy set her glass down with a satisfied sigh, her smile returning. "See? Not so bad, right?"

Kelly nodded, the alcohol helping to calm her nerves. "Not so bad," she agreed, a tentative smile forming on her lips.

After a while of swinging to the beats, Candy led them with confidence through the bustling club to a VIP section. A bouncer, tall and imposing, nodded to Candy and lifted the velvet rope, allowing them entry into the exclusive area.

The VIP section was a stark contrast to the main club. It was dark, with overstuffed sofas and easy chairs scattered around. Silhouettes of men and women moved in silent harmony, their bodies swaying to their own private rhythms. The atmosphere was thick with an almost visible sense of desire.

Candy gracefully sank into one of the luxurious sofas, catching the eye of a passing waitress. She plucked two champagne glasses off the tray and handed one to Kelly. "Watch... and learn," she said with a knowing smile.

Kelly was entranced by the scene around her. The room was warm, the air thick with the scent of perfume and sweat. "It's... kinda dark... and uh... warm in here," she murmured, her voice barely audible over the soft murmur of the room.

Candy leaned back in her chair, her eyes never leaving Kelly. The grinding lap dancers and their captivated partners were a sight to behold. Kelly fidgeted in her seat, feeling a mixture of discomfort and fascination. Sensing her unease, Candy leaned over, her fingers gently stroking Kelly's hair, her breath warm against Kelly's neck. "It just takes letting go," she whispered, her voice a soft purr.

Kelly began to run her hand over her own arm, the sensation sending shivers down her spine. She moved her hand across her chest, softly caressing herself, her body responding to Candy's encouragement. Candy noticed and smiled, a hint of triumph in her eyes. "That's it, feel yourself taking part," she urged.

One of the dancers, a striking woman with flowing hair and

an air of confident seduction, noticed Kelly watching. She moved gracefully towards Kelly, her movements smooth and feline. She crossed in front of Kelly and then behind her, letting her hands trail down from Kelly's shoulders to her thighs. "Why just watch? We can party if you want," the dancer whispered, her voice silky and inviting. "I'll even give you ladies two for one."

Kelly felt a jolt of nervous excitement. She was drawn to the dancer's touch, the feel of her hands on her body was intoxicating. The dancer leaned in closer, her lips brushing against Kelly's ear. "Maybe we should go somewhere more private?" she suggested, her voice a seductive whisper. She kissed Kelly softly, her lips lingering for a moment. Kelly, her mind swirling with the alcohol and the heady atmosphere, nodded.

The dancer pointed to an almost invisible door on a nearby wall. She stood up, taking Kelly's hand, and led her away. Candy watched them go, a satisfied smile playing on her lips.

The dancer opened the door and motioned for Kelly to step inside. "Be with you in just a minute," she said, her voice promising secrets and delights.

The room was almost pitch black, illuminated only by the flickering glow of a single candle. Kelly looked around, her eyes trying to adjust to the darkness. The room was small, intimate, with a large chair positioned in front of a wall-sized mirror. She could see her own reflection, her wide eyes and nervous expression staring back at her.

"I have to be nuts," Kelly muttered to herself, turning to leave. But a voice stopped her.

"Be patient," came the soft, familiar tones of Candy.

Kelly turned back, her heart pounding. She looked around for Candy, but all she saw was her own reflection and the dim outlines of the room. Suddenly, the mirror lit up, revealing the next room. It was larger, with a plush sofa facing another empty one. A man sat alone on the sofa, his back turned to the mirror.

Kelly paused, curiosity piqued. "What's going on?" she whispered, her voice barely above a breath.

Candy emerged from the shadows behind her, a drink in her hand. She stirred it with her finger, then slid the glass up Kelly's arm, the cool condensation leaving a trail on her skin. She placed the glass to Kelly's lips. "No, I don't want..." Kelly started, resisting.

"It's time to find out what it is you want," Candy insisted, tilting the drink into Kelly's mouth. Kelly hesitated, then swallowed, the liquid burning a path down her throat.

"Enjoy the ride," Candy whispered, her voice a seductive promise.

Kelly's eyes began to glaze over as she slid into the chair, her gaze fixed on the larger room revealed by the mirror. Inside, the dancer entered, moving with a sensual grace. She began to strip seductively for the man, her body a fluid motion of desire and temptation. Kelly watched her body responding to the scene. She began to moan slightly, the effects of the drink amplifying her senses.

As the dancer dropped to her knees, her head moving into the man's lap, Kelly felt a rush of heat. When the dancer raised her head again, it was now Kelly who saw herself dancing for the man. Her movements were uninhibited, filled with sensual abandon. She danced, losing herself in the moment, the lines between reality and fantasy blurring as she embraced her own desires.

Kelly's head rolled back, her eyes reflecting the maelstrom of confusion and desire raging within her. She was caught in a pool of sensations, her body responding to stimuli that her mind struggled to process. The room around her seemed to fade, the dim light of the candle flickering as if to the rhythm of her racing heart. She felt a warmth spreading through her, an intoxicating blend of fear and arousal.

In the adjoining room, the dancer now straddled the man, her movements a mesmerizing display of raw sexuality. Her body arched and swayed with a rhythm that was both primal and seductive. As she threw herself backward, the man's hands roamed her body, caressing and teasing. Each touch sent shivers of pleasure through her, her moans growing louder, more desperate.

With each undulation of her hips, the dancer seemed to draw closer to a crescendo, her movements becoming more frenetic. As she returned upright, it was no longer the dancer on the man's lap. In the flickering light of the mirror, it was Kelly who now straddled the faceless stranger, her body moving with an instinctive grace.

Kelly's senses were overwhelmed by the man's touch. His hands roamed her body with a practiced ease, fingers trailing fire across her skin. He gripped her hips, guiding her movements, each thrust sending waves of pleasure crashing through her. Kelly's moans grew louder, more insistent, a validation to the mounting ecstasy she felt.

She swung her body with wild abandon, riding the man with a fervor that surprised even her. His kisses were hungry, his lips and tongue exploring her neck, her collarbone, the swell of her breasts. When he buried his face in her chest, Kelly felt a surge of power and vulnerability all at once, the duality adding to the intensity of the moment.

The pace quickened, the sounds of their union filling the room. The friction of their bodies created a symphony of gasps and moans, each one a note in the crescendo of their shared desire.

Kelly's breath came in ragged pants, her body slick with sweat, her muscles tensing and releasing in a rhythm as old as time.

The man's hands clutched at her more urgently, his grip tightening as he too neared his climax. Kelly felt the heat coiling deep within her, a molten core of pleasure ready to erupt. She rode him harder, faster, driven by a need that had consumed her.

Their movements became a blur, a fevered dance of flesh and passion. Kelly's cries grew louder, her body convulsing as the orgasm tore through her. The man's own release followed, his grip on her hips almost bruising as he buried his face deeper into her chest, his own groans mingling with her cries of ecstasy.

For a moment, time stood still. The air around them seemed to hum with the aftershocks of their climax, the heat of their exertion hanging like a tangible presence in the room. Kelly's body slowly relaxed, her head rolling back again as she caught her breath, her skin tingling with the remnants of pleasure.

In the flickering light of the candle, Kelly saw her reflection in the mirror, her face flushed, her eyes glazed. The confusion and desire that had warred within her now settled into a strange, satiated calm. She had crossed a threshold, one that she couldn't uncross.

***

Kelly snapped her eyes open with a start, her heart pounding against her ribcage. The room was dim, illuminated only by the flickering glow of the candle. Her surroundings seemed to waver, the edges of her vision blurred as if she were peering through a fogged glass. She took a deep breath, the lingering scents of sweat, perfume, and something indefinably primal filling her nostrils.

Her gaze fell upon the dancer in the adjoining room. Kelly struggled to focus, her mind grappling with the fragments of her recent experience. Each time she blinked, the scene before her shifted, as if the room itself were alive and breathing.

A figure leaned over her, and Kelly's vision sharpened just enough to recognize Candy's familiar form. Candy's eyes were filled with concern, her brows knit together as she scrutinized Kelly's face. The worry etched on Candy's features was a stark contrast to her usual confident demeanor.

"Kelly, are you okay?" Candy's voice seemed to echo in Kelly's ears, the words elongated and distorted.

Kelly tried to respond, but her mouth felt dry, her tongue was heavy. She managed a weak nod, her mind still clouded with the remnants of her earlier trance. The edges of her vision darkened, and she felt a peculiar detachment, as if she were floating above her own body, observing the scene from a distance.

Another figure came into view, leaning over her from the opposite side. The man from the other room—Houston—looked down at her, his face a mask of unreadable emotion. Kelly's heart skipped a beat, her mind racing to process his sudden appearance. His presence was disconcerting, a jarring reminder of the intensity of the scene she had just witnessed.

Kelly's eyes fluttered, struggling to focus on their faces. The room seemed to spin around her, and she felt a wave of dizziness wash over her. She tried to latch onto their words, to pull herself back to reality, but it was like grasping at smoke.

The dimly lit room began to blur further, the figures of Candy and Houston melding into shadows. Kelly's consciousness wavered, the sounds around her fading into a distant hum. She closed her eyes, surrendering to the enveloping darkness, her last thought a jumbled mix of confusion and curiosity about what had just transpired.

As her senses dulled and the world slipped away, she felt a strange sense of peace. She drifted into unconsciousness, the candle's flicker the last light she saw before the darkness claimed her.

Kelly woke slowly, her head throbbing and her vision blurry. The soft light filtering through the windows seemed painfully bright, and she squinted against it, trying to piece together her fragmented memories. As her surroundings gradually came into focus, she realized she was in the pool house at Lorenso's mansion, the familiar scent of chlorine mingling with the morning air.

She sat up, the silk sheets sliding off her body, and looked around in a panic. The room spun slightly, her disorientation making it hard to grasp reality. Her heart pounded in her chest as she tried to remember how she got here. The events of the previous night were a hazy blur, images and sensations jumbled together in her mind.

Taking a deep breath, Kelly steadied herself and swung her legs over the side of the bed. She stood up, wincing as a wave of dizziness washed over her. Steadying herself on the edge of the nightstand, she took a moment to gather her thoughts. The pool house, with its plush furnishings and serene ambiance, felt like a stark contrast to her inner turmoil.

Kelly walked into the kitchen, her steps unsteady but determined. The smell of freshly brewed coffee and buttered toast filled the air, a sharp contrast to the tension she felt. Candy stood by the counter, casually eating a piece of toast. She looked up as Kelly entered, a playful smile on her lips.

"Hey, Sleepyhead," Candy said, her tone light and teasing.

Without warning, Kelly stormed over, anger blazing in her eyes. Before Candy could react, Kelly swung her fist, connecting with

Candy's jaw with a solid thud. Candy stumbled back, dropping her toast and sprawling across the kitchen floor.

"What the hell did you do to me?!" Kelly screamed, her voice shaking with fury and fear.

Candy wiped her mouth, checking for blood. Her playful demeanor vanished, replaced by a serious, calculating look. She pushed herself up on one elbow, her eyes narrowing as she regarded Kelly.

"Nothing you didn't need," Candy replied, her voice cold and measured.

"Bullshit!" Kelly spat, her hands clenched into fists at her sides.

Candy slowly got to her feet, brushing herself off. She walked to the freezer, her movements deliberate and pulled out a bag of frozen peas. Pressing it to her chin, she winced slightly.

"Nothing happened," Candy said, her tone firm. "You took a little trip, that's all. No need to get physical."

Kelly glared at her, her chest heaving with suppressed rage. The room seemed to close in around her, the walls pressing in as she tried to make sense of Candy's words.

"I think you loosened a tooth," Candy muttered, inspecting the frozen peas.

"You're lucky that's all I did," Kelly shot back, her voice trembling.

Candy's eyes flashed with anger. "No, you're lucky I don't full-on bitch-slap your whining ass. It was just some fun… that's all. You seemed to like it."

"That's not the point," Kelly said, her voice cracking. "I can't remember what happened. I don't know what was real and what I dreamed."

Candy's expression softened slightly, a hint of sympathy creeping into her eyes. "Is there a difference?"

"The difference is I didn't get to choose," Kelly said, her voice barely above a whisper.

Candy sighed, lowering the bag of peas. "I just opened a door. What was behind it is on you. Besides, trust me… You needed it."

Kelly turned to leave, pausing at the doorway. She looked back over her shoulder, her eyes still blazing with anger and confusion.

"Next time, ask first."

Candy watched her go, taking a sip of her coffee. She cringed, the heat causing her to press the frozen peas back to her chin. The room fell silent, the tension lingering in the air long after Kelly had gone.

Chapter Eleven

The sun suspended high in the cloudless sky, emitting a brilliant glow over the tropical paradise that was the island of Cayman. Palm trees swayed gently in the breeze, their leaves rustling softly. The turquoise waters lapped at the pristine white sandy beaches, and the distant sound of waves provided a soothing soundtrack to the idyllic scenery. The vibrant colors of blooming hibiscus and bougainvillea added splashes of red and pink to the lush greenery. This island was a haven of tranquility and beauty.

A man in a long black silk robe and flip flops strolled down a dimly lit hallway, whistling a cheerful tune. His steps were light and carefree, an air of nonchalance surrounding him. The robe swished around his legs as he walked, the flip flops making soft slapping sounds against the polished wooden floor. He paused in front of a heavy wooden door, the only one in the otherwise barren hallway. With a casual flick of his wrist, he turned the brass doorknob and began his descent down a narrow staircase.

The stairs creaked under his weight, the only sound breaking the eerie silence.

As he reached the bottom, he pulled a chain hanging from the ceiling. A single bare bulb flickered to life, throwing a weak, yellowish glow over the small, cluttered room. The dim light revealed a space filled with discarded furniture, old boxes, and dusty cobwebs. The air was musty, carrying the faint scent of decay. The man moved with purpose, pulling out a ring of keys from his robe pocket. He approached a heavy metal door, the sound of metal scraping against metal echoing through the room as he unlocked it.

The door swung open with a creak, and a low, muffled grunt emanated from the darkness beyond. The man stepped into the room, his figure silhouetted against the dim light. He pulled a switch, and a harsh, bright light flooded the room, revealing a disturbing scene.

In the center of the room, a middle-aged, plump man lay tied to a metal bed. His skin was marred with hundreds of small, scabbed circles, as if he had been repeatedly stabbed with a sharp object. His mouth was taped shut, his eyes wide with terror behind a pair of swimming goggles. The light reflected off the lenses, giving his frightened eyes an almost surreal, exaggerated look.

The man in the robe whistled a merry tune as he walked to a nearby trashcan. He lifted the lid and pulled out a handful of bird seeds, the small grains trickling through his fingers. Still whistling, he approached the bound man, who let out muffled yells and thrashed against his restraints. The bound man's eyes followed the birdseed, widening in terror as the man in the robe scattered it over his prone body.

With a casual flick of his wrist, the man opened a small door in the wall. Six enormous brown roosters strutted out, their beady eyes glinting in the light. They pecked furiously at the ground, their sharp beaks clicking against the concrete floor. The bound man tried to shake them off, his body thrashing wildly as the roosters approached.

Suddenly, a playful tune rang out, and the man in the robe pulled out his cell phone. He stepped away from the bed, the light catching his face for the first time. It was Jimmy, his expression one of mild annoyance as he answered the call.

"Talk to me," Jimmy said, his tone casual.

There was a pause as he listened, his brow furrowing slightly. "Houston! How the hell are you, man?" he exclaimed, his voice laced with surprise.

Another pause followed, during which Jimmy's expression shifted from surprise to irritation. "No, no, it's cool. I'm just feeding my roosters," he said, rolling his eyes.

The conversation continued, Jimmy's annoyance growing with each passing second. "Oh, sure, I can set that up, but why?" he asked, his tone impatient.

His eyes widened in shock. "WHAT! You gotta be fucking kidding me!" he shouted, his free hand clenching into a fist.

There was another pause, longer this time, as Jimmy processed what he was being told. "Right, right. I'll do it, but you better have one hell of a story when I see your ass," he said, his tone resigned.

Jimmy hung up, shaking his head in disbelief. He turned to the man tied to the bed, who was frantically trying to keep an eye on the roosters now pecking the birdseed scattered across his body. The man's muffled screams of terror filled the room, his eyes darting back and forth as he tried to fend off the birds.

"Alright, Mr. Todd, seems I have chores, so our talk about your outstanding balance will have to wait. I need to make a quick phone call," Jimmy said, his tone almost apologetic.

With a swift motion, Jimmy picked up one of the roosters and tossed it onto the bound man's chest. The bird flapped its wings wildly, trying to find its footing as the man let out a muffled scream. Jimmy didn't wait to see what happened next. He turned on his heel and exited the room, closing the door behind him.

As the door clicked shut, the man's muffled screams were abruptly cut off, replaced by the unsettling silence of the basement room. The only sounds that remained were the frantic pecking of the roosters and the faint, fading echoes of terror.

***

Back at the manicured lawn of Candy and Lorenzo's lavish home. The driveway gleamed, its cobblestones meticulously cleaned and polished. Lorenzo's luxury SUV glided smoothly up the drive and into the garage, the engine purring softly before falling silent. Lorenzo's figure of muscle towered with frustration as he stepped out of the vehicle. His shoulders slumped, and a frown marred his handsome features.

Inside the spacious kitchen, Candy sat perched on a sleek, modern stool, idly picking at a vibrant salad. The kitchen, with its marble countertops and state-of-the-art appliances, gleamed under the soft afternoon light filtering through the large windows. Lorenzo entered, his presence filling the room with an air of barely contained anger.

"Hey baby, how was the meeting?" Candy's voice was soft and soothing, a practiced blend of concern and affection.

Lorenzo slammed his briefcase onto the counter, running a hand through his hair in exasperation. "Fucking sucked. They aren't going to trade me."

Candy's expression shifted to one of sympathy. "Oh Papi, I'm sorry."

Lorenzo's hands clenched into fists, his knuckles white. "Fucking bastards, after all I did for that team."

Candy set her salad aside and slid off the stool, moving gracefully towards him. "Can I fix you something to eat?"

Lorenzo shook his head, his eyes dark with frustration. "Nah, I ain't hungry."

With practiced ease, Candy nuzzled against him, her lips brushing his neck seductively. "Nothing I can do for you, baby?"

Lorenzo pushed her away, a scowl deepening the lines on his face. "Jesus, Candy, give it a rest, huh?"

Undeterred, Candy picked up a forkful of salad and tried to spoon it into Lorenzo's mouth. His reaction was swift and violent as he slapped her hard across the cheek, sending her sprawling across the kitchen floor. Candy held her cheek with both hands, tears welling in her eyes as she looked up at him.

"What the hell did you do that for?" she asked, her voice trembling.

Lorenzo loomed over her, his anger palpable. "Didn't I say I wasn't hungry? You have nothing that can satisfy me at the moment. Try something like that again, and you won't get off with just a slap."

Candy scrambled to her feet, trying to move away, but her short skirt caught on a hook by the wall, tearing part of it away and exposing her panty less bottom. The fresh sight of her bare skin momentarily distracted Lorenzo, making him pause.

"On second thought, Candy," Lorenzo said, his tone shifting. "I guess there is something you can help me with."

He moved closer, spanking her exposed ass hard enough that she let out a cry of pain. Grabbing her roughly, he dragged her towards him, pressing her against his hardened member. He spanked her again, even harder this time, eliciting another cry, this one louder, more pained.

Lorenzo ignored her cries, turning her around and bending her over the countertop. With a rough motion, he ripped the skirt from where it was caught, tearing it further. Wetting his hand with his tongue, he thrust it between her legs, fingering her carelessly. Candy cried out again, the pain evident in her voice, her soul was probably not ready for this at the moment. She had always been the prepared type, anywhere and anytime but not this time or probably they hadn't gotten to that point.

Without any gentleness, Lorenzo pulled his hand away and yanked down his pants. He thrust himself into her, and despite the roughness, Candy couldn't deny the pleasure she felt. His movements were fierce and relentless, driving her to the brink of madness. She was beginning to enjoy it. His thrusts had always had its way of driving her crazy she always loved it.

Candy managed to speak between her moans, "Lorenzo, let's continue in the bedroom—"

But he only pounded harder and harder, each thrust hitting the deepest parts of her. The sound of their bodies colliding filled the kitchen, loud and raw. He lifted her, placing her on top of the counter and continuing his assault.

The intensity lasted only a few minutes, but it felt like an eternity. As Lorenzo was about to climax, he pulled out and made Candy kneel before him. With a final thrust, he released himself onto her face, leaving her gasping and dazed on the kitchen floor.

Candy wiped her face, trying to regain her composure as Lorenzo pulled up his pants. She looked up at him, her eyes filled with a mix of anger, pain, and lingering desire.

Lorenzo simply smirked, turning away from her. "After this week, the season is over and I have to play another year on this fucking team."

Candy's anger faltered for a moment, as she quickly regained her composure. "I have an idea."

Lorenzo's eyes narrowed suspiciously. "Yeah, what?"

"Well," Candy began, her tone carefully measured, "it's been so rough on you this year. I haven't done anything to help."

Lorenzo's laugh was bitter. "You're a goddamn pain in my ass most of the time."

Candy's smile remained fixed, though it no longer reached her eyes. "That's what I was saying. Well, I thought it would do us some good to get away. You know, just the two of us."

Lorenzo snorted. "A vacation? Spending more money, that's your big plan? Forget it, I got shit I gotta do."

Candy stepped closer, her voice dropping to a soothing whisper. "Baby, you need to get some rest too. There's nothing that can't wait. Besides, do you really want to explain the team's season and your efforts to get traded to reporters for a month? By the time we get back, it will be long forgotten."

Lorenzo hesitated, the tension in his shoulders easing slightly. "That's true. Where you wanna go? Vegas, LA, how about New York?"

Candy's eyes sparkled with anticipation. "I was thinking of something a little more tropical, a little more… private." She produced a glossy brochure from behind her back and laid it on the counter in front of him. The brochure featured stunning images of the Cayman Islands — pristine beaches, luxurious resorts, and crystal-clear waters.

"The Cayman Islands," Lorenzo read aloud, intrigued despite himself. "Never heard of it."

Candy leaned in closer, her voice a seductive whisper. "It's very hot right now, the new place to be."

Lorenzo picked up the brochure, flipping through the pages. "Really?"

Candy nodded, her smile growing more confident. "Imagine it, Papi. Just you and me on a beautiful beach, no one to bother us, no stress, no reporters. Just us."

Lorenzo's eyes lingered on the pictures of the idyllic beaches and luxurious accommodations. "It does look nice," he admitted, his voice softening.

Candy placed her hand on his arm, giving it a gentle squeeze. "You deserve a break, Lorenzo. We both do. Let's just get away from everything for a little while."

Lorenzo sighed, the weight of his anger and frustration beginning to lift.

Candy's face lit up with genuine joy as she saw he was on the bridge of falling for the scheme. "Papi, you sure won't regret it!"

Lorenzo allowed a small smile to tug at the corners of his mouth but still not uttering anything.

Candy tugged at his shirt and he finally said something. "What if I think of accepting this your proposal? I have no time for shits like this," Smiling widely, her earlier tears forgotten in the excitement of their upcoming trip. "I'll make all the arrangements. You just relax and get ready to enjoy yourself."

As Lorenzo watched Candy bustling around, his thoughts began to drift to the sandy beaches and clear waters of the Cayman Islands. For the first time in a long while, he felt a glimmer of hope and anticipation.

"I do not think this is actually going to work out so do not get ahead of yourself."

Candy nodded eagerly. "Just think about it."

As she turned to leave the kitchen, she cast a sly glance over her shoulder, her heart skipping a beat when she saw Lorenzo still engrossed in the brochure. A triumphant smile played at her lips as she slipped out of the room with her half-ripped skirt, the promise of a successful plan warming her from within.

***

The living room, furnished with high-end modern decor, was dimly lit by the afternoon sun streaming through the large bay windows. A plush, stylish sofa sat in the center, facing a massive flat-screen TV mounted on the wall. The TV blared with its audio, capturing the attention of everyone present. Lorenzo, dressed in casual athletic wear, sat on the couch, his face etched with frustration and concern. Candy, elegantly dressed in a form-fitting dress, perched beside him, her expression a mix of anger and determination. Kelly, looking uncomfortable, lingered near the edge of the room, her eyes darting between the TV and the tense couple.

The news anchor's voice cut through the room, delivering a shocking update. "In a developing story, a woman has accused a star football player of assault. While she has chosen to keep his name undisclosed, she has come forward requesting a settlement from the player's side, stating that this is all she needs and that she is not here to ruin his career. The alleged assailant is said to be a key player on the session leading team."

Candy's eyes narrowed as she glanced at Kelly, signaling her to leave. Kelly, sensing the rising tension, quietly slipped out of the room, her footsteps barely audible on the thick carpet.

Candy turned her gaze to Lorenzo, her eyes blazing with anger. "That is your doing, right?"

Lorenzo didn't reply, his jaw clenched tightly. His eyes stayed fixed on the screen, but his mind was clearly elsewhere.

"You have me in the house, and you're still out there, spoiling your name, huh?" Candy's voice was sharp, cutting through the room like a knife.

"Just shut up," Lorenzo snapped, his frustration boiling over. He rubbed his temples, trying to fend off an impending headache.

"I will not!" Candy's voice rose, matching his intensity. She stood up from the couch, her body language radiating anger and disbelief. "You think this is acceptable behavior?"

"It was a mistake," Lorenzo muttered, his voice lacking conviction. He ran a hand through his hair, visibly agitated. "I'm positive it was all planned. I know that girl wasn't my type, but I woke up in bed with her, and I thought it was a drunk, consensual thing."

"You call drugging someone consensual?" Candy retorted, her voice dripping with sarcasm and disgust. She crossed her arms over her chest, glaring at him.

"I was the one drugged, Candy," Lorenzo insisted, his tone defensive. He looked at her, his eyes pleading for her to believe.

"This will affect your career," Candy warned, her eyes never leaving his. She took a step closer, her tone softer but still firm. "You know how these things can escalate."

"Not if I give her the money she wants," Lorenzo replied, his voice hardening with resolve. He leaned back on the couch, trying to appear nonchalant, but the tension in his body betrayed him.

"You think money is everything?" Candy shot back, her tone incredulous. She shook her head, clearly exasperated. "You can't just buy your way out of everything, Lorenzo."

"It is," Lorenzo responded flatly, his eyes meeting hers with a challenging look. "Money can solve this."

Candy shook her head, her expression a mix of disappointment and anger. "Ignorant man. This is more reason for taking a vacation. Settle the lady, and we'll be out of town. No other stress about the topic to witness."

Lorenzo hesitated, the weight of her words sinking in. He sighed, rubbing his face with his hands. "Hm."

Candy stood up, smoothing her skirt and looking down at him. "Once again, think about it, Lorenzo. This is your chance to fix things before they get worse." She leaned over, placing the glossy brochure on the coffee table in front of him.

Lorenzo's eyes scanned the images, the tension in his shoulders easing slightly.

Candy nodded, her eyes sparkling with anticipation. "Just think about it. We can get away from all this stress. No reporters, no scandals. Just us, in paradise."

Lorenzo looked up at her, his expression thoughtful. "You really think this will help?"

Candy smiled, her confidence returning. "I know it will. Settle things with that girl, and we can be on our way. No other stress, no other distractions."

Lorenzo sighed, his resolve weakening. "Alright, I'll think about it."

Candy straightened up, her smile widening. "Good. We need this, Lorenzo. You need this."

She left him there, alone with his thoughts, the TV still blaring in the background. As she walked away, a satisfied smile tugged at the corners of her lips. She had planned this whole incident when he was planning on backing away from the vacation, knowing that it would push Lorenzo toward the vacation she had been eager to take. Now, it was definitely going to work out.

***

Lorenzo turned onto his street, the familiar row of houses standing like silent sentinels in the warm evening light. The sky was very warm on this particular day, just how he liked it. He could see the roofs of his neighbors' houses, the perfectly trimmed lawns, and the occasional child playing in the yard. It was a peaceful scene, one that contrasted sharply with the turmoil of his thoughts.

As he approached his house, Lorenzo slowed the car, the tires crunching softly on the gravel driveway. His mansion stood at the end of the cul-de-sac, its white facade catching the last rays of the setting sun. The neatly maintained lawn was bordered by a low, white picket fence, and a row of colorful flowers lined the walkway leading to the front door.

He pulled the car into the driveway, the engine purring quietly before he turned it off. The sudden silence was almost deafening, filled only with the distant chirping of crickets and the rustle of leaves in the gentle evening breeze. Lorenzo sat there for a moment, his hands resting on the steering wheel, his mind filled with a series of thoughts and emotions.

His gaze drifted to the house, the place that had been his refuge and his battleground. The windows were dark, the interior lights not yet turned on. It gave the house an empty, almost eerie feeling, as if it was holding its breath, waiting for his next move.

Leaning back in his seat, he took a deep breath. The familiar scent of leather and the faint aroma of air freshener filled his nostrils, a small reminder of the everyday routines that had been disrupted by his turbulent relationship with Candy. He closed his eyes for a moment, trying to center himself, to find some clarity amidst the chaos.

When he opened his eyes, his gaze was drawn to the flower beds near the front porch. Candy had planted those flowers, carefully selecting each one for its color and fragrance during their early time together. It was the third month he met her. He remembered the day they had worked together in the garden, her laughter ringing out as they teased each other, the sun warming their backs. It had been one of those rare, perfect days, when everything seemed to align, and their love felt unbreakable.

But those days had become increasingly rare, overshadowed by arguments and misunderstandings. Lorenzo couldn't shake the feeling that their relationship was becoming excessively toxic, a black hole pulling them deeper into conflict. Even when he tried to show love, it didn't come out the way it should, twisted and tainted by their constant battles. The affection he once felt now seemed buried under layers of resentment and frustration.

He knew that Candy couldn't leave him in spite of the toxicity. And he wasn't planning to leave her either.

Lorenzo sighed deeply, his mind churning with the realization that something had to change. They couldn't continue like this, stuck in a cycle of love and hate. He knew he wanted Candy more for her looks, but for now that was enough to sustain them or better still, that was enough to make him keep her.

He sighed, running a hand through his hair, the frustration and confusion evident in his expression. The coolness of the evening air seeped through the open window, a welcome respite from the heat of his emotions. He knew he couldn't stay in the car forever, that he had to face whatever awaited him inside.

Gathering his resolve, Lorenzo opened the car door and stepped out, the gravel crunching beneath his shoes. He walked slowly towards the front door, each step measured, as if he was approaching an uncertain future. The key felt heavy in his hand as he inserted it into the lock, the click of the mechanism echoing in the quiet evening. This was like the first time he ever felt this unsure of anything.

Pushing the door open, he stepped inside, the familiar scent of home greeting him. The hallway was dimly lit, the shadows stretching long and thin across the wooden floor. He paused for a moment, listening to the stillness, the quiet hum of the refrigerator, the only sound breaking the silence.

As he closed the door behind him, Lorenzo felt a mix of anticipation and dread. He knew that a conversation with

Candy was inevitable that they needed to address the issues festering between them. But his anticipation wasn't born out of a desire to mend things, it was rooted in a need to reassert his control, to remind her who was really in charge.

Taking a deep breath, he moved further into the house, the soft glow of the living room light guiding him. Candy was sitting on the couch, her posture tense, her eyes flicking up to meet his as he entered the room. She looked both vulnerable and defiant, a mirror of his own conflicting emotions, though his were far more calculated.

"Hey," he said softly, breaking the silence, his tone deceptively gentle.

"Hey," she replied, her voice equally soft but edged with the awareness of their unspoken power struggle.

Lorenzo sat down beside her, the weight of the moment pressing down on them. He couldn't feel the ting of those earlier days anymore, but he had chosen to own Candy. He knew she couldn't leave him, and he wasn't ready to leave her either. That confidence allowed him to treat her as he pleased, knowing she was trapped in this toxic dance with him.

As he settled next to Candy, his mind began to whirl with new thoughts. They had exchanged soft greetings, but his attention was only half on their conversation. He couldn't shake the nagging suspicion that had been growing ever since Candy brought up the idea of a vacation.

Lorenzo leaned back, trying to appear casual, but his thoughts were far from relaxed. What was Candy's real motive for suggesting this trip? Was she simply looking for a way to reconnect, to rekindle the spark that had dimmed between them? Or was there something more behind her insistence on a getaway?

He studied her out of the corner of his eye, watching the way she fiddled with the hem of her shirt, her eyes darting around the room as if looking for an escape route. Lorenzo had always admired Candy's spontaneity, her love for adventure. But this felt different. It felt calculated.

"Candy," he began slowly, choosing his words with care, "about the vacation... why now?"

She looked up at him, already expecting such words from him, her eyes narrowing slightly. "Why not now? We both need a break, Lorenzo. Things have been tense, and I thought... I thought it might help us." She knew the best way to toy with him emotionally, and that's where she was headed.

Lorenzo felt her response was reasonable, almost too reasonable. He nodded, but he wasn't convinced. Was she hoping for something specific to happen on this trip? His mind jumped to the idea that had been gnawing at him ever since she'd suggested the vacation: did she expect him to propose?

The thought made his heart race. Marriage had been a distant topic for them, something they joked about but never seriously discussed. Was this Candy's way of nudging him toward that commitment? Lorenzo wasn't sure if he was ready for that step, especially given their recent way of life and his struggle.

He cleared his throat, trying to sound nonchalant. "Do you think... I mean, were you hoping for something special to happen on this trip?"

Candy's eyes flashed with something he couldn't quite decipher.

Was it hope? Anxiety? She took a deep breath before answering, her voice steady but her fingers still fidgeting with her shirt so he can think she's probably being petty. "Lorenzo, I just want us to have a good time together, to remind ourselves why we're still in this. If something special happens, then great. But I'm not pushing for anything."

Her words were reassuring, but Lorenzo's mind was still spinning. He needed to understand her intentions, to figure out if this vacation was a genuine attempt to mend their relationship or if there was an expectation lurking beneath the surface.

"Candy are you… are you expecting me to propose?" he asked bluntly, unable to hold the question back any longer.

Candy's eyes widened as she almost burst into laughter, surprise evident on her face. She had never seen a future with him. "What? No, Lorenzo, I wasn't expecting that. I just wanted us to have a chance to be together, away from all the stress and the fighting." She feigned a concerned look to make him fall for her words.

Lorenzo exhaled, relief washing over him. Maybe he was overthinking things, letting his insecurities cloud his judgment. But he couldn't shake the feeling that there was more to this than Candy was letting on.

As he settled deeper into the couch, Lorenzo's thoughts shifted again. He knew Candy's manipulative tendencies well, and he was certain she was plotting something. But he had his own plans. He wasn't about to let her get the upper hand. Their relationship might be toxic, but he thrived on the chaos, the power dynamics that played out between them. He wasn't ready to let go of that control.

Their relationship was riddled with manipulation and control, both parties were sure the conversation on the vacation was far from over and Candy is stopping at nothing to make it happen. Her plan was all in her head and no matter how he was sensing something wrong he can never think of it to the extent of what she has in mind.

Chapter Twelve

The office of Dr. Lawrence Robert Koch was a cramped and cluttered space, and this proved the years of neglect and decay. Dust and cobwebs clung to every surface, giving the room an abandoned, almost haunted feel. In the darkened waiting area, framed diplomas that once stood as proud symbols of achievement now hung crookedly on the walls, their glass fronts smeared with grime. The frames themselves were coated in a thick layer of dust, the gold trim tarnished and dull. The names and dates on the certificates were barely legible, the ink faded with time and neglect. A single flickering bulb made an eerie, intermittent light, creating ghostly shadows that danced across the walls and floor, accentuating the disarray. The bulb buzzed faintly, adding to the unsettling atmosphere. Papers were strewn haphazardly across the floor and the desk, some crumpled and yellowed with age, others torn and stained, as if tossed aside in a fit of frustration or apathy. The clutter created an image of utter chaos, a stark contrast to the room's former glory.

In the inner sanctum of the office, the disarray continued unabated. The small space was dominated by a battered leather couch, its once rich brown surface now cracked and faded, the stuffing protruding from several gaping tears. Slumped on the couch in a tangle of limbs was Dr. Koch, a man in his late 50s, whose appearance spoke volumes of his decline. His once sharp features were softened by age and a lifestyle of excess, his eyes sunken and surrounded by dark circles, his cheeks hollow. His hair, once neatly trimmed, was now a wild tangle of gray, and his face was covered in a few days' worth of unkempt stubble.

Clinging to him was a young, half-naked woman, her presence showed the doctor's desperate attempts to stave off loneliness and decay. She was draped across him, her scant clothing disheveled, her makeup smeared from a night of excess. Beside the couch, on the grimy floor, lay a bottle of cheap scotch, its amber contents nearly depleted. The bottle's label was peeling, the glass was smudged with fingerprints. Dr. Koch's hand dangled precariously above it, his fingers twitching slightly, as if he had passed out mid-swig. The room smelled faintly of stale alcohol and sweat, the air thick with a sense of desolation and ruin.

A hand entered the frame, lightly slapping the doctor awake. Dr. Koch jerked slightly, mumbling incoherently as he tried to rouse himself. "Hmp, ugh, what's that, who's there?" he muttered, his eyes barely opening.

Jimmy, standing tall and imposing, his face partially obscured by the shadows, replied curtly, "Lose the bitch."

The doctor struggled to sit up, managing with great effort to shift into an upright position. His movements were sluggish, his mind foggy from the alcohol. Jimmy motioned for the young woman to leave, and she did so hurriedly, gathering her clothes and slipping out of the office without a word, casting a fearful glance at Jimmy as she exited.

Jimmy crossed the room with purposeful strides, shoving papers off an overstuffed chair before sitting down. He adjusted the only lamp in the room, directing its harsh light straight at Dr. Koch, who squinted back in discomfort. The light illuminated Jimmy's stern face, highlighting his determined expression.

"Perhaps the gentleman could lower the light? It's a bit disorienting," Dr. Koch suggested, attempting to maintain some semblance of dignity despite his disheveled appearance.

Jimmy's voice was cold and unforgiving. "You know who I am, right? We're, like, communicating here, right?" His tone was laced with sarcasm and menace.

"Most assuredly," Dr. Koch responded, his voice wavering slightly. "I am familiar with your needs."

Jimmy leaned forward, his eyes boring into the doctor. "Excuse me for saying so, but... you're a fucking drunk. How do I know you can deliver?" His words were sharp, cutting through the room's stillness.

Dr. Koch straightened, trying to appear more composed. "Dear Sir, I am more than a common drunk. I have been the senior medical examiner of this fine island paradise for over a decade. I am above reproach, a man of my word," he declared, his tone attempting to convey confidence.

The doctor attempted to look dignified, sitting up as straight as his inebriated state would allow. Jimmy, unimpressed, stood and approached him. Reaching behind his back, Jimmy drew out an automatic pistol, swiftly cocking it and pressing the muzzle against Dr. Koch's forehead.

The doctor's eyes widened in confusion and fear. "Let me ask you this, Doc, you know what this is?" Jimmy's tone was menacing, the cold steel of the gun pressing into the doctor's skin.

"I believe it's a large caliber weapon," Dr. Koch stammered, his voice barely a whisper, his eyes locked on the gun.

Jimmy's eyes narrowed. "Good. Maybe you're not a total hump. Now, what's my name?"

"I'm sorry... but, at the moment it eludes me," Dr. Koch admitted, his voice trembling as sweat began to bead on his forehead.

"Keep it that way. Do your part, and you walk away a rich man.

Make me think for a second you're a risk..." Jimmy pulled the trigger, and the gun clicked harmlessly. Dr. Koch flinched violently, a look of sheer terror on his face, his breath coming in quick, shallow gasps.

"Are we communicating, Doctor?" Jimmy asked, his voice deadly calm, his eyes never leaving the doctor's.

"You have made yourself very clear..." Dr. Koch replied, his voice shaking, his body trembling as he tried to regain control.

Jimmy tossed an overstuffed envelope onto the sofa next to the doctor. With shaky hands, Dr. Koch picked it up and peeked inside, his eyes widening at the sight of the cash. The bills were neatly stacked, a small fortune crammed into the envelope.

"You get the rest when we get the death certificate," Jimmy said, his tone brokering no argument. "Lay off the sauce. I want you clear-headed."

"Stopping drinking is no way to do that, young man," Dr. Koch quipped, attempting a weak smile, his attempt at humor falling flat in the tense atmosphere.

Jimmy's glare silenced him immediately. "Not another drop," the doctor quickly amended, his voice barely above a whisper.

Jimmy holstered his gun and exited the office, leaving Dr. Koch to exhale a sigh of relief. The doctor looked down at the bottle of scotch on the floor, hesitating for a moment. With a dejected look, he picked up the bottle, and after a brief pause, he tossed it out of an open window, the sound of shattering glass echoing in the night.

As the bottle shattered on the ground outside, Dr. Koch leaned back on the couch, the weight of the situation settling heavily on his shoulders. The night was far from over, and the price of his actions loomed large in the dimly lit room. He ran a hand through his disheveled hair, the reality of his predicament sinking in.

***

The calm, reflective surface of a swimming pool was shattered as Kelly burst through the water, gasping for air. She pushed her hair back, her eyes wide with curiosity. The moon hung low in the sky, its light dimmed by fast-moving clouds. Mist hung heavily in the air, adding an ethereal quality to the scene. A waterfall cascaded over a corner of the pool, its flow illuminated by a soft blue light, creating a mesmerizing display.

As Kelly's eyes adjusted to the dim light, she noticed a shadow moving behind the wall of water. Drawn by an inexplicable urge, she moved closer, her movements tentative yet resolute. The figure of a man materialized in front of her, his face obscured by the veil of water. Kelly's heart raced, her breath quickening as she reached through the cascading water. Her fingers brushed against the man's body, the sensation sending shivers down her spine.

Her curiosity turned to desire as she was pulled into the water, enveloped in the arms of her unseen lover. Behind the waterfall, the two figures became one, their bodies entwined in a passionate embrace. The blue light cast an otherworldly glow, highlighting their movements as they succumbed to their hunger and lust.

In the stillness of the night, the bedroom was bathed in the soft, dappled light of the moon. The curtains fluttered gently with the night breeze, casting intricate patterns across the room. On the bed, Kelly lay restless, her body tossing and turning as if fighting unseen forces. Beads of sweat glistened on her forehead, her hands clutching the sheets, her fingers digging into the fabric as she ground her teeth. The air was thick with tension, her breaths coming in shallow, rapid gasps as she struggled against the grip of her dreams.

Suddenly, she stopped. Her body went rigid, and she drew in a hushed breath, her eyes snapping open realizing it was only a dream.

Meanwhile, in the bustling heart of South Beach, Candy was driving alone with the top down, her hair whipping in the wind. The neon lights and the vibrant nightlife surrounded her, creating a stark contrast to the serene and mysterious scene at the pool. Her cell phone rang, and she slipped on a headset, answering the call with a confident smile.

"Hello?" she said, her tone smooth and controlled.

The only response was the sound of shallow, labored breathing on the other end. Candy's smile widened.

"Kelly, are you okay?" she asked, her voice tinged with amusement.

"I… I had a dream," Kelly's voice trembled, filled with a mix of confusion and excitement.

"Good for you," Candy replied, her tone soothing yet firm. "You're on your way to a better place. You're ready for the next step. Stop by my loft around 11 tonight. I'll have a surprise waiting. And Kelly, try to dress for the occasion."

She hung up the phone, her smile never fading as she dialed another number.

"Hey… yeah…" she said, her voice dropping to a conspiratorial whisper. After a brief pause, she continued, "We got her."

As she drove through the lively streets, Candy's mind raced with anticipation. Everything was falling into place. She had Kelly right where she wanted her and tonight would be a night to remember. The city lights blurred around her, but her focus remained sharp. The plan was in motion, and nothing could stop it now.

***

The loft was an expansive space, its size emphasized by the lofty ceilings that soared above. The second floor extended over a quarter of the area, leaving the rest open and filled with an airy sense of freedom. The ceiling itself was a masterpiece, constructed entirely of glass panes that provided an unobstructed view of the night sky. The moon hovered low and luminous, stars scattered across the inky blackness like diamonds on velvet. The effect was breathtaking, the celestial display lending the room an ethereal quality.

Easels were propped against the walls, canvases haphazardly strewn about the floor, as if long abandoned by an artist who had once called this space their sanctuary. At the far end of the room, a wall of enormous windows stretched from floor to ceiling, framing a picturesque scene of boats bobbing gently in a nearby marina. The water's surface reflected the moonlight, creating a shimmering world that contrasted with the dark outlines of the vessels.

As the scene unfolded, a pair of high heels could be seen, their stiletto tips just grazing the wooden floor. The heels belonged to Kelly, her legs encased in sheer garters that peeked tantalizingly from beneath the hem of her skirt. She moved with sultry confidence, her coat swinging in a wide arc as she shrugged it off and let it fall to the floor. The wooden planks creaked softly under her feet, adding to the ambient sound of the quiet night.

Candy's voice broke the silence, her tone smooth and almost seductive. "One million dollars. It can change your life, but it comes with a price. Can you take a life for one million dollars and live with yourself?"

Kelly's gaze darted around the room, searching for the source of the voice which she already knew belonged to Candy. The space was filled with tables and canvases, the dim lighting casting long shadows that obscured much of the room's detail. Her head turned sharply as the distinct click of high-heeled shoes echoed through the loft, capturing her attention. She stood still, her posture tense, staring straight ahead.

"I'm not going to kill anyone," Kelly declared, her voice steady but laced with underlying tension.

Candy's response came smoothly, almost dismissively. "You're already in it. You might not get your hands dirty, but you're in the mix."

Kelly's eyes flickered with unease as she saw a shadow flit through the darkened loft. "Why am I here, Candy? What is it you want?"

Candy's reply was simple yet loaded with implications. "Trust. It's important that we are able to trust each other, Kelly."

Emerging from the shadows, Candy revealed herself, her hands clasped behind her back. "Do you trust me, Kelly?"

Kelly's hesitation was palpable. "I did. I'm not so sure anymore."

Candy's approach was slow, deliberate. She brushed against Kelly as she passed, the contact brief but charged. From behind her back, Candy produced a long black silk scarf, moving with fluid grace as she placed it over Kelly's eyes, blindfolding her.

"Do you trust yourself?" Candy's voice was a whisper now, intimate and probing.

Kelly stood still, her breath hitching slightly as Candy tied the blindfold securely. Though tentative, she did not resist. Candy began to circle Kelly slowly, her hand trailing over Kelly's body with a light, almost reverent touch.

"So many struggles raging inside you," Candy murmured, her tone soft and hypnotic. "So much desire waiting, hiding."

As Candy moved away, the sound of another set of footsteps filled the space. Kelly's head turned slightly, her breathing becoming more rapid, anticipation and fear mingling in her chest. The footsteps grew closer, and soon Houston came into view, his approach confident and deliberate. He drew near to Kelly, his lips hovering just inches from her neck. The warmth of his breath against her skin elicited a soft moan from Kelly, her body reacting instinctively.

From her perch on a nearby table, Candy watched the unfolding scene with a keen eye. "That's it," she encouraged, her voice a blend of authority and reassurance. "Trust yourself, trust me, let yourself go."

In that moment, the loft seemed to pulse with the collective intensity of their emotions. The interplay of light and shadow, the soft rustle of clothing, and the quiet hum of the night outside all coalesced into a charged atmosphere, setting the stage for what was to come.

Houston moved behind Kelly, his presence both commanding and reassuring. His hands began their journey at her calves, gliding sensuously upwards. The warmth of his touch contrasted with the coolness of the room, sending shivers through Kelly's body. His fingers traced the curves of her legs, pausing momentarily to savor the smoothness of her skin before continuing their ascent. As his hands reached her thighs, he applied gentle pressure, his palms flattening to cover more surface, and Kelly's breathing deepened in response.

Houston's hands moved over her hips with a firm yet tender grip, as if he was committing every curve to memory. He lingered at her waist, his thumbs brushing the sensitive area just above her hip bones, eliciting a soft gasp from Kelly. His fingers then trailed up to her back, before moving to her shoulders, where he squeezed gently, massaging away any tension.

Reaching around her body, Houston's hands found Kelly's breasts, cupping them with deliberate care. The warmth of his palms and the firmness of his grip sent a wave of heat through her. He pulled her closer, their bodies melding together as he buried his face in the crook of her neck. His breath was hot against her skin, and she could feel the faint prickle of his stubble. Lost in the moment, Kelly rolled her head back, her eyes fluttering closed as she surrendered to the pleasure of his roaming hands.

In one fluid, practiced motion, Houston spun Kelly around to face him. Their lips met in a kiss that was both passionate and hungry. Their bodies pressed tightly together, the kiss growing deeper and more fervent with each passing second. Kelly's fingers found their way to Houston's hair, tangling in the thick strands as she pulled him closer.

As he laid Kelly flat on her back on a nearby table, his hands working feverishly to rip off her shirt. He buried his face in her chest, his mouth exploring every inch of her exposed skin. Kelly's moans filled the loft, her back arching as Houston's hand drifted between her legs. She reached out blindly, seeking the touch of the stranger she couldn't see.

Candy watched from a distance, her gaze fixed on the couple.

Her eyes sparkled with arousal as she observed Houston lift Kelly effortlessly. His hands roamed over her body, caressing and exploring with a possessive intensity. As he continued to kiss and grope her, Kelly's hands moved with urgency, tearing at his belt with desperate fingers. She fumbled with the buckle, her frustration evident as she struggled to free him from his clothes. Her need to feel his skin against hers, unhindered by fabric, drove her movements, each touch more frantic than the last.

Houston responded to her urgency, his own hands working feverishly to assist her. He pulled her even closer, their bodies now fully aligned, the heat between them visible. Kelly's fingers finally succeeded, the belt coming undone, and she pushed his pants down, her hands exploring the newly exposed skin with a hunger that matched his.

From across the room, Candy slid her hands down her chest, feeling the heat, her breath quickening as she observed the raw intensity between Houston and Kelly.

Houston and Kelly's breaths came in ragged gasps, their bodies moving in sync. Houston pushed Kelly's skirt up, his hands trembling with desire as he ripped off her panties. With a swift motion, he rolled her onto her stomach, her legs dangling off the edge of the table. He mounted her from behind, and Kelly let out a loud cry, their bodies moving together in wild, unrestrained abandon.

Houston's grip on Kelly's hair tightened, pulling her head back as he kissed her fiercely. Their movements grew more frantic, each thrust bringing them closer to the edge. They both climaxed in a shared moment of intense release, their cries echoing through the loft.

As the waves of pleasure subsided, Houston gently laid Kelly back on the table, stepping away to pull up his pants. He faded into the shadows, leaving Kelly blindfolded and breathless, her body still trembling from the experience. Candy approached her, untying the blindfold with gentle hands and helping her to sit up. She kissed Kelly softly, a lingering promise of more to come, before she too walked out, leaving Kelly alone in the dark, half-dressed and reeling from the night's events.

***

Candy stepped out of the bathroom, her phone pressed to her ear as she spoke in hurried whispers. The morning sun streamed through the bedroom windows, casting a soft glow across the room, illuminating the polished wood floors and the neatly made bed. Candy's voice was low and urgent.

"Ok, I'll be there..."

She abruptly hung up the phone as she spotted Lorenzo standing by the dresser, his presence unexpected. Her eyes widened in surprise and she flashed a bright smile.

"Ay Papi, you're back! I didn't think you were coming home till tomorrow?"

She hurried over to him, her movements graceful and fluid, and threw her arms around his neck, planting a kiss on his lips. Lorenzo remained stiff and unresponsive, barely acknowledging her affection.

"Who the fuck was that on the phone?" he demanded, his voice cold and hard.

Candy's smile faltered. She tried to maintain a casual tone, but there was an edge of defensiveness in her voice. "The travel agent. I have to pay for the tickets and take our passports to their office for verification today."

Lorenzo's scowl deepened, his eyes narrowing suspiciously. "I never said I was going. Whatever the fuck islands, what the hell are we supposed to do down there?"

Candy's frustration bubbled to the surface. She took a step back, her hands gesturing emphatically as she spoke. "We eat, drink, gamble a little, and do each other."

Lorenzo snorted, his derision unmistakable. "That ain't a vacation."

Candy's patience snapped. Her voice rose, filled with

exasperation. "Then fine, I'll go by myself. Jesus, Lorenzo, I'm fucking trying here. I guess that's just a waste of time, huh?"

Without waiting for a response, Candy spun on her heel and stormed out of the bedroom, her footsteps echoing sharply against the polished wooden floor. The hallway was dimly lit, unlike the tension-filled room she had just left. She paused, leaning against the cool, smooth surface of the wall, her breath coming in short, angry bursts. Her heart pounded in her chest, a drumbeat of frustration and fury. The coolness of the floor beneath her bare feet was a welcome respite, a grounding sensation amidst the series of thoughts.

She closed her eyes, taking a moment to center herself sincs the hallway was silent. She focused on the rhythm of her breathing, the rise and fall of her chest, willing herself to calm down. The scent of polished wood and faint traces of Lorenzo's cologne lingered in the air, mingling with the faint saltiness of the ocean breeze seeping through the open window at the end of the hall.

From inside the bedroom, Lorenzo's voice called after her, softer now, carrying a hint of regret. "Candy, hey Candy, wait up. Don't be that way."

A small, involuntary smile tugged at the corners of Candy's lips, a fleeting moment of triumph. She quickly composed herself, wiping away any trace of satisfaction from her face. She drew in a deep breath, letting her shoulders relax, and replaced her expression with one of vulnerability and hurt. The transformation was seamless, a practiced facade that masked her true feelings.

Turning around, she walked back into the bedroom, her footsteps now softer, almost hesitant. The room was bathed in the soft glow of late afternoon sunlight filtering through the curtains. Lorenzo stood near the bed, his posture tense, his hands clenching and unclenching at his sides. As she approached, her expression softened, her eyes wide with a feigned hurt.

"I just want us to have some time together, Lorenzo. Is that really too much to ask?" Her voice was gentle, almost pleading, each word carefully chosen to evoke a response.

Lorenzo's shoulders slumped slightly, the anger in his eyes dimming, replaced by a flicker of remorse. He ran a hand through his hair, sighing deeply. "Alright, alright. We'll go. Just... don't go running off like that, okay?"

Candy nodded, her expression earnest, though inside she felt a thrill of victory. "Thank you, Lorenzo," she said softly, stepping closer to him. She reached out, her fingers grazing his arm in a gesture of reconciliation. "I just want us to be happy."

Lorenzo's gaze softened further, the tension in his body easing as he wrapped an arm around her shoulders. "Yeah, me too," he murmured. “Let’s just… make the most of our time, okay?”

Candy leaned into him, The moment was bittersweet, a fragile truce in the ongoing battle of wills between them.

Candy nodded, stepping closer to him and wrapping her arms around his waist. She rested her head on his chest, feeling the tension slowly drain from his body as he wrapped his arms around her in return. Resting her head against his chest, listening to the steady rhythm of his heartbeat. “I think that’s a great idea,” she whispered, a contented smile playing on her lips. The room seemed to breathe a sigh of relief as the conflict between them eased, leaving behind a fragile peace. The morning sunlight continued to pour in, with a warm, golden light over their embrace.

Chapter Thirteen

Candy sat in a dimly lit booth at the back of Moody's Pub, her fingers idly tracing the rim of a tequila bottle.

The pub was a smoky, crowded space, filled with the low hum of conversation and the occasional clink of glasses. The wooden paneling on the walls was dark and worn, and the air carried the scent of spilled beer and fried food. Candy's eyes flicked to the entrance as she awaited Kelly's arrival.

Kelly walked into the pub, her eyes scanning the room with cautious air. There was something different about her tonight— an aura of confidence that seemed to set her apart from the rest of the patrons. She spotted Candy and made her way over, weaving through the crowd with a purpose. As she slid into the booth across from Candy, she offered a nod of approval.

"Nice place," Kelly remarked, her tone slightly sardonic.

Candy shrugged, pouring herself a shot of tequila. "Not my choice," she replied, her voice edged with irritation.

Kelly raised an eyebrow, her curiosity piqued. "Not your choice? When is anything not your choice? What are we doing here?"

Candy didn't respond immediately. Instead, she glanced toward the door, her gaze sharpening. "Meeting someone. In fact, there he is now."

Kelly turned her head and saw Houston entering the pub. He stopped at the bar, ordered a beer, and then headed toward their booth. His presence was commanding, and he carried himself with an air of casual confidence. As he approached, he raised his beer in a silent toast to Kelly, his eyes assessing her.

"Kelly, meet Houston," Candy introduced, her voice holding a note of formality.

Houston looked at Kelly over, his gaze lingering. "We've met," he said, taking a sip of his beer.

Kelly's eyes flicked to Candy, seeking an explanation. Candy, however, looked away, a small smile playing on her lips. The tension between them was obvious.

"Oh...I see. Well, this is embarrassing," Kelly said, her voice tinged with both amusement and awkwardness.

Houston chuckled, his expression warm. "Why? You rock."

Candy's patience seemed to wear thin as she cut in. "Look, this isn't a blind date, okay? We've got work to do, alright?" Her tone was sharp, brooking no argument.

Houston shrugged, unfazed. He reached for the tequila bottle, poured himself a shot, and downed it in one smooth motion. "So what's the plan?" he asked, his eyes locking onto Candy's.

As Candy began to outline their strategy. Her voice became the focal point, clear and decisive, as she laid out the details of their operation. Her outline was very narrative that it all felt real like it was already taking place before them

The sunlight streamed into the backyard, casting a warm glow over the scene. Lorenzo lounged by the pool, earbuds in, listening to music on his iPod. His muscular frame was relaxed, eyes closed behind dark sunglasses, completely unaware of the unfolding plans around him.

In the background, Candy's voice continued to outline the plan. "First, we need to get Kelly invited to the Cayman Islands. That shouldn't be too hard."

The scene played out as the sliding glass door of the house opened, and Kelly emerged, wrapped in a plush white robe. Her hair was tousled, giving her a carefree, yet composed look. She hesitated for a moment, noticing Lorenzo by the pool, before stepping out fully.

"Oh, I'm sorry," Kelly said, feigning surprise and innocence. "I didn't know you were here. Candy told me I could use the pool during my lunch break, but if it bothers you..."

Lorenzo pulled out his earphones, the music faintly audible. He glanced up, his eyes briefly narrowing in assessment before softening. "Don't worry about it, go ahead," he said, waving her off with a dismissive yet curious gesture.

Kelly nodded, giving him a polite smile. She walked to the edge of the pool, her movements deliberately graceful. She untied her robe and let it slip to the ground, revealing an innocent yet flattering swimsuit that clung to her figure in all the right places. Lorenzo, despite his attempts to remain indifferent, couldn't help but lower his sunglasses slightly for a better look.

With a fluid motion, Kelly dove into the pool, breaking the surface with barely a splash. She swam a few laps, her strokes even and confident, all the while aware of Lorenzo's gaze following her every move. Emerging from the water, she ran her hands through her hair, slicking it back and revealing the subtle curve of her neck and shoulders. Lorenzo watched, his interest piqued despite himself.

Candy's voiceover continued, her tone dripping with calculated determination. "He will begin to loose guard at this point. It'll be the perfect cover. He won't suspect a thing."

Kelly climbed out of the pool, the water glistening on her skin. She wrapped the robe back around herself and gave Lorenzo a final, lingering glance before heading back into the house. Lorenzo watched her go, his mind filled with temptation.

As Kelly disappeared inside, Lorenzo leaned back in his chair, a thoughtful expression crossing his face. Candy's plan will already be in motion at that time, and every piece falling perfectly into place.

Candy, Kelly, and Houston still occupied a secluded booth as Candy detailed the plan to the others. The table was cluttered with shot glasses and a nearly empty bottle of tequila, evidence of their lengthy plotting session. Candy leaned back, a cigarette dangling from her fingers, exhaling a plume of smoke that swirled lazily in the dim light.

Candy's voice cut through the haze, her tone confident and slightly slurred from the alcohol. "Once we get him interested, he should do the rest," she said, her eyes flicking between Kelly and Houston, assessing their commitment to the plan.

Kelly nodded, her earlier confidence now bolstered by the tequila coursing through her veins. Houston raised his beer in a mock toast before taking a long swig. The trio sat in a conspiratorial silence, the gravity of their scheme settling over them like the smoky air.

* * *

The sunlight streamed into the kitchen, giving a warm glow on the polished surfaces. Kelly, dressed in a uniform that clung to her curves more than it probably should, stood on a chair, diligently cleaning the windows. Her attire, intentionally chosen for its provocative cut, showcased her figure in a way that was hard to ignore.

Lorenzo entered the kitchen, his steps slowing as he took in the scene before him. Kelly, perched precariously on the chair, was reaching for a corner of the window that seemed just out of her grasp. The view from his angle offered an unobstructed look at her behind, framed perfectly at eye level.

Sensing his presence, Kelly turned her head slightly and smiled. "Hi, Mr. Steel," she greeted, her voice sweet and innocent. "Could you just do me a huge favor? I tip over every time I try to get that corner. Could you spot me?"

Lorenzo, caught off guard but intrigued, moved closer. "Sure," he replied, positioning himself behind her. As Kelly leaned further to reach the elusive corner, Lorenzo placed his hands on her hips to steady her. The touch was electric, sending a thrill through Kelly that she didn't bother to hide.

She wiped the corner clean, then pretended to lose her balance, falling back into Lorenzo's arms. They both laughed, the sound light and carefree, but there was an undercurrent of something much more intense. Kelly looked up at him, her eyes twinkling with mischief and something deeper.

Candy's voice continued to weave through the scene as she laid out the blueprint of their elaborate scheme. "We get him more involved," her voice echoed, "and let nature take its course."

Lorenzo found himself drawn further into Kelly's orbit. Her charm and the seemingly innocent accidents were all part of the meticulous plan Candy had crafted. As Kelly slipped from Lorenzo's grasp, she straightened herself, giving him a coy smile before turning back to her work.

The seeds of the plan were taking root, each encounter designed to entangle Lorenzo deeper into their web. Candy's outline, articulated over drinks and smoke-filled air, was coming to life in the bright, sunlit kitchen. Every glance, every touch, was calculated to ensure their success, and as Lorenzo left the kitchen, thoughts of Kelly lingered longer than they should have.

The low hum of conversation and clinking glasses created a murmur of background noise that felt like a cloak of anonymity around them. Candy leaned forward, her eyes glinting with a blend of determination and cunning as she directed her next word to Kelly.

"We don't have to worry about being obvious," Candy said, her voice carrying a casual confidence. "Lorenzo thinks every woman wants him, so it will just be a matter of time before he makes his move."

Houston took a long drag from his cigarette, exhaling slowly as he nodded in agreement. Kelly, sipping her tequila, seemed to be lost in thought, yet her confidence was still there. The trio, united in their scheme, painted a picture of calculated deceit, each playing their part in a plan meticulously crafted by Candy.

Candy's mind whirred with the details of the plot they were about to set in motion. She could see every step clearly, envisioning how each move would unfold. It was like a carefully choreographed dance, where every participant had a specific role, and she was the conductor of this symphony of deception.

The scene transitioned to the sunlit bedroom of Candy and Lorenzo's home. Kelly, dressed in a modest yet subtly provoca- tive outfit, moved around the room with deliberate grace, making the bed with care.

As Kelly fluffed the pillows and smoothed the sheets, Lorenzo entered. His presence was imposing, with confidence and arrogance, that filled the room. Kelly glanced up, a perfect blend of innocence and allure in her eyes.

"Hi Mr. Steel, I'll be through here in just a sec," Kelly said, her voice soft and sweet, tinged with a hint of nervousness that she had practiced to perfection.

Candy's voice narrated the scene unfolding in the bedroom.

"It never fails," Candy's voice echoed in Kelly's mind. "Every time Lorenzo makes a move on someone I know, he always starts the same way. He'll ask you..."

Lorenzo's eyes lingered on Kelly, as he moved closer to the bed, sitting down with a practiced casualness that was anything but.

"So, Kelly, how are you and Candy getting along?" Lorenzo asked, his voice smooth, masking the predatory gleam in his eyes.

Candy's voice continued, guiding Kelly through her response. "Here's the answer he's looking for."

Kelly turned to Lorenzo, her expression a perfect mix of sympathy and admiration.

"She's okay," Kelly said, her voice filled with a touch of wistfulness. "She's a very lucky woman, Mr. Steel. I hope she appreciates it."

Lorenzo's face lit up with a smile, his ego stroked just as Candy had predicted. He leaned in a bit closer, the scent of his cologne mixing with the fresh linen of the bed.

"I'm not sure she does," Lorenzo said, his tone feigning vulnerability. "And it... it hurts sometimes."

Kelly placed a comforting hand on his shoulder, her touch light yet deliberate.

"You poor man," she said softly, her eyes locking onto his with genuine concern.

Candy's voice echoed with satisfaction. "Now, we've got him."

Back in the smoky confines of Moody's Pub, Candy leaned back in the booth, a satisfied smile playing on her lips.

"I'll pretend I hurt my shoulder," she said, her mind already working through the logistics. "Some reason that would make it make sense that you come with us... Lorenzo will jump at the chance."

Houston poured himself another shot of tequila, his eyes fixed on Candy.

"And if he gets suspicious?" he asked, his voice low and gruff.

Candy shook her head, her confidence unshaken. "He won't. By the time he realizes what's happening, it'll be too late. He'll be in too deep to back out."

Kelly, now fully immersed in her role, nodded in agreement. The plan was simple yet brilliant, relying on Lorenzo's predictability and ego. Candy's manipulation was subtle, weaving a web of deceit that ensnared Lorenzo without him even realizing it.

The bedroom scene played out like a script in Kelly's mind. She could see Lorenzo's reaction, feel his touch, hear his words. Every detail had been anticipated, every move calculated. As she finished making the bed, she knew that the real performance was about to begin.

Lorenzo watched her, his gaze lingering on her curves. Kelly felt a surge of confidence. She knew she had him right where Candy wanted him.

Candy's voice continued to outline the plan, her words precise and measured.

"We'll keep him intrigued," she said, her eyes flicking to Kelly and then to Houston. "Kelly, you'll be the bait. Make him feel like he's the one in control, the one making the decisions. But remember, every step he takes is one we've planned."

Houston nodded, his expression serious. "And if he gets wise?" he asked, his tone carrying a hint of concern.

Candy's smile was cold and calculating. "He won't. By the time he realizes what's happening, it'll be too late. He'll be in too deep to back out."

Kelly's role was now clear in her mind. She was the key to this plan, the alluring distraction that would keep Lorenzo occupied while Candy and Houston pulled the strings.

In the outline Candy was laying, as she moved to leave the bedroom, Lorenzo caught her hand, his grip firm yet gentle.

"Thank you, Kelly," he said, his voice sincere. "I don't know what I'd do without you."

Kelly smiled, a hint of sadness in her eyes. "You're welcome, Mr. Steel," she replied, her voice soft.

Back at the pub, Candy continued to detail the final steps of the plan.

"We'll make sure he feels needed," she said, her voice unwavering.

"He'll think he's the one in control, but in reality, we're the ones pulling the strings."

Houston poured another drink, his eyes never leaving Candy's face. "And if something goes wrong?" he asked.

Candy shook her head. "Nothing will go wrong," she said firmly. "We've planned for every contingency. Trust me, this will work."

Kelly, now fully committed to her role, nodded. She knew that Candy's plan was foolproof. All they needed to do was execute it perfectly.

The game had begun, and they were ready to play it to the end.

The night wore on, and the pub's atmosphere grew more relaxed, but the trio's focus never wavered. They knew that the stakes were high, and they were prepared to do whatever it took to achieve their objective.

The following day, in the bedroom of Candy and Lorenzo's home, Candy continued to unfold the plan. In the outline scene they were crafting, Kelly, dressed in her flattering uniform, moved through the house. Every interaction with Lorenzo carefully calculated every word and gesture designed to draw him further into their trap.

Lorenzo, oblivious to the machinations around him, played his part perfectly. His ego and desires made him an easy target, and Kelly's charm and allure only served to draw him in further. The web of deceit tightened around him with every passing moment.

Candy watched from the sidelines, her eyes sharp and focused. She knew that the success of their plan hinged on Kelly's performance.

Then she proceeded, "I'll pretend I hurt my shoulder, for some reason that would make it make sense that you come with us... Lorenzo will jump at the chance," Candy said, her tone confident and assured.

She went on with the final part of her outline with the scene of the outline displaying the blazing sun of St. Lucia greeted them as they stepped off the plane. With her arm in a sling, she descended the steps carefully. Behind her, Kelly and Lorenzo followed, laughing and joking together, their spirits high. The vibrant colors of the airport, with palm trees swaying in the gentle breeze, set the stage for the next act of their scheme.

An establishing shot of the White Sands Resort highlighted its exclusivity, which was the one Candy planned on booking. The luxurious resort catered to the elite, its pristine beaches and opulent architecture promising a haven of indulgence and relaxation.

Lorenzo and Candy entered their lavish suite, the grandeur of the room lost on them as they focused on the plan. Candy's voice narrated the unfolding events with precision.

"Once we arrive, I'll feign a headache, complain about my arm, anything I can," Candy's voice echoed in the background, outlining her strategy.

Lorenzo and Candy sat in a cabana, looking bored as they watched the poolside activities. Kelly, in a revealing bikini, was the center of attention, her vivacious energy drawing all eyes, including Lorenzo's. She laughed and flirted, her carefree act was a stark contrast to the calculated plot simmering beneath the surface.

"It shouldn't take much of this to get Lorenzo to make a move. A couple of days at the pool..." Candy's voice continued, the plan progressing smoothly.

The dance club was alive with pounding music and twirling lights, a pulsating crowd filling the dance floor. Lorenzo and Candy, her arm in a chic matching sling, sat watching the revelry. Kelly was again the star, dancing with wild abandon and enjoying herself immensely. Lorenzo's gaze followed her every move, his interest growing with each passing moment.

"A couple of nights... Lorenzo will be like a dog in heat," Candy's voice-over continued, confident in her ability to manipulate the situation.

In the cool, elegant lobby of the resort, Lorenzo spotted Kelly passing through. He stopped her, leading her to a quiet corner, the anticipation in his eyes unmistakable.

"He'll suggest another hotel... you'll suggest the Rainforest," Candy's voice explained, the plan unfolding with perfect precision.

Lorenzo entered the luxurious presidential suite, his footsteps light on the plush carpet. The room was bathed in the soft glow of afternoon sunlight filtering through the large windows, which offered a breathtaking view of the pristine beach and azure ocean beyond. Candy lay in the grand king-sized bed, her arm still secured in a sling, creating a stark contrast to the opulence surrounding her.

Lorenzo's face was a blend of poorly concealed excitement and a thin veneer of concern. He approached the bed with casual air, trying to mask the eagerness that sparked his eyes.

"I was thinking about doing some exploring," he began, his voice attempting a nonchalant tone. "You feel up to it? There's supposed to be a pretty cool rainforest thing around here."

Candy shifted slightly in the bed, her eyes narrowing as she looked up at him. "Rainforest?" she echoed, her voice tinged with skepticism and feigned doubt.

"Yeah, Rainforest," Lorenzo repeated, nodding enthusiastically. "You know it's vanishing. I kinda wanted to see it... you know... before it's gone." His eyes betrayed his true intentions, flickering with a hidden agenda that Candy could easily read.

Candy sighed softly, raising her injured arm slightly to emphasize her point. "I'm not sure I'm up for that, Lorenzo," she said, her voice filled with an air of reluctance and resignation.

Lorenzo glanced at her arm, the sling a reminder of her supposed injury. "That's right, you should probably get some rest... you know, rest the arm," he said, his words filled with apparent concern, though his relief was barely concealed.

Candy offered him a gentle, reassuring smile. "Don't worry about me, honey," she replied, her voice sweet yet firm. "You go have a nice time."

He hesitated for a moment, his eagerness visible as he searched her face for any sign of hesitation. "You sure?" he asked, his tone almost pleading, hoping for her affirmation.

"Go ahead," Candy insisted, her smile widening as she reassured him once more. Her eyes held a knowing glint, confident in the success of the plan she had so meticulously crafted.

He leaned in for a kiss before exiting. As soon as the door closed behind him, Candy picked up the phone and dialed, her expression shifting to one of triumph.

"He's on the way," she said, hanging up with a smile. She then removed the sling, her satisfaction evident.

Back in the dimly lit booth of Moody's Pub, Candy continued her detailed explanation.

"You see, the beauty is since he's stepping out on me, he'll keep your little rendezvous a secret," Candy explained, her tone confident.

Houston, skeptical but intrigued, raised an eyebrow. "How do you know he's going to follow your little sex kitten here?

There's lots of other beach bunnies that wouldn't be as risky."

"The risk is the appeal to him, it gets him on more than some random fuck. He has all of those he wants during road trips," Candy replied, her eyes glinting with certainty.

Lorenzo emerged from a small liquor store, a bag in hand, glancing around before heading off. Candy's voice narrated his movements with precise calculation.

"We'll be able to use the clerk to establish a time and the fact that he was drinking," Candy's voice-over explained, each step carefully planned.

Lorenzo, still carrying the bag from the liquor store, approached the valet to rent a Land Rover ATV. The vehicle was rugged, with a roll bar and no doors, perfect for the terrain he planned to explore. The valet attempted to explain the Rover's features, but Lorenzo, charged with anticipation, was impatient to leave. He sped off, gears grinding, as the valet watched with a cringe.

"You'll tell him to pick you up down the road, just to be sure," Candy's voice continued, laying out the logistics.

On a scenic road lined with trees, Kelly waited, keeping an eye out for Lorenzo. When he skidded to a stop in the Land Rover, Kelly smiled and jumped in, her excitement contagious.

"We'll follow behind you. If you do your job, Lorenzo will never notice," Candy's voice reassured, the plan nearing its climax.

An old pickup truck, driven by Houston with Candy beside him, passed by, discreetly following the Land Rover.

Kelly glanced casually behind them, spotting the pickup truck rounding a bend and keeping a safe distance. She turned back to Lorenzo, who was adjusting to the rear-view mirror. Sensing an opportunity, Kelly slid her hand up his leg, her charm distracting him completely.

"You'll be perfectly safe," Candy's voice promised, confident in their control over the situation.

The Land Rover came to a stop in a small clearing at the edge of a cliff, a cascading waterfall creating a picturesque backdrop.

The table in Moody's Pub was now littered with more empty bottles, used limes, and shot glasses. Candy continued her explanation, pulling out a small vial of white powder.

"This is a spider venom... some kind of neural inhibitor. Lots of these kinds of spiders around our vacation spot, so even if it comes up, no problem. You make the drinks, slip this in… Lorenzo wouldn't be able to move in 5 minutes," Candy said, her voice confident and unwavering.

Kelly, though confident, voiced a concern. "What if it doesn't work?"

"It'll work, guaranteed to knock a rhino's dick in the dirt it'll work," Candy assured, her conviction unshaken.

Houston chimed in. "Even if it doesn't, we'll be close by."

Kelly, still uneasy, asked, "So what are you gonna do? The guy's a football player, not some scared accountant."

Houston pulled back his jacket, revealing a large automatic weapon. "Hey, do I look like I know any accountants? Don't worry about the jock, okay?"

Candy's confidence was infectious. "Everything's going to work alright!"

Houston unceremoniously dumped an unconscious Lorenzo into the Land Rover, starting the engine and dropping it into gear. The vehicle lurched forward, pitching over the edge of the cliff and slamming against a large rock before plunging down. The collision was horrific, a violent mix of metal, glass, flesh, and bone.

Candy leaned back, her expression one of triumph. "And that's it. A tragic accident. Dr. Koch, the island's coroner, will make sure it's written up that way. Right?"

Houston nodded. "It's already handled."

Candy's smile widened. "Then once we have the death certificate, no one can touch us. We come back here… you guys get your money, and we all go our separate ways."

Houston, still skeptical, asked, "Just that easy?"

Candy's confidence was unshakable. "Just that easy."

Chapter Fourteen

The sun was blazing high in the clear blue sky as the airliner touched down at Owen Roberts International Airport in the Cayman Islands. The tires screeched slightly upon contact, a sound that momentarily pierced the airport's steady hum of activity. The plane taxied smoothly towards the gate, its powerful engines emitting a deep, resonant hum that reverberated through the air.

The airport itself was a hive of activity. Vacationers, with their colorful attire and wide-brimmed hats, mingled with locals who moved with practiced efficiency. The energy was clear with a mix of excitement from those eager to start their tropical getaway and the routine hustle of airport staff ensuring everything ran smoothly. The scent of saltwater mingled with the distant aroma of island cuisine, hinting at the adventures awaiting each traveler.

As the plane came to a halt, ground crew members swiftly maneuvered the stair ramp into place, their movements precise and coordinated. The door of the airliner swung open with a soft hiss, and a flight attendant appeared in the doorway. Her bright smile was as warm as the island sun, a welcome for the passengers who had endured the long flight.

One by one, travelers began to file out, their expressions a blend of relief and anticipation. They squinted against the brilliant sunlight, adjusting their sunglasses and hats as they descended the stairs. The bright colors of the island landscape, lush green palms, sparkling turquoise waters, and pristine white sands beckoned them forward, promising relaxation and adventure.

Candy was among the first to step out, her sharp attire a contrast to the casual vacationers around her. She moved with an air of grace and purpose, each step deliberate and confident. The sling cradling her arm did little to diminish her poise instead, it seemed to add an element of intrigue. Her eyes, sharp and focused, gleamed with the intent of someone who had carefully planned for the days ahead.

As she descended the stairs, her gaze never wavered, taking in every detail of her surroundings. The warm breeze tousled her hair, carrying with it the scent of the sea. Behind her, Lorenzo emerged from the plane, struggling with the weight of their luggage. His posture was less composed, his movements slower and marked by the fatigue of their journey. Beads of sweat dotted his forehead, and he shifted the bags uncomfortably as he tried to keep up with Candy's brisk pace.

Lorenzo's face was a mask of weariness, his eyes dull with exhaustion. The bags he carried seemed to weigh him down further, each step an effort. Yet, despite his obvious fatigue, there was a glimmer of anticipation in his eyes which was a hint of excitement for what lay ahead. As he followed Candy down the stairs, the contrast between them was evident.

Together, they stepped onto the sun-warmed tarmac, ready to embark on the next phase of their crafted scheme. The bright, vibrant landscape of the Cayman Islands seemed almost surreal against the backdrop of their calculated intentions, a paradise masking the perilous path they were about to tread.

The doorway of the plane remained empty for a moment, creating a brief pause in the steady stream of disembarking passengers. Then, Kelly appeared. She stepped out onto the ramp, her eyes scanning the surroundings. Her movements were deliberate, her confidence radiating as she descended the stairs, ready to play her part in the unfolding plan.

The tropical air enveloped them, warm and fragrant with the scent of the sea and blooming flowers. The lively energy of the Cayman Islands was palpable, a stark contrast to the controlled environment of the plane. Candy, Lorenzo, and Kelly moved through the airport with each step bringing them closer to the culmination of their meticulously crafted scheme.

Candy's sharp attire and composed demeanor belied the machinations behind her poised exterior. Her arm in a sling was more than just a prop but also a symbol of the lengths they were willing to go to ensure their plan's success. As she moved forward, she glanced back at Lorenzo, who was struggling under the weight of their luggage, his face a picture of exhaustion.

Lorenzo's burdened state was part of the plan, a calculated move to play on his ego and desires. Candy's careful planning had ensured that every detail was accounted for, every possibility anticipated. Her mind raced with thoughts of what was to come, the careful dance of manipulation and deceit that would play out in the days ahead.

Kelly, walking a few steps behind, was the final piece of the puzzle. Her presence was a crucial element, her role carefully scripted to entice and ensnare Lorenzo. As she took in the vibrant surroundings, her mind was set on the task at hand. The tropical paradise of the Cayman Islands was the perfect backdrop for their plot, a place where desires and ambitions could easily be manipulated and exploited.

Together, they moved through the bustling airport. The plan was no longer a distant concept but a living, breathing reality, unfolding with each step they took. The tropical heat, the sounds of the island, and the anticipation in the air all served as a prelude to the events that would soon transpire.

Candy, Lorenzo, and Kelly were now on the stage they had set, their roles clearly defined. The plan was in motion, and there was no turning back. As they stepped out into the bright sunlight of the Cayman Islands, the wheels of their scheme were turning, each moment bringing them closer to the final act. The die was cast, and the only thing left was to see how the story would unfold in the idyllic yet treacherous paradise of the Cayman Islands.

Houston stood across the tarmac, his eyes fixed on Kelly as she descended the stairs from the plane. His gaze shifted to Lorenzo and Candy, taking in the scene with a keen, calculating expression. From his vantage point, he could see the trio clearly, their movements were precise. The sun beat down on the Cayman Islands, casting a harsh light on the unfolding drama.

Beside Houston, Jimmy fidgeted impatiently, his restlessness evident in every exaggerated movement. "Jeez, man, we were just fucking here four days ago. Did you leave a bag or something? Come on, man, what the fuck are we doing here?" he grumbled, his voice edged with frustration and confusion.

Houston's eyes never left the trio they were surveilling. He replied, his tone steady and deliberate, "Protecting our interests."

Jimmy's frustration boiled over, his patience snapped. "What fucking interests!? You tell me to set shit up, you don't tell me why. You're here four fucking days, and you still haven't told me shit," he spat out, his tone a mix of anger and bewilderment. His eyes bore into Houston, seeking answers that had been withheld for too long.

Houston finally turned to face Jimmy, his expression unreadable, a mask of calm that only served to infuriate Jimmy further. "It's complicated, and I wasn't sure how you'd react," Houston said, his voice measured, as if he was explaining something trivial.

Jimmy's patience was wearing perilously thin. "Well, you're about three minutes from me feeding your nuts to my roosters, so one way or another..." he threatened, his voice dropping to a low, menacing growl. His eyes narrowed, and the tension between them became almost palpable.

Houston couldn't help but chuckle at Jimmy's threat. "All right, but don't say I didn't warn you," he said, placing a reassuring, albeit slightly condescending, arm around Jimmy's shoulders. The two of them began to walk towards an old, rusted pickup truck parked nearby. The truck, with its dented body and chipped paint, looked as if it had seen better days, a stark contrast to the pristine rental jeeps that lined the entrance of the resort.

As they strolled across the tarmac, Houston started to speak, his voice low. "Remember that time we were in Mexico a while back..." He began, his tone was casual, but there was an underlying tension taking on a storytelling tone, a sense of gravity that hinted at the seriousness of their current situation.

The two men continued their conversation, their figures gradually disappearing into the distance as they approached the weathered pickup truck. The sun glinted off the truck's rusty exterior, a contrast to the pristine beauty of the Cayman Islands around them.

Houston's mind was filled with a series of thoughts as he recounted the events in Mexico. Every detail of their current situation was intertwined with past experiences, lessons learned, and the web of deceit they were now navigating. He knew that Jimmy's impatience was justified, but there were layers to their plan that required careful handling, secrets that couldn't be divulged too soon.

As they reached the truck, Houston opened the driver's side door and climbed in, with Jimmy following suit on the passenger side. The truck's engine roared to life with a throaty rumble, and they pulled away from the airport, the sound of gravel crunching under the tires echoing in the still air.

The Cayman Islands stretched out before them, a tropical paradise masking the darker undercurrents of their mission. Houston's mind was sharp, his instincts honed. Protecting their interests required more than just physical presence but also demanded a keen understanding of human nature, the ability to anticipate moves, and the resolve to act when the time came.

As they drove away, the airport and its bustling activity faded into the background, replaced by the vibrant landscape of the islands. The scent of saltwater and blooming flowers filled the air, a deceptive contrast to the tension simmering beneath the surface. Houston's thoughts remained focused on Candy, Lorenzo, and Kelly, each playing their part in a larger game that was only beginning to unfold.

Houston knew that the days ahead would be challenging, filled with unexpected twists and turns. But he was ready. The stakes were high, and failure was not an option. As the truck sped along the coastal road, Houston's resolve hardened. Protecting their interests was more than just a task but was a necessity, a driving force that pushed him forward, no matter the cost.

"So, there we were. A perfect plan... but then again, things don't always go the way you think they will." Candy's subconscious mind thought.

The bustling lobby of the White Sands Resort was in vuew, its elegant design complemented by the vibrant activity of vacationers moving about. The focus was now tightly on Lorenzo, his expression was one of confusion and reluctance.

"Rainforest? Like up in the woods? Hellll no, I ain't climbing around a mountain for a piece of ass!" Lorenzo's voice boomed with disdain. "I'm Lorenzo Steele. You want me to rent a Jeep to hit it? Hell no, let's just go round back the tennis courts. They got some kind of huts or some shit."

Kelly, standing beside him, paused and looked around the busy lobby. Her eyes caught sight of Houston, who was watching them intently from across the room. The plan was going awry, but Kelly's quick thinking kicked in. She suddenly pushed Lorenzo into a corner, her movements swift and decisive. Grabbing his crotch with one hand, she buried her head into his neck, pinning him against the wall with her other arm.

"You think I am gonna be inspired by a hut back of some tennis courts?" Kelly whispered, her voice a mix of seduction and challenge. Her eyes locked onto Lorenzo's, daring him to defy her.

Lorenzo, caught off guard by her boldness and the intensity of her gaze, stammered, "Inspired, huh? What's that?"

Kelly's eyes glinted with determination, a sly smile playing on her lips. "Something you won't see behind the tennis courts," she murmured, her breath warm against his skin as she leaned in closer. Her tongue traced a slow, deliberate line along the curve of Lorenzo's ear, sending shivers down his spine and igniting a fire in his veins.

Lorenzo's resistance began to crumble, his bravado melting under her touch. His eyes glazed over with desire as he felt the electricity between them. "Really?" he managed to say, his voice tinged with both curiosity and longing.

Kelly pressed her advantage, her voice dropping to a sultry whisper that was almost a purr. "Really, your call... Mr. Steel." She let the last words linger in the air, a tantalizing promise wrapped in a challenge.

Her hand moved with calculated precision, sliding up Lorenzo's chest. Her fingers, cool and confident, found his nipples and gave them a sharp twist. Lorenzo winced, a mixture of pain and pleasure flashing across his face. The sensation was intense, unexpected, and it only fueled his desire further.

"Yeah, where are those jeeps at?" he finally conceded, his voice breathy and eager. His facade of indifference shattered, revealing a man completely under Kelly's spell.

As Kelly stepped back slightly, she could see the effect she had on him. Lorenzo's eyes were dark with lust, his breathing ragged. The playful yet determined glint in her eyes assured him that whatever lay ahead would be worth every risk. She had him exactly where she wanted him, and the game was just beginning.

As the scene played out, the lobby's background noise seemed to fade, leaving only the charged interaction between Kelly and

Lorenzo. Their surroundings blurred, and for a moment, it was as if they were the only two people in the room. Kelly had turned the situation around, her quick thinking and bold actions keeping their plan on track.

Houston, still watching from his vantage point, nodded slightly in approval. Kelly had managed to steer Lorenzo in the right direction, but the game was far from over. The stakes were high, and every move counted.

As they moved toward the rental desk to inquire about the jeeps, the plan continued to unfold, each step bringing them closer to their ultimate goal. The Cayman Islands, with its lush landscapes and hidden dangers, awaited them, ready to test their resolve and cunning at every turn.

Candy sat parked near the entrance of the White Sands Resort, her red pickup truck idling as she eyed a row of rental jeeps. Dressed inconspicuously in dark glasses and a wide-brimmed hat, she smoked nervously, her fingers tapping the steering wheel in a jittery rhythm. With a quick, frustrated flick, she tossed her cigarette out the window, then reached into her purse, pulling out a small vial. She dipped her little finger into the white powder, then quickly sniffed coke into both nostrils, her body visibly relaxing as the drug took effect.

Her moment of relief was shattered by a harsh voice. "What the fuck are you doing? Where'd you get that shit?" Candy jumped, startled, and turned to see Houston's face glaring at her through the open window. In her shock, she dropped the vial and fumbled to catch it, but it slipped through her fingers and fell to the floor of the truck.

"God damn it, Houston!" Candy cursed under her breath, bending down to retrieve the small vial that had slipped from her grasp. Her movements were quick and frantic, her fingers trembling as she picked it up from the dusty ground. Meanwhile, Houston walked around the front of the truck with measured steps, his face a mask of irritation and concern. The tropical sun beat down on them, casting shadows across the tarmac.

As Houston climbed into the driver's seat, he shot Candy a stern look. "You don't need to be fucked up, Candy. Put that shit away," he ordered, his voice firm and unyielding, leaving no room for argument. His eyes, though hard, held a flicker of concern for her well-being.

Candy straightened up, the vial clenched tightly in her hand. She was visibly agitated, her chest rising and falling with rapid breaths. "I'm just trying to level out, alright? Killing someone isn't a daily thing for me," she snapped back, her voice laced with desperation and a hint of vulnerability that she rarely showed. The stress of their plan was taking its toll, and she was struggling to maintain her composure.

Houston sighed, the tension in his shoulders easing slightly as he softened his gaze. "They should be out in a minute. Just relax," he said, trying to offer some semblance of reassurance. His tone was gentler now.

Candy glanced nervously towards the entrance of the terminal, her eyes scanning the crowd for any sign of their accomplices. She spotted Kelly emerging from the doorway, her movements purposeful and confident. "There goes Kelly," Candy said, her voice barely above a whisper. She watched as Kelly glanced over at them briefly before making her way down the road, disappearing behind a cluster of lush trees that bordered the environment.

Houston followed her gaze, his eyes narrowing as he spotted their target. "There's Lorenzo," he noted, pointing towards the line of rental jeeps where Lorenzo was engaged in a conversation with an attendant. His posture was relaxed and exuded casual arrogance, a stark contrast to the tension that gripped Candy and Houston. Lorenzo laughed at something the attendant said, clearly enjoying his role as the center of attention.

Candy's grip on the vial tightened as she watched Lorenzo. The plan was already in motion, and there was no turning back now. She could feel her heart pounding in her chest, each beat echoing the countdown to their fateful confrontation. She and Houston shared a moment of silent understanding, knowing that the next steps they took would irrevocably change the course of their lives. The tropical breeze rustled the leaves of the nearby palm trees, a stark reminder of the paradise they found themselves in and the dangerous game they were playing within it.

"Cheap fuck's probably trying to get a discount," Candy muttered under her breath, her disdain evident as she noticed Lorenzo was beginning to spend much more time than required. Houston twisted the key in the ignition, the truck's engine sputtering and groaning but refusing to catch. They shared a tense, fleeting smile, a momentary release of nervous energy, before Houston tried again. This time the engine moaned louder, but still, it didn't start.

"Not good," Houston said, his voice strained with frustration, the muscles in his jaw tightening.

Candy's eyes widened with growing anxiety as she glanced back at Lorenzo. "He's leaving," she announced, urgency creeping into her tone as she watched Lorenzo finish his transaction and move towards the jeeps.

Houston remained calm, his focus unwavering. He tried the ignition once more, and this time the engine roared to life with a deafening clatter. He quickly slammed the truck into gear, the vehicle lurching forward. Their progress was abruptly halted as a group of rowdy youths in an overloaded jeep skidded to a stop in front of them, blocking their path. The boys were laughing and shouting, oblivious to the tense situation they had just interrupted.

"FUCK!" Houston shouted, slamming on the brakes, his knuckles white as he gripped the steering wheel tightly. His eyes darted around, searching for a way out of the unexpected blockade.

Candy's panic was palpable, her voice rising in pitch. "Gotta go, gotta go, gotta go," she urged, her fingers drumming anxiously on the dashboard as she thought the road will be cleared.

Houston's hand shot under the sea with frustration clearly on his facet, emerging with a sleek automatic pistol. His expression was steely, determination etched into his features. But before he could take any drastic measures, Candy quickly grabbed his wrist, her grip firm and insistence. She shook her head vehemently, her eyes wide with warning. "No," she mouthed silently, nodding towards the front of the truck where the boys were still horsing around, oblivious to the tension inside the cab. She signaled for patience, her gaze steady and imploring.

Houston took a deep breath, his fingers reluctantly loosening around the weapon as he lowered it. His shoulders sagged slightly, the tension in his body easing just a fraction. Their eyes locked in a brief moment, a silent agreement passing between them. He placed the gun back under the seat, taking another deep breath to steady himself. The moment of panic had passed, replaced by a resolute calm as they waited for their path to clear.

Chapter Fifteen

Lorenzo's eyes lingered on Kelly, his gaze intense enough to undress her right there in the car. His stare was a deliberate violation, stripping away any semblance of comfort she might have found in the small space they shared. Kelly shifted uneasily in her seat, tugging at her clothes as if adjusting her outfit could shield her from his predatory look. The soft cotton of her top suddenly felt too thin, too revealing under his scrutiny. She kept her face neutral, projecting an innocence that belied the unease twisting in her stomach, but the slight tremor in her hands gave her away.

Lorenzo's lips curled into a knowing smile. He enjoyed watching her squirm, reveling in the power he held over her. Kelly was trying her best to maintain composure, but the way she fidgeted, straightening her skirt, and smoothing her blouse, only fueled his satisfaction. She acted like one who was trapped, both physically in the car and emotionally in his web, though she knew exactly what she was doing and what needed to be done. Her innocence, real or feigned, didn't matter to him, it was just another layer to peel away.

Kelly's eyes darted toward the window, searching for something to distract herself from Lorenzo's unwavering attention. She didn't dare meet his gaze, knowing that doing so would only invite more of his silent taunts. Instead, she focused on the world outside, where life continued as normal, unlike the simmering tension that filled the car. She hoped really badly to see Candy's car behind them, to show she was not alone in this.

Meanwhile, across town, Candy and Houston had been sitting in the pickup truck for what felt like an eternity. The waiting was wearing on them both, the air inside the cab thick with frustration and unspoken fears. Candy's hands gripped the steering wheel, knuckles white, as she stared ahead, trying to keep her anxiety at bay. Houston was beside her, equally tense, his eyes flicking between the side mirrors and the windshield, searching for any sign of movement.

The scenario had dragged on far longer than either of them had anticipated. What should have been a quick in-and-out operation had turned into an extended stakeout, and neither was pleased. They were losing precious time, and with it, the advantage they'd hoped to gain.

A flash of red and blue lights in the side mirror caught Houston's attention. He turned his head slightly to see a local police car pulling up behind the rowdy youths' jeep that had blocked their path earlier. The officer stepped out, smiling at the partying kids as if they were nothing more than harmless troublemakers.

"Let's just sit tight, okay?" Candy's voice was steady, but Houston could hear the strain beneath it. She was holding it together, but just barely.

"We're losing them," Houston muttered, frustration edging into his tone. His mind was racing, trying to calculate how much longer they could afford to wait before they missed their window of opportunity entirely.

"Well, if a cop sees me running around, that's not gonna help," Candy shot back, her voice sharp. She didn't need Houston reminding her of the stakes, they were all too clear. But the last thing she needed was to draw unwanted attention from law enforcement.

Houston let out a sigh, leaning back in his seat. "Your friend, your fiancé, your call," he said, the words dripping with resigned frustration. He hated feeling powerless, hated sitting there while time slipped away from them, but he knew Candy was right. They couldn't afford to make a move while the cop was on the scene.

Candy's eyes flicked to the rearview mirror, catching a glimpse of the officer laughing with the kids. "Shit!" she hissed under her breath. They were stuck, and there was nothing she could do about it.

The seconds ticked by each one stretching out into what felt like an eternity. The cop lingered by the jeep, clearly enjoying the interaction, oblivious to the tension simmering in the pickup truck behind him. Candy and Houston exchanged a look, a silent acknowledgment of the precarious position they were in. They were on the verge of losing everything they'd worked for, and all they could do was wait.

Finally, after what felt like hours, the cop gave the kids a friendly wave and walked back to his car. Houston sat up a little straighter, his hand hovering over the door handle, ready to spring into action the moment the coast was clear. But Candy held up a hand, signaling him to stay put. They couldn't afford to rush, not now.

The police car pulled away, its lights still flashing, and Candy let out a breath she didn't realize she'd been holding. "Okay," she said, her voice low and urgent. "We're clear."

Houston didn't need to be told twice. He reached for the gearshift, eyes locked on the road ahead. But just as he was about to throw the truck into the drive, a new complication arose, a group of pedestrians crossing the street, taking their time as if they had all the time in the world.

"Goddamn it!" Houston swore, slamming his hand on the dashboard. They were so close, yet still so far from making their move.

Candy gritted her teeth, her patience fraying. "Hold on," she said through clenched teeth, her eyes narrowing as she watched the group slowly make their way across the road. The moment they were clear, she'd ask Houston to gun it, consequences be damned.

Finally, the last pedestrian stepped onto the sidewalk, and Houston didn't hesitate. He slammed his foot on the gas, and the pickup lurched forward, tires squealing as they peeled out of their spot. Candy gripped the dashboard, bracing himself as they sped down the road, every second counting.

They had lost precious time, but they weren't out of the game yet. As they roared down the street, both Candy and Houston knew that the next few moments would be critical. They were running out of options, but they were not about to give up. Not now. Not ever.

***

The tension between him and Kelly grew as Lorenzo navigated the winding roads of the Cayman Islands. The sun cast long shadows across the tropical landscape, illuminating the dense foliage with a golden hue. Palm trees swayed gently in the breeze, and the scent of saltwater lingered in the air. But for Lorenzo, the serene beauty of the surroundings did nothing to quell the growing feeling gnawing at him.

Kelly had mentioned a spot, a secluded place where they could steal away for a private rendezvous. But as they drove, the road seemed to stretch endlessly, twisting and turning with no clear destination in sight. Lorenzo's grip on the steering wheel tightened, his knuckles turning white as he shot quick, annoyed glances at Kelly, who sat beside him in the passenger seat.

Kelly's demeanor was a mix of innocence and unease. She tugged at the hem of her dress, fidgeting under Lorenzo's intense gaze. Her fingers played nervously with a loose thread, her eyes darting around the car as if searching for something to anchor herself. The playful spark that usually danced in her eyes was dimmed, replaced by a cautious awareness of Lorenzo's growing impatience.

The silence between them was heavy, broken only by the occasional hum of the jeep's engine as it powered up yet another incline. Lorenzo's thoughts raced, his mind alternating between frustration and desire. He couldn't understand why finding this spot was so difficult. Kelly had been confident when she mentioned it, but now, her uncertainty seemed to mirror his own mounting doubts.

"Are you sure it's this way?" Lorenzo finally snapped, his voice cutting through the tension like a knife.

Kelly bit her lip, her gaze dropping to her lap. "I think so," she replied, though her tone lacked conviction. "I mean, it should be just up ahead."

"Should be?" Lorenzo echoed, his voice laced with sarcasm. "We've been driving for what feels like forever, Kelly. We don't have time to waste, especially with Candy waiting back in the room."

Kelly cringed slightly at the mention of Candy, her discomfort evident. She noticed that there was no longer any sign of her car and she had been trying to buy time all this while but still, her car was nowhere to be found.

"I'm sorry," Kelly murmured, her voice barely above a whisper. She sneaked a glance at Lorenzo, who was now glaring at the road ahead with a mix of frustration and determination. "I just thought... you'd like it. It's supposed to be really beautiful and secluded."

Lorenzo exhaled sharply, trying to temper his irritation. He didn't want to completely lose his cool, but the situation was testing his patience. He stole another glance at Kelly, noting how she tugged at her dress, her nervousness almost written all over her. Despite everything, there was something about her that kept him tethered, something that made him unable to fully let go of his desire to control the situation and her.

The jeep continued its journey up the winding road, the tires crunching over the gravel and loose stones. The road narrowed as they ascended a small hill, the foliage on either side growing denser, closing in around them. Lorenzo's eyes scanned the landscape, looking for any sign that they were nearing the elusive spot Kelly had mentioned. But all he saw were more trees, more underbrush, and no hint of the seclusion Kelly had promised.

Finally, as they crested the hill, Kelly's voice broke the silence. "There," she said, pointing ahead. "I think it's around here."

Lorenzo squinted in the direction she indicated, his eyes narrowing as he focused on a small, unmarked path that veered off from the main road. The path was barely visible, partially hidden by overgrown bushes and shaded by a canopy of palm trees. It didn't look like much, but something about it seemed to resonate with Kelly's earlier description.

Without a word, Lorenzo slowed the jeep and turned onto the path. The vehicle jolted as it left the paved road and rumbled over the uneven ground. Branches brushed against the sides of the jeep, and the undergrowth crunched beneath the tires. Kelly shifted in her seat, her earlier discomfort returning as they ventured deeper into the secluded area.

Lorenzo's jaw was set, his focus entirely on the path ahead. He wanted to see this spot, to finally put an end to the uncertainty that had been gnawing at him since they set out. Kelly, meanwhile, could feel the intensity of his gaze on her, even when he wasn't looking directly at her. It was as if he could see through her, stripping away any pretense of innocence she tried to maintain.

The path eventually widened into a small clearing, surrounded by towering palm trees and thick vegetation. The sunlight filtered through the leaves, casting dappled shadows on the ground. It was quiet, almost eerily so, the only sound being the distant chirping of birds and the soft rustle of the breeze through the trees.

She quickly told Lorenzo to stop at some point that she quickly needed to ease herself, she needed to stall a little bit more as she was sure she would lose her mind if Candy and Houston didn't appear on time. Also, she checked the stuff given to her by Candy if it was still with her.

His foot slammed down on the brake pedal, the jeep's tires screeching in protest as the vehicle skidded to a stop. Dust and gravel sprayed up from beneath the tires, creating a small cloud that momentarily obscured Kelly from view when she stepped out. When she was done the dust was very much still in the air. She didn't flinch, though; instead, she moved quickly, almost instinctively, toward the passenger side door. Her movements were fluid and practiced, as though she had been anticipating this exact moment.

Lorenzo barely gave her time to settle into the seat. As soon as she was in, he reached out, his large hand wrapping around the back of her head, fingers tangling in her hair. With a rough pull, he brought her closer, his lips crashing down on hers with a fierce intensity. There was nothing gentle about the kiss, it was raw, filled with the pent-up tension and frustration that had been building for days. Kelly responded, though her movements were less confident, more cautious. She could feel the heat radiating from his body, but her mind was elsewhere.

As their lips parted, Kelly's eyes darted toward the rearview mirror, her gaze scanning the road behind them. Her heart pounded in her chest, each beat a reminder of the anxiety that had been gnawing at her all day. The road behind them was empty, just as it had been before, but that did nothing to ease the knot of worry in her stomach.

"So, where's this place at?" Lorenzo's voice was low, almost a growl, as he leaned back into his seat. His eyes were still dark with the remnants of desire, but there was something else there too—a simmering impatience.

Kelly swallowed, her mind racing as she tried to piece together the directions. "Uh, I think there's a sign up ahead," she said, her voice betraying a hint of uncertainty. She glanced out the window, her fingers fiddling nervously with the hem of her shirt. The unease was evident in every movement.

Lorenzo wasn't convinced. He knew this wasn't just about finding the right turnoff. Something about Kelly's behavior was setting off alarm bells in his mind. "We could stop and ask for directions... Maybe get a drink?" Kelly suggested to her tone light, but Lorenzo wasn't buying it.

He shot her a sharp look, his frustration bubbling to the surface. "We ain't got time to get a drink, shit, do you realize Candy is back in our room?" His voice was harsh, cutting through the air like a knife.

Without waiting for a response, Lorenzo hit the brakes hard. The jeep skidded to a stop once again, tires biting into the gravel with loud screech. Kelly winced at the sudden motion, her hand instinctively grabbing the edge of her seat to steady herself. For a moment, neither of them spoke. The tension that had been building throughout the drive hung in the air, heavy and oppressive.

Lorenzo's eyes scanned the area around them, looking for something familiar. Then he spotted it: a small, weathered sign partially hidden by the overgrowth. He threw the jeep into reverse, the tires spinning momentarily before gripping the road and sending the vehicle backward. The sign came into clearer view as they drew closer, its faded letters spelling out

"CAYMAN RESERVE" in chipped paint. It was tilted slightly, as if it had been standing there, unnoticeable earlier

"This it?" Lorenzo asked, his voice low and measured.

Kelly nodded slowly, her earlier confidence now replaced with hesitant uncertainty. "Yeah... this is it."

Lorenzo didn't waste any time. He spun the steering wheel, wheeling the jeep around in a tight turn. The front of the vehicle clipped the sign, causing it to bend even further, the post groaning under the strain. Without a second thought, Lorenzo accelerated, the jeep lurching forward onto the narrow path leading into the reserve.

The road ahead was narrower, less maintained, with thick vegetation encroaching on either side. Palm fronds brushed against the side of the jeep as they sped along the path, the sound of their rustling mingling with the distant calls of tropical birds. The deeper they drove into the reserve, the more isolated they felt, as if they were leaving the world behind and entering a hidden enclave known only to a few.

Kelly's heart was still racing, but now it wasn't just fear that gripped her, it was a growing sense of foreboding. She glanced behind them again, but the road they had come from was quickly disappearing from view, swallowed up by the dense foliage. She couldn't shake the feeling that they were being followed, though there was no sign of another vehicle in sight.

Lorenzo, on the other hand, was focused on the path ahead. His hands were steady on the wheel, his jaw set in a determined line. The thought of Candy waiting back in their room gnawed at him, but it also fueled his urgency. He had no intention of letting things spiral out of control. This trip was supposed to be about getting things done, not getting distracted.

The jeep bounced over a small dip in the road, causing Kelly to grab the dashboard for support. She cast another quick glance at Lorenzo, but his expression was unreadable, his attention fully on the road.

They drove deeper into the reserve, the path winding and twisting like a labyrinth. Every turn seemed to take them further from the main road, deeper into the heart of the island. The trees grew taller, their thick canopies blocking out the sun in places, casting the path into shadow. The air grew denser, and more humid, as they ventured further, the smell of earth and vegetation filling their lungs.

As they rounded another bend, the road opened up slightly, revealing a clearing up ahead. Lorenzo slowed the jeep, his eyes narrowing as he scanned the area. There was no sign of anyone else, no other cars, no buildings, just the wild beauty of the reserve stretching out before them.

Kelly's tension didn't lessen, even as they slowed. If anything, it grew more intense. The further they drove, the more isolated they became, and the more she wondered when Candy and Houston would catch up.

Finally, Lorenzo brought the jeep to a stop at the edge of the clearing. He cut the engine, and for a moment, the only sound was the soft rustling of leaves in the breeze. The silence was heavy, filled with unspoken questions and unresolved tensions.

Lorenzo finally turned to look at her, his eyes dark and unreadable. He leaned back in his seat, studying her with an intensity that made Kelly squirm. His gaze seemed to strip away the layers she had tried to put up, leaving her feeling exposed and vulnerable.

"Alright," Lorenzo said, his voice calm but with an underlying edge. "We're here. Now what?"

Kelly hesitated, unsure of how to answer. "Let's just... take a moment," She suggested, her voice soft as she tried to mask her uncertainty. "It's beautiful here. We could... enjoy it together."

Lorenzo's gaze didn't waver. "Enjoy it together?" he echoed, the words laced with skepticism. He leaned closer, his presence filling the small space between them. "And what exactly are we supposed to enjoy, Kelly? This place? Or each other?"

The air was thick with the scent of earth and foliage, a sensory overload that would have enchanted most, but Lorenzo was focused on one thing only, the rendezvous spot Kelly had assured him would be perfect for their little escape.

The waterfall, not far from where they parked, provided a soothing, rhythmic backdrop. Lorenzo glanced over at Kelly. She was already stepping out of the jeep, moving with a nervous energy that hadn't gone unnoticed by him.

Kelly's figure stood out against the natural beauty of the environment, her light clothing contrasting with the rich greens and browns of the surrounding foliage. There was a hint of apprehension in the way she looked around, her eyes darting from one side of the clearing to the other, as though she were expecting something—though what, Lorenzo couldn't tell.

She walked a few paces ahead and laid out a blanket on the soft grass, glancing back at Lorenzo with a forced smile. The nervousness was still there, but she tried to hide it behind a playful facade. Lorenzo, however, wasn't in the mood for pretense. The journey to this secluded spot had been long and frustrating, and he was eager to get down to business.

He watched her for a moment longer, observing how she smoothed out the blanket and adjusted her clothes, before he stepped out of the jeep. The moment his boots hit the ground, he felt a surge of energy—an intensity that had been building up inside him since they left the main road. Without warning, he strode over to Kelly, his movements swift.

Before she could react, Lorenzo grabbed her from behind, his large hands gripping her shoulders. Kelly let out a small gasp as he roughly spun her around to face him, and without hesitation, he pulled her close, bending her backward slightly as his lips claimed hers in a deep, possessive kiss. It was a kiss that left no room for softness or hesitation—an assertion of dominance that communicated exactly what he wanted.

Kelly's initial surprise gave way to a hesitant response. She kissed him back, though with a cautious edge, as if unsure of where this was going. As Lorenzo's hands moved to her top, starting to lift it off her, Kelly placed her hands on his chest, gently pushing him back.

"Easy there," she murmured, her voice slightly breathless. "Let's not rush this. How about a drink?"

Lorenzo's dark eyes narrowed slightly, a mix of annoyance and desire flashing across his features. "I didn't come all the way up here to have a drink, ya know?" His voice was low and gravelly, laced with the frustration that had been simmering beneath the surface.

Kelly hesitated, sensing the tension in his tone. She knew she had to tread carefully, Lorenzo wasn't someone who liked to be teased or denied. But at the same time, she needed to maintain some control over the situation, to keep things from spiraling out of her grasp.

She stood up slowly, stepping out of Lorenzo's reach. With a coy smile, she reached for the hem of her top and, in one fluid motion, lifted it over her head, revealing a lacy, seductive bra beneath. The fabric clung to her skin, accentuating her curves in a way that was both enticing and provocative. She leaned down slightly, positioning herself so that her chest was just inches from Lorenzo's face. He instinctively tried to move closer, his lips parting slightly as if to touch her, but Kelly pulled back just enough to keep him at bay.

"I'll make us something," she said, her voice light and teasing. "You lose that shirt."

Lorenzo watched her with a dark, smoldering intensity, his eyes tracing every movement she made. He didn't respond verbally, but there was a challenge in his gaze that made it clear he wasn't playing games. He reached for the hem of his shirt and pulled it off, tossing it aside without a second thought. His muscular chest and arms were now fully exposed, the sunlight filtering through the trees casting highlights on his tanned skin.

Kelly turned away, her heart pounding in her chest. She could feel his eyes on her, burning with a desire that was as intense as it was dangerous. Her hands trembled slightly as she walked back to the jeep, reaching into the back seat where she had stashed a small cooler. As she did, she felt for the small vial she had hidden in her pocket earlier. Her fingers closed around it, and she pulled it out with a quick, furtive motion.

Stealing a glance over her shoulder, Kelly made sure Lorenzo wasn't watching too closely. His attention was still on her, but he seemed more interested in the show she was putting on than in what she was doing with her hands. Fighting to keep her nerves in check, Kelly uncapped the vial and emptied its contents into one of the plastic cups she had brought along. The powder dissolved almost instantly, blending with the liquid in the cup.

With a practiced motion, Kelly tore some mint leaves from a small sprig she had brought and sprinkled them into the cup over a few cubes of ice. She poured a shot of rum over the mixture, then filled the rest of the cup with soda, stirring it with her finger to blend the ingredients. The coolness of the ice contrasted with the heat of her nerves, and she briefly considered licking the liquid off her finger but stopped herself. Instead, she wiped her hand on her shorts, trying to calm the tremor that had started in her hands.

Kelly put on her best smile as she walked back to Lorenzo, holding out the drink. "Here you go, baby," she said, her voice soft and seductive, but with an underlying tension that she hoped he wouldn't notice.

Lorenzo took the cup from her but didn't immediately drink. Instead, he set it down on the ground beside the blanket, his gaze never leaving hers. "You know," he said, his voice low and gravelly, "this park thing ain't all that bad. Makes a motherfucker feel like Tarzan."

Kelly let out a small laugh, though it was more out of nerves than amusement. She raised her own cup, offering a toast. "How about a toast?" she suggested, trying to keep the mood light.

But Lorenzo wasn't interested in toasting. He was interested in her. Before she could raise her cup to her lips, he grabbed her, pulling her down into his lap. His hands roamed over her body, his lips finding their way to her chest. Kelly tensed slightly, her mind racing as she tried to stay in control of the situation. She knew she had to play along, at least for now.

As Lorenzo's hands moved to undress her further, Kelly reached down and started to unbuckle his belt. She slid it out from the loops of his jeans, holding it in front of her as if considering what to do next. She ran the length of the belt through her hands, a small smile playing on her lips as an idea formed in her mind.

She took Lorenzo's hand, trying to guide it toward the nearest tree. "Let's try something different," she suggested, her voice soft and coaxing. "How about I tie you up? You can be my Tarzan, and I'll be your Jane."

Lorenzo's eyes darkened with suspicion. He wasn't one to give up control easily, and the idea of being tied up didn't sit well with him. "What the fuck is this?" he demanded, his voice sharp.

Kelly forced herself to stay calm, to keep her voice light and playful. "Come on, it's just a game. If you won't try my mojito, I'll make you. It'll be fun."

But Lorenzo wasn't in the mood for games. He had been patient up until now, but his patience was wearing thin. The frustration that had been building up inside him since they arrived in the clearing was starting to boil over. He wasn't interested in being tied up or playing games, he was here for something much more straightforward.

"I ain't got time for games," Lorenzo growled, his tone leaving no room for argument.

Kelly swallowed hard, realizing that her plan was quickly unraveling. She had hoped to distract him, to keep him occupied long enough for the drink to take effect, but it was clear that Lorenzo wasn't going to be easily swayed. The tension between them was visible, a tightrope that she was precariously balancing on.

"There's always time for games," Kelly insisted, though her voice lacked the confidence it had before. She continued to try to wrap the belt around Lorenzo's wrist, but he wasn't cooperating. He was too focused on her, too intent on getting what he wanted.

The struggle between them intensified as Kelly tried to maintain control, but Lorenzo wasn't having it. His frustration reached its breaking point, and with a sudden burst of anger, he threw her off him, standing up abruptly.

Kelly landed hard on the blanket, her breath knocked out of her as she looked up at Lorenzo in shock. The anger in his eyes was unmistakable, a dangerous glint that made her heart race with fear.

"What the fuck is wrong with you, bitch?!" Lorenzo shouted, his voice echoing through the clearing.

Chapter Sixteen

Candy and Houston had finally managed to free themselves from the spot where they had been stuck for what felt like an eternity. The tension in the car was thick, both of them acutely aware of the precious time slipping away. The sun was beginning to dip below the horizon. The air inside the pickup truck was heavy with anticipation and unspoken concerns.

As they left the main road, the surroundings grew more secluded. The thick vegetation of the Cayman Islands seemed to close in around them, the once wide and smooth path now narrowed into a more rugged terrain. The road ahead forked into two distinct directions, each leading deeper into the dense wilderness. The decision now lay before them on deciding which route to take.

Candy's eyes darted between the two options. The signpost they had seen earlier, also noticed by Kelly and Lorenzo, had provided no clear guidance. She bit her lip, the weight of the situation pressing down on her. Calling Kelly now would be too risky as it could jeopardize the entire plan, and they were already running late.

"What do you think?" Candy finally asked, her voice tinged with urgency.

Houston gripped the steering wheel, his gaze shifting from one path to the other. "I'd say we go with the one that looks clearer," he suggested, nodding towards the road on the right. It was slightly wider, the ground more even, as if it had been traveling more frequently. "Seems like a safer bet."

Candy nodded, though the uncertainty gnawed at her. "Okay, let's go," she agreed, trying to keep her anxiety at bay. They couldn't afford any more delays.

Houston steered the truck down the right-hand path, the tires crunching over the gravel and dirt. For a moment, the tension in Candy's chest eased as they moved forward, but that relief was short-lived. A sudden jolt shook the vehicle, and the engine sputtered before dying completely. The truck lurched to a halt, and an ominous silence settled over them.

"Damn it," Houston muttered, pounding the steering wheel in frustration. He tried turning the key in the ignition again, but the engine only coughed weakly in response.

Candy's heart sank. They were now officially over thirty minutes late. Her mind raced with all the possible scenarios that could be unfolding. Was Kelly okay? Could she handle the situation on her own? What if something went wrong?

Different "what ifs" started crossing Candy's mind, each one more unsettling than the last. She could feel the panic rising, her thoughts spinning out of control. But before she could spiral any further, the engine roared back to life, jolting the truck forward.

Candy let out a breath she didn't realize she'd been holding, but her relief was tempered by something else. Out of the corner of her eye, she noticed Houston staring at her. It wasn't just a casual glance, there was something darker behind his gaze, a look she knew all too well. Lust, raw and unmistakable, was written all over his face.

As the truck picked up speed again, Houston turned to her with a grin that made Candy's skin crawl. It was a lousy, leering grin, the kind that made his intentions all too clear.

"You can't make me," Candy shot back, her voice cold and firm.

Houston chuckled, the sound low and suggestive. "It's not like we haven't done it in the car before," he said, his smirk widening. "Back in those days, remember?"

Candy narrowed her eyes at him, her patience wearing thin. "Just drive, Houston," she ordered, her tone leaving no room for argument.

For a moment, he looked like he might push further, but something in Candy's expression must have warned him off. He turned his attention back to the road, though the smirk didn't completely leave his face. Candy, however, was done with the conversation. She turned her gaze out the window, focusing on the passing trees and the fading light, trying to block out the discomfort by gnawing at her.

As they continued down the path, the road began to narrow once again, the vegetation encroaching from both sides. The clear, broad path they had chosen was now anything but, and Candy couldn't shake the feeling that they had made the wrong choice. But there was no turning back now. All they could do was press on and hope they reached their destination before it was too late.

***

Lorenzo's patience was wearing thin. The lush surroundings of the secluded spot, meant to be a perfect hideaway, now felt suffocating. The idea of a playful, romantic escape had turned into something else entirely. The tension in the air was thick, not the kind that led to teasing banter or lighthearted flirting, but a heavy, oppressive force pressing down on them both.

Kelly, sensing Lorenzo's frustration, had tried to keep things light, to delay what seemed inevitable. She'd attempted to steer them towards a more relaxed pace, hoping to extend the moment and perhaps change the direction of the encounter. She suggested the spiked drink, tried to distract him with a game, anything to make him drink, to keep him from diving straight into what he actually wanted. But it was clear to her now that Lorenzo wasn't interested in playing along.

"Look," Lorenzo growled, his voice edged with irritation, "I ain't about playin' here. You know why we're here, so what the fuck is your problem?"

Kelly hesitated, her hands trembling slightly as she reached for the drink she'd prepared earlier. "I...I...here, have a drink, baby," she stammered, her voice barely steady as she tried to calm the storm brewing in his eyes.

But Lorenzo wasn't having it. His hand shot out, slapping the cup from her grasp with a force that sent it flying. The drink spilled across the blanket, the liquid soaking into the fabric as the cup rolled away into the underbrush. The sharp crack of the slap reverberated in the air, a stark reminder of the shift in his mood.

"I didn't come up here for a drink!" he snapped, his tone final, leaving no room for argument or hesitation. The games were over.

In a swift, predatory movement, Lorenzo stood on the blanket, his body pinning Kelly's against the rough bark of the tree behind her. His hands were rough, urgent, as they tore at her clothes, pulling off her bra and ripping down her shorts with a force that left no doubt about his intentions. Kelly struggled instinctively, her body tensing as she tried to push him away, but Lorenzo was too strong, his grip too firm. She had felt this moment was coming, even though the reality of it was far more intense than she had anticipated. But she had hoped Candy would be there before it happened.

"Yea, now you're gonna see something more worthwhile," Lorenzo muttered, his voice a low, dangerous growl as he pressed her harder against the tree. The bark bit into her back, the rough surface scraping against her skin, but that discomfort was nothing compared to the pressure of Lorenzo's weight bearing down on her.

At that moment, something inside Kelly shifted. She stopped resisting, her body going still as she thought she could accept what was happening. A strange curiosity took hold, a desire to see what lay beyond this point of no return. She had pushed him to this when she thought he would consume the drink in no time, and now she wanted to experience it fully, to immerse herself in the raw, unfiltered intensity of Lorenzo's desire. Her resistance faded slightly, replaced by a different kind of tension, one that hummed just beneath the surface of her skin.

As Lorenzo pushed her legs apart forcefully, his hands rough and unyielding, Kelly's mind raced. This was far from the gentle, tender moments she had shared with Houston. This was something darker, something primal. And yet, as the initial shock wore off, she found herself responding to it, her body betraying her with a surge of adrenaline that quickened her pulse and sent a flush to her cheeks.

As Lorenzo's grip tightened, a sudden surge of fear coursed through Kelly's veins, igniting a desperate need to escape. Her initial surrender to the moment shattered, replaced by a frantic struggle as she tried to push Lorenzo off her with all the strength she could muster. Her hands pressed against his chest, her nails digging into his skin, but it was as if she were pushing against an immovable force. She kicked her legs, twisted her body, and thrashed beneath him, but it was futile. Lorenzo was just too strong, his weight and power overwhelming her every attempt to break free. Each frantic movement only seemed to fuel his determination, making her feel even more trapped and helpless beneath him.

Lorenzo slapped her hard across the face as he noticed her attempt to flee, a stinging blow that left her gasping. But instead of recoiling, Kelly found herself leaning into the sensation, her breath catching in her throat as a new kind of heat spread through her body. It was a twisted, conflicted response, but it was there, nonetheless.

He pushed her legs open wider with a lot more force than the previous, his hands bruising as he gripped her thighs. He yanked down his pants, the fabric rustling in the quiet of the forest, and positioned himself between her legs. The roughness of his actions, the sheer force of his presence, overwhelmed Kelly, leaving her no choice but to surrender to the moment.

And yet, despite the harshness, there was a part of her that welcomed it. The way Lorenzo took control, the way he commanded her body, stirred something deep within her. It was wrong, twisted even, but it was undeniably powerful. The pain, the pleasure, the confusion—it all blurred together until she could no longer tell where one ended and the other began.

Lorenzo's movements were relentless, driven by an intensity that bordered on feral. He took her with a force that left her breathless, each thrust sending shockwaves through her body. The world around them faded, the only thing that mattered was the raw, unbridled connection between them.

The rough bark of the tree dug into her back, but the pain only heightened the experience, blending in a way that left her reeling.

Lorenzo's pace quickened, his breath coming in ragged gasps as he neared the edge, each movement more frantic and desperate than the last. He was completely lost in the moment, driven by a primal need that consumed him entirely, leaving no room for thought, reason, or the awareness of Kelly's growing fear. All that mattered to him was the heat of her body beneath him, the way her reluctant form was trapped under his control, and the delusion that she was yielding to his every move. But for Kelly, this was a nightmare she couldn't escape. She didn't want any of it—her mind was racing, her thoughts filled with horror and despair. Every touch, every forceful thrust, only deepened her terror. Silently, she prayed, her heart pleading for Candy and Houston to burst in and save her from this torment. But the minutes dragged on, and no one came to her rescue. Her whispered prayers echoed unanswered as she remained trapped under Lorenzo, her hope fading with every passing second.

Fighting back with every ounce of strength she could muster, Kelly found herself powerless against his relentless force. Despite her desperate attempts to resist, he overpowered her, his actions driven by a violent intensity that left her breathless and terrified. Her struggles were in vain as he took her with a brutal and unyielding force, his every move a stark contrast to the stillness of the surrounding nature, which stood as a silent and indifferent witness to the harrowing scene unfolding under its watch. The trees, the wind, and the distant calls of wildlife remained eerily quiet, offering no comfort or refuge as Kelly was forced to endure the brutality of Lorenzo's assault.

He leaned back against the rough bark of the towering tree when he was through, a self-satisfied smile playing on his lips. The island around them buzzed with the sounds of nature. But at this moment, all of that seemed like background noise to Lorenzo, who was basking in the afterglow of what had just transpired. He stretched his legs out in front of him, crossing one ankle over the other, and tilted his head back to stare up at the sky, which was barely visible through the thick tangle of leaves and vines overhead.

Kelly lay beside him on the ground, curling her body into a tight ball. Her arms were wrapped around her knees, which were drawn up to her chest, and she stared straight ahead with wide, unblinking eyes. Her breathing was shallow and rapid, each breath coming out in short, almost gasping spurts. Her skin was pale, a stark contrast to the dark earth beneath her, and a thin sheen of sweat glistened on her forehead. She felt cold, despite the warmth of the tropical air, and she shivered slightly as a gentle breeze rustled the leaves above them.

Lorenzo, oblivious to her distress, reached over and gave her a light poke with his finger, aiming for her side in an attempt to get her attention. When she didn't respond, he poked her again, a little harder this time, his smile fading slightly as he glanced over at her. "Hey," he said, his voice carrying a tone of casual indifference. "What's the matter?" He waited for her to say something, but she remained silent, her gaze still fixed on some distant point in front of her. She didn't even seem to notice him.

A flicker of irritation crossed Lorenzo's face as he shifted his weight slightly, trying to make himself more comfortable against the sculpture behind him. "Ah, Christ, come on," he muttered, more to himself than to her. "Stop acting like you didn't enjoy it, okay?" His words were edged with impatience, as though he couldn't understand why she wasn't reacting as he expected her to.

He stared at her for a moment longer, his brow furrowing in confusion. Kelly's blank expression unnerved him. Lorenzo shook his head, pushing the thought aside. Maybe she was just tired or pretending so he wouldn't know she enjoyed it as well. With a grunt, he pushed himself to his feet, brushing off his pants as he did so. The ground was damp beneath him, and he could feel the moisture soaking into the fabric of his jeans. He grimaced slightly, then turned his attention back to Kelly, who hadn't moved an inch. He watched her for a moment, then shrugged and began walking toward the jeep, which was parked a short distance away, just beyond the edge of the clearing.

***

As the pickup truck rumbled along the winding road, Candy's eyes were glued to the scenery outside, every nerve in her body taut with tension. The tropical landscape of the Cayman Islands blurred past the windows, but Candy's mind was too preoccupied to appreciate the beauty of the island. She barely noticed the swaying palm trees or the vivid bursts of colorful flowers that dotted the roadside. All she could think about was the clock ticking away and the pressure mounting as the minutes slipped by. Houston, seated beside her, kept his focus on the road ahead, his grip on the steering wheel firm but relaxed in contrast to Candy's visible anxiety.

"Shit!" Candy cursed under her breath, her voice tinged with frustration and worry. Her eyes darted back and forth, scanning the road as if searching for something, anything, that could lead them to their destination. They had already been driving for far too long, and with every passing minute, Candy's sense of urgency grew.

Houston glanced at her, his expression calm, but his eyes betrayed a flicker of concern. He knew they were running out of time. "We'll find them," he said in a low, reassuring tone, though the uncertainty in his voice was unmistakable. Candy's tension was contagious, and even though Houston tried to maintain a facade of confidence, the truth was, he was just as anxious as she was even though he didn't know why he was.

Candy didn't respond to Houston's attempt at comfort. Her attention was fully consumed by the task at hand. Her eyes flicked between the road ahead and the dense foliage on either side, searching desperately for any sign that they were on the right path. The road stretched out before them, seemingly endless, and for a moment, Candy feared they had gone too far away from the planned spot. She opened her mouth to say something, perhaps to suggest turning back, when something caught her eye.

"There, there, stop!" Candy's voice cut through the air, sharp and commanding. She pointed frantically at something just barely visible ahead. It was a sign, bent over and almost hidden by the thick undergrowth that bordered the road. The letters were partially obscured by the foliage, but Candy didn't need to read them to know this was it.

Houston reacted instantly to her command, slamming on the brakes. The tires screeched against the asphalt, and the truck lurched violently as it came to an abrupt halt. Candy braced herself against the dashboard, her heart pounding in her chest. For a moment, everything was still, the roar of the engine replaced by the faint rustling of leaves in the breeze. The sudden stop sent a cloud of dust swirling around the truck, momentarily blocking their view.

As the dust settled, Candy and Houston could clearly see the sign Candy had pointed out. It was bent over, its once straight post now leaning precariously to one side as if it had been knocked down recently. The sign had clearly seen better days, its paint faded and chipped, but it was still legible. Candy squinted at it, trying to make out the words as Houston maneuvered the truck closer.

"This has to be it," Candy muttered to herself, her voice barely audible over the sound of the truck's engine. Her mind raced, trying to remember if Kelly had mentioned anything about a sign or a turnoff. She wasn't sure any longer even though she typically planned this with Kelly, but there was something about this place that felt right—or at least, it felt like the only option they had left.

Houston didn't wait for further confirmation. With a swift turn of the wheel, he spun the truck around and steered it down the narrow side road that branched off from the main one. The tires crunched over loose gravel as they left the asphalt behind and ventured onto the uneven terrain of the side road.

The truck bounced and jolted over the bumpy ground, making the ride uncomfortable and slow. Candy gripped the edge of her seat, her knuckles turning white as she held on tightly. Every jolt sent a fresh wave of anxiety through her, but she forced herself to stay focused. There was no turning back now.

"Are you sure this is the road we drafted in our?" Houston asked, his voice betraying a hint of doubt as he navigated the rough terrain. The truck's headlights illuminated the path ahead, but the dense foliage made it difficult to see far.

Candy hesitated for a moment, biting her lip as she considered his question. "I don't know," she admitted finally, her voice tinged with uncertainty. "But we don't have much choice. We're running out of time." She didn't need to say more, Houston knew as well as she did what was at stake.

They continued down the narrow path, the tension in the air thickening with every passing second. The sounds of the island's nature echoed through the environment, creating a symphony of distant calls and rustling leaves, but inside the truck, the silence between Candy and Houston was loud.

Candy kept her eyes trained on the path ahead, her mind racing with possibilities. What if they were too late? What if they were heading in the wrong direction? The thought of Kelly waiting for them, alone and vulnerable, filled her with dread alongside a dead man. Not even an ordinary man, but a football celebrity. She couldn't shake the feeling that they were running out of time, that every second counted, and that they were already too late.

Finally, after what felt like an eternity, the narrow path began to widen slightly, opening up into a small clearing. The environment loomed all around them, but the road here was more defined as if it had been used more frequently. Candy scanned the area, searching for any sign that they were in the right place.

"Is this it?" Houston asked, slowing the truck to a crawl as they entered the clearing. He looked around, trying to spot anything that might give them a clue as the whole scenario had just turned over, it was not going as planned. Candy squinted, her eyes scanning for any hint of movement in the surrounding but the Island was totally deserted. "I think so," she said uncertainly. "But I don't see anything. Maybe we're still too far off."

Her unease deepened as they drove further down the isolated path. The silence of the island, usually a source of peace, now felt oppressive, like a weight pressing down on her chest. She began to regret their decision to carry out their plan during this time of year, a time when the island was nearly deserted. Candy had meticulously chosen this period, knowing that visitors were rare, hoping it would give them the privacy they needed. But now, that very isolation was turning against them.

"If there were more people around, we could've just asked for directions," Candy thought, biting her lip as the realization sank in. The caretakers of the area were known to be scarce, only showing up when called upon through the island's customer care service. But making that call was out of the question as it could draw unwanted attention and raise suspicions. They were on their own, and every decision felt like it carried the weight of their entire plan.

Her thoughts were interrupted when she suddenly caught sight of something familiar through the dense secluded area below. A vehicle, partially obscured by the foliage, was parked just off the road. Candy's heart skipped a beat as recognition set in, it was the same vehicle Kelly and Lorenzo had taken. The sight of it sent a jolt of contentment through her. She grabbed Houston's arm, her voice urgent. "Stop the truck, now!"

Houston's reaction was immediate. He hit the brakes, bringing the truck to a halt. The vehicle skidded slightly on the gravel, coming to rest at an angle that gave them a clear view of the road ahead. Candy's pulse quickened as she opened the door and stepped out, motioning for Houston to follow her. They moved quietly, their footsteps barely making a sound on the soft earth as they approached the parked vehicle.

As they neared, Candy's anxiety grew. Something felt off, a sense of foreboding that she couldn't shake. Her eyes darted around, scanning the area for any sign of Kelly or Lorenzo. But the closer they got, the more her fear turned to dread. The vehicle was abandoned, its doors slightly ajar as if someone had left in a hurry. The air around them was thick with the scent of damp earth and something else, something metallic that made Candy's stomach churn.

Rounding the side of Lorenzo's parked vehicle, they stopped in their tracks. What they saw made Candy's blood run cold. There, on the ground, was Kelly, her clothes stained with blood, kneeling with her face down. The sight was like a punch to the gut, leaving Candy momentarily paralyzed with shock.

"No... no, no, no..." Candy whispered, her voice trembling as she took a step forward. Houston remained silent, his expression unreadable as he stared at the scene before them. Candy's mind raced, trying to process what she was seeing. Kelly's posture was one of defeat, her body slumped forward as if she had been abandoned by every ounce of strength. The blood on her clothes told a story that Candy didn't want to hear, a story of violence and desperation.

Candy's breath hitched as she stood beside Kelly, reaching out with trembling hands. "Kelly," she called softly, hoping for any sign of life, any indication that her girl was still with them. But Kelly didn't move, her body eerily still. Candy's heart pounded in her chest, a sickening rhythm that echoed the fear clawing at her insides.

Houston stood far away from the scene, his face grim. He didn't say a word, but Candy could feel his tension, the way his muscles were coiled like a spring ready to snap. The isolation of the island, once a strategic advantage, now felt like a trap, leaving them vulnerable and with nowhere to turn.

Her mind raced with the implications. How had this happened? What had gone wrong? And most importantly, where was Lorenzo? She scanned the area again, her eyes darting back to the vehicle and then to the surroundings. The Island was thick, its shadows hiding whatever secrets lay within.

Chapter Seventeen

Just a few minutes ago, Lorenzo had stood up and headed over to the jeep, his frustration and anger were visible as he turned his back on Kelly. Around them, nature seemed

to hold its breath, the stillness of the Island a contrast to the turmoil brewing within. Kelly watched him go, her body tense and her mind racing. Every step he took away from her felt like a countdown, the seconds ticking by as she weighed her options, her fear and anger battling for control.

Lorenzo's pace was deliberate, each footfall heavy with the weight of his intentions. But as he approached the jeep, his back turned to her, something inside Kelly snapped. The fear that had been simmering beneath the surface erupted into a violent resolve, a desperate need to take control of the situation before it spiraled completely out of her grasp.

Without thinking, Kelly lunged for the nearest object she could find, which was a thick branch that had fallen from one of the towering trees surrounding them. Her fingers wrapped around the rough bark, the texture digging into her skin as she lifted it with trembling hands. She barely recognized herself in that moment, driven by a primal instinct to protect herself, to finish her mission at any cost.

Lorenzo reached the jeep, oblivious to the danger behind him, his mind too focused on his own anger and frustration to notice the shift in the air. But as he reached for the door handle, Kelly moved. Her body propelled by a surge of adrenaline, she swung the branch with all the strength she could muster. The branch arced through the air in a wide, deadly swing, connecting with the back of Lorenzo's head with a sickening thud.

He staggered, his hand reflexively going to the back of his head as he dropped to one knee. He looked down at his hand, now slick with blood, and then back up at Kelly, shock and disbelief flooding his features. He couldn't believe what had just happened, couldn't believe that she had dared to strike him.

"You fucking bitch," he spat, his voice dripping with venom as he struggled to comprehend the betrayal.

But Kelly didn't hesitate. There was no room for doubt, no time for second-guessing. She raised the branch again, her breath coming in ragged gasps, her heart pounding in her chest like a war drum. The branch came down with brutal force, connecting with Lorenzo's head once more, driving him onto his back.

His body hit the ground hard, his vision blurring as the pain exploded through his skull. The tall buildings, the Island nature around him spun, the trees and the sky merging into a dizzying whirl of color and light. But before he could gather his thoughts, before he could even attempt to get back up, Kelly was on him again. She stood over him, the branch held high above her head, her eyes wild with fear and determination.

There was no hesitation this time, no pause to consider the consequences. Kelly brought the branch down again, and again, each blow landing with a sickening thud, the impact rever- berating through her arms and down to her core. Lorenzo's body convulsed with each strike, his hands flailing weakly in an attempt to defend himself, but it was no use. Kelly was relentless, her desperation fueling her strength as she fought to end this once and for all.

The environment around them remained eerily silent, as if the world itself was holding its breath, waiting for the outcome. The only sounds were the dull thud of the branch against flesh and bone, and Kelly's ragged breathing as she poured every ounce of her being into the attack.

Finally, when her arms could no longer lift the branch, when her body was trembling from exhaustion and the weight of what she had just done, she let the branch slip from her grasp. It fell to the ground beside Lorenzo's motionless body, the blood- soaked wood, a stark reminder of the violence that had just taken place.

She stumbled back, her legs barely holding her up as the adrenaline began to fade, leaving behind a cold, hollow emptiness. Her breath came in short, shallow gasps, her chest heaving with the effort. The wild look in her eyes slowly began to fade, replaced by a dawning horror at what she had just done.

Kelly's hands were shaking uncontrollably, her fingers still stained with Lorenzo's blood. She stared at them, as if trying to convince herself that this wasn't real, that this hadn't just happened. But the evidence was all around her, the blood on her hands, the lifeless body lying at her feet.

She took a few shaky steps backward, her legs finally giving up as she dropped to her knees. The reality of what she had just done crashed over her like a wave, threatening to drown her in guilt and fear. She had killed him. Lorenzo was dead, and she had been the one to end his life.

The weight of that realization was crushing, and for a long moment, Kelly could do nothing but stare blankly ahead, her mind numb to everything around her. She had acted out of desperation, out of a primal need to survive, but now that the immediate danger had passed, all she was left with was the crushing guilt and the knowledge that she could never take this back.

As she knelt there, the cold earth beneath her, Kelly began to regret everything that had led them to this moment. She regretted agreeing to come to this godforsaken island, to carry out this reckless plan at a time when no one else would be around, most especially the ones she planned the whole thing alongside.

Her mind raced with the possibilities, the what ifs that now seemed pointless to consider. If only there had been someone else on the island, someone who could have intervened, someone who could have stopped this before it had gone too far. But there was no one, and now, she was left to deal with the aftermath on her own.

It was at this moment that Candy arrived at the scene. Her heart pounded in her chest, each beat a frantic drum as she pushed through the underbrush. She was so focused on the urgency of the situation that she failed to notice the subtle signs of chaos unfolding before her. The bloodstained ground and the eerie silence of the forest seemed to close in around her as she approached.

Candy's gaze swept over the area, her eyes searching for clues, for any hint of what had happened. It was then that she spotted Kelly, kneeling on the ground, her body glued to the spot she was kneeling and her face down. Kelly's clothes were smeared with dark, splotchy stains, the blood stark against the fabric. The sight was enough to stop Candy in her tracks, her breath catching in her throat.

Kelly, overwhelmed by her own distress, had not even noticed the presence of the vehicle nor Candy's arrival. Her mind was trapped in a state of numb shock, and she was kneeling on a blanket, a piece of fabric that Lorenzo had used earlier. The blanket was now draped over Lorenzo's head and wrapped around him to the toe, concealing the horrifying truth of what lay beneath.

Candy's heart raced as she saw the bloodied state of Kelly. She was immediately struck by the horrific realization that something had gone terribly wrong. She moved closer, her eyes scanning the scene for more details, but her view was obscured by the blanket. The ghastly sight of Kelly's condition was enough to make her stomach churn, but she still couldn't see Lorenzo's body lying beneath the blanket.

Houston, who had been trailing behind her, decided to move closer to the scene. His eyes fell upon the blanket, and he instinctively called out, his voice a strained whisper cutting through the oppressive silence.

"What's a blanket doing here?" Houston asked, his tone edged with concern and confusion.

Candy's response was laced with a mixture of dread and uncertainty. "I don't think Kelly is conscious. I mean, look at her, she's completely covered in blood."

Houston, moving with caution, bent over to examine Kelly's

face. He gently lifted the tip of her face to get a better view, his eyes widening as he took in sight before him. Kelly's face was pale and her eyes were wide open, but they seemed vacant, lost in a state of shock.

"It looks like she's in shock," Houston said, his voice barely more than a murmur, as he straightened up and turned to Candy. His own shock was evident in the way his hands trembled slightly.

"What the hell really happened here?" Candy asked, her voice breaking as she struggled to comprehend the gravity of the situation.

Houston's response was cut off by his own gasp of horror as he pulled the blanket off the heap on the ground. The sight that greeted him made his blood run cold. The blanket, now thrown aside, revealed Lorenzo's lifeless body sprawled on the Island floor, blood pooling around him in dark, menacing stains. Houston's face contorted with disbelief and horror.

"Holy Christ," Houston exclaimed, his voice choking with shock.

Candy, too, was struck speechless. Her mind raced, struggling to piece together the fragments of what had just happened. She had hoped for answers, for some semblance of clarity, but all she found was the chilling evidence of violence and despair.

Desperate to understand, Candy dropped to her knees beside Kelly, grabbing her shoulders and shaking her gently. "Kelly, what the hell happened?" she demanded, her voice a mixture of urgency and frustration. "You need to tell me."

Both Candy and Houston were now fully confronted by the gruesome reality before them. The serene, almost idyllic setting seemed to mock the horror of the scene, the stark contrast heightening their sense of disorientation. Candy's hands shook as she tried to process the sight, her mind grappling with the enormity of the tragedy that had unfolded.

For a moment, everything seemed to stand still, the reality of what they were seeing too horrifying to fully comprehend.

Candy felt a cold chill run down her spine, her mind struggling to process the scene before her. This was not what they had expected, not what they had planned for. Everything had gone horribly, tragically wrong.

Houston's voice finally broke the silence, cutting through the thick tension in the air. "We're fucked," he muttered, the words slipping out before he could fully grasp their meaning.

Candy turned to him, moving a lot closer, her face pale but her eyes hard with determination as she fully got a grip of herself and emotions as a whole. "It's fine," she said, the words coming out more forceful than she intended. She was trying to convince herself as much as she was trying to convince him. "We can fix this. We just need to think."

Houston shook his head, his gaze locked on Lorenzo's lifeless body. The blood, dark and still wet, glistened in the setting sunlight, a grim reminder of the brutality that had just occurred. "She beat the shit out of him," Houston said, his voice heavy with disbelief. "It doesn't look like an accident."

Candy's mind raced, searching for a solution, a way out of this nightmare. "It will," she said, more to herself than to Houston. "Don't forget he's about to roll down a fucking mountain."

Houston's eyes widened as the implication of her words sank in. "What exactly do we say happened?" he asked, his voice barely above a whisper.

Candy's expression hardened as she met his gaze. "Lorenzo happened," she said simply. There was no need to explain further. The brutality of what had just occurred was evident, and there was no turning back now. "Get him in the jeep. I'll check on Kelly."

Candy moved away, her steps deliberate, but her mind was still reeling. She couldn't afford to lose control, not now. They had to get out of this, and they had to do it quickly. As she approached Kelly, who was still kneeling on the ground, lost in her own world of shock, Candy felt a pang of something that she hadn't allowed herself to feel before—pity.

Houston, meanwhile, looked down at Lorenzo's bloody body with a mixture of revulsion and grim resignation. There was no dignity in death, not like this. Lorenzo's face, once full of life and arrogance, was now a lifeless mask, blood seeping from the deep gashes Kelly had inflicted. Houston crouched down, hesitating for just a moment before reaching out to grab Lorenzo by the shoulders.

"Tough luck, bubba," Houston muttered under his breath, the words more for himself than for Lorenzo. "Slave to the wand, die by the wand, that's what my Pops always told me." The old saying seemed bitterly ironic now, a hollow echo of wisdom that felt out of place in the face of such raw violence. Houston paused, his mind wandering back to his father's voice, the lessons he had tried to impart, before shaking his head and pushing the thoughts away.

With a grunt, he began the grim task of dragging Lorenzo's body towards the rental Jeep's truck. The dead weight was heavier than he expected, the resistance of the lifeless form against the ground only adding to the difficulty. Blood smeared across the ground, leaving a trail that Houston tried not to look at, tried not to think about. Every movement felt laborious, as if the air itself had thickened, resisting his every effort.

As Houston struggled with Lorenzo's body, Candy knelt beside Kelly. The sight of her friend, bloodied and dazed, was a jarring contrast to the Kelly she knew. This was not the confident, sharp-tongued woman who she had planned the whole event with. This was someone else, someone broken. Candy gently reached out, placing a hand on Kelly's shoulder, trying to draw her attention.

"Kelly," Candy said softly, her voice laced with concern. "Kelly, can you hear me?"

Kelly's eyes slowly focused, blinking as if coming out of a trance. She looked at Candy, but there was no recognition in her gaze, only a blank, haunted stare.

"Kelly, you're in shock," Candy said, her voice steady despite the panic rising in her chest. "We need to get you out of here."

Kelly didn't respond, her body stiff and unyielding. Candy bit her lip, trying to hold back the frustration that was bubbling up inside her. This was not the time for emotions, not the time for weakness. She needed to stay strong, for both of them.

In the background, Candy could hear Houston grunting as he finally managed to heave Lorenzo's body into the back of the jeep. The sickening thud of the corpse hitting the metal floor sent a shiver down her spine, but she forced herself to focus on Kelly.

Candy shook her head, trying to clear the fog of panic that threatened to overwhelm her. She had to think clearly and had to act quickly. "What the hell happened?" she whispered, the question directed more at herself than anyone else.

***

Kelly sat in the passenger seat of the pickup truck, her body trembling as she stared blankly ahead, lost in the chaotic storm of emotions swirling within her. Her usually sharp, calculating mind felt numb, overtaken by the trauma of what had just occurred. The deserted island outside, with its dense greenery above the sand, seemed to close in on her, making it harder to breathe, harder to think. Everything felt surreal, like a twisted dream she couldn't wake up from.

Candy, sitting next to her, watched Kelly with concern. She could see the shock written all over her friend's face, the haunted look in her eyes. She knew that Kelly was trying to process the horror of what she had done, the violence she had unleashed in that desperate moment. Candy reached out, wrapping an arm around Kelly's shoulders, offering a semblance of comfort in this nightmarish situation.

"You, okay?" Candy asked softly, her voice tinged with worry. She knew it was a loaded question, one that had no easy answer, but she needed to keep Kelly grounded, to pull her back from the edge.

Kelly blinked, her gaze shifting slightly, but she didn't look at Candy. Instead, she continued to stare ahead, her mind replaying the gruesome scene over and over. "Are you serious?" Kelly finally replied, her voice flat, almost hollow. It was clear that she was still in shock, her emotions buried beneath the weight of what had just happened.

Candy bit her lip, trying to maintain her composure. She knew they couldn't afford to fall apart now. They had to keep moving, had to get away from this place before the reality of their situation caught up with them. "Kelly, we have to get going," Candy urged gently but firmly. "It's not smart to be hanging around here."

She nodded slowly, her movements mechanically, as if she were on autopilot. "I know," she murmured, her voice barely audible. "I... I can't believe..." Her voice trailed off, the words she wanted to say lost in the fog of her mind.

Candy tightened her grip on Kelly's shoulder, trying to reassure her. "He didn't give you a choice," she said firmly, her voice filled with conviction. "You did what you had to do." But even as she said the words, Candy couldn't help but feel the weight of their truth. Lorenzo would have died very easily if only he had taken the drink, he pushed Kelly to the brink, forcing her hand in the most brutal way possible.

Before Kelly could respond, Houston appeared outside the pickup truck, his face grim and determined. He had been busy setting things in motion, ensuring that they covered their tracks as best they could. He knew the stakes were high, and there was no room for error. "Ready," he said curtly, signaling that it was time to move.

Candy gave Kelly's shoulder a final squeeze before exiting the pickup. She didn't say anything, but the look she gave Kelly was filled with silence. As she stepped out of the truck, Candy's expression hardened, her focus shifting to the task at hand. She walked towards the jeep where Lorenzo's body slumped in the driver's seat, his head resting awkwardly against the steering wheel, a macabre reminder of the violence that had transpired.

Candy stopped a few feet away from the jeep, staring at the lifeless form of her former fiancé. The disdain she felt for him was clear, a bitter taste in her mouth. This man, who had once been a significant part of her life, had become a twisted reflection of everything she despised. "See you on the other side," Candy muttered under her breath, her words filled with a cold finality. There was no love lost between them, only a deep, simmering resentment that had now reached its inevitable conclusion.

With a deep breath, Candy turned on her heel and headed back to the pickup truck, her mind already shifting to the next step in their plan. Houston, meanwhile, approached the jeep with a grim sense of purpose. He held a rag in his hand, ready to execute the final part of their cover-up. As he reached the vehicle, Houston glanced down at Lorenzo's lifeless body, a fleeting look of contempt crossing his features. Without wasting any time, he reached into the jeep, starting the engine with a practiced ease. The sound of the engine rumbling to life was unnervingly normal, as if it were just another day, just another drive.

Houston then lifted Lorenzo's limp leg, placing it on the clutch as he shifted the jeep into gear. The motion was precise, calculated, as Houston worked to ensure that everything would appear as an unfortunate accident. He took one last look back at Candy and Kelly, who were watching from the pickup, before lifting Lorenzo's leg off the clutch. The jeep lurched forward, its tires crunching over the underbrush as it sped towards the edge of the cliff.

Candy and Kelly watched in tense silence as the jeep sped toward its final destination. The vehicle crashed through a patch of bushes, scattering debris before it hit a series of rocky outcrops along the coastal area. The jeep jolted violently, its metal scraping against the rugged terrain. As it skidded off the last of the rocks, it plunged over the edge of a cliff, not too high but enough to send a shiver down their spines.

Houston walked toward the edge, peering down into the darkness below. He waited, his breath held, for the inevitable sound that would signal the end of this part of their nightmare. And then it came—a massive explosion that erupted into the night, sending a fireball shooting up into the sky. The flames flickered against the backdrop of the night, a stark reminder of life that had just been extinguished. The jeep was gone, reduced to nothing but a smoldering wreckage far below.

Satisfied, he turned away from the edge and began walking back to the pickup. The heat from the explosion warmed his back as he moved, but he didn't look back. There was nothing left to see, nothing that he wanted to remember. As he approached the truck, Houston could see the worry etched into Candy's face, the fear that still gripped Kelly's features.

"Hard part's over, ladies," Houston said as he climbed into the driver's seat. He could see the doubt in Kelly's eyes, the lingering fear that this nightmare was far from over.

Kelly shook her head, her voice trembling as she spoke. "It doesn't feel that way," she admitted, her gaze dropping to her hands, which were still stained with blood. The reality of what she had done, of what they had all done, was sinking in, and it felt like a weight she would never be able to lift.

Houston didn't have a response for that. But he also knew that they couldn't afford to dwell on it now. They had to keep moving, had to put as much distance between themselves and this place as possible. Without another word, Houston backed up the pickup truck, the tires kicking up dirt as they reversed onto the road.

Candy glanced at Kelly, her heart heavy with worry. She could see the toll this was taking on her friend, but there was nothing she could do to make it better.

Chapter Eighteen

The streets were alive with the hum of activity, but towering above it all was a sleek, modern high-rise, the headquarters of a powerful and successful insurance company. Its gleaming glass façade reflected the urban landscape, a fortress of steel and glass that dominated the skyline, exuding an air of authority and impenetrable success.

A taxi pulled up smoothly to the curb in front of the building, its engine idling softly as it came to a halt. The door swung open, and a man stepped out, his presence immediately commanding attention. He wore a long, dark coat that brushed the ground as he moved, the fabric catching the light in subtle waves. His figure was tall and imposing, shoulders squared with the quiet confidence of someone who knew exactly who he was and what he was capable of.

His face was chiseled and stern, with sharp, angular features that hinted at a life lived on the edge. There was something predatory in his gaze, a piercing intensity that gave him the look of a wolf among sheep. His eyes, a cold shade of steel, scanned his surroundings with a calculated precision, missing nothing and revealing nothing in return. He was a man who had seen much and trusted little.

Pausing for a moment, he tilted his head back slightly, allowing his gaze to travel up the towering height of the high-rise. The building loomed above him, a symbol of power and wealth, but the man's expression remained unreadable. He was not impressed, nor was he intimidated. This was just another structure, another place where deals were made and lives were altered. And today, it would be the site of something far more significant.

With a deliberate motion, he reached into the inner pocket of his coat and pulled out a slim silver case. Flipping it open with a practiced flick of his thumb, he extracted a single cigarette, placing it between his lips with the ease of long habit. His other hand retrieved a lighter, the metallic click echoing softly in the late afternoon air as the flame flared to life. He cupped the lighter to his face, shielding the flame from the slight breeze as he lit the cigarette, inhaling deeply.

The tip of the cigarette glowed a bright orange as he took his first drag, the smoke curling up around his face like a veil. He exhaled slowly, the smoke drifting lazily into the air, blending with the city's constant swirl of activity. For a brief moment, he simply stood there, cigarette in hand, surveying the world around him. The pedestrians who hurried past, the cars that zipped by on the busy street, the office workers scurrying in and out of the building—

none of it escaped his notice.

But his attention was not on these minor details for long. He had come here with a purpose, and it was time to set things in motion. He flicked the cigarette butt onto the pavement, grinding it under the heel of his polished shoe with a final, decisive twist. Then, with one last glance at the high-rise, he adjusted the collar of his coat and began to move.

His steps were measured, purposeful, each one carrying him closer to the entrance of the building. The glass doors reflected his image as he approached, a shadowy figure with an aura of controlled menace. He was not just entering an office; he was stepping onto a battlefield, one where the stakes were high and the consequences could be severe.

As he reached the doors, he paused, if only for a fraction of a second, as if savoring the moment. The faintest hint of a smile tugged at the corner of his mouth—barely noticeable, but there. Then, without hesitation, he pushed through the doors and disappeared into the building's gleaming interior, leaving the chaos of the city behind as he entered a different kind of arena, one where his true game was about to begin.

Quinn Jessop, a man in his late thirties, sat alone in the room, the heavy silence broken only by the soft, rhythmic ticking of a clock on the wall. Spread out before him on the polished oak table were numerous files and photographs, each one a piece of a complex puzzle that only he seemed capable of solving. The air was thick with the scent of paper, ink, and the faint but unmistakable aroma of cigarette smoke. His sharp eyes scanned the documents, his mind already piecing together the story they told, a story that was as troubling as it was inevitable.

The room was a stark contrast to the sleek, modern offices outside its door. Here, the lighting was muted, almost suffocating, with only a single desk lamp casting a pool of yellowed light over his work. The walls were lined with old bookshelves, their contents a testament to the kind of knowledge that wasn't found in any corporate handbook.

He leaned back in his chair, the leather creaking softly beneath him as he drew slowly on his cigarette. The end of it glowed a dull red, the smoke curling lazily up toward the ceiling, where it mingled with the shadows. His expression was one of practiced indifference, a mask that betrayed nothing of the thoughts running through his mind. He was a man who had seen too much and learned too little to be easily impressed or intimidated.

His moment of solitude was interrupted by the sound of the door creaking open. Ron White, a man in his mid-fifties with the unmistakable air of a corporate executive, entered the room. Ron was the epitome of the company man, dressed in a tailored suit that spoke of wealth and power, but his demeanor was far from confident. There was nervous energy about him, a slight hesitation in his step, as if he was walking into something he didn't fully understand or control.

Ron's eyes flickered to the cigarette in Quinn's hand, and a look of mild disapproval crossed his face. "You know you're not supposed to smoke in the building, Quinn," he said, his voice carrying the forced authority of someone who knew he wouldn't be listened to.

He didn't bother to reply immediately. Instead, he took another long, deliberate drag on his cigarette, his gaze never leaving Ron. The smoke swirled around him as he exhaled slowly, the tension in the room thickening with each passing second. Finally, he spoke, his voice low and gravelly, tinged with the kind of cynicism that only years of dealing with people like Ron could produce. "Well, you didn't call me to help with this penny ante shit."

Ron shifted uncomfortably, his eyes darting to the files spread out on the table. He knew Quinn was right, whatever had brought them here wasn't ordinary by any means. "No," Ron admitted, his tone grudging. "There's a slew of VPs gathering with worried looks."

His lip curled in a faint, almost dismissive smile. "VPs always worry," he said, his words laced with a kind of amused disdain. To him, the corporate hierarchy was nothing more than a collection of nervous men in expensive suits, each one more terrified of losing his position than actually solving the problems that landed on his desk. They were pawns in a game they barely understood, and Quinn had little patience for their fears.

"Yea, but not you, huh?" Ron shot back, though his voice lacked conviction. He was trying to regain some control of the conversation, but it was clear that Quinn wasn't the type to be easily swayed by corporate posturing.

Quinn's smile faded, replaced by a look of mild irritation. "What's the point?" he replied, his tone flat. "Worrying doesn't change anything. It doesn't make problems go away, and it sure as hell doesn't fix them."

There was a moment of silence as the two men regarded each other, the tension in the room palpable. Ron, despite his position, felt a growing unease in Quinn's presence. There was something about the man, his confidence, his detachment, his utter lack of concern for the rules that governed everyone else, that made Ron feel out of his depth.

Quinn took one last drag from his cigarette before stubbing it out in the ashtray with a slow, deliberate motion. The sound of the smoldering ash being crushed echoed in the stillness, a final punctuation to their conversation. He leaned forward, his eyes narrowing as he met Ron's gaze head-on. "So, what's really going on, Ron? You didn't drag me in here just to watch VPs squirm. What's the play?"

Ron hesitated, his mouth opening as if to speak, but no words came out. He knew that whatever he said next would set things in motion, and there was no turning back once Quinn was involved. Taking a deep breath, he finally spoke, his voice barely above a whisper. "There's something bigger, Quinn."

His eyes flickered with interest for the first time since Ron had entered the room. He leaned back again, the faintest hint of a smile playing at the corners of his mouth. "Now we're talking," he said, his tone almost casual. "Tell me everything."

***

Quinn and Ron strode through the bustling corridors of Allied Insurance, their footsteps echoing off the polished marble floors. The open-plan offices on either side were filled with corporate drones, each one busy with their tasks, yet unable to resist glancing up as the two men passed. The presence of Quinn Jessop sent a ripple of curiosity and unease through the ranks. His very appearance in the building was enough to stir whispers.

As they approached a corner, their path was suddenly blocked by a group of employees spilling out of a nearby conference room. The group seemed momentarily paralyzed by the sight of Quinn, their conversations halting as they made way for the two men. Beyond them, the door to the conference room was still open, and Quinn's sharp eyes caught sight of two men deep in conversation inside. As if sensing his gaze, one of the men turned, his eyes widening in recognition.

"Quinn Jessop!" The man, Baxter, exclaimed with a mix of surprise and amusement. His voice carried across the hallway, drawing even more attention. "Well, look at that, William—it's the A-Team."

William, the other man, chuckled in response, his laughter filled with a kind of derisive camaraderie. Baxter wasn't done yet, though, he saw an opportunity to make a scene and wasn't about to let it pass. "Hey... maybe William could show my friend here what makes a big-time investigator like you worth all that money," Baxter taunted, a smug smile tugging at the corners of his mouth.

Quinn's expression remained unreadable, his eyes flicking briefly over Baxter before settling into a look of mild disinterest. He had dealt with men like Baxter before, corporate types who believed that their position within the company gave them some sort of authority over him. In truth, they were little more than annoyances, gnats buzzing in his ear, easily ignored or swatted away.

Ron, sensing the tension, leaned closer to Quinn. "Just ignore the prick. He's looking to push your buttons," he muttered, his voice low and filled with annoyance. The hallway had grown quieter as the employees who had exited the meeting hung back, their interest piqued by the unfolding drama. They tried to appear inconspicuous, but their glances toward Quinn and Baxter betrayed their curiosity.

Quinn let out a slow, deliberate breath, the corners of his mouth twitching into a faint smile. "Shouldn't take long," he said, his voice calm and composed, as he moved past Ron and into the conference room.

The room was spacious, dominated by a long, glossy table that was now littered with files and documents. Quinn could feel the eyes of the onlookers boring into his back, but he paid them no attention. Baxter, relishing the opportunity to grandstand, stepped up to the table with a smug air of superiority.

"You have two claims," Baxter began, his tone dripping with condescension. "One we've investigated for over 30 man-hours and are positive is legitimate. The other was investigated by our team, and after a three-month investigation, we've determined it's fraudulent."

As he spoke, Baxter picked up a file, removing about three sheets stapled together. He placed them face down on the table with a flourish, then repeated the action with another file, laying the second stapled sheet next to the first. The spectators outside strained to get a better view, their curiosity piqued by the challenge Baxter had laid out.

"The question is," Baxter continued, his smile widening, "can you tell which is legit and which is the fraud from just the claim form?"

Ron, who had followed Quinn into the room, looked at the two identical sheets and shook his head. "That's bullshit, Baxter. There isn't any information on that form," he protested, his voice laced with frustration.

Baxter, however, was not deterred. He was enjoying this far too much to back down now. "Oh, come on," he sneered. "Big-time cop quits and becomes a highly overpaid dick for hire. We'd all like to see the skills."

For a moment, Quinn didn't respond. He simply stared at Baxter, who seemed to take Quinn's silence as a victory. The smug executive was satisfied that he had embarrassed the seasoned investigator in front of the crowd. But Quinn had seen through the game from the moment he stepped into the room.

"Are you sure your findings are right?" Quinn asked finally, his voice calm, almost casual.

"Without a doubt," Baxter replied confidently, though there was a flicker of uncertainty in his eyes.

Quinn's gaze shifted to the table, then back to Baxter. He noticed the way Baxter's fingers twitched slightly as he ran them through his hair, the subtle shift in his posture as he tried to play to the crowd. It was all Quinn needed. He didn't even have to look at the claim forms to know the answer. His hand hovered over one form, then the other, as if weighing them in his mind. He could see Baxter's confidence waver, his eyes darting nervously between the two files. Quinn allowed a small, knowing smile to touch his lips as he finally picked up one of the forms and tossed it at Baxter.

Baxter caught it, his eyes scanning the document quickly. The change in his expression was instantaneous as he was clearly shocked. He had chosen the correct one. The smugness drained from Baxter's face, replaced by confusion and frustration. Quinn, satisfied with the outcome, turned to leave, his movements deliberate and unhurried.

William, who had been watching with a mixture of fascination and disbelief, stepped forward. "But… you didn't even look at them," he stammered, still trying to process what had just happened.

Quinn paused at the door, glancing back over his shoulder. "Didn't have to," he said simply. "Answers aren't where people tell you they are. When someone has a secret, they won't tell ya. You just gotta be able to see it."

He turned his gaze to Baxter, whose face was now a mask of irritation and embarrassment. "You shouldn't have looked at which was which," Quinn added with a slight smirk. "Let's play poker sometime."

With that, Quinn exited the room, leaving Baxter fuming in his wake. Ron, who had been watching the exchange with barely concealed amusement, couldn't help but grin as he followed Quinn down the hallway.

"Nice," Ron said, catching up to Quinn. "So, how did you know?"

Quinn shrugged, his expression casual. "Fifty-fifty chance," he replied. "I just played human nature. Picked the second one he put down."

Ron shook his head in admiration. "You got balls, my friend," he said, clapping Quinn on the back as they continued down the hallway, leaving the murmurs and whispers of the onlookers behind them. He didn't respond, but the faint smile on his face spoke volumes. He had played the game, and once again, he had won.

***

Quinn and Ron entered the supreme boardroom in Allied

Insurance, which was their main destination. The room was filled with a collection of executives in suits, each seated on plush couches and chairs. They all wore expressions of deep concern, their postures tense and alert, a clear indication that something serious was at stake. At the head of the long, polished wood table sat VP of Allied Insurance, Richards, his face set in a grim mask of determination.

Quinn surveyed the room, his sharp eyes taking in the anxious faces around him. "Jeez, y'all look like your golden parachutes just failed," he quipped, attempting to lighten the mood, though his words only seemed to deepen the frowns of the assembled executives.

"Sit down, Mr. Jessop," Richards said curtly, clearly not in the mood for jokes.

"Alright," Quinn replied, his tone nonchalant as he slid into a chair. The tension in the room was palpable, but he remained unfazed, his act cool and collected.

Richards wasted no time, sliding a file across the smooth, glossy surface of the table toward him. "What's the biggest life insurance policy this company has ever paid out?" he asked, his voice carrying the weight of someone who was deeply invested in the answer.

Quinn caught the file, flipping it open with practiced ease. "Ten million," he replied without missing a beat. "Jonas Wilmington, some rich steel guy. Eighteen beneficiaries, clean."

Richards nodded, acknowledging Quinn's quick recall. "Are you familiar with Lorenzo Steele?" he asked, his eyes narrowing slightly.

He looked up from the file, a flicker of recognition crossing his face. "The football player?" he responded.

"Ex-football player," Richards corrected, his tone grave. "He died two days ago on the island of Grand Cayman in some off-road accident."

Quinn's brows furrowed slightly as he processed the information. He returned his attention to the file, scanning the details inside. "Accidental death, money, young fiancée... no brainer," he said, his tone suggesting that he had seen many similar cases.

Richards, however, was not convinced. "She's not a suspect. Her alibi checked out; that's not the problem," he explained, his frustration evident.

Quinn looked up again, his interest piqued. "Then what is the problem?" he asked, leaning back in his chair, his eyes fixed on Richards.

Richards took a deep breath, his expression growing even more serious. "We'd rather not pay two hundred fifty million dollars to the beneficiary," he said, his voice low. "You're booked on the next flight."

Quinn stared at Richards for a moment, the enormity of the figure settling in. Two hundred fifty million dollars was a staggering sum, even for a company as large as Allied Insurance.

There was clearly more to this case than met the eye. With a nod, Quinn closed the file and stood up, ready to dig deeper into the mystery that awaited him in Grand Cayman.

***

The cabin of the airplane was lowly lit, with only a few overhead lights casting pools of soft, yellow light onto the seats below. Quinn Jessop sat alone, absorbed in a large file spread out across his tray table. The steady hum of the engines created a soothing background noise, but his mind was far from relaxed. He flipped through the documents, his eyes narrowing as he scanned the contents with the focus of someone who knew there was more at stake than what was immediately visible.

He paused at a newspaper clipping from the sports section, showing a photo of Lorenzo Steele at a signing event with the Miami team. Steele's broad smile and the sea of cheering fans around him captured the peak of his career. Leaning back in his seat, his thoughts already piecing together the implications of Steele's death.

He remembered the conversation with Richards back at the office. Richards had explained how team owners, often using their attorneys as intermediaries, found ways to compensate star players outside of the usual salary caps and financial regulations. Insurance policies had become a popular tool for this purpose, with teams purchasing high-value policies for players and setting their maturity dates to coincide with the end of the players' contracts. It was a clever maneuver, allowing teams to effectively pay more without breaching any official limits.

Quinn smirked, thinking about the ingenuity of it all. "Smart motherfuckers," he muttered to himself, impressed by the crafty way the system had been gamed.

As he continued to leaf through the file, he pulled out a photo of a young woman in a cheerleading uniform. The caption read:

Brazilian Candy. The picture, taken during her cheerleading days, showed her flashing a bright, confident smile. Quinn raised an eyebrow, a wry grin forming on his face. "Very tasty... I'll bet you're a dancing bitch, ain't ya?" he mused, wondering what role she played in the unfolding drama. There was something about her that seemed out of place, something that hinted at a deeper story.

His mind drifted back to the details of the case. Steele had died in the final year of his contract, triggering the insurance policy's maturity. It was an accidental death, but the policy had an added rider that doubled the payout in such cases. That meant a payout of two hundred fifty million dollars, an eye- watering sum that could make anyone's head spin.

Shaking his head, he was still trying to wrap his mind around the amount. "Holy shit," he whispered, realizing why Allied Insurance was so eager to get to the bottom of this. Two hundred fifty million wasn't just a loss, it was a catastrophe, a potential sinkhole that could swallow profits and credibility whole.

Closing the file but keeping it on his lap, Quinn sat back and stared out the window into the inky darkness. The situation was far more complicated than he'd initially thought. There were layers to this case, layers that hinted at deception, greed, and possibly even murder. He knew he needed to stay sharp. Whatever awaited him in Grand Cayman wasn't going to be straightforward. The stakes were high, and he couldn't afford to miss a single detail.

As the plane soared through the night sky, Quinn continued to gaze out into the void, his mind already working through the possibilities, preparing for whatever was to come.

Chapter Nineteen

Quinn Jessop stepped out of the airport terminal, blinking against the bright Caribbean sun. He squinted as his eyes adjusted, the sudden shift from the dim interior of the plane and airport to the brilliant daylight catching him off guard. The warm, salty breeze of the island hit him, carrying with it the sounds of tourists chattering and the distant hum of planes taking off and landing. It was a stark contrast to the cold, sterile environment of the insurance offices he had left hours ago.

Quinn slung a garment bag over his shoulder and reached into his pocket for his sunglasses. Sliding them on, he let out a low whistle, scanning the busy airport grounds. The parking area was a chaotic mix of taxis, rental cars, and people hustling to their destinations. His eyes darted from one taxi to another, looking for a ride. Spotting a cab parked under the shade of a palm tree with its driver leaning against the door, Quinn raised his hand and signaled.

The driver, a middle-aged man with a wide-brimmed hat and a toothy grin, nodded and climbed into the car, pulling it around to where Quinn stood. Quinn tossed his bag into the back seat before sliding in himself, the cool air conditioning a welcome relief from the midday heat. As the taxi pulled away from the curb, Quinn settled into his seat, watching the airport slowly disappear behind them.

His mind wandered back to his conversation with Richards. He could almost hear the man's voice in his head, stern and un- yielding. Richards had been clear about the stakes: *Mr. Jessop, you have always produced results. This is certainly an occasion when results would be greatly appreciated.* The words echoed in Quinn's mind, a reminder of the high expectations placed on him. It wasn't just about solving a case; it was about protecting the company's bottom line from a massive payout that could have severe repercussions.

Quinn glanced out the window as the taxi navigated through the narrow, winding streets of Grand Cayman. The island was beautiful, with its lush greenery and turquoise waters, but he knew better than to get lost in its charm. There was a job to do, and he was here to do it. Two hundred fifty million dollars was on the line, and Allied Insurance was counting on him to get to the bottom of Lorenzo Steele's death and the circumstances surrounding it.

He leaned back in his seat, feeling the rhythm of the road beneath him. The scenery blurred as the taxi sped up, and Quinn's thoughts sharpened. He needed to gather as much information as possible, connect the dots, and figure out what really happened to Lorenzo

Steele. The clock was ticking, and there was no time to waste.

As the taxi turned onto a main road, Quinn could see the ocean stretching out in the distance, its surface glittering under the sun. Somewhere out there, answers were waiting to be uncovered.

***

Candy stood on the balcony of the presidential suite, the breeze gently rustling her hair as she smoked a cigarette. Her mind was racing with thoughts of everything that had happened. She took a final drag and then flicked the cigarette over the railing, watching as it spiraled down to the street below. With a sigh, she turned and walked back into the suite, the luxury of the room a stark contrast to the turmoil in her head.

Her eyes drifted to the adjoining door that led to Kelly's room. She needed to talk to her, but just as she was about to move, a knock at the suite's main door froze her in place. She hesitated, her heart beating faster. The knock came again, louder this time, echoing through the quiet of the suite.

Candy took a deep breath, steeling herself. She smoothed her dress, straightening her posture, and walked over to the door. She opened it cautiously, but there was no one there. Frowning, she stepped into the hallway and glanced down it just in time to see a bellman walking away.

"Sorry, I slipped it under the door," the bellman called back over his shoulder, turning to acknowledge her.

Candy looked down and saw a manila envelope lying at her feet. She nodded absently, closing the door behind her. "Thanks," she muttered, but the door was already shut, muffling her voice.

She stared at the envelope, her mind spinning with possibilities. With a tentative nudge of her foot, she pushed it. It felt heavy. Reluctantly, she picked it up and carried it over to the small table in the suite. She sat down, turning the envelope over in her hands, and then, with a sudden burst of frustration, she tore it open.

As the envelope ripped, she recoiled slightly, letting it drop to the table. A single photo poked out from the torn opening—a corner just visible. She reached out with trembling fingers, grabbed the envelope, and shook it, letting the contents spill out across the table.

Dozens of photographs scattered in front of her. Each one was worse than the last. Images of Kelly and Candy at the scene of Lorenzo's murder filled the table, the grim reality of what they had done captured in stark, undeniable clarity. Blood, bodies, and the look of shock and fear on their faces.

Candy's breath hitched when she saw a photo of herself saying goodbye to Lorenzo, his lifeless body slumped over in the driver's seat, blood pooling around him. Her hands shook as she tossed the photo aside, her eyes scanning the rest of the pictures. Then she noticed a small scrap of paper among the photographs. Picking it up, she unfolded it and read the scrawled message:

JUST IN CASE FYI.

"Shit," she whispered under her breath, the weight of the situation pressing down on her. She had hoped for a clean getaway, but this was a clear reminder that they were far from out of the island.

Candy stood abruptly, crossing the suite in quick strides. She flung open the door to the adjoining room where Kelly was sleeping. The noise jolted Kelly awake, and she bolted upright in bed, eyes wide and unfocused.

"Hey," Kelly mumbled, rubbing her eyes and trying to shake off the remnants of sleep.

"Time to get up," Candy said, her voice tense.

Kelly blinked a few times, still groggy. "That's okay, I've slept enough. Is everything okay?"

Candy's jaw tightened as she spoke, "Well, Sleeping Beauty, we just got pictures delivered of us at the scene of Lorenzo's murder."

Kelly's eyes widened in shock, all traces of sleep gone in an instant. "What!?" she exclaimed, scrambling out of bed.

Candy nodded toward the other room. "Go look for yourself."

Kelly rushed past her, entering the main suite and grabbing the photos. She sifted through them frantically, her disbelief growing with each one she saw.

"It's just Houston," Candy explained, trying to keep her voice calm. "I told you we have a history. As soon as they finish the inquiry and issue the death certificate, we're out of here."

Kelly looked up from the photos, her face pale. "I guess the plan hasn't gone that well to this point, huh?"

Candy forced a smile, though her nerves were frayed. "We're fine. The plan's fine. We just stick to the story, and in a couple of days, we'll be home. This will all be over. No one can touch us."

Kelly didn't look convinced, but she nodded, clutching the photographs tightly in her hands. The tension in the room was thick, but Candy knew they had no choice but to keep moving forward. There was no turning back now.

***

The sun blazed down on Quinn Jessop and Inspector Philip LaReine as they navigated the rocky terrain of the Cayman Islands cliffside. The sea breeze carried the scent of salt and seaweed, whipping through their clothes and rustling the sparse vegetation that clung to the cliff's edge. Below, the turquoise waters of the Caribbean crashed against the rocks, sending sprays of foam high into the air.

They approached the spot where Lorenzo Steele's jeep had veered off the narrow, winding road and plunged over the edge, tumbling down to the jagged rocks below. The ground at the top of the cliff was dry and dusty, with patches of wiry grass and scrub brush. There were no obvious signs of an accident, no skid marks or disturbed earth, nothing to indicate a sudden swerve or loss of control.

Quinn squinted against the bright sunlight, scanning the area carefully. "So, the guy just drove over the side?" he asked, his voice laced with skepticism. He gestured toward the edge of the cliff, where the ground dropped away sharply to the rocky shore below. "No dead animals, no big rocks, no signs of an accident. Nothing?"

Inspector LaReine, a tall, stern man in his 30s with a commanding presence and a thick Caribbean accent, stood with his arms crossed, his posture rigid. His dark eyes were unreadable behind a pair of aviator sunglasses, his expression calm but wary. He wore a crisp white shirt rolled up to his elbows, the light fabric fluttering slightly in the wind.

"The accident was at the bottom, yes?" LaReine replied evenly, his tone giving nothing away. He watched Quinn closely, trying to gauge the American's intentions and measure his resolve.

Quinn frowned, clearly not satisfied with the response. "So, the investigation's over? Just like that?"

LaReine let out a slow, deliberate breath, clearly holding onto his patience. "It is unclear what your purpose is here, monami.

This is a local matter. We have conducted our inquiry, and the coroner has established that no crime has been committed. You are chasing the wild goose."

Ignoring the inspector's curt dismissal, Quinn continued to survey the scene. He walked slowly along the cliff's edge, his eyes combing the ground for any signs of foul play. The dry soil and sparse vegetation offered little in the way of clues, but Quinn was thorough, taking in every detail with a trained eye.

As he moved, something caught his attention—a small patch of disturbed dirt near a cluster of rocks. He crouched down for a closer look, noticing a few crushed leaves and a tuft of disturbed grass. Producing a pair of tweezers from his jacket pocket, Quinn carefully picked up the leaves, holding them up to his nose and sniffing them.

Quinn stood up, turning to LaReine and holding the leaves out. "What's that smell like?" he asked, his voice calm but probing.

LaReine hesitated for a moment, clearly reluctant to engage with the American further. Then, with a resigned sigh, he leaned in and took a cautious sniff of the leaves. His eyebrows rose slightly, a flicker of surprise crossing his otherwise stoic face. "Mint. I believe it is mint."

Quinn's eyes lit up, a flash of recognition sparking in his gaze. "Mint! That's it!" He quickly pulled out a small plastic baggie from his coat pocket, carefully placing the leaves inside and sealing it with a snap. He tucked the baggie away with a satisfied nod, his mind already working through the implications of this new piece of evidence.

LaReine watched Quinn's actions with a bemused smile. "You find this amusing, Mr. Jessop?" he asked, wiping his brow with a neatly folded handkerchief. The sun was relentless, and he adjusted his hat, a straw fedora, to better shield his eyes. "What about those tracks, backing up? Fleeing the scene, one might say."

Quinn looked up from the ground, his expression turning thoughtful. "Interesting theory," he replied, glancing at the faint tire tracks that seemed to lead back from the cliff's edge, barely visible in the dry dirt and loose gravel.

LaReine chuckled softly, shaking his head. "It appears to you that we are not interested in doing our job, eh? Not like your Law and Order or CSI, where everything is so clear-cut and the guilty are always caught within the hour."

Quinn shrugged, trying to keep his tone light and non-confrontational. "Look, I'm just doing my job. Nothing personal. Just looking for answers."

LaReine's expression softened slightly, but his eyes remained sharp, unyielding. "And I am doing my job. I balance a thin line on this little island. It is often difficult to police those who put food on your table. This is an accident...unfortunate. Perhaps it is more, but here, I arrest those I can convict."

Quinn nodded, understanding the unspoken complexities that LaReine was alluding to. "What about the wife?" he asked, shifting the conversation.

LaReine's lips curled into a small smile, as if the question amused him. "You mean his fiancé, an exquisite beauty," he said, his voice almost wistful. "Obviously, she is distraught. A tragic loss for her, losing her man so young."

"Obviously," Quinn echoed, his mind racing with possibilities. The words hung in the hot, humid air between them, heavy with unspoken questions and unresolved tensions.

As they stood there, surrounded by the sounds and smells of the Cayman Islands coastline, Quinn knew that the answers he was looking for wouldn't come easily. This wasn't just about a simple accident or a straightforward investigation; there were layers to this case, layers that he would have to peel back one by one if he wanted to get to the truth. And he was more than ready to do just that.

***

Houston and Jimmy strolled down a narrow street in the Cayman Islands, far from the polished tourist attractions nor like the reserved place they carried out the plan on Lorenzo. The area was a stark contrast to the postcard image of paradise that most visitors carried home. Here, the buildings were worn, their once-bright paint faded and chipped by the sun and salt air. The locals, dressed in everyday attire rather than the typical beachwear, moved about their routines with a purposeful gait, casting occasional glances at the two strangers.

Jimmy ducked into a small, dimly lit bar with a faded sign reading "Fleur Del Mar." Houston lingered outside for a moment, his gaze sweeping the street as if searching for someone or something. After a beat, he shook his head and followed Jimmy inside.

Inside the bar, the air was thick with the smell of rum and sweat. The small lighting cast shadows across the cracked wooden floor, and a low murmur of conversation filled the space. A few ceiling fans turned lazily, doing little to combat the oppressive heat. Locals occupied most of the tables and barstools, nursing drinks and engaging in quiet conversations. It was clear this was a place where peoplecame to escape or perhaps to be forgotten.

Houston made his way to the bar, where Jimmy was already waiting with two glasses of dark rum in hand. He passed one to Houston with a knowing nod, and they navigated through the scattered patrons, finding an empty booth near the back. The seat was torn, the table sticky, but it offered a semblance of privacy.

Jimmy leaned back in his seat, eyeing Houston carefully. "You look worried," he said, his voice low but sharp, cutting through the hum of the bar.

Houston took a sip of his drink, his expression guarded. "I'm fine," he replied curtly, though his eyes told a different story.

Jimmy wasn't convinced. "I can't believe you hooked up with that bitch again," he continued, shaking his head in disbelief. "When are you gonna learn, huh? She's trouble, man. Capital fucking T trouble."

His jaw tightened, and his grip on the glass firm. "I'd fucking kill her," he muttered, his voice laced with anger. "But we won't get our money back that way."

Jimmy scoffed, rolling his eyes. "Fuck the money. Money ain't hard to come by," he said dismissively. "There's always another job, another hustle."

Houston set his glass down with a hard thunk, his eyes flashing with determination. "I want her money, our money," he said fiercely. "It's payback."

Jimmy leaned in, his tone turning serious. "You better make sure you know what you're doing, buddy," he warned, his gaze fixed on Houston. "I don't think just having those photos is gonna be enough. I don't think you understand, this chick has you under her thumb."

He shook his head, his expression hardening. "This time, it's different," he insisted, more to himself than to Jimmy.

Jimmy raised an eyebrow, skepticism etched on his face. "How's it any different?" he challenged. "Oh yeah, this time you get to fuck other chicks."

A slow, grim smile spread across Houston's face. "This time, I'm ready," he said with conviction.

Jimmy sighed, finishing his drink in one gulp. He stared at his partner for a while, trying to gauge his resolve. "Dude...you better be," he finally said, his voice carrying a mix of doubt and concern.

***

Dr. Lawrence Robert Koch sat behind his large mahogany desk, surrounded by a sea of paperwork. He adjusted his reading glasses and leaned closer to a document, the pages rustling slightly under the ceiling fan's soft whirr. The sunlight streaming through the window highlighted the dust particles floating lazily in the air. The distant sound of waves crashing against the shore provided a soothing, almost rhythmic background noise to his otherwise mundane afternoon.

The door creaked open, pulling Dr. Koch's attention away from his paperwork. He looked up, frowning slightly, the lenses of his glasses reflecting the light.

"Hello? Who's there?" he called out, his voice tinged with a mixture of curiosity and annoyance at the interruption.

The door swung open-wide, and Inspector Philip LaReine stepped inside. The Inspector wore a crisp police uniform, his posture exuding authority. Behind him followed Quinn Jessop, with a rumpled suit and a sharp, calculating gaze that took in every detail of the cluttered office.

"Inspector LaReine, Doctor," the Inspector announced, his tone courteous but firm. "If we could have a moment of your time?"

Dr. Koch nodded, his expression softening into a professional smile as he gestured towards a well-worn leather sofa against the wall. "Of course, gentlemen, please have a seat. I assume this is about Mr. Steele. Terrible tragedy, just terrible," he said, his voice adopting a somber tone befitting the situation.

Inspector LaReine and Quinn moved towards the sofa, but Quinn remained standing, choosing to lean casually against the wall, his arms crossed. LaReine introduced him with a nod, "This is Mr. Jessop. He's an investigator from the insurance company looking into Mr. Steele's policy."

Dr. Koch's eyes flickered with interest as he regarded Quinn, his expression inscrutable. "Yes, of course. Anything I can do to help," he said, settling back into his chair and clasping his hands together on the desk.

Quinn didn't waste time with pleasantries. "You examined the body, Doctor?" he asked directly, his voice steady and authoritative.

He nodded slowly, his brow furrowing slightly. "Yes, yes, I did. The body was badly burned in the crash. There was severe trauma, all consistent with an automobile accident of this nature. Very tragic."

Quinn leaned forward slightly, narrowing his gaze as he scrutinized the doctor's response. "Did you perform a toxicology report?" he asked, his tone probing.

Dr. Koch blinked, momentarily taken aback by the question. "A tox report?" he echoed, as if buying time to think. Then he quickly recovered, nodding. "Oh, you mean a toxicology report. Yes, we did one. No drugs or sedatives were found, just alcohol, and quite a bit of it, actually. It's my opinion that the accident was a result of excessive drinking."

Quinn's expression remained unreadable, but there was a slight tightening around his eyes. "Drinking?" he prompted, his voice carrying a hint of skepticism.

The doctor sighed, a resigned look crossing his face. "Yes, it's very sad. Unfortunately, it's all too common in these cases. People come here on vacation, they let loose, and sometimes they don't realize their limits."

Considering this for a moment, Quinn then glanced around the cluttered office, taking in the medical books and anatomical models scattered about. "May I see the body?" he asked suddenly, catching Dr. Koch off guard.

"The body?" He repeated, his eyebrows shooting up in surprise.

"Yes," Quinn replied, maintaining a calm demeanor. "Just a formality, really."

He shook his head, his expression apologetic. "I'm sorry, Mr. Jessop, but the body has already been sent to the mortuary for cremation. It wouldn't do you much good now, I'm afraid. The process is mostly done."

Quinn raised an eyebrow, his lips pressing into a thin line. "So quickly?" he asked, a note of suspicion creeping into his voice.

Offering a faint, reassuring smile. "I believe Mrs. Steele intends to scatter his ashes here in the Cayman Islands," he explained smoothly. "She wanted everything done as soon as possible, I assume for closure."

"Of course," Quinn said softly, nodding as if he understood perfectly.

The doctor's ears perked up at the tone in Quinn's voice. "Excuse me?" he asked, his curiosity piqued.

Quinn leaned forward, his gaze sharp and unwavering. "Dr. Koch, would it surprise you to learn that Mrs. Steele stands to collect a large sum of money from her man's insurance policy?" he asked pointedly.

His expression didn't change, but a flicker of something—surprise, perhaps, crossed his eyes. "He was a sports figure, wasn't he? I would think he would carry considerable insurance," he replied diplomatically, choosing his words carefully.

Quinn nodded, studying the doctor's face intently. "What's the Mrs. like? I haven't had the chance to meet her yet," he said, throwing out the question casually, almost as an afterthought.

Dr. Koch hesitated, his eyes narrowing slightly as he considered his response. "I have never had the pleasure," he replied finally, his voice measured.

"Really?" Quinn said, feigning surprise. "I hear she's quite attractive."

Dr. Koch forced a polite smile, shifting slightly in his chair. "Well, Mrf. Steele was quite a notable man, handsome and well- built, from what I've heard. I assume his wife would be similarly striking."

Quinn's eyes narrowed further. "Oh, so you've seen Mr. Steele?" he pressed, his tone sharp.

Dr. Koch shook his head quickly. "No, no," he clarified. "I saw him for the first time on my table."

Quinn leaned back, his gaze never leaving the doctor. A small, knowing smile tugged at the corner of his mouth. "So… there was enough of the body to see he's cute?" he asked, his voice laced with subtle sarcasm. "Maybe I should take a look, huh?"

He looked over at Inspector LaReine, who simply raised his eyebrows and shrugged, staying silent. The room fell into a tense silence as both men stared at the doctor, waiting for his response. The doctor shifted uncomfortably, the situation pressing down on him like the humid island air.

***

The sterile room of the Cayman Islands mortuary felt cold, despite the island's humid heat pressing against its walls from outside. A faint smell of formaldehyde hung in the air, mingling with the scent of antiseptic cleaners. Metal drawers lined one side of the room, each marked with a small, silver plaque indicating the body it held. The atmosphere was filled with an unsettling quiet that only the dead seemed to understand.

Dr. Koch stood at the head of a long, stainless-steel table, his face a mask of professional detachment. To his right was Quinn Jessop, his posture tense and his expression a mixture of skepticism and impatience. Inspector Philip LaReine, the stoic local police officer, observed the scene with a cautious eye, while a mortician, dressed in a plain white coat, prepared to reveal the body of Lorenzo Steele.

With a nod from the mortician, one of the metal drawers slid open with a soft metallic clang, revealing a black body bag inside. The mortician carefully unzipped the bag, exposing the charred remains of Lorenzo Steele. The once-athletic man was now reduced to a blackened, barely recognizable figure. The sight of the charred corpse was jarring—a grim reminder of the violent end that had befallen him.

Dr. Koch cleared his throat, breaking the silence. "As you can see, the trauma is consistent with the type of accident reported. Severe burns, multiple fractures... a tragic, but straightforward case."

Quinn's eyes narrowed as he stared at the body, his mind racing with questions and doubts. "Well, he's definitely dead," he remarked dryly, his voice tinged with sarcasm.

Inspector LaReine glanced at Quinn, his expression unreadable. "Was there a doubt?" he asked, arching an eyebrow.

Quinn shrugged, his gaze shifting back to Dr. Koch. "Nothing is ever that simple," he muttered, his tone flat. "How was identification made?"

Dr. Koch hesitated for a moment before responding. "Dental records," he replied, adjusting his glasses nervously. "Finger- prints were no good—too much damage."

Quinn's jaw tightened. "No identification from the wife?" he pressed, his suspicion evident in his voice.

Inspector LaReine stepped forward, shaking his head slightly. "It was not needed. Why further upset the poor woman?" he replied, his tone placating.

Quinn let out a short, humorless laugh. "Yeah, no one wants that," he said sarcastically.

Reaching into his pocket, Quinn pulled out a small digital camera. The device clicked softly as he powered it on, but before he could lift it to take a photograph, Dr. Koch quickly stepped in front of him, blocking his view.

"No, no photographs," He said firmly, his voice rising slightly with agitation. "Inspector, that is unacceptable."

Quinn's expression darkened, his patience wearing thin. "We

are entitled to gather evidence," he insisted, his tone challenging. "We have a stake in this."

He shook his head, his face flushing with indignation. "But it is improper," he argued, his voice trembling with a mix of anger and frustration. "Photographs, especially when the individual is any type of celebrity, are coveted. Allowing the public to see them presents the loved ones with undue hardship."

Quinn rolled his eyes, his frustration boiling over. "Oh, give me a fucking break," he snapped. "No pictures, and they're going to cremate this guy tomorrow? What the hell are you trying to hide?"

The doctor's face turned red with anger. "I am insulted by the insinuation," he said stiffly, his voice cold and clipped.

Inspector LaReine raised a hand, attempting to diffuse the tension. "Perhaps the autopsy photos, Doctor?" he suggested, his tone calm but firm.

Dr. Koch hesitated, clearly uncomfortable with the idea. "Again, I am uncomfortable with allowing access to—"

"I think it will be fine, Doctor," Inspector LaReine interjected, cutting him off. He turned to Quinn, his expression stern but fair. "Mr. Jessop, I will have the Doctor forward all pertinent files and photographic evidence to you. Would that satisfy your need to document the incident?"

Quinn paused, weighing his options. He knew he was being stonewalled but decided to pick his battles. "I suppose I don't have a choice," he muttered begrudgingly.

Inspector LaReine nodded, satisfied with the compromise. "Good, then everyone's happy," he said, signaling to the mortician.

The mortician nodded in return and carefully zipped the body bag back up. With a soft thud, he slid the drawer closed, the sound echoing in the quiet room like a final punctuation mark to the grim scene.

Quinn watched the drawer disappear into the wall, his mind still churning with questions and doubts. He turned to leave, muttering under his breath, "Not everyone, Monsieur," as he walked out of the cold, sterile mortuary and back into the warm, chaotic reality of the Cayman Islands.

***

The presidential suite of the luxurious Cayman Islands resort is an elegant blend of modern amenities and tropical charm. The suite's opulence is marred by an underlying tension, as Candy Steele emerges from the bedroom, cradling a drink in her good hand.

Her gaze flits around the suite, a mixture of weariness and anxiety in her eyes. As she moves toward the coffee table, she retrieves her purse and discreetly pulls out a small vial of cocaine.

The tiny glass vial glints in the fading light, promising a temporary escape from her troubles. Just as she is about to open it, a sudden knock at the door startles her, causing her to fumble with the vial. She quickly shoves it back into her purse, her heartbeat quickening.

The door to the adjoining room opens slightly, and Kelly peeks in, her face etched with concern. "Candy, are you alright?" she whispers urgently.

Candy, composing herself, gestures for Kelly to retreat. "Go back inside," she says in a hushed tone, her expression serious. Kelly nods and closes the door, leaving it slightly ajar. Candy takes a deep breath, her hand instinctively moving back to the sling supporting her injured arm, a prop she uses to garner sympathy and deflect suspicion.

She approaches the suite's main door cautiously, glancing through the peephole. Her eyes widen slightly as she recognizes Inspector LaReine standing in the hallway, flanked by a man she hasn't seen before. After a moment's hesitation, she opens the door, plastering on a cordial smile.

"Inspector," she greets him with feigned surprise. "What a pleasant surprise to see you again."

Her gaze shifts to the man beside him, taking in his sharp suit and the skeptical look in his eyes. There's an aura of authority around him that sets her on edge.

"And you've brought a friend," she continues, her voice dripping with false charm. "How nice. Please, come in."

Inspector LaReine steps inside, nodding politely. "This is Monsieur Quinn Jessop," he introduces. "He is an investigator from Allied Insurance in New York."

Candy's smile falters for a split second, replaced by a flicker of confusion. "Allied Insurance?" she repeats, masking her uncertainty.

LaReine nods again, his tone neutral. "Your fiancé's insurance company. We need just a moment of your time."

Candy leads them to the suite's opulent sitting area, her movements deliberately slow as she favors her injured shoulder. The plush armchairs and a glass-topped coffee table create an intimate yet tense atmosphere. Quinn follows, his eyes never leaving Candy, studying her with an intensity that makes her uncomfortable.

"Can I offer you a drink?" Candy asks, her voice smooth but strained.

Inspector LaReine shakes his head politely. "No, thank you, Madam. I am on duty."

Quinn, however, remains unfazed. "I'll have one," he replies nonchalantly.

Turning to Quinn, she smiles, a practiced gesture she has perfected over the years. "What would you like, Mr. Jessop?" she asks, emphasizing his last name as if testing its familiarity.

Quinn leans back in his chair, his expression bemused. "How about a mojito?" he suggests with a slight smirk. "I hear they're all the rage. And please, call me Quinn."

Candy's smile tightens. "I have scotch, bourbon, and vodka," she replies with a hint of irritation. "What's in a mojito?"

Quinn raises an eyebrow, feigning surprise. "I thought everyone in Miami knew how to make a mojito."

Candy's eyes flash with annoyance, but she keeps her composure. "I'm not everyone, Quinn," she retorts.

She reaches for the phone on the side table and dials the number for the adjoining room. "Kelly, I need you," she says, her tone commanding. After a brief pause, Kelly appears in the doorway, her face pale and uncertain as she takes in the unfamiliar guests.

"Kelly, would you be a dear and fix Mr... Quinn a drink?" Candy asks, her voice smooth but edged with impatience.

Quinn waves his hand dismissively. "Scotch is fine. On the rocks," he says, abandoning the mojito pretense.

She nods nervously and moves to the suite's wet bar. Candy watches her go, then turns back to Quinn, her expression curious. "I wasn't aware Lorenzo carried a policy with your company," she remarks casually, trying to steer the conversation.

Quinn leans forward, his gaze unwavering. "That surprises me, can I call you Mrs. Steele."

Candy's smile becomes a little more genuine, her eyes sparkling with a hint of mischief. "Call me Candy," she insists. "Everyone does."

Suddenly, a loud crash interrupts the moment as Kelly drops a glass. The sound of shattering glass fills the room, drawing everyone's attention.

"I'm sorry! I'm so sorry!" Kelly exclaims, flustered as she quickly kneels to pick up the broken pieces.

Candy rolls her eyes, trying to appear annoyed but secretly enjoying the distraction. "My apologies," she says to the men, her tone slightly exasperated. "Since my arm has been hurting, having Kelly around to help has been a godsend."

Quinn's eyes linger on Kelly for a moment before shifting back to Candy. "I'm sure she comes in very handy," he replies, his words laced with double meaning. "What happened, by the way?" he asks, nodding toward her sling.

Candy shrugs, feigning indifference. "I think I... pulled something," she says vaguely, her eyes flickering to his. "How much did you say my husband's policy was for?"

Quinn gives her a cool smile. "I hadn't," he says, leaving the question hanging in the air.

Kelly, still visibly nervous, hands him his scotch. "Thank you," he says, taking the glass and offering her a reassuring smile.

"You're welcome," She murmurs, retreating quickly to the adjoining room. As she closes the door behind her, she leaves it slightly ajar, a small gap that Quinn notices.

"Mind if I smoke?" Quinn asks, shifting his attention back to Candy.

"Not at all," Candy replies, matching his gaze. "Light two."

Quinn reaches into his pocket and pulls out a silver lighter. He picks up two cigarettes from the table, lighting them with practice ease. He hands one to Candy, who takes it with her good hand.

Inspector LaReine clears his throat, breaking the tension. "Perhaps, Madam, you could recount your movements the afternoon of your Lorenzo's tragic accident," he suggests, his tone professional.

Candy tilts her head, her eyes narrowing slightly. "Any particular reason?" she asks, her voice edged with suspicion.

He leans back, exhaling a cloud of smoke. "I'm the curious type," he says, his eyes never leaving hers.

Candy holds his gaze for a moment before sighing, feigning resignation. "I'm afraid it's not very interesting," she begins. "Lorenzo wanted to go for a ride on the island. I wasn't really up to it. He had a few drinks at lunch, but he seemed okay when he left."

Inspector LaReine nods, taking notes. "He was remembered by the clerk at a nearby liquor store purchasing quite a quantity of liquor," he adds, glancing up at her.

Candy shrugs again. "He liked to entertain," she says dismissively. "I stayed back. I was very tired."

Quinn raises an eyebrow. "So you just hung out by yourself all afternoon?" he asks, his tone skeptical.

She smiles, a slow, knowing smile. "I was very tired," she repeats. "Well, no, Kelly was with me. She brought me lunch."

He leans forward slightly, his interest piqued. "So just you and Kelly, huh?"

Her smile turns into a smirk. "Most men would say that was enough," she replies smoothly.

A charged silence fills the room as Candy and Quinn lock eyes, a silent understanding passing between them. Inspector LaReine notices the exchange and clears his throat, breaking the moment.

"Well, the hour is getting late," he says, rising from his seat. "Madam, my sincere condolences."

Candy stands as well, a polite smile on her lips. "Thank you, Inspector," she says graciously.

Quinn watches her closely, spinning his lighter between his fingers. As the Inspector heads toward the door, Quinn lingers, taking one last look around the room.

As he reaches the door, he suddenly stops and turns back, holding up the lighter. "Oops, almost stole your lighter," he says with a sheepish grin.

He tosses the lighter across the room toward Candy, aiming for her injured side. She doesn't move, her expression unreadable as the lighter sails past her and crashes into a large floor vase behind her, shattering it into pieces. She glances at the broken vase, then back at Quinn, a slight smirk tugging at her lips.

"Oh, was I supposed to catch that?" she asks innocently, pausing for effect. "Sorry."

Quinn chuckles, shaking his head. "Yeah, me too," he says, a hint of amusement in his voice.

With that, he turns and exits the suite, Inspector LaReine following closely behind. As soon as the door closes, Candy's smile fades. She exhales sharply, her demeanor shifting from charming hostess to cold and calculating.

Kelly reenters from the adjoining room, her face pale and anxious. "What was that about?" she demands. "Why did that guy want to talk to you?"

Candy turns to face her, her expression hardening. Without warning, she backhands Kelly across the face, sending her sprawling backward onto the couch. Kelly gasps, stunned, as Candy looms over her, grabbing her by the collar and yanking her up.

"Listen to me, you stupid bitch," Candy hisses, her voice low and menacing. "Fuck up again, and I'll bury you. This is done, it's over. There's nothing to do... but fuck up and get caught."

She tightens her grip, her eyes blazing with fury. "I'm not getting caught," she growls.

Kelly chokes, her eyes wide with fear. "Alright... alright," she gasps, nodding frantically.

She releases her, shoving her back onto the couch. Kelly pushes her away, her hands shaking as she tries to regain her composure. "You didn't say anything about an investigator," she mutters, her voice trembling.

Candy waves her off dismissively. "It won't matter," she says coldly. "We scatter that son of a bitch's ashes and get the hell off this island. Once we're back in Miami, no one can touch us."

Without another word, Candy turns and strides toward her bedroom, leaving Kelly to stare after her, still shaking and on the verge of tears.

Chapter Twenty

The bustling night scene at Miami International Airport is a mix of travelers hurrying to their destinations and the bright lights of the city beyond. The airport's exterior is illuminated by a series of neon signs and large glass windows that reflect the headlights of cars streaming in and out of the terminal. Palm trees sway gently in the warm evening breeze, adding a distinctly tropical vibe to the otherwise busy atmosphere.

Inside, the airport is a hive of activity. Passengers disembark from their flights, greeted by eager loved ones waiting just beyond the gate. The air is filled with the sounds of laughter, chatter, and the occasional cry of a child overwhelmed by the commotion. Among the sea of faces, Candy Steele emerges from the gate, her arm still in a sling, her expression one of impatience. She glances back to see Kelly struggling to keep up, laden with their bags.

Candy pushes her way through the crowd, her movements abrupt and annoyed as she shoulders past slow-moving passengers. Her face is set in a mask of determination, her eyes scanning the area as she moves swiftly toward the baggage claim. Kelly trails behind, her face flushed and her arms straining under the weight of the bags. The two women move with a silent but shared purpose, their footsteps echoing on the polished airport floors.

As they reach the baggage claim, Candy's eyes dart around, scanning the faces of the other travelers. Her expression is tense, her gaze never resting in one place for long. Kelly notices her unease but keeps silent, focusing instead on the carousel as it begins to churn out bags.

Outside, the air is cooler, with a slight breeze blowing in from the ocean. Candy and Kelly push through the glass doors leading out of the terminal. The automatic doors slide open with a soft hiss, revealing a throng of reporters and photographers waiting just outside. The flashing lights of cameras immediately illuminate their faces, creating a stark contrast against the dark night sky. The noise level rises sharply as reporters shout questions, their voices overlapping in a chaotic jumble of sound.

Kelly freezes for a moment, her eyes wide with shock as she takes in the scene. "Oh Christ, what are they doing here?" she mutters under her breath, glancing nervously at Candy. "I didn't think there would be press waiting for us."

Candy turns her back to the doors for a brief moment. She uses her good arm to adjust her hair and smooth her clothing, transforming her annoyed expression into one of the carefully curated despair. Her eyes glisten as if on the verge of tears, her lower lip quivering just enough to convey vulnerability.

"I did," she replies coolly, her voice tinged with a calculated mix of bitterness and sorrow. She reaches out and takes Kelly's arm, gripping it tightly for support. The gesture is both protective and controlling, her fingers digging into Kelly's skin just enough to communicate her need for control in this situation.

"Just let me handle it," She says softly, her voice firm despite the wavering in her tone. She gives Kelly a meaningful look, a silent command to follow her lead without question.

Together, they step forward, moving through the automatic doors and into the fray. The reporters immediately close in around them, a wall of bodies pressing forward, microphones thrust out like weapons. Camera flashes burst continuously, blinding Candy and Kelly as they navigate through the crowd.

Candy's face is a picture of anguish as she holds up her good hand to shield her eyes from the blinding lights. "Please, please, not now," she pleads, her voice cracking with emotion. "I'm just trying to get home."

The reporters, undeterred by her plea, continue to shout questions, their voices chaotic blend of curiosity and accusation.

"Candy how are you feeling after your husband's tragic accident?" one reporter yells, thrusting a microphone inch from her face.

"Do you have any comments on the ongoing investigation?" another shouts, elbowing a colleague out of the way.

"Is it true you've been named a person of interest?" a third asks, his tone sharp and probing.

Candy's eyes widen slightly at the last question, but she quickly recovers, shaking her head vehemently. "No, no, I'm just here to grieve in peace," she insists, her voice breaking. She leans heavily on Kelly, who is trying her best to remain composed amidst the chaos.

"Please," Candy begs, her face contorting with feigned anguish, "I just need some space. Please respect my privacy during this difficult time." She wonders why they kept calling Lorenzo her husband.

The crowd of reporters continues to press in, but with Kelly's support, she manages to push through, navigating her way toward a waiting black limousine. The vehicle is parked just outside the terminal, its engine running and the driver standing by the open rear door.

Candy and Kelly quickly climb into the back seat, slamming the door shut behind them. As the ride pulls away, the reporters continue to shout questions and snap photos, their faces a mixture of frustration and triumph at having captured the moment. Candy watches them through the tinted rear window, her expression hardening once more as the airport fades into the distance.

***

The sleek, black limousine glides through the quiet streets, approaching the grand entrance of Lorenzo's upscale Miami home. As it nears the property, the glow of flashlights and camera flashes becomes visible, revealing a sizable crowd of reporters and onlookers gathered outside the gates.

The press members jostle for position, holding up microphones and shouting questions as the limousine slows to a crawl. Beyond the gate, a sea of flowers lines the walkway, their petals shimmering under the soft glow of candles held by somber football fans. Many are wearing jerseys with Lorenzo's number, and some hold signs that read "R.I.P. Lorenzo" and "We Love You." A makeshift memorial has formed at the gates, with photographs, handwritten notes, and candles flickering in the night breeze, their flames casting eerie shadows on the faces of the mourners.

Inside the limousine, Candy leans forward, peering through the tinted window at the unexpected display. Her face contorts in both disbelief and irritation as she takes in the scene.

"You gotta be kidding me," she mutters, her voice barely audible over the murmurs of the crowd outside.

The limousine rolls up to the front gate, which swings open upon their arrival, allowing the vehicle to pass through. The gate closes promptly behind them, cutting off the clamor of the crowd. The driver parks the limousine in the circular driveway, coming to a smooth stop in front of the grand entrance. He steps out swiftly, moving around to open the passenger door.

Kelly steps out first, her face reflecting wariness. She quickly turns to help Candy, who carefully maneuvers her way out, her arm still in a sling. Candy keeps her head down, her face hidden beneath a veil of apparent grief, playing the part of the bereaved widow for any onlookers who might be watching.

The driver begins to unload the bags from the trunk, setting them neatly on the ground beside the limo. Candy and Kelly make their way toward the front door, their footsteps echoing softly on the stone pathway. As they approach, Kelly reaches out for the handle, ready to open the door and step inside.

But before her hand can grasp the doorknob, the door swings open from the inside. Standing in the doorway is Jimmy, as the new house manager.

"Welcome home," Jimmy says, his voice calm and steady.

Candy and Kelly exchange a quick, surprised glance. They hadn't expected anyone to be there waiting for them. Most especially not Jimmy.

The door shuts behind Jimmy with a quiet thud, enveloping the foyer in an uneasy silence. As soon as the sound of the crowd outside fades, Candy's demeanor changes dramatically. She yanks off her sling and hurls it across the room, her face contorted with rage.

"What the fuck are you doing here?!" she snaps, her voice a sharp whisper that slices through the air. Her eyes are fiery, blazing with anger and panic.

Jimmy remains unfazed by her outburst. He stands calmly, arms crossed over his chest, watching her with an almost bemused expression.

"I'm your new security," he says matter-of-factly. He turns his attention to Kelly, who stands awkwardly to the side, unsure of where to look or what to do. "And you are?" he asks, raising an eyebrow.

Kelly opens her mouth to respond, but Candy cuts her off before she can get a word out.

"Forget her," She barks, waving a dismissive hand in Kelly's direction. She takes a step closer to Jimmy, her body tense and her voice rising with frustration. "Are you nuts? Don't you think having a man hanging around the house right after my husband died is a little... STUPID?!"

Jimmy's expression remains calm, almost bored. "You're smart, you'll figure out a way to explain it," he says coolly, shrugging as if her concerns are trivial.

Candy throws her hands up in exasperation. "I've got half the city watching me, an insurance investigator dogging my every move, and now this?" she hisses, her voice dripping with incredulity.

Jimmy steps forward, his demeanor becoming more serious. "Deal with it, Candy," he says firmly, locking eyes with her. "You know our history. This is the only way it's gonna work."

For a moment, the two of them stand face-to-face, locked in a silent battle of wills. Candy's chest heaves with anger, but he doesn't budge, his calm confidence unshaken. Finally, he turns and walks away, leaving Candy and Kelly standing alone in the foyer with the luggage scattered around them.

As Jimmy disappears down the hallway, Candy lets out a frustrated growl and turns away, pacing back and forth. Kelly remains silent, her eyes darting between Candy and the direc- tion he went. She fidgets nervously, unsure of what to say or do.

Candy stops pacing and slumps against the wall, her expression a mix of anger and defeat. "This is just perfect," she mutters under her breath, rubbing her temples as if trying to ward off a headache.

"As if things weren't complicated enough already."

Kelly finally gathers the courage to speak. "What are we going to do now?" she asks hesitantly, her voice barely above a whisper.

She is straightening up, her eyes narrowing as a determined look crosses her face. "We stick to the plan," she says firmly, her voice resolute. "We keep our heads down, we play the grieving widow and friend, and we get through this. No mistakes, no slip-ups. Got it?"

Kelly nods quickly, swallowing hard. "Got it," she echoes, her voice shaky.

Taking a deep breath, Candy tried to calm herself. "Good," she says, her tone softer now but still edged with tension. "Now, let's get these bags upstairs and figure out our next move."

Kelly bends down to pick up the bags, and Candy watches her for a moment before turning and heading towards the staircase, her mind racing with thoughts of what to do next. As she ascends the stairs, the weight of the situation presses down on her, but she forces herself to stay focused.

***

Houston pushed open the door to the cheap motel room, the salt of the ocean filled the air, mixing with the staleness of the room. The faint sound of crashing waves could be heard in the distance, barely muffled by the thin, flimsy walls. He tossed a duffel bag onto the bed, causing the mattress to sag under its weight, and flicked on the television mounted to the wall. The screen flickered to life, casting a bluish glow across the room, highlighting the peeling wallpaper and stained carpet.

Reaching behind his back, Houston pulled out a large automatic handgun, its metallic surface catching the light for a brief moment. He placed it on the nightstand with a thud, the weight of the weapon a stark contrast to the fragile, worn-out furniture around it. He threw himself onto the bed, the springs creaking loudly under his weight, and began flipping through the channels on the television with a weary, disinterested expression.

Images flashed quickly across the screen until he paused on a local news broadcast. A pair of perfectly polished news anchors sat behind a sleek desk, their faces set in serious expressions as they shifted to a new story.

"Turning to the tragic death of Miami football star Lorenzo Steele," the anchorman said, his tone somber, "reporter Miriam Walker was at Miami International when his fiancee, former cheerleader Candy Steele, arrived from the vacation cut short by tragedy."

The scene on the television changed, cutting to live feed outside

Candy and Lorenzo's luxurious home. A crowd of fans held a candlelight vigil, their faces illuminated by the soft, flickering glow of dozens of candles. Signs expressing love and condolences for the fallen star filled the background, creating a sea of grief and support.

In front of this backdrop stood Miriam Walker, a reporter with a sympathetic expression, holding a microphone. "Just days after departing from this very terminal, happy and celebrating the end of the football season, one of Miami's most glamorous couples was rocked by the tragic accident that claimed the life of this rising football star," she reported.

As Miriam spoke, the broadcast transitioned into a montage of still photos and video clips of Lorenzo Steele's career highlights. Powerful tackles, triumphant touchdowns, and his charismatic smile played across the screen, showing a man full of life and potential.

"Bursting onto the scene in his second year," Miriam's voice continued over the footage, "Lorenzo Steele seemed headed for superstardom. Brash, outspoken, but always ready at game time... 'Hard Steele,' as he was known, was poised for a huge breakout season."

Houston watched, his eyes narrowing at the sight of Lorenzo's smiling face. Reaching into his duffel bag, he pulled out a bottle of tequila. He twisted the cap off with a swift flick of his thumb and took a long, deliberate swig, the burn of the liquor a familiar comfort. His eyes remained glued to the screen, the news report now cutting to footage from earlier in the day.

The screen showed Candy and Kelly emerging from the airport, cameras flashing and reporters crowding around them. Candy's face was a mask of grief, her expression distraught and tear- streaked.

"I... I can't really find the words..." Candy stammered, her voice trembling with emotion. "Lorenzo was my life... he loved this city, loved his team... he..."

Her voice broke, and she reached into her purse, pulling out a delicate handkerchief to dab at her eyes. Her entire body seemed to sag under the weight of her sorrow. Kelly, as the supportive friend, wrapped an arm around Candy's shoulders, gently guiding her away from the pressing crowd of microphones and cameras.

"Lorenzo Steele will be remembered for his exciting play on the gridiron," Miriam's voice narrated as the footage showed Candy being led away, "but to his beautiful woman, he will always be missed. Miriam Walker, Miami International Airport, reporting."

Houston watched his face impassive as the news segment ended. He took another swig from the tequila bottle, his gaze still fixed on the television. He raised the bottle in a mocking toast, a crooked smile pulling at the corners of his lips.

"Jimmy was right... you are dangerous goods," he muttered to himself, his voice low and filled with a bitter edge.

As the news anchor moved on to the next story, Houston's attention was caught by the mention of Lorenzo's contract.

"Sources close to the team report that Lorenzo Steele's contract carried an enormous insurance rider," the anchorman stated. "While no amount was mentioned, sources claim the policy was standard for a star athlete and was not related to his death."

A flash of anger crossed Houston's face. His jaw clenched tightly, and his grip on the tequila bottle tightened until his knuckles turned white. In a sudden burst of rage, he hurled the bottle across the room. It shattered against the wall, sending shards of glass and a spray of liquor flying in all directions.

"FUCK!" he yelled, the curse echoing in the small, quiet space. The TV continued to play in the background, the anchors moving on to other news, but Houston wasn't listening any- more. His chest heaved with frustration, his mind racing with thoughts of betrayal and anger. He paced back and forth across the small room, the weight of the gun on the nightstand, a constant, heavy presence in the corner of his mind.

***

A nondescript rental car sat parked discreetly across the street from Candy and Lorenzo's house, blending into the shadows of the quiet suburban neighborhood. Inside the car, Quinn leaned back in the driver's seat, his face partially illuminated by the faint orange glow of his cigarette. He took a long drag, exhaling a thin stream of smoke that quickly dissipated into the night air. His eyes were fixed on the house, observing every detail, every movement, as if he were a predator waiting for the perfect moment to strike.

Upstairs in the bedroom, Candy stood by the window, peeking through a narrow gap in the heavy drapes. She stared down at the street below, her expression a mix of irritation and exhaustion. Outside, a few die-hard fans still maintained their candlelight vigil, their faces cast in a soft, flickering glow. Among them were a scattering of dead flowers and wilted wreaths, remnants of earlier tributes left to honor Lorenzo.

Candy sighed, her breath fogging up the cold glass as she muttered under her breath. "How long are they going to do this? Jesus Christ, he wasn't that good a player."

Behind her, Kelly lay sprawled on the bed, her hands resting behind her head as she stared up at the ceiling. She chuckled softly, her voice carrying a hint of sarcasm. "It's really a testament to football fans. Music fans are that devoted. You wouldn't catch tennis fans still hanging around this long."

Candy turned to give Kelly an unimpressed look, one eyebrow raised. "Funny."

She began pacing the room, her movements restless and agitated. She was like a caged animal, trapped in her own home, unable to escape the eyes of the public and the weight of her grief. "I'm going nuts. I gotta get out of here," she blurted out, her frustration bubbling to the surface.

Kelly propped herself up on her elbows, her expression turning serious. "Not a good idea," she cautioned. "We're probably being watched."

Candy threw her hands up in exasperation. "Well, we've been back three weeks. How long do I have to mourn?"

Kelly gestured towards the window with a nod. "Till they go home," she replied matter-of-factly.

Candy sighed again, more heavily this time, her shoulders slumping in defeat. She turned back to the window, her eyes scanning the small group of fans still gathered outside. She felt a pang of anger mixed with helplessness. All she wanted was for this to be over, to move on with her life and leave the tragedy behind. But as long as the fans remained, so did the reminders of what she had done.

Jimmy rummaged through the nearly empty refrigerator, pushing aside a carton of eggs and a half-empty jug of milk. The shelves were mostly bare, save for a few forgotten leftovers and a jar of pickles. He grumbled under his breath, annoyed at the lack of options. Just as he was about to slam the refrigerator door shut, his cell phone rang. He pulled it out of his pocket, glancing at the caller ID before answering.

"Yeah, go," he said tersely, still irritated. He listened intently as the voice on the other end spoke, his expression darkening with each passing second. "What? ... Yeah, yeah, sure." With a heavy sigh, he hung up and slammed the refrigerator door shut with a force that rattled the contents inside.

He left the kitchen and headed to the room, pushed open the bedroom door, his face set in a serious expression. Candy was sitting on the edge of the bed, her posture tense, as she stared out the window. Hearing Jimmy's heavy footsteps, she turned to face him.

"You got a call," Jimmy said bluntly, holding out the phone toward her.

Candy hesitated for a moment, a flicker of uncertainty crossing her face. Reluctantly, she took the phone from him, already dreading the conversation that awaited her. Pressing the phone to her ear, she spoke with a tone that mixed irritation with caution.

"This isn't smart," she muttered.

Houston's voice crackled over the line, laced with impatience and anger. "Don't tell me about smart. You get your ass here now."

Candy's grip tightened on the phone, her knuckles turning white. "How the hell am I supposed to do that?" she snapped back, her frustration bubbling over.

"Fucking do it, Candy!" He barked, his voice sharp and commanding.

Before she could respond, the line went dead. "Wait, what... Houston? Houston? Damn it!" she yelled, her voice echoing off the walls. In a fit of rage, she hurled the phone across the room. It shattered against the wall, pieces scattering across the floor.

Jimmy, who had been standing nearby, jumped at the sound of the phone smashing. "Hey! What the hell?" he exclaimed, his eyes wide with surprise.

Candy's chest heaved with anger and frustration. She ran a hand through her hair, her mind racing with thoughts of Houston's demands and the impossible situation she found herself in. She knew things were spiraling out of control, but she felt powerless to stop it.

Jimmy watched her carefully, his expression softening slightly. "What did he say?" he asked, his voice calmer now, trying to understand the severity of the situation.

She didn't respond immediately, still trying to process everything. She stared at the broken phone on the floor, the reality of her predicament sinking deeper. "He wants me to go to him," she finally said, her voice barely above a whisper. "But I don't know how the hell I'm supposed to do that."

Jimmy nodded slowly, understanding the dilemma. "We'll figure it out," he said, trying to offer some reassurance. "But first, we need to get you out of here without anyone noticing."

Candy glanced at him, her eyes filled with a mix of fear and determination. "Yeah," she said softly, her voice trembling slightly. "Yeah, we do."

Quinn sat in his nondescript rental car, a cigarette dangling lazily between his lips. His eyes were fixed on the house ahead, barely visible behind the gated entrance. As he took a slow drag, the gate began to creak open. Candy's sleek 600SL convertible, its top down, emerged from the driveway. Kelly sat beside her in the passenger seat, her face tense with anticipation. Candy paused at the street, glancing in the rearview mirror. Noticing Quinn's car, she smirked, a glint of mischief in her eyes.

Quinn quickly flicked his cigarette out the window and shifted his car into gear, ready to follow.

She drove cautiously down the city street, her eyes darting between the road ahead and the rearview mirror. She caught sight of Quinn's car tailing them and tightened her grip on the wheel. A sly smile tugged at her lips as she adjusted her hand on the shifter.

"Hold on," She muttered, more to herself than to Kelly. She shifted into a lower gear, and the car roared to life, surging forward with a burst of speed. The engine growled as they weaved through traffic, narrowly missing a couple of cars. Quinn was quick to react, punching the gas to keep up.

Inside Candy's car, Kelly braced herself, her knuckles turning white as she clutched the edge of her seat. She glanced nervously over her shoulder, catching sight of Quinn's car gaining on them.

"I hope you know what you're doing," Kelly shouted over the roar of the wind.

Candy's expression was set, focused. "This wasn't my idea, remember?"

Without warning, she yanked the wheel hard to the right, spinning the car into a narrow alley. The tires screeched against the pavement, and they barely avoided a stack of garbage cans. Behind them, Quinn slammed on his brakes, his car skidding as he attempted to make the sharp turn. His sedan grazed the side of a fence, but he quickly straightened out and floored it, blasting through a group of garbage cans, sending them flying in all directions.

She checked her rearview mirror, her eyes wide and focused. The adrenaline coursed through her veins as she navigated the tight alley, dodging obstacles at every turn.

"LOOK OUT!" Kelly screamed, her voice filled with panic.

She snapped her attention back to the front and saw the massive rear end of an SUV stopped dead ahead. She slammed on the brakes, cutting the wheel hard to avoid a collision. The car swerved around the SUV, just as another vehicle barreled through the intersection. The car narrowly missed them, crashing into a parked car with a deafening crunch. Candy didn't waste a second as she floored the gas again, the tires squealing as they shot through the intersection, narrowly avoiding two more cars.

"Wow," She breathed, her heart racing. She risked a quick glance at Kelly, who was gripping the dashboard with both hands. "I mean, wow!"

Kelly glanced back, her face pale. "Tell me we lost him. Tell me we lost him!"

She checked the mirror again and saw Quinn's sedan charging through the chaos they had left behind, weaving through the intersection.

"Okay," She muttered, trying to keep her voice steady. Kelly twisted in her seat to look back. "SHIT!"

Quinn on the other hand tightened his grip on the wheel, his eyes locked on Candy's taillights. "Okay, now I got it. It's crazy time, huh? Alright, okay, here we go, gloves are off, baby," he muttered to himself, his jaw clenched with determination.

Candy pushed the car harder, taking sharp corners and cutting through gas stations, desperately trying to lose Quinn. Her mind raced with possibilities. Finally, she had an idea.

"Take off your top," Candy ordered suddenly, her voice urgent. Kelly shot her a confused look. "What?"

"Take it off!" She insisted, her tone leaving no room for argument.

Kelly hesitated, still baffled. "Alright, I'm trying to be more open but..."

"Kelly, just shut up and take off your top! We gotta lose this guy!"

Grumbling under her breath, she complied, pulling off her shirt and tossing it aside. "I don't see how this is gonna help," she muttered.

"Lose the bra," Candy commanded, her eyes flicking between the road and Kelly.

Kelly raised an incredulous eyebrow. "Candy, I know you think of them as weapons, but..."

"HURRY UP!" She snapped, her focus back on the road.

With a resigned sigh, Kelly unclasped her bra and held her hands over her chest. "Satisfied?"

Candy took a quick glance over and smirked. "Nice. When I tell you, get ready for a full-on flash."

Staring at her, wide-eyed. "A what?" She blurted.

"Flash! When I tell you, jump up and flash whoever's looking."

"I can't—"

"Hey, it's not brain surgery. You stand up, wave your arms, go WOOOOO! Got it? God, do I have to do everything?"

Candy turned a corner onto a street lined with bustling nightclubs, the neon lights casting colorful reflections on the wet pavement. She honked the horn furiously and slammed on the brakes, skidding sideways to a stop in the middle of the street.

"NOW!" Candy shouted.

Kelly shot her a hard look but quickly stood up, grabbing the spoiler for balance. "WOOOOOOOOO!" she yelled, waving her arms wildly.

The crowds on either side of the street erupted in cheers, people rushing forward to see what the commotion was about. Candy glanced behind them and saw Quinn's car approaching. They needed a bigger distraction.

"You gotta sell it more," Candy urged.

Kelly hesitated for a split second, then reached down, grabbed her by the shirt, and pulled her into a kiss. The two women leaned into each other, their hands roaming over each other's bodies. The crowd gasped, then exploded into a frenzy of cheers and applause, rushing into the street and blocking traffic.

Kelly pulled away and dropped back into her seat, breathless. "Hey, come on, let's go."

Candy blinked, momentarily stunned by the kiss, but quickly snapped back to reality. She saw Quinn's car turning the corner behind them, but the street was now filled with screaming, excited club-goers.

Candy waved cheekily at Quinn, then floored the gas pedal. The 600SL roared to life, peeling away through a gap in the crowd.

Quinn slammed on the brakes as he reached the edge of the mob. He laid on the horn, but the crowd, fueled by the excitement of the spectacle, refused to budge. Realizing he wasn't going anywhere, he threw his hands up in frustration and slammed his fists on the steering wheel.

"Damn it!" He shouted, watching helplessly as Candy's car disappeared into the night.

***

Candy and Kelly pushed through the heavy wooden door of Moody's Pub. The moment they stepped inside, they burst into laughter, their voices echoing in the low-ceilinged room. They headed straight to the bar, Candy leading the way with an easy confidence.

The bartender, a grizzled man in his fifties, caught sight of them and gave a knowing smile. As Candy approached, he slid a bottle of tequila across the bar to her. "On the house," he said with a wink.

"Thanks, Jake," Candy replied, catching the bottle with one hand. She turned, her eyes scanning the room until they landed on Houston, who was sitting in the far corner. His expression was dark, his brows furrowed as he stared at them from across the room.

Kelly leaned in closer to Candy, her voice low. "Jeez, he looks pissed."

She smirked, unfazed by Houston's glare. "Leave him to me," she said coolly, strutting confidently toward the corner table.

Houston didn't even blink as they approached. He kept his eyes locked on Candy, his expression a mix of anger and frustration. As they reached the table, Candy didn't waste any time. She poured herself a shot of tequila, tossing it back like it was water.

Houston's eyes flicked to Kelly for a moment, then back to her. "Why's she here?" he asked, his voice low and menacing.

"I needed the company," Candy replied with a shrug, pouring herself another shot.

His fist came down hard on the table, making both women jump. "Tell me about the money, Candy," he demanded, his eyes burning with intensity.

Candy played dumb, her face a picture of innocence. "What money?"

His patience snapped, and he slammed his fist down again. "Quit jacking me around. The insurance money, Candy. When were you gonna tell me about that?"

She rolled her eyes, unfazed by his anger. "You're getting your end," she said, her tone dismissive.

Houston leaned in, his voice growling low. "I'm getting shit. Wasting your husband when he's insured for two hundred fifty million...not real smart."

Kelly's eyes widened in shock. "How much?" she asked, her voice barely a whisper.

He turned his gaze to her, his expression incredulous. "You didn't know either?" he asked, his tone dripping with sarcasm.

Sighing and rolling her eyes again. "It's not the way it sounds," Candy insisted.

Kelly looked at Candy, her face pale. "Are you crazy? Do you know what kind of heat that will bring down?"

She waved off her concern with a flick of her wrist. "We can handle it. No one thinks it was anything but an accident."

Houston leaned back in his chair, shaking his head in disbelief. "What do you think, they're gonna cut you a check and forget it? You start writing checks to your maid here and some random career criminal, and no one's gonna say anything?"

"We're dead, we're dead," Kelly muttered, her voice shaking.

Candy rolled her eyes. "What's the difference? If no one suspects, what's the difference?"

Houston's eyes narrowed, his voice dropping to a dangerous whisper. "Shares for starters, increased risk, increased return. I want my share. Don't forget, I have a lovely photo essay of you and your little playmate here doing in old Lorenzo. So let's be realistic."

Kelly's face went even paler. "I can't believe this is happening," she whispered, her voice filled with dread.

Candy fixed Houston with a cold stare. "You know, Houston, we have always understood each other. I always thought you had balls. This is no time to turn soft. I know what I'm doing."

His face hardened. "The hell you do. Settle with the insurance company."

She blinked, taken aback. "What?!"

"Settle," He repeated firmly. "How much money do you need,

Candy? Make them an offer. If you don't, we're all going down for this."

She took another shot of tequila, her mind racing. "So what do we do?" she asked finally.

Houston's voice was steady, his plan already formed. "We set up a numbered account in the Cayman Islands, funnel the money there, and all take an equal share, then go our separate ways."

Her face twisted with disdain. "The hell with that."

Houston leaned forward, his eyes boring into hers. "The hell with you. Don't fuck with me on this."

She sneered. "So we put the money somewhere only you can get it? How stupid do you think I am?"

Houston's jaw clenched. "I'm not giving you another chance to screw me over."

The table fell silent for a moment, the tension thick in the air. Finally, he spoke again, his voice softer but still firm. "It's the only way it works, Candy."

She considered his words, then nodded slowly. "Then I want some insurance."

Houston frowned, confused. "What?"

"Give Kelly access to the account you set up," Candy demanded.

Kelly's eyes widened in shock. "Me?" she stammered.

She nodded. "You'll still have what you want," she said to Houston, "and I'll feel more secure... just in case."

Kelly shook her head, panic creeping back into her voice. "Don't put me in the middle of this. I'm already freaked."

Houston studied Kelly for a long moment, then nodded. "Alright."

Kelly looked between them, bewildered. "Alright? Alright? What the hell are you guys talking about?"

He stood, downing a shot of tequila in one gulp. "I'll set it up. You deal with the insurance company. All the money in the world won't do us any good if we're in prison, Candy."

With that, Houston turned and walked away, leaving the two ladies sitting in stunned silence.

Kelly turned to Candy, her eyes wide with confusion and fear. "What just happened?"

She shrugged, her expression cool and detached. "Nothing," she said, her voice calm. "Just the price of doing business."

Chapter Twenty-One

Candy walked with sharp precision down the hall of Allied Insurance, her designer heels clicking with purpose. Dressed in an elegant, tailored business suit, she was the picture of both authority and style. She carried an air of unshakable confidence, her head held high as she followed Ron through the series of offices. Her eyes remained forward, never once wavering as she neared the room where the meeting awaited her. Every detail of her look was carefully considered, her impeccable makeup, her perfectly coiffed hair, and the understated luxury of her accessories. Candy's clear intention was to command attention, and it was clear she had no intention of being underestimated.

Ron led the way and opened the door with practiced ease, stepping aside to allow Candys's entry. The door creaked slightly as it swung open, revealing a spacious conference room that boasted polished wooden walls, expensive artwork, and a long table made of mahogany that gleamed under the overhead lights.

Two figures were seated at a sleek, glass table, Richards and Quinn. Both looked up as she entered.

"Ms. Steele, this is Mr. Richards, and I believe you've already met Mr. Jessop," Ron introduced, stepping back as Candy walked confidently into the room.

Candy's eyes briefly flicked to Quinn Jessop, who sat with an expression of measured calm, his fingers interlaced on the table. She offered a polite smile. "Nice to see you again, Mr. Jessop."

"Good morning," Richards greeted with a nod, his voice carrying authority but laced with politeness.

"Morning, Richards. Quinn," Candy replied with a polite smile, her tone professional yet warm.

Quinn returned the smile and echoed the greeting before motioning to the empty seat across from him. "Candy, please take a seat."

She moved with graceful precision, taking her seat at the table while maintaining eye contact with the two men before her. For a brief moment, silence filled the room, tension simmering just beneath the surface. The hum of the air conditioner was the only sound, underscoring the unspoken thoughts that passed between them.

Richards, the company vice president with a demeanor that suggested he had seen it all in his years, finally broke the silence. He leaned forward slightly, adjusting his glasses. "Ms. Steele, let me first express, on behalf of all of us, our sincere condolences for your loss."

Her expression softened, though only by a fraction. "Thank you, Mr. Richards. It has been difficult, but I'm grateful that Lorenzo took such good care of things. He was a sweet and caring man, always thinking ahead."

Quinn leaned back in his chair with a small smirk that didn't reach his eyes. "Two hundred fifty million is a lot of caring."

Candy's gaze flicked to him, cool and composed, though there was a hint of steel behind her eyes. "He was that kind of guy," she replied with an air of casual indifference. "But let's not beat around the bush, gentlemen. I'm not here to waste time. It's clear that Mr. Jessop feels there's something suspicious about my fiancé's death."

The air in the room grew noticeably heavier. Richards cleared his throat, carefully choosing his words. "No one is directly implying that you were involved in Mr. Steele's passing. However, given the substantial amount of money involved, it's our duty to investigate and ensure that there are no... irregularities in the claim."

Candy's posture stiffened slightly, though her expression remained impeccably controlled. "Irregularities?" she echoed, her tone just short of icy. "He was drunk and drove off a cliff. What exactly is irregular about that?"

The atmosphere was taut like a rope stretched to its limit.

Richards maintained his professional reaction, though there was a subtle shift in his eyes as he sensed the tension rising. "Ms. Steele, I understand this is a difficult time, but we have procedures to follow, especially when dealing with a claim of this size. We simply want to ensure everything is in order."

She crossed her legs, leaning back slightly in her chair. Her expression was one of measured patience, though there was an unmistakable undercurrent of challenge in her gaze. "I'm fully aware of your procedures, Mr. Richards. What I'm wondering is if this is about more than just the money. Perhaps someone here thinks there's more to the story?"

Quinn's eyes met hers, and for a moment, the two locked in a silent battle of wills. He spoke with an edge that suggested he wasn't easily intimidated. "Let's just say that the circumstances of Mr. Steele's accident raise questions. But as Mr. Richards said, we're not here to make baseless accusations. We just want to make sure everything checks out."

Candy smiled, though it was more a show of her teeth than anything warm. "Of course. I wouldn't expect anything less from Allied Insurance. After all, thoroughness is key, isn't it?"

Richards interjected, sensing the need to steer the conversation back on track. "Ms. Steele, we understand you're managing a lot right now. If you feel more comfortable with legal representation, we're more than willing to accommodate."

Her smile widened, though it didn't reach her eyes. "Thank you, but I think I can handle reading the amount on a cheque. I don't need an attorney for that."

"Moreso, you're not yet legally married to this man" He cornered, trying to gain more stand.

"Yet my name is always attached to every damn thing." She charged back.

There was a beat of silence as the implication hung in the air. Candy was making it clear she wasn't a woman who could be easily intimidated or delayed. She knew exactly what she wanted and she wasn't about to let anyone stand in her way.

Richards gave a measured nod, maintaining his professionalism. "We appreciate your confidence, Ms. Steele. Our goal is simply to ensure that all parties are protected and that everything is above board."

Her gaze never wavered as she leaned slightly forward, her voice calm but with an edge that cut through the air like a knife. "I trust that your investigation will be thorough and fair. But let me be clear, I expect this matter to be resolved promptly. I won't tolerate unnecessary delays."

Quinn's eyes narrowed, and he leaned forward slightly as if testing her resolve. "We're just doing our job, Ms. Steele. But when two hundred fifty million dollars is on the line, you can understand why we have to be meticulous."

Candy's eyes met his stare with unwavering confidence. "Of course, Mr. Jessop. And I'm sure you understand that I expect what's mine to be delivered without unnecessary complications."

The room went silent again and the anxiety of the room became thickened with each passing second. It was a battle of wits, with each side testing the other's boundaries. Despite the polite words exchanged, there was an undercurrent of suspicion, mistrust, and unspoken threats.

Richards sensed the standoff couldn't continue without escalating. He leaned back, offering a conciliatory smile. "Let's go for a short break, Ms. Steele. We appreciate your cooperation."

Candy uncrossed her legs and stood with the same elegance she had when she entered. "Thank you, gentlemen. I look forward to hearing from you."

With that, she turned and walked out of the room, leaving behind the unmistakable scent of her expensive perfume. As the door clicked shut behind her, the two men exchanged glances.

Quinn's smirk returned, though there was a hardness to it now. "She's playing it cool, but she's nervous. You could see it in her eyes."

Richards sighed, rubbing the bridge of his nose. "Maybe. Or

maybe she's just exactly what she appears to be, a woman who wants what's owed to her."

Quinn shook his head, a glint of suspicion in his eyes. "Nobody plays it that cool unless they've got something to hide. I don't buy it, Richards. Something's off here."

Richards stared at the door, deep in thought. "We'll see. For now, let's focus on the investigation. If there's something to find, we'll find it."

The room fell into an uneasy silence, the men now caught between the line of their professional duties and the growing sense that this case was anything but routine. The stakes were high, and they all knew that one wrong move and the consequences could be far-reaching.

After a few moments, Richards broke the silence. "Ron," he called, his voice carrying experience and authority.

Ron, who had been sitting quietly near the door, immediately stepped forward. "Yes, sir?"

"Call Ms. Steele back in," Richards instructed. "I think it's time we got to the bottom of this, and I want to see how she reacts when we push a little harder."

Ron nodded and quietly slipped out of the room to carry out the instructions. He leaned forward, steepling his fingers as he looked at Quinn. "What do you think?"

Quinn shrugged, his expression skeptical. "She's hiding something. I mean what I said earlier, the cool confidence, the deflections, and how quickly she tried to take control of the conversation, and it all felt rehearsed. I've seen it before."

Richards nodded thoughtfully. "Maybe. Or maybe she's just tired of being under suspicion and wants to get this over with. Either way, we need to see if she cracks under pressure."

They exchanged a few more words, discussing potential angles for their line of questioning. They both knew that the stakes were high, and any misstep could lead to a costly payout or worse a legal battle. After a few minutes, the door opened, and Ron re-entered with Candy following close behind.

She walked back into the room with the same grace and confidence as before, her designer heels barely making a sound on the polished floor. She moved with an air of purpose, her face composed and calm, giving away nothing. Without waiting for an invitation, she returned to her seat and crossed her legs, folding her hands neatly in her lap. Her eyes flicked between Richards and Quinn, her expression polite but expectant.

"Gentlemen," she began smoothly, "I hope we're not going to waste more of each other's time."

Richards allowed a small smile, leaning forward slightly. "Thank you for your patience, Ms. We just need to clarify a few things. We wouldn't want any unresolved questions hanging over this case."

She nodded once, her expression unchanged. "Of course. I'm happy to clear up any questions you might have. But as I mentioned earlier, I do have other engagements to attend to, so let's be efficient, shall we?"

Quinn watched her closely, his eyes narrowing as he reached into his briefcase and pulled out a small plastic bag. He tossed it onto the table in front of Candy with a soft thud. The bag contained a few crushed green leaves, preserved in a clear plastic seal. Candy's eyes flicked to the bag with mild interest, but her expression remained indifferent.

"Know what those are?" Quinn asked, his voice casual but laced with a subtle challenge.

She raised an eyebrow, feigning ignorance. "No, I don't. Should I?"

Quinn leaned back in his chair, crossing his arms over his chest. "Mint leaves," he said, watching her closely for any reaction.

Candy gave a small, dismissive shrug. "And?"

Quinn's eyes hardened and his tone sharpened. "I found them at the scene of your husband's accident. The funny thing is, when I had them analyzed, they came back with traces of a particular spider venom. Not enough to kill a man, but certainly enough to incapacitate him. Now, isn't that interesting?"

Candy's expression remained calm, though there was the faintest hint of amusement in her eyes. "My husband was hardly a 'normal' man, Mr. Jessop. He was a professional football player strong, fit, and very much in peak physical condition. Something like that wouldn't have affected him the way it might affect someone else."

Quinn leaned forward, pressing his point. "Kinda an odd thing to turn up at a crash site, though, don't you think? Especially when combined with everything else."

Candy didn't flinch. She kept her voice steady, her eyes locked on his. "So, there are no spiders on the Island? Is that what you're getting at, Mr. Jessop?"

Quinn's lips curled into a smirk. "Oh, there are plenty of spiders in that area. It's full of them. The question is, how do traces of venom from a rare species end up on mint leaves found at the scene of your husband's so-called 'accident'?"

She leaned back, uncrossing and recrossing her legs with practiced ease. "Well then, it sounds like what you have is nothing more than a natural occurrence. There's nothing strange about it, is there?"

Quinn didn't back down, sensing an opportunity to push

further. "On its own, maybe not. But when combined with some other curious facts, it does raise questions. Like why someone would choose that particular area to go driving alone, late at night. And why traces of alcohol in your husband's system don't seem consistent with the usual behavior of a disciplined athlete."

Her expression remained cold and composed, but there was an edge in her voice now. "You're fishing, Mr. Jessop. My husband was a grown man who made his own decisions. If he chose to have a drink or two, that was his business. But to imply there's something more nefarious at play here without concrete evidence is irresponsible at best."

Quinn's smirk faded slightly as he leaned in, his voice dropping to a near whisper. "I don't have to imply anything. The facts speak for themselves. And the fact that you're trying so hard to brush them off tells me you're hiding something."

Candy's eyes narrowed, her composure still intact but with a hint of icy disdain now creeping into her tone. "I'm not hiding anything, Mr. Jessop. What I'm tired of is being treated like a suspect in my own man's death. I'm here for what's rightfully mine, and I don't have time to indulge baseless theories."

Richards, sensing the exasperation of the matter escalating, stepped in with a calming gesture. "Let's not get ahead of ourselves here. We're all just trying to understand the full picture. We're simply exploring every angle, as is our obligation. We're not making any accusations."

She shifted her gaze to Richards, her voice smooth as silk but carrying an unmistakable edge. "Exploring every angle? Fine. But I won't be bullied, Mr. Richards. Here's what I suggest, I'm not interested in your money if it means being dragged through the mud and lynched in the media. I have a reputation to protect, and I won't let this turn into a circus."

The room fell silent, the air filled with unspoken words. Candy's challenge hung in the air, a test to see how far they were willing to push. Quinn's eyes remained locked on hers, but it was Richards who finally spoke, his tone measured and professional.

"We're not looking to create any unnecessary complications. We just need to complete our due diligence. Once we've done that, this matter can be put to rest."

She leaned forward slightly, her gaze unflinching. "Good. Then I suggest you do just that. Investigate, cross your T's, dot your I's, and get this over with. Because I won't be waiting forever."

Quinn watched her with calculating eyes, still unconvinced. "We'll be thorough. You can count on that."

Her lips curled into a faint smile, more mocking than friendly. "I'm sure you will. And I'll be here when you're ready to issue the cheque."

With that, she stood, her movements fluid and deliberate. She smoothed the front of her suit, adjusting her jacket with a graceful flick of her hand, her eyes swept the room one last time, locking onto each man's gaze with a combination of allure and confidence. She moved with the grace of someone who knew she was in control, her presence commanding attention without a word. The atmosphere in the room thickened, and every man except Quinn fell into her trap. Even Richards seasoned and calculating look, couldn't completely hide his momentary distraction.

"Yes, I do have a suggestion," she said smoothly, her voice wrapping around the words like velvet. "It's clear that an ongoing battle doesn't suit either of us. So, here's what I propose fifty million dollars, Mr. Richards. That's the amount I'll settle for one cheque, fifty million dollars, and I'm out of your hair.

I'll never be bothered by Allied Insurance again, and this whole thing goes away."

Candy moved slowly across the room, her heels clicking softly against the floor as she reached into her purse. The man's eyes followed her every move, captivated by her poise. She took out a slim, leather-bound folder and placed it on the table with deliberate care. "My lawyer came up with this little agreement. Since no charges have been filed and none will be, this should resolve all matters related to my husband's death. Or so they tell me."

"Your fiance" Quinn corrected but she didn't reply, not even spare him a glance.

She pushed the contract across the table toward Richards, who remained silent as he glanced at it. There was a long pause as her offer hung in the air like a dare.

"Take it or leave it," she continued. "I'm happy to go the distance on this, and if it comes to that, I'd probably win. We both know that."

Richards didn't immediately reach for the contract, but his calculating eyes were already weighing the risks and benefits. Candy could see the wheels turning in his mind. She allowed herself a small, confident smile, knowing she had backed them into a corner.

She turned as if to leave, then paused with a perfectly timed flick of her hand. "Oh, I almost forgot there's additional ten million for a foundation in Lorenzo's name. It's a nice tax deduction for you, and the least I can do to honor his memory. I'll be expecting your call."

Richards studied her with sharp eyes as she finished her proposal, the room was tense with unspoken thoughts and calculations. Her confident act never wavered, even as Richards leaned forward, clasping his hands together in contemplation.

He broke the silence. "Ms. Steele, you've certainly given us something to think about. But before we proceed, I need a moment to discuss this privately with my colleagues."

Candy's smile remained, but her eyes hardened slightly. "Of course, Mr. Richards. But don't take too long I don't have all day."

With that, she stood gracefully and headed toward the door. Just before leaving, she paused, her fingers lingering on the doorknob. "I'll be outside, but let's not drag this out. I expect an answer shortly." With a final, meaningful glance at the room, she closed the door behind her, leaving the three men inside.

Candy stepped into the hallway, her sharp heels echoing slightly against the polished floor as she walked. The calm and controlled exterior she maintained was masking the quick calculations running through her mind. She walked to the end of the hall, stopping at a large window overlooking the bustling city below. She stood there, taking in the view while subtly checking her watch. Every passing second felt like a silent countdown, a test of how long they'd take before they caved to her terms.

Back inside the room, Richards leaned back in his chair, rubbing his temples as if trying to ease the tension building there. He exchanged a glance with Quinn, whose expression was still hard with suspicion and doubt.

"She's good," he murmured, almost to himself.

Quinn leaned forward, his voice low but edged with frustration. "So, we're really going to let her get away with this? You know she's behind Lorenzo's death. All the signs are there."

Richards sighed, tired of the back-and-forth. "It doesn't matter what we suspect. There's no solid proof that could hold up in court, and you know how costly a full investigation would be let alone a legal battle. The media would have a field day. And even if we went all in, we could still lose. This offer lets us cut our losses and move on."

Quinn clenched his jaw, still unhappy. "And what happens when she tries this again? What if she gets bolder?"

Richards shook his head. "She's smart enough to know not to push her luck. She's won this round, but it's likely her last big score. We need to think about the business and what's at stake here. We can't afford a scandal especially not one that risks our reputation and revenue streams."

He made his decision with a finality that left no room for debate. He straightened in his seat and buzzed the intercom. "Ron, ask

Ms. Steele to join us again."

Candy stood near the window, her patience running thin. She had expected them to take time to deliberate, but they were pushing it. Just as she considered returning to the room uninvited, Ron appeared with a neutral expression.

"They're ready for you, Ms. Steele," he said with practiced politeness.

She turned, giving Ron a curt nod before striding back down the hallway. She opened the door without hesitation, walking into the room with the same confidence as before. Closing the door behind her, she faced the men, noting the change in the atmosphere. Richards looked resigned but resolved, while Quinn's scowl barely hid his frustration.

"Well?" she asked, raising an eyebrow.

Richards didn't waste any more time. "We'll accept your terms, Ms. Steele. Fifty million, and we consider this matter closed. But first, there are a few documents you'll need to sign." He slid the cheque across the table, accompanied by a stack of legal papers.

Her eyes flickered with satisfaction as she saw the check. It was the final piece she needed. She walked forward, picked up the pen, and signed the documents with quick, fluid motions. As she did, the room was silent except for the soft scratch of pen on paper.

Once finished, she looked up, her smile sharp. "Pleasure doing business with you, gentlemen. You can rest assured, you'll never hear from me again."

Richards gave a curt nod. "We trust you'll keep your end of the bargain, Ms. Steele. Any future complications, and we won't be so accommodating."

Candy didn't flinch at the implied threat. "I have no intention of revisiting this chapter," she replied smoothly, tucking the check and copies of the signed documents into her purse. "Consider this matter resolved."

Without waiting for a response, she turned and walked toward the door. As she opened it and stepped out, she couldn't resist one final parting shot. "I'll be in touch if I decide to set up that foundation. It might be a nice way to honor Lorenzo's legacy, don't you think?"

She didn't wait for a reply, closing the door behind her with a soft click. The room was left in heavy silence, Richards and Quinn exchanging a long look.

Outside the building, she emerged from the sleek, glass-walled skyscraper with the same poise she had displayed inside. She paused for a moment, slipping on a pair of dark sunglasses that added a final touch to her stylish ensemble. She moved with an air of triumph, the check in her purse felt like a seal of victory. As she reached the curb, she looked toward the street, she saw her cab waiting by the curb, the door open and ready.

Her lips curved into a satisfied smile as she strode toward the car. But beneath the surface, her mind was still racing, calculating her next move. She slid into the backseat of the car, and as it pulled away, she allowed herself a moment of satisfaction. But even as she settled back, a new set of calculations began to run through her mind.

They say every move in business is a gamble. You bet big, you win big or you lose it all. I've stacked the deck in my favor, but this game isn't over until I cash in. Fifty million dollars now I just need to make sure I keep it.

The city blurred past the windows as the car sped away, carrying Candy toward the next phase of her plan.

She stared out the window as the cityscape blurred past. Her expression remained serene, but inside, she replayed the events of the last few weeks like a chess game in her mind. Every move had been carefully orchestrated, every piece positioned with precision. But the final hurdle was proving to be more challenging than anticipated.

She knew there was just one more obstacle settling up. Houston was right handing over millions without raising suspicions was going to be tricky. Even with Allied signing off on the contract, they wouldn't take kindly to losing fifty million dollars any more than two hundred fifty. But I've got the cheque I just need the right place to cash it.

The car continued through the busy streets, the hustle and bustle of the city fading as they headed toward more secluded areas. Her mind continued to race, considering every possible angle. She couldn't afford any mistakes now, not when she was this close to closing the deal.

The car made a turn onto a quieter street, lined with towering trees that blocked out most of the sunlight. The car slowed as they approached a gated estate. The high iron gates swung open silently as the car rolled through, disappearing into the shadow of tall, manicured hedges. They drove up a winding driveway until they reached the entrance of an elegant mansion. The car stopped, and the driver stepped out to open the door for her.

She stepped out and took in the grand estate with a casual glance as if it were nothing out of the ordinary. But her mind was already calculating her next move. She wasn't here for the scenery, she was here to meet someone who could help her with the final piece of the puzzle.

***

The study was dimly lit, with heavy mahogany furniture and shelves lined with old leather-bound books. The air smelled faintly of cigar smoke and aged whiskey. Candy sat in a high- backed chair across from Houston. He had the kind of influence and connections that could make problems disappear, but nothing came cheap with him.

"So," Houston drawled, leaning back in his chair, "you've managed to get this far. Impressive, but we're not quite done yet, are we?"

Her eyes met his, her expression unwavering. "No, we're not. I need to make sure this deal goes smoothly. Allied may have signed the contract, but I need your help to ensure they don't have second thoughts or find a loophole."

Houston chuckled, a low, rumbling sound. "You know how these things work, darling. Fifty million is still a lot of money to lose, and those insurance boys don't like to part with their cash without a fight. But I've got connections. For the right price, I can make sure everything is airtight."

Candy's smile was icy. "I'm prepared to pay, Houston. But let's not pretend this is just about money. I need assurances no loose ends, no surprises. Can you guarantee that?"

Houston's eyes glittered with amusement. "For you? I can make anything happen. But remember, Candy, once you cross this line, there's no going back. Are you ready for that?"

She didn't hesitate. "I crossed that line a long time ago."

He nodded approvingly. "Good. Then we'll proceed. I'll take care of everything on my end. You focus on tying up the loose ends in your circle. When the dust settles, you'll be sitting pretty and they'll be none the wiser."

She stood, her decision made. She extended her hand, and Houston took it with a firm grip. "Pleasure doing business with you, as always," he said with a sly grin.

"The pleasure's all mine," She replied, her voice laced with a hint of steel.

As she left the mansion, her mind was already racing ahead, planning her next steps. The game was almost over, but she knew better than to let her guard down. One misstep and everything could come crashing down around her. But if she played it right if she stayed two steps ahead she'd be free and clear, with fifty million dollars in her pocket and her future secured.

Chapter Twenty-Two

Candy sat by the window in her lavish hotel suite, gazing out at the cityscape. The cheque for fifty million dollars lay on the coffee table, a tangible reminderof her victory. But now, she and Houston had to figure out how to liquidate the funds quickly without raising suspicion. The longer the money sat in an account, the greater the chance the insurance company could connect the dots or uncover something that might invalidate the settlement. Time was ticking.

Houston paced the room, deep in thought. "We need to move fast. We can't just deposit that kind of money anywhere without eyebrows being raised. The banks will ask questions, and that's not a risk we can afford."

Her eyes narrowed as she considered their options. "You're right. We need to get rid of the check without attracting attention. The insurance company might get curious, and if they decide to dig deeper, everything we've built could come crashing down."

Houston stopped pacing, a sly grin creeping across his face. "I've got it. What about a casino? They're used to dealing with large sums of money, and they won't blink twice at someone cashing out big. Plus, we could make it look like we won the money there. Clean and simple."

Candy's expression remained thoughtful. It was a smart plan, but she wasn't about to take unnecessary risks. "I like the idea, but we need to be careful. The last thing we want is to show up at a place where you're known. We need somewhere discreet, somewhere they won't question a big payout."

Raising an eyebrow. "You've got a place in mind?" He questioned.

Candy nodded slowly, a plan forming in her mind. "There's an Indian casino on the outskirts of Miami the Miccosukee Casino & Resort. It's perfect. They handle large transactions without much oversight, and they're not under the same scrutiny as the major Vegas casinos. We can move the money there and no one will be the wiser."

Houston's grin widened. "Smart. We cash out there, no alarms, no red flags. By the time anyone thinks to check, it'll be too late. They won't find a trace."

Candy stood, her mind made up. "We do this fast and clean. No mistakes. Once the money is in our hands, we disappear.

Let's get moving."

***

At the parking lot outside the Miccosukee Casino & Resort,

Miami Strip, a sparkle of the Bentley Azure shone under the dim streetlights as Houston waited in a deserted parking lot behind a construction site. The air was heavy with tension, the kind that settles in just before a crucial move. Moments later, a sleek Jaguar convertible pulled in, and Candy stepped out, accompanied by Kelly.

Houston got out of the Bentley, a smirk on his face as he took in the sight of Candy. "How'd you like the ride?" he asked, running his hand over the polished exterior of the car.

Candy raised an eyebrow, her tone laced with sarcasm. "How the hell did you get a Bentley?"

Houston shrugged nonchalantly. "Gotta show money if you're playing in big leagues."

Candy shook her head but couldn't help the smirk that tugged at her lips. "You're sure you can pull this off?"

"Woman, please," Houston shot back with a cocky grin.

Kelly, who had been watching the exchange nervously, interjected. "Do what exactly? But what about the insurance guy? Wat if he figures this out?"

Candy's expression hardened, but there was a cold confidence in her voice. "I'm going to lose the money as soon as I have it in hand. Once it's gone, there's nothing anyone can do, no matter how much they want to dig. It'll be too late."

Kelly still looked uneasy. "But what if he puts it all together? You know he won't just let this slide."

Candy stepped closer to Houston, wrapping an arm around him while keeping her eyes on Kelly. "If he knew anything, he'd have busted us already. We're in the clear."

Houston nodded, but something about his demeanor shifted. "Jimmy's handling some business with friends. We're covered."

Candy's patience had worn thin. "It's not about the money, Houston," she snapped. "I didn't endure three years with Lorenzo just to end up with pocket change."

Houston's voice was laced with frustration. "Fifty million isn't exactly pocket change."

Candy's eyes narrowed, a sly smile curling on her lips. "I was aiming for two hundred fifty million."

Kelly, her voice trembling, pleaded, "Candy, what are you doing? Stop this."

But Candy was past reasoning. She raised her gun, first pointing it at Houston, before swinging it toward Kelly. With cold precision, she pulled the trigger. The bullet struck Kelly in this shoulder, sending her reeling back against her car. A second shot followed, and Kelly crumpled to the ground, lifeless.

Houston's instincts kicked in. He drew his own gun, aiming it directly at Candy. But she remained unfazed, her expression unreadable.

"What the hell are you doing?" Houston's voice was edged with disbelief and fury.

Candy's tone was icy, devoid of remorse. "We didn't need her anymore."

Scanning the empty lot for any witnesses, Houston moved cautiously toward Kelly's body, checking for a pulse.

"Don't you think finding her dead will raise some red flags?" he asked, still trying to wrap his head around the sudden betrayal.

Candy's response was callous. "We'll be long gone by then. Dump her at that construction site nearby, and no one will ever find her."

Houston shook his head in disgust. "You're a heartless bitch, Candy."

Unbothered, Candy turned and walked to her car. "Don't mess with me, Houston. I owed you this much. Now clean up the mess. I'll see you at the game."

Candy stepped back into the shadows, her eyes narrowing as she left Houston standing alone in the dimly lit parking lot. His gaze drifted toward the lifeless body of Kelly, sprawled across the cold concrete. A chill crept through the night air, wrapping around him as he fought to process the scene before him. But there was no time to linger Candy had made it clear: this was now his burden to bear.

"Don't play games with me, Houston," she had warned moments earlier, her tone icy and detached. "I owed you this much. Get rid of her. I'll see you at the game."

With those final words, she turned and sauntered away, the click of her heels echoing ominously in the silence. Her confidence was unwavering, each step measured and deliberate as she disappeared into the darkness, leaving Houston with only his thoughts and the grim task ahead of him.

Candy didn't look back. The world she navigated was one where hesitation meant weakness, and Candy Steele was anything but weak. As she left behind the grim scene, her mind had already moved on to the next step in her plan a plan she would execute with the same precision and poise that defined her every move.

***

Inside the Miccosukee, the atmosphere was a stark contrast to the desolate parking lot. The plush VIP check-in area radiated opulence, with soft lighting, gilded accents, and the delicate clinking of glasses echoing in the distance. It was a sanctuary tailored to the tastes of those who lived beyond the reach of the ordinary where every need was met before it could even be expressed.

Candy glided through the entrance, her sharp eyes taking in

every detail. A smiling young woman appeared almost immediately, offering her a flute of champagne with a polished grace. Candy accepted the glass, but her mind was elsewhere as she sipped the effervescent liquid. The woman vanished as seamlessly as she had appeared, leaving Candy to survey the room.

Her attention was drawn to a small, expensive-looking desk where a well-groomed man in a perfectly tailored suit stood. He rose smoothly, his eyes meeting hers with the practiced ease of someone accustomed to catering to the elite.

"Welcome to the Miccosukee," he said, his voice smooth and professional. "My name is Duncan, and I am the VIP concierge. How may I assist you?"

Candy didn't waste time with pleasantries. "I'd like a room, Duncan," she said, her tone cool and direct.

Duncan's brow furrowed slightly, though his smile remained in place. "Was your reservation through our VIP check-in?" he asked, his voice tinged with polite curiosity. "I didn't have an arrival scheduled."

Candy's lips curved into a faint smile, but there was no warmth in it. "It was a last-minute trip," she said, reaching into her purse. "Maybe this will clear things up."

She began rummaging through her bag, her movements deliberate as she searched for what she needed. Duncan's patience wore thin, though his expression remained composed. "I'm sure I could have one of our front office personnel assist you if you're unsure of" "Got it!" Candy interrupted, pulling out a small slip of paper and handing it to him. Duncan accepted it with a hint of reluctance, his annoyance barely concealed. He glanced at the paper briefly before slipping on his glasses for a closer inspection. Candy leaned against the marble counter in the luxurious Miccosukee VIP lounge, eyeing Duncan with a confident smile. She knew she had him in the palm of her hand now that he'd seen the check. She enjoyed watching people squirm under the weight of her wealth, the way their demeanor shifted as they realized who they were dealing with.

"I'd like to deposit that into an account here at the hotel," she said casually, her voice smooth like silk. "And I feel like playing a little tonight. Poker, maybe. Is everything okay?"

Duncan was already on his feet, his once distant and slightly dismissive attitude replaced by eager attentiveness. The check had done its job.

"Whatever you'd like, Ms. Steele," he said with a broad, professional smile that now carried a hint of genuine respect. "The Miccosukee's entire staff is at your disposal. Would you care to see a show while you're in town? How long will you be staying?"

Candy let the question hang in the air as she tapped her nail lightly on the counter. "I'll let you know," she said with a mysterious smile. She turned on her heel and walked away, leaving Duncan scrambling to ensure everything would be set up perfectly for her.

***

The neon lights buzzed above the dingy entrance of the strip bar. The area was grimy, the kind of place where shadows clung to the corners and unsavory deals went unnoticed. Jimmy stumbled out of the bar, his face flush from hours of cheap drinks and questionable company. He was grinning, clearly having had a great time, as he fumbled with his pack of cigarettes. The first match sputtered out in the wind, followed by the second, leaving him cursing under his breath as he tried again.

Jimmy was sighted down the street, his movements were watched through the windshield of a dark, nondescript car. The engine rumbled quietly as the vehicle rolled forward, inching closer to its target. Jimmy had no idea he was being followed as he finally managed to light his cigarette. He took a long drag, oblivious to the approaching danger, and began to wander down the street.

Around the corner, in an empty, dimly lit street, he fumbled with his keys, searching for the right one to unlock his beat-up car. The street was silent, save for the distant hum of the city. Just as he found the right key, a dark sedan pulled up beside him. Curious and a little irritated, Jimmy leaned down, trying to peer into the passenger window. The glass was tinted, revealing nothing.

He straightened up and squinted into the window. "Hey... what're you doing here?" he asked, his voice slurred from the night's indulgences.

The answer came not in words but in action. A gloved hand rose from within the car, holding a silenced pistol. The sound of the gun firing was barely more than a whisper, but its impact was immediate. Jimmy staggered back, pressing against his car as blood blossomed across his chest. Confusion clouded his eyes as he looked down at his hands, which were suddenly slick with blood.

"Hey?" he managed to choke out, but the plea was futile.

The gun fired again four more times. Each shot was precise, methodical, ensuring the job was done. Jimmy's body jerked with every hit, the bullets tearing through him until his strength gave out. His fingers fumbled toward his waistband where he kept his own gun, but it was too late. The dark sedan's tires squealed as it sped away into the night, leaving him to crumble to his knees before collapsing face down onto the cold pavement, dead.

***

Candy surveyed the casino floor from a balcony, her gaze drifting over the tables below where fortunes were made and lost in the span of a few hands. The lights reflected off the lavish décor, casting everything in a golden glow. She felt a thrill coursing through her veins; she thrived in places like this, where the stakes were high, and the players even higher.

A man in an expensive suit approached her from behind. He carried himself with the authority of someone who managed more than just money but also he managed egos, expectations, and secrets.

"Ms. Steele?" the man asked as he stepped closer.

"Yes?" she replied without taking her eyes off the tables. "Your game is ready," the man informed her.

She finally turned to look at him, a slight smile playing at the corners of her lips. "Thank you," she said smoothly.

The man gestured for her to follow, leading her through the casino floor, past the sounds of clattering chips and the occasional cheer or groan from the players. They moved deeper into the heart of the casino, away from the crowds and into a more exclusive area reserved for the high rollers.

"I'm sorry about your husband," the man said, his voice respectful but tinged with curiosity. "He was one hell of a player."

Candy didn't flinch. She kept her tone even as she replied, "He was. But I'm here to play my own game now."

The man nodded and pushed open a small, intricately carved door. Inside was a room that screamed opulence velvet chairs, rich wood paneling, and a low-lit ambiance designed for both comfort and intimidation. A round poker table dominated the center of the room. Seated around it were some of the biggest names in the world P. Deville, Ian Crump, Vic Ticanio, and, to Candy's surprise, Houston. Each of them had stacks of chips in front of them, ready to play.

A bartender stood behind a fully stocked bar, and two beautiful cocktail waitresses hovered nearby, ready to attend to any need.

The pit manager cleared his throat, capturing the attention of everyone in the room. "Gentlemen, this is Ms. Steele. The table rules are simple: no limit. The house will draw our usual percentage. Enjoy your game, and if there's anything else you need, just ask."

With that, the man exited, leaving Candy to take her place at the table. She slid into a chair, crossing her legs with a casual grace that belied her readiness. "Call me Candy," she said, flashing a smile that was both sweet and deadly.

P. Deville leaned forward, his grin wide and charming. "Candy, Candy, sweet thing. I'm Deville, P. Deville. What's your game?"

Candy's eyes twinkled with mischief. "I play them all."

Crump snorted, unable to resist interjecting. "Candy? What kind of name is that? Is it French? We should be playing in Atlantic City, not here in Miami. I thought we were playing in Atlantic City."

Vic Ticanio, ever the entertainer, leaned in and whispered to Candy, "Don't mind Ian he has relaxation issues." He gave her a conspiratorial wink.

Candy's gaze shifted to Houston, who hadn't said a word yet. There was a history between them, a tension that hung in the air like a loaded gun. She arched an eyebrow and asked coyly, "And your name?"

"Houston," he replied simply, his voice steady and unreadable.

Crump, never one to stay quiet for long, chimed in, "I think I own something in Houston."

P. Deville clapped his hands together, eager to get the game started. "Now that everyone's all friendly and introduced, let's play!"

The dealer got to work, shuffling the cards with practiced precision. The game was seven-card stud, and the atmosphere shifted as the first round of betting began. Chips clattered onto the table as each player assessed their hand, trying to outwit and outbluff the others. It was a game of skill, strategy, and nerves just the way Candy liked it.

As the night wore on, the game grew more intense. A montage of action flashed across the table: chips changing hands, fortunes rising and falling, the players' faces hardening as the stakes got higher. Drinks flowed freely, and the room grew hazy with cigar smoke. Everyone's true character came out under the pressure Crump's arrogance, Wayne's charm, Diddy's playful confidence, and Houston's cold calculation. But Candy? She remained an enigma, cool and composed as she played her cards with deadly precision.

Hours passed, and the once lively table had thinned out. One by one, the others either ran out of chips or simply gave up, leaving only Candy and Houston still in the game. The tension between them was palpable now, each sizing the other up as they prepared for the final showdown.

"You've built quite the stack there," she observed, her voice a seductive purr. "Care to raise the stakes?"

P. Deville shook his head, leaning back in his chair. "I'm out," he said, tapping out with a rueful grin.

Houston's gaze never left Candy's. "Deal me in," he said, his voice low and full of challenge.

Candy's eyes glittered as she looked straight at Houston, daring him to match her.

She leaned back in her chair, her eyes gleaming with mischief. The other players at the table, who had been dozing or growing weary from the long hours, suddenly snapped back to attention when she calmly announced, "One million dollars."

P. Deville's eyes widened, and he leaned forward, the playful grin gone from his face. "Say what?" he asked, unable to believe what he'd just heard.

Candy's voice remained smooth and confident. "I'm betting one million."

The dealer, who had been dealing cards with routine efficiency all night, suddenly froze. He shot a glance at her, his hand hovering over the deck, and then discreetly pushed a hidden button under the table. It was a signal, a call for backup when things got a little too intense.

"Is there a problem?" Candy asked, her tone laced with a hint of challenge.

The dealer cleared his throat. "That's a very large bet, ma'am."

Candy's lips curved into a sly smile. "I thought this was Miami. No limits, right?"

Before the dealer could respond, the pit manager, a sharp-eyed man with slicked-back hair, entered the room. He leaned down to listen as the dealer whispered the situation in his ear. The manager straightened up and addressed Candy directly. "Ms. Steele, the stakes are indeed unlimited in a private game like this, and it's up to the players to agree on the bets. However, the casino cannot guarantee funds in these situations."

Candy barely blinked. "I'm sure we can all pay our bills," she replied coolly, casting a quick glance at the others around the table.

Vic Ticanio, always quick to maintain his gentlemanly persona, raised his hands in a gesture of surrender. "Well, it's too rich for my blood," he said, smiling ruefully as he pushed his chair back from the table.

Crump, ever the businessman, leaned in with a calculating look. "Can I bet property?" he asked, his voice dripping with his usual bravado.

P. Deville rolled his eyes and shook his head. "Ian, you always ask, and we always say no. Chill out."

Candy chuckled, enjoying the spectacle. But then, all eyes turned to Houston. He had been quiet, observing with an unreadable expression as he slowly rolled a thick cigar between his fingers. He looked at Candy, then at P. Deville, before finally speaking.

"I'm in," Houston said, pushing his stack of chips into the growing pot. He reached for a slip of paper, scribbled a quick signature, and tossed it in as well. The room buzzed with anticipation as the dealer dealt the next cards.

P. Deville drew a jack, Candy pulled a queen, and Houston received an eight of spades. Everyone's attention locked onto the players' faces as they discreetly checked their hole cards.

Candy didn't waste any time. She leaned forward slightly, her gaze locked on Houston as she announced her next move. "Five million," she said, tossing another slip of paper into the pot as casually as if she were ordering another drink.

P. Deville's jaw dropped. "Are you for real? Did you say FIVE million?"

Candy met his incredulous stare with a serene smile. "Yes, I did."

P. Deville shook his head in disbelief. "Girl, you're crazy."

Houston, unfazed, leaned back in his chair, took a long puff of his cigar, and slowly exhaled a cloud of smoke. "Raise five million," he said, his voice low and steady.

P. Deville whipped his head around to stare at Houston. "You're nuts too. I'm out," he said, throwing his hands up in surrender. He was done playing at this level, and he wasn't about to risk everything against these two wild cards.

Candy and Houston locked eyes across the table, the tension crackling between them like electricity. "Well, it looks like it's just you and me, cowboy," Candy said, her voice dripping with both challenge and charm.

The dealer, sensing the heightened stakes, took a deep breath before flipping the next cards. Candy drew another queen, while Houston was dealt a ten of hearts. The two players studied their new cards, but their focus never wavered from each other.

Candy's smile widened, but there was a sharp edge to it now. "Feeling lucky, huh?" she taunted.

Houston's eyes glinted as he replied, "Born lucky."

The mood in the room was tense, the cocktail waitresses had stopped moving, frozen in place as they watched the high-stakes drama unfold. The bartender, who had been polishing glasses absentmindedly, now leaned against the bar, watching with rapt attention.

Candy's fingers drummed lightly on the table as she considered her next move. The thrill of the game was intoxicating. She loved the rush, the adrenaline of pushing boundaries and seeing who would blink first. She picked up another slip of paper and signed it with a flourish before tossing it into the pot. "Let's see if you can keep up," she purred.

Houston didn't flinch. He casually adjusted his jacket, took another drag from his cigar, and then leaned forward to match her bet without a word. The dealer dealt the final cards, and the atmosphere in the room grew even more charged. Candy drew a third queen a deadly trio that gave her a powerful hand. Houston's card, a six of diamonds, seemed to give him nothing of consequence.

But there was something in Houston's expression that made

Candy hesitate. He wasn't rattled; if anything, he looked more confident than ever. Candy knew that a good poker face could be deceptive, but she also knew Houston wasn't someone who bluffed easily.

The others around the table held their breath as Candy leaned in, her eyes narrowing. "All in," she said, pushing the last of her chips and another signed slip into the pot.

Houston's expression remained inscrutable. He leaned back in his chair, studying her with those cold, calculating eyes. Then, in one fluid motion, he pushed all his chips into the center as well, signing his final slip with a deliberate flourish before tossing it onto the pile.

The dealer's hands trembled slightly as he prepared to reveal the hole cards. Everyone in the room was on edge, waiting to see who would walk away with everything on the line.

"Show 'em," Candy said, her voice a little tighter than before. She flipped over her hole cards to reveal her deadly hand three queens, a formidable combination.

But Houston didn't flinch. He slowly revealed his cards, one by one, until the final combination came into view. He had a straight an unlikely, but devastating, hand that beat her queens.

Candy's confident smile faltered for a fraction of a second, but she quickly masked it with a graceful nod. "Well played," she said, forcing herself to remain poised even as she felt the sting of defeat.

Houston leaned forward slightly, his eyes locking onto hers as he replied, "You put up one hell of a fight, Candy. But in the end, luck's always on my side."

The dealer began to rake in the massive pile of chips, paper slips, and cash. The game was over, but the energy in the room remained charged as the reality of what had just happened settled in. Candy had lost big, but she wasn't someone who would walk away easily. She had more moves to make, and this was just one chapter in a larger game.

As she stood up, adjusting her dress with a practiced flick of her wrist, she shot Houston a look that promised this wasn't the end. "You might've won tonight," she said with a sly grin, "but this is the nightlife, baby. The night's still young."

With that, she turned and walked out of the room, her heels clicking confidently against the polished floor, leaving the others to wonder what her next move would be.

Houston watched her go, a small, satisfied smile playing on his lips. The game had gone exactly as he'd planned, but he knew Candy well enough to know she wasn't done yet. This was just the beginning, and he was more than ready for whatever she had in store next.

As the door closed behind her, the room slowly came back to life. The tension broke, and the remaining players began to stir, murmuring to each other about the high-stakes game they'd just witnessed. But for Candy and Houston, the night wasn't over—it was only the start of something much bigger, something that would pull them deeper into the dark, glittering world of power, money, and deception.

And in that world, no one played fair.

***

In the executive office was a world away from the chaos of the casino floor. The space was tastefully decorated with rich mahogany furniture, thick carpets, and subdued lighting. Behind the imposing desk sat a distinguished man in his mid- fifties, impeccably dressed and radiating calm authority. This was the General Manager of the Miccosukee, and he was not someone easily rattled. He eyed Houston with a measured look, drumming his fingers on the desk.

"So, things got a little out of hand, wouldn't you say?" the General Manager asked, his tone even, though his eyes were sharp.

Houston leaned back in his chair, unbothered. "I feel pretty good about it," he replied with a casual shrug.

The General Manager nodded slowly. "Yes, I understand that." He paused, choosing his words carefully. "But your winnings come from the young lady, not the casino. We're just the intermediary."

Houston's expression hardened. "I don't care if you're her daddy. I just care about getting paid."

The General Manager leaned forward slightly, folding his hands. "Ms. Steele has funds deposited with the hotel to settle her debt. It's an odd coincidence, really… the amounts being so similar."

"Less the casino's commission," Houston added, his tone sharp.

"Of course," the General Manager agreed smoothly. "It's just a matter of transferring the funds. However, the IRS will need to be informed."

Houston's eyes narrowed. "What does that mean?"

"It means fifty million is more than the casino can cash on the spot," the General Manager explained patiently. "We're also waiting for Ms. Steele's funds to clear."

"How long?" Houston asked, his voice edged with suspicion.

The General Manager steepled his fingers, considering. "I can give you four million now. The rest will be transferred to any account you choose as soon as the funds clear."

Houston didn't immediately respond. Instead, he scanned the room, taking in the opulent surroundings before focusing back on the General Manager. "I guess you're good for it," he finally said, standing up.

He reached across the desk and grabbed a piece of paper and a pen, quickly jotting down a long account number. He handed it over with a cool expression. "You can give that name and number to the IRS."

The General Manager raised an eyebrow as he glanced at the paper. "The Caymans? I'll arrange the transfer personally," he said smoothly, reading the name Houston had written. "Mr... Tully."

***

In the room, Houston stood by the large windows of his suite, gazing out at the glittering lights of the Las Vegas Strip. A glass of scotch was in his hand, and a satisfied smile played on his lips. The duffel bag at his feet was packed with stacks of cash, millions in crisp bills. He picked up a cigar and lit it, taking a slow drag as he savored the moment. But his relaxation was interrupted by a sharp knock at the door.

His instincts kicked in immediately. Houston's expression darkened as he set down his drink and grabbed a large automatic pistol from the nearby table. He moved silently toward the door but stopped short, opting instead to check the secondary entrance to the suite. Opening it a crack, he peered out cautiously, gun at the ready.

Down the hall, Houston spotted Candy approaching. She was dressed in a short coat, her eyes fixed on him as she sauntered forward.

His grip tightened on the gun, but he kept it concealed behind his back. Candy reached him and offered a coy smile.

"I know I shouldn't be here, but I got lonely," she said softly, her voice dripping with seductive charm. "Can I come in?"

Houston didn't lower the gun. He waved it at her, making his distrust clear. "Sorry, but you've got a bad track record," he replied, eyes narrowing with suspicion.

But Candy didn't flinch. Instead, she slowly unbuttoned her coat, revealing that she was wearing nothing but a garter and

a lacy bra underneath. "Figured you'd be worried about that," she said with a smirk. "Wanna frisk me?"

She spun around slowly, showing off her figure while letting Houston take in every detail. His eyes remained cold, but he couldn't entirely hide his interest. Still, he wasn't letting his guard down. He motioned for her to go inside, then quickly checked the hallway again before stepping back in and closing the door behind him.

The game between them was far from over, and both of them knew it. Candy's charm and allure might be powerful weapons, but he was always ready for the next hand no matter what the stakes might be.

Chapter Twenty-Three

The highway stretched out, shimmering under the hot sun as Houston chirped the alarm on his Bentley, locking it with a final glance. With a smirk, he left the pristine luxury car behind and jumped into the passenger seat of a dusty minivan. The van's tires screeched as it sped off, kicking up dirt and debris, leaving the gleaming Bentley coated in a cloud of filth. The dust lingered in the air, slowly settling over the abandoned car like a veil.

Candy's voice echoed in the distance, recounting the aftermath. "Some guys just don't let things go. I thought I had it all figured out. Guess I was wrong."

Inside the mini-van, Houston sat calmly, his eyes fixed on the side-view mirror. He watched the Bentley slowly fade out of view, now nothing more than a dirty memory. A twinge of regret crossed his face.

"I hate to dump that car," he muttered, more to himself than anyone else.

The driver was revealed to be Kelly, cigarette dangling from her lips. She was almost unrecognizable from the timid woman she used to be. Her once-soft features were now hardened, eyes cold and calculating.

"That bitch had it coming," Kelly spat, exhaling a plume of smoke. "How did you know she'd use your gun to shoot me?"

Houston's lips curled into a sly grin. "This is Vegas, baby. Sometimes you just roll the dice."

Kelly shot him a sidelong glance, neither surprised nor satisfied by his answer. She knew better than to expect straightforward explanations from a man like Houston.

In the crystal-clear waters of a serene bay, a luxurious yacht was anchored, basking in the sun. A small water minivan darted across the waves, heading directly for the gleaming vessel. Standing at the front of the minivan was Houston, his eyes locked on the yacht as it drew nearer. The boat rocked gently as the van pulled alongside, and Houston grabbed the ladder, swiftly climbing aboard. They came down from the van and carried their bags, abandoning the van.

Houston strode across the deck, heading to the front of the boat. There, lying on a sunbed, was Kelly. She was no longer the plain maid; she radiated confidence, wearing a sleek designer bikini that accentuated her newfound aura of power. Her sunglasses slid down her nose as she peered over them, her face breaking into a bright smile when she saw Houston.

"Hey," he called out.

Kelly lowered her sunglasses, a smile spread across her face as she saw him. She leaped up and threw her arms around and he planted a passionate kiss on his lips.

"And the money?" she asked, her eyes gleaming with anticipation.

"Arrived this morning," Houston replied with a satisfied grin.

Her reaction was filled with instantaneous joy and triumph. She threw her arms around him again, and this time, Houston scooped her up, carrying her below deck to the cabin.

The two of them were lost in a frenzy of wild passion. Kelly was no longer the timid maid she once was. She was a new woman bold, fierce, and in complete control of her desires. The tangled sheets told the story of their intense connection, a fusion of lust and triumph.

The cabin was quiet now after the wild sex, with only the soft sound of the ocean outside. Houston lay in the bed, his body nestled in the midst of tangled sheets. Kelly entered the room, holding two glasses. She handed one to Houston.

"Mojito?" she offered with a grin.

Houston chuckled, taking the glass. "You've really developed a taste for those things," he observed, taking a sip.

She raised her glass, her smile mischievous. "To us, and to Candy. We couldn't have done it without her."

Houston raised his glass in agreement. "Payback's a bitch," he said with a smirk, "and so was she."

They both downed their drinks in one smooth motion. As Kelly leaned in to kiss him, there was a brief moment of connection before she pulled away.

"I'll be right back," she murmured, her tone soft but determined.

As she disappeared up the stairs, Houston reached for his shirt, but a sudden pain shot through his arm. He winced, rubbing at the spot. Something felt off. He tried to shake it off, but a growing sense of unease gnawed at him.

He could hear the hum of the yacht's engines starting up, and the sound of the anchor being raised. The uneasy feeling intensified as he struggled to get to his feet, his legs suddenly weak. The world around him began to spin, and his vision blurred.

A sickening realization hit him and something was very wrong.

He staggered toward the door, desperate to make it topside, but his limbs were uncooperative, each movement a struggle. His mind raced as he fought to stay conscious, but the poison because that's what it had to be was working fast, shutting down his body bit by bit.

Through the haze, he could hear Kelly's laughter drifting down from above. She had played with him, just like they had played Candy. He'd been so sure he had control, so sure he was the one orchestrating everything. But Kelly had learned from the best and now she was making her final move.

Darkness closed in as Houston collapsed onto the cabin floor, his mind clinging to one last thought: In Vegas, you roll the dice... but eventually, everyone craps out.

Up on deck, Kelly smirked, her expression ice-cold as she steered the yacht away from the tranquil bay, leaving Houston to fight for his life below. The game had never really been about the cards or money. It was always about who could play their hand the best and Kelly had just played hers flawlessly.

Houston's legs felt like lead as he stumbled to the bathroom door, clutching the walls for support. His vision blurred and the world seemed to sway beneath his feet. When he finally managed to get the door open, he froze in shock.

Standing inside, grinning like a cat with a canary, was Candy. Her eyes sparkled with a wicked delight, a sight he thought he'd never see again.

"Hi, honey," she said, her voice dripping with mock sweetness. "Nice seeing you again."

Before he could react, she swung back and delivered a hard punch straight to his jaw. The blow sent him reeling backward, and he collapsed onto the bed. She shook her hand, wincing from the impact.

"Ouch," she muttered, rubbing her knuckles as if the punch had hurt her more than him.

The yacht drifted lazily in the open ocean, surrounded by nothing but endless blue. The sun was already setting in the cloudless sky, casting a warm glow over the tranquil waters.

On the deck, Houston lay flat on his back, slowly blinking his eyes open. All he could see was the empty sky above him, a perfect picture of peace if it weren't for the situation he was in.

His vision focused, and he saw Kelly standing over him, cigarette in hand. Her lips curled into a smile as she looked down at him.

"He's awake," she called out.

Candy appeared beside her, and together, they grabbed Houston's limp arms and dragged him across the deck. His muscles refused to cooperate, and though he wasn't tied up, he was as helpless as a ragdoll. They propped him up against the side of the boat, his back pressed against the rail. His eyes darted between the two women, anger and fear battling within him.

"What the hell are you doing?" he growled, his voice thick with frustration.

Candy tilted her head, feigning innocence. "Houston, you don't seem happy to see me."

She mimicked her "death scene," snorting and grabbing her nose in exaggerated mockery. Her performance was disturbingly accurate.

"You've got to admit, it was pretty convincing," she said with a sly grin.

"Fucking bitch," he spat, his words laced with venom.

Candy smirked and turned to Kelly. "He doesn't seem too thrilled to see me."

Kelly ran her fingers through his hair, playing with it as if he were a pet. He tried to jerk away, but his body barely responded.

"I think he's just overwhelmed," Kelly said, her voice smooth as silk.

"What the hell did you do to me?" He demanded, his voice strained as he fought the weakness spreading through him.

Kelly's smile widened. "Spider venom. We had a little leftover. It's amazing stuff, don't you think?"

His mind raced. Spider venom of course. That's why his body was shutting down, his muscles betraying him.

"How.... how did you even get it?" he stammered, trying to piece it all together.

Candy's smile never wavered. "Oh, you must be really confused. Let me clear things up for you."

"See, it all started when Tully called to tell me you were back in town and looking for me. That slimeball actually thought he could blackmail me."

Candy leaned back, disgust clear on her face as she recalled the memory.

"Gross, but necessary. Once I handled Tully, I knew I needed help, so I called Kelly."

Houston's eyes narrowed. "You knew each other?" Kelly's voice was a matter of fact. "We grew up together."

"Kelly was working as a paralegal when I found her," Candy explained. "She specialized in contracts."

Kelly chimed in, her voice full of pride. "That's right. I'm the one who discovered the insurance policy scam."

Candy raised her glass in a mock toast. "Nicely done, by the way. Brilliant work."

She beamed. "Thank you. You're so sweet."

Candy continued, "All we had to do after that was track you down in Los Angeles."

"Men are so predictable, she said as she reminded him of the past."

Houston stared at the two women in front of him, the truth finally sinking in. They had played him from the start, pulling every string, setting him up for the ultimate betrayal.

Candy leaned in close, her face inches from his. "You thought you were the one in control. But in Vegas, you should know, the house always wins."

Kelly traced her fingers along Candy's body before turning her attention back to Houston. She leaned in close, offering him a sip from her glass. He turned his head away, refusing her.

"Just trying to be nice," she said, her voice deceptively sweet. "Go to hell," Houston shot back, his tone dripping with defiance.

Kelly's expression hardened, and without warning, she back-handed him across the face. Blood trickled from the corner of his mouth, but instead of flinching, he laughed.

"I should've known," he muttered, spitting out blood. "Women like you can't stand each other. The fact that you two got along should've clued me in."

Kelly smirked. "Oh honey, you never had a chance."

Candy circled him with a knowing smile, her voice teasing as she spoke. "I know you, Houston. You always like to hedge your bets. You couldn't resist having someone on the inside."

Kelly stepped closer, her tone mocked. "You have to admit, I played the part exactly the way you wanted."

Houston gave a resigned nod. "Yeah, you did."

Candy leaned in, kissing Kelly on the lips. "She sure did," she echoed, the words laced with cruel satisfaction. "Kelly made sure you did exactly what we needed. The rest," she paused, letting the weight of the unspoken settle in, "well, you know I how that played out. You even did us a favor by taking care of Tully. Saved us the trouble."

Houston's thoughts raced as he tried to piece it all together. "And Jimmy?" The question burned on his tongue, even though he dreaded the answer.

Kelly's voice was crisp, cutting through his thoughts like a blade. "I handled that."

{Flashback}

At the Sleazy strip bar, Jimmy stumbled out of a dingy strip bar, squinting against the neon lights. Kelly's car idled nearby, waiting for him. As he turned the corner, the car rolled up beside him. Recognizing her, Jimmy leaned into the open window with a grin, but before he could say a word, Kelly raised her gun and pulled the trigger. The shot was quick, merciless, and left Jimmy crumpled on the pavement.

{Flashback ends}

Houston's face was a mask of anger and confusion. He stared

at Candy, his dark eyes burning with intensity. "Why did you settle with the insurance company?" he demanded, his voice rising above the sound of the waves. "If we were all dead, no one would be able to touch you."

Candy leaned casually against the railing, her expression calm and composed, almost amused. "Ah, but you were right," she replied, her voice laced with a hint of mockery. "I couldn't start writing checks to strangers. Not to mention, I'd rather have fifty million and you dead than two hundred million and have to keep looking over my shoulder."

Houston's jaw clenched, his fists balled at his sides. "I would have found you," he growled, his voice filled with venom.

Her smile widened, her eyes glinting with amusement and cruelty. "I know, Papi. That's what makes killing you so much fun."

Kelly emerged from the cabin below, her hair tousled by the wind, a playful smile on her lips. "The funny part," she chimed in, "was we hadn't thought about having Candy shoot me until you brought it up. Since you thought she would, it was too good to pass up."

Candy chuckled softly, shaking her head. "Personally, I think my death performance was better," she said, turning to her with a playful grin.

She rolled her eyes, a teasing smirk playing on her lips. "Really? I thought I nailed it," she replied, her tone light and sarcastic.

{Flashback}

Under the glow of the streetlights, the empty parking lot in downtown Atlanta was eerily silent. The shadows stretched long across the asphalt, the only sound being the distant hum of traffic. Candy sat in the driver's seat of her car, the engine idling softly.

Houston stood over Kelly, who lay sprawled on the ground, blood pooling beneath her. She groaned softly, then slowly raised herself onto one elbow, a mischievous smile spread across her face. Houston's eyes widened in shock, his mind racing to process what he was seeing.

Candy watched from the car, her eyes locked onto Houston's face. She could see the realization dawning on him, the pieces of the puzzle finally coming together. With a satisfied smirk, she shifted the car into gear and drove away, leaving Houston standing over Kelly.

{Flashback ends}

Back on the yacht, Houston's face was pale, his eyes wide with disbelief. "You're both nuts," he muttered, shaking his head in disbelief.

Candy laughed, a light, carefree sound that seemed out of place given the circumstances. "Oh now, come on," she said, her voice dripping with mock sympathy. "If I wasn't dead, you wouldn't have destroyed the pictures. You caught us off guard with that one. Hell, we knew you were watching us. Why do you think we acted everything out for you?"

Houston's face contorted with rage, his hands trembling with barely restrained fury. "You played me," he snarled, his voice low and dangerous.

Her eyes gleamed with triumph. "Like a fiddle, Papi," she replied, her voice smooth and confident. "And now, it's time to end the game."

She stepped closer to Houston, her eyes never leaving him. The tension between them was clear, a silent battle of wills playing out in the space between them. For a moment, it seemed as if Houston might lash out, his body tensing as if to strike. But then, slowly, he relaxed, his shoulders slumping in defeat as she walked away.

From a secluded vantage point on a rocky beach, Houston crouched low, concealed behind a cluster of jagged rocks. The wind whipped through his hair as he watched Candy and Kelly on the yacht anchored just off the shore. They were deep in conversation, their body language relaxed and intimate. Houston's eyes narrowed as he tried to decipher their words from a distance, a growing sense of dread gnawing at him.

The yacht bobbed gently on the waves. He stood weakly on the deck, staring intently at Candy and Kelly, who stood together near the helm. The air was thick with tension, an undercurrent of finality hanging between them.

"So, what now?" Houston asked his voice tightly with suspicion.

Candy exchanged a knowing glance with Kelly before turning her attention back to him. "Well, we talked about it," she began, her tone casual yet firm.

Kelly nodded in agreement. "We really did," she added, her expression serious. "But we both felt there was no way we could let you live."

Candy shrugged, her face devoid of any emotion. "It's nothing personal," she said with a small, almost apologetic smile.

Chiming in, her voice soft but unwavering. "It's really not," Kelly agreed, her eyes fixed on his face.

Candy took a step closer to Houston, her gaze locked onto his. "We'll both miss your..." she trailed off, searching for the right word.

"Talents," Kelly finished for her, a smirk playing on her lips.

She leaned in, placing a hand on Houston's shoulder as she gave him a deep, lingering kiss. Houston stood rigid, his eyes wide with shock and confusion.

"You always knew how to treat a lady, Houston," Candy murmured against his lips, her voice a husky whisper.

Before he could react, Kelly slid into his lap, wrapping her arms around his neck. She kissed him deeply, her lips moving with a slow, deliberate passion. When she finally pulled away, she looked him in the eyes, her expression a mix of sorrow and resolve.

"I'll actually miss you," she said softly. "I've had fun with you."

He blinked, his mind racing as he tried to process what was happening. "You can't trust her, you know," he said urgently, his voice laced with desperation. "She'll kill you too."

Kelly glanced at Candy, a faint smile on her lips. "She's not the murdering type," she replied, her tone light and almost dismissive.

Without warning, she shifted her position, kicking the wall behind Houston with a sudden, forceful movement. A hidden door sprang open, and Houston tumbled backward, his arms flailing as he fell overboard into the ocean.

He hit the water with a splash, sinking beneath the surface for a moment before bobbing back up. He struggled to stay afloat, his eyes wide with panic as he treaded water, helpless and exposed.

The two ladies leaned over the railing, watching him with cold, detached expressions. "He was a nice guy," Candy remarked, her voice calm and unaffected.

"Sure was," Kelly agreed, her gaze steady as she watched Houston struggle.

She tilted her head, with a thoughtful look on her face. "Did you ever know what his real name was?" she asked.

Kelly shook her head, a small frown creasing her brow. "I don't think he ever told me," she admitted.

"Bob," She said simply, her tone flat and emotionless.

In the churning waves, Houston's movements grew weaker, his head dipping below the surface for longer intervals. Finally, he slipped beneath the water one last time, disappearing from view. The duo stood in silence for a moment, watching the spot where he had vanished.

Then, as if on cue, they both burst into laughter, the sound loud and carefree against the backdrop of the open sea.

Candy turned to Kelly, a playful glint in her eyes. "Where to now?" she asked, her tone light and breezy.

She thought for a moment, her smile widening. "I think we should visit that doctor in the Cayman Islands," she suggested. "Just to be safe."

Candy nodded, a satisfied smile spread across her face. "Good idea," she agreed.

Together, they walked towards the helm, their laughter mingling with the sound of the waves. The yacht glided smoothly through the open ocean, its bow cut through the water with effortless grace as they sailed towards its next adventure...

Made in the USA
Middletown, DE
21 February 2025

71639476R00143